Spanish
ESCAPE

ESCAPE
COLLECTION

April 2017

May 2017

June 2017

July 2017

August 2017

September 2017

Spanish
ESCAPE

Carol
MARINELLI

Maisey
YATES

Catherine
MANN

MILLS
&
BOON

Published in Great Britain 2017
By Mills & Boon, an imprint of HarperCollins*Publishers*
1 London Bridge Street, London, SE1 9GF

SPANISH ESCAPE © 2017 Harlequin Books S.A.

The Playboy of Puerto Banús © 2013 Carol Marinelli
A Game of Vows © 2012 Maisey Yates
For the Sake of Their Son © 2014 Catherine Mann

ISBN: 978-0-263-93098-6

09-0417

Our policy is to use papers that are natural, renewable and recyclable products and made from wood grown in sustainable forests. The logging and manufacturing processes conform to the legal environmental regulations of the country of origin.

Printed and bound in Spain
by CPI, Barcelona

THE PLAYBOY OF
PUERTO BANÚS

CAROL MARINELLI

For Anne and Tony
Thank you for all your love and support.
It means so much.

C xxxx

Carol Marinelli is a Taurus, with Taurus rising, yet still thinks she is a secret Gemini. Originally from England, she now lives in Australia and is the single mother of three. Apart from her children, writing romance and the friendships forged along the way are her passion. She chooses to believe in a happy-ever-after for all and strives for that in her writing.

CHAPTER ONE

'ESTELLE, I PROMISE, you wouldn't have to do anything except hold Gordon's hand and dance....'

'And?' Estelle pushed, pulling down the corner on the page she was reading and closing her book, hardly able to believe she was having this conversation, let alone considering going along with Ginny's plan.

'Maybe a small kiss on the cheek or lips...' As Estelle shook her head Ginny pushed on. 'You just have to look as if you're madly in love.'

'With a sixty-four-year-old?'

'Yes.' Ginny sighed, but before Estelle could argue further broke in, 'Everyone will think you're a gold-digger, that you're only with Gordon for his money. Which you will be...' Ginny stopped talking then, interrupted by a terrible coughing fit.

They were housemates rather than best friends, two students trying to get through university. At twenty-five, Estelle was a few years older than Ginny, and had long wondered how Ginny managed to run a car and dress so well, but now she had found out. Ginny worked for a very exclusive escort agency and had a long-term client—Gordon Edwards, a politician with a secret. Which was why, Ginny had assured her, nothing would happen or be expected from Estelle if she took Ginny's place as his date at a very grand wedding being held this evening.

'I'd have to share a room with him.'

Estelle had never shared a room with a man in her life. She wasn't especially shy or retiring but she certainly had none of Ginny's confidence or social ease. Ginny thought the weekends were designed for parties, clubs and pubs, whereas Estelle's idea of a perfect weekend was looking around old churches or ruins and then curling up on the sofa with a book.

Not playing escort!

'Gordon always takes the sofa when we share a room.'

'No.' Estelle pushed up her glasses and returned to her book. She tried to carry on reading about the mausoleum of the first Qin Emperor but it was terribly hard to do so when she was so worried about her brother and he *still* hadn't rung to let her know if he had got the job.

There was no mistaking the fact that the money would help.

It was late Saturday morning in London, and the wedding was being held that evening in a castle in Scotland. If Estelle was going to go then she would have to start getting ready now, for they would fly to Edinburgh and then take a helicopter to the castle and time was fast running out.

'Please,' Ginny said. 'The agency are freaking because they can't get anyone suitable at such short notice. He's coming to pick me up in an hour.'

'What will people think?' Estelle asked. 'If people are used to seeing him with you…'

'Gordon will take care of that. He'll say that we had an argument, that I was pushing for an engagement ring or something. We were going to be finishing soon anyway, now that I'm nearly through university. Honestly, Estelle, Gordon really is the loveliest man. There's so much pressure on him to appear straight—he simply cannot go to this wedding without a date. Just think of the money!'

Estelle couldn't stop thinking about the money.

Attending this wedding would mean that she could pay her brother's mortgage for an entire month, as well as a couple of his bills.

Okay, it wouldn't entirely solve their dilemma, but it would buy Andrew and his young family a little bit more time and, given all they had been through this past year, and all that was still to come, they could certainly use the reprieve.

Andrew had done so much for her—had put his own life on hold to make sure that Estelle's life carried on as normally as possible when their parents had died when Estelle was seventeen.

It was time for Estelle to step up, just as Andrew had.

'Okay.' Estelle took a deep breath and her decision was made. 'Ring and say that I'll come.'

'I've already told him that you've agreed,' Ginny admitted. 'Estelle, don't look at me like that. I know how badly you need the money and I simply couldn't bear to tell Gordon that I didn't have someone else lined up.'

Ginny looked more closely at Estelle. Her long black hair was pulled back in a ponytail, her very pale skin was without a blemish, and there was no last night's make-up smudged under Estelle's green eyes because Estelle rarely wore any. Ginny was trying not to show it but she was actually more than a little nervous as to what a made-up Estelle would look like and whether or not she could carry it off.

'You need to get ready. I'll help with your hair and things.'

'You're not coming near me with that cough,' Estelle said. 'I can manage.' She looked at Ginny's doubtful expression. 'We can all look like tarts if we have to.' She smiled and Ginny laughed. 'Though I don't actually have anything I can wear…would anyone notice if I wore something of yours?'

'I bought a new dress for the wedding.' Ginny headed to the wardrobe in her bedroom and Estelle followed.

Estelle's jaw dropped when she held the flimsy gold fabric up.

'Does that go under the dress?'

'It looks stunning on.'

'On *you*, perhaps…' Estelle said, because Ginny was a lot slimmer and had a tiny pert bust, whereas, though small, Estelle was curvy. 'I'm going to look like…'

'Which is the whole point.' Ginny grinned. 'Honestly, Estelle, if you just relax you'll have fun.'

'I doubt it,' Estelle said, wrapping her long dark hair in heated rollers at Ginny's dressing table, and setting to work on her face under her housemate's very watchful eye. Gordon was supposed to be a womanizer, and somehow Estelle had to get the balance right between looking as if she adored him while being far, far too young for him too.

'You need more foundation.'

'More?' Estelle already felt as if she had an inch on.

'And lashings of mascara.'

Ginny watched as Estelle took out the heated rollers and her long dark hair tumbled into ringlets. 'Okay, loads of hairspray…' Ginny said. 'Oh, and by the way, Gordon calls me Virginia, just in case anyone mentions me.'

Ginny blinked a few times when Estelle turned around. The smoky grey eyeshadow and layers of mascara brought out the emerald in her green eyes, and the make-up accentuated Estelle's full lips. Seeing the long black curls framing her friend's petite face, Ginny started to believe that Estelle could carry this off.

'You look amazing! Let's see you in the dress.'

'Won't I change there?'

'Gordon's schedule is too busy. Once you land I would imagine you'll be straight into the wedding.'

The dress was beautiful—sheer and gold, it clung everywhere. It was far too revealing but it was delicious too. Ginny gaped when Estelle wobbled on very high shoes.

'I think Gordon might dump me.'

'This,' Estelle said firmly, 'is a one-off.'

'That's what I said when I first started at the agency,' Ginny admitted. 'But if it goes well…'

'Don't even *think* it!' Estelle said as a car tooted in the street.

'You'll be fine,' Ginny said as Estelle nearly jumped out of her skin. 'You look stunning. I know you can do this.'

Estelle clung onto that as she stepped out of her cheap student accommodation home. Teetering on the unfamiliar high heels, she walked out of the drive and towards a sleek silver car, more than a little terrified to meet the politician.

'I have amazing taste!'

Gordon greeted her with a smile as his driver held open the door and Estelle climbed in. He was chubby, dressed in full Scottish regalia, and he made her smile even before she'd properly sat down.

'And you've got far better legs than me! I feel ridiculous in a kilt.'

Instantly he made her relax.

As the car headed for the airport he brought Estelle up to speed. 'We met two weeks ago…'

'Where?' Estelle asked.

'At Dario's…'

'Dario who?'

Gordon laughed. 'You really don't know anything, do you? It's a bar in Soho—sugar daddy heaven.'

'Oh, God…' she groaned.

'Do you work?' Gordon asked.

'Part-time at the library.'

'Maybe don't mention that. Just say you do a little bit of modelling,' Gordon suggested. 'Keep it all very vague, or say that right now keeping Gordon happy is a full-time job.' Estelle blushed and Gordon noticed. 'I know. Awful, isn't it? I seem to have created this terrible persona.'

'I'm worried that I shan't be able to pull it off.'

'You'll be fine,' Gordon said, and he went through everything with her again.

They practised their story over and over on the short flight to Edinburgh. He even asked after her brother and niece, and she was surprised that he knew about their plight.

'Virginia and I have become good friends this past year,' Gordon said. 'She was ever so upset for you when your brother had his accident and when the baby was born so unwell…' He gave her hand a squeeze. 'How is she now?'

'Waiting for surgery.'

'Just remember that you're helping them,' Gordon said as they transferred to the helicopter that would take them to the castle where the very exclusive wedding was being held.

As they walked across the immaculate lawn Gordon took her hand and she was grateful to hold onto it. He really was nice—if they had met under any other circumstances she would be looking forward to this evening.

'I can't wait to get inside the castle,' Estelle admitted. She'd already told Gordon she was studying ancient architecture.

'There won't be much time for exploring,' Gordon said. 'We'll be shown to our room and there will just be time to freshen up and touch up your hair and make-up before we head down for the wedding.'

'Okay.'

'And just remember,' Gordon said, 'this time tomorrow it will all be over and you'll never have to see any of them again.'

CHAPTER TWO

THE SOUND OF seagulls and the distant throb of music didn't wake Raúl from his slumber; instead they were the sounds that soothed him when he was startled in his sleep. He lay there, heart pounding for a moment, telling himself it was just a dream, while knowing that it was a memory that had jolted him awake.

The gentle motion of his berthed yacht almost tempted him back to sleep, but then he remembered that he was supposed to be meeting with his father.

Raúl forced his eyes open and stared at the tousled blonde hair on his pillow.

'*Buenos días,*' she purred.

'*Buenos días.*' Raúl responded, but instead of moving towards her he turned onto his back.

'What time do we leave for the wedding?'

Raúl closed his eyes at her presumption. He had never actually asked Kelly to join him as his guest, but that was the trouble with dating your PA—she knew your diary. The wedding was to be held this evening in the Scottish Highlands. It was nothing for Raúl to fly from Spain to Scotland for a wedding, but Kelly clearly thought that a few weeks out of his office and in his bed meant she was automatically invited.

'I'll speak to you about that later,' Raúl said, glancing at the clock. 'Right now I have to meet with my father.'

'Raúl…' Kelly turned to him in a move that was suggestive.

'Later,' he said, and climbed out of bed. 'I am supposed to be meeting with him in ten minutes.'

'That wouldn't have stopped you before.'

He took the stairs and walked up onto the deck, picking his way through the debris and the evidence of another wild Raúl Sanchez Fuente party. A maid was already starting the mammoth clean up and she gave a cheery wave to Raúl.

'*Gracias,*' she said as he gave her a substantial cash bonus without apologising for the mess. She did not mind his excesses—Raúl paid and treated her well, unlike the owners of some of the yachts, who expected her to work without complaint for very little.

Raúl put on his shades and walked along the Puerto Banús marina, where his yacht was moored. Here, Raúl belonged. Here, despite his decadent ways, he fitted in— because he was not the wildest. Raúl could hear a party continuing on, the music throbbing, the sound of laughter and merriment carrying across the sparkling water, and it reminded Raúl why he loved this place. Rarely was it ever silent. The marina was full of luxurious yachts and had the heady scent of filthy money. Ludicrously expensive cars were casually parked, all the fruits of serious wealth were on display here, and Raúl—dishevelled, unshaven and terribly beautiful—blended in well.

A couple of tourists stumbling home from a club nudged each other as Raúl walked past, trying to place him. For he was as good-looking as any film star and clearly he was *someone*. People-watching was a regular activity in Puerto

Banús, for amongst the tourists and locals were the rich, the famous and the notorious too.

Raúl scored two out of three—though he *was* famous in the business world.

Enrique, his driver, was waiting for him, and Raúl climbed in and gave a brief greeting, and then sat silently as he was driven the short distance to the Marbella branch of De La Fuente Holdings. He had no doubt as to what his father wanted to discuss, but his mind was going over what Kelly had just said.

'That wouldn't have stopped you before.'

Before what? Raúl asked himself.

Before he lost interest?

Before the chase had ended?

Before she assumed that a Saturday night would be shared?

Raúl was an island.

An island with frequent visitors and world-renowned parties, an island of endless sun and unlimited luxury, but one who preferred guests not to outstay their welcome, only allowed the superficial. Yes, Raúl was an island, and he intended to keep it that way. He certainly didn't want permanent boarders and he chose not to let anyone get too close.

He would never be responsible again for another's heart.

'I shan't be long,' Raúl told Enrique as the car door was lifted and he climbed out.

Raúl was not looking forward to this conversation, but his father had insisted they meet this morning and Raúl just wanted it over and done with.

'Buenos días.' He greeted Angela, his father's PA. 'What are you doing here on a Saturday?' he asked, because Angela usually flew home to her family for the weekend.

'I am trying to track down a certain Spaniard who said he would be here at eight a.m.,' Angela scolded mildly. She was the one woman who could get away with telling Raúl how it was. In her late fifties, she had been employed by the company for as long as Raúl could remember. 'I've been trying to call you—don't you ever have your phone on?'

'The battery is flat.'

'Well, before you speak with your father I need to go through your diary.'

'Later.'

'No, Raúl. I'm flying home later this morning. This needs to be done now. We also need to sort out a new PA for you—preferably one you *don't* fancy!' Angela was less than impressed with Raúl's brief eye-roll. 'Raúl, you need to remember that I'm going on long service leave in a few weeks' time. If I'm going to train somebody up for you, then I need to get on to it now.'

'Choose someone, then,' Raúl said. 'And you're right; perhaps it would be better if it was someone that I did not fancy.'

'Finally!' Angela sighed.

Yes, after having it pointed out to him on numerous occasions, Raúl was finally accepting that mixing business with pleasure had consequences, and sleeping with his PA was perhaps not such a good idea.

What was it with women? Raúl wondered. Why, once they'd made it to his bed, did they decide that they could no longer both work *and* sleep with him? Raúl could set his watch by it. After a few weeks they would decide, just as Kelly now had, that frequent dates and sex weren't enough. They wanted exclusivity, wanted inclusion, wanted commitment—which Raúl simply refused to give. Kelly would be found another position—or paid off handsomely, if that was what she preferred.

'All your flights and transfers are arranged for this afternoon,' Angela said. 'I can't believe that you'll be wearing a kilt.'

'I look good in a kilt.' Raúl smiled. 'Donald has asked that all the male guests wear them. I'm an honorary Scotsman, you know!' He was. He had studied in Scotland for four years, perhaps the best four years of his life, and the friendships he had made there had long continued.

Bar one.

His face hardened as he thought of his ex, who would be there tonight. Perhaps he *should* take Kelly after all, or arrive alone and get off with one of his old flames just to annoy the hell out of Araminta.

'Right, let's get this done…'

He went to walk towards his father's office but Angela called him back. 'It might be an idea to have a coffee before you see him.'

'No need,' Raúl said. 'I will get this over with and then go to Sol's for breakfast.' He loved Saturday mornings at Sol's—a beautiful waterfront café that moved you out quickly if you weren't one of the most beautiful. For people like Raúl they didn't even bother with a bill. They wanted his patronage, wanted the energy he brought to the place. Yes, Raúl decided, he would head there next—except Angela was calling him back again.

'Go and freshen up and I will bring you in coffee and a clean shirt.'

Yes, Angela was the only woman who could get away with speaking to him like that.

Raúl went into his own huge office—which was more like a luxurious hotel suite. As well as the office there was a sumptuous bedroom, and both rooms were put to good use. Heading towards the bathroom, he glanced at the bed and was briefly tempted to lie down. He had had two, possibly three hours' sleep last night. But he forced himself on to the bathroom, grimacing when he saw himself in the mirror. He could see now why Angela had been so insistent that he freshened up before facing his father.

Raúl's black eyes were bloodshot. He had forgotten to shave yesterday, so now two days' worth of black growth lined his strong jaw. His usually immaculate jet-black hair was tousled and fell over his forehead, and the lipstick on his collar, Raúl was sure, *wasn't* the colour that Kelly had been wearing last night.

Yes, he looked every inch the debauched playboy that his father accused him of being.

Raúl took off his jacket and shirt and splashed water on his face, and then set about changing, calling out his thanks to Angela when he heard her tell him that she had put a coffee on his desk.

'*Gracias!*' he called, and walked out mid-shave. Angela was possibly the only woman who did not blush at the sight of him without a shirt—she had seen him in nappies, after all. 'And thanks for pointing me in this direction before I meet with my father.'

'No problem.' She smiled. 'There is a fresh shirt hanging on the chair in your office also.'

'Do you know what it is that he wants to see me about?' Raúl was fishing. He knew exactly what his father would want to discuss. 'Am I to be given another lecture about taming my ways and settling down?'

'I'm not sure.' Only now did Angela's cheeks turn pink. 'Raúl, please listen to what your father has to say, though. This is no time for arguments. Your father is sick…'

'Just because he is ill, it does not necessarily make him right.'

'No,' Angela said carefully. 'But he does care for you, Raúl, even if he does not easily show it. Please listen to him… He is worried about you facing things on your own…' Angela saw Raúl's frown and stopped.

'I think you *do* know what this is about.'

'Raúl, I just ask that you listen—I can't bear to hear you two fighting.'

'Stop worrying,' Raúl said kindly. He liked Angela; she was the closest thing to a mum he had. 'I have no intention of fighting. I just think that at thirty years of age I don't have to be told my bedtime, and certainly not who I'm going to bed *with*…'

Raúl got back to shaving. He had no intention of being dictated to, but his hand did pause. Would it be such a big deal to let his father think that maybe he was actually serious about someone? Would it hurt just to hint that maybe he was close to settling down? His father was dying, after all.

'Wish me luck.' Raúl's voice was wry as, clean-shaven and bit clearer in the head, he walked past Angela to face his father. He glanced over, saw the tension and strain on her features. 'It will be fine,' he reassured her. 'Look…' He knew Angela would never keep news from his father. 'I *am* seeing someone, but I don't want him getting carried away.'

'Who?' Angela's eyes were wide.

'Just an old flame. We ran into each other again. She lives in England but I'm seeing her at the wedding tonight…'

'Araminta!'

'Stop there…' Raúl smiled. That was all that was needed. He knew the seed had been sewn.

Raúl knocked on his father's door and stepped in.

There should have been flames, he thought afterwards.

Or the smell of sulphur. Actually, there should have been the smell of car fuel and the sound of thunder followed by silence. There should at least have been some warning, as he was walked through the door, that he was returning to hell.

CHAPTER THREE

ESTELLE FELT AS if everyone knew what a fraud she was.

She closed her heavily made-up eyes and dragged in a deep breath. They were standing in the castle grounds, waiting to be led to their seating, and some pre-wedding drinks and nibbles were being served.

Why they hell had she agreed to this?

You know why, Estelle told herself, her resolve hardening.

'Are you okay, darling?' Gordon asked. 'The wedding should start soon.'

He'd been nothing but kind, just as Ginny had promised he would be.

'I'm fine,' Estelle said, and held a little more tightly onto his arm, just as Gordon had told her to do.

'This is Estelle.'

Gordon introduced her to a couple and Estelle watched the slight rise of the woman's eyebrow.

'Estelle, this is Veronica and James.'

'Estelle.' Veronica gave a curt nod and soon moved James away.

'You're doing wonderfully,' Gordon said, squeezing her hand and drawing her away from the mingling wedding guests so that they could speak without being overheard. 'Maybe you just need to smile a bit more,' he suggested gently, 'and, I know it calls for brilliant acting, could you try and look just a little more besotted with me? I've got my terrible reputation with women to think of.'

'Of course,' Estelle said through chattering teeth.

'The gay man and the virgin,' Gordon whispered in her ear. 'If only they knew!'

Estelle's eyes widened in horror and Gordon quickly apologised. 'I was just trying to make you smile,' he said.

'I can't believe that she *told* you!'

Estelle was horrified that Ginny would share something as personal and as sensitive as that. Then again, she could believe it—Ginny found it endlessly amusing that Estelle had never slept with anyone. It wasn't by deliberate choice; it wasn't something she'd actively decided. More that she'd been so shell shocked by her parents' death that home-work and books had been her escape. By the time she'd emerged from her grief Estelle had felt two steps behind her peers. Clubs and parties had seemed frivolous. It was ancient ruins and buildings that fascinated her, and when she did meet someone there was always a panic that her virgin status must mean she was looking for a husband. More and more it had become an issue.

Now it would seem it was a joke!

She'd be having strong words with Ginny.

'Virginia didn't say it in a malicious way.' Gordon seemed devastated to have upset her. 'We were just talking one night. I really should never have brought it up.'

'It's okay,' Estelle conceded. 'I guess I am a bit of a rarity.'

'We all have our secrets,' Gordon said. 'And for tonight we both have to cover them up.' He smiled at her strained expression. 'Estelle, I know how hard it was for you to agree to this, but I promise you have nothing to feel nervous about. I'm soon to be a happily married man.'

'I know,' Estelle said. Gordon had told her on the plane about his long-term boyfriend, Frank, and the plans they had made. 'I just can't stand the disapproving looks and that everyone thinks of me as a gold-digger,' she admitted. 'Even though that's the whole point of the night.'

'Stop caring what everyone thinks,' Gordon said.

It was the same as she said to Andrew, who was acutely embarrassed to be in a wheelchair. 'You're right.'

Gordon lifted her chin and she smiled into his eyes. 'That's better.' Gordon smiled back. 'We'll get through this together.'

So Estelle held onto his arm and did her best to look suitably besotted, ignoring the occasional disapproving stare from the other guests, and she was just starting to relax and get into things when *he* arrived.

Till that moment Estelle had thought it would be the bride who would make an entrance, and it wasn't the sight of a helicopter landing that had heads turning—helicopters had been landing regularly since Estelle had got there— no, it was the man who stepped out who held everyone's attention.

'Oh, my, the evening just got interesting,' Gordon said as the most stunning man ducked under the blades and then walked towards the gathering.

He was tall, his thick black hair brushed back and gleaming, and his mouth was sulky and unsmiling. His Mediterranean colouring should surely mean that he'd look out of place wearing a kilt, but instead he looked as if he'd been born to wear one. Lean-hipped and long-limbed, but muscular too, he could absolutely carry it off.

He could carry me off right now, Estelle thought wildly—and wild thoughts were rare for Estelle.

She watched as he accepted whisky from a waiter and then stood still. He seemed removed and remote from everyone else. Even the women who flocked to him were quickly dismissed, as if at any minute he might simply walk off.

Then he met her eyes.

Estelle tried to flick hers away, except she found that she couldn't.

His eyes drifted down over the gold dress, but not in the disapproving way that Veronica's had. Although they weren't approving either. They were merely assessing.

She felt herself burn as his eyes moved then to her sixty-four-year-old date, and she wanted to correct him—wanted to tell him that the rotund, red-faced man who was struggling with the heat in his heavy kilt and jacket was not her lover. Though of course she could not.

She wanted to, though.

'Eyes only for me, darling,' Gordon reminded her, perhaps picking up on the crackle of energy crossing the lawn. His glance followed Estelle's gaze. 'Though frankly no one would blame you a bit for looking. He's completely divine.'

'Who?' Estelle tried to pretend that she hadn't noticed the delicious stranger—Gordon was paying her good money to be here, after all—but she wasn't fooling anyone.

'Raúl Sanchez Fuente,' Gordon said in a low voice. 'Our paths cross now and then at various functions. He owns everything but morals. The bastard even looks good in a kilt. He has my heart—not that he wants it…'

Estelle couldn't help but laugh.

Raúl's eyes lazily worked over the guests. He was questioning now his decision to come alone. He needed distraction tonight, but when he had thought of the old flames that he might run into he had been thinking of the perky breasts and the narrow waists of yesteryear, as if the clock might have stopped on his university days. Instead the hands of time had moved on.

There was Shona. Her once long red hair was now cut too severely and she stood next to a chinless wonder. She caught his eye and then blushed unbecomingly and shot him a furious look, as if their once torrid times could be erased and forgotten by her wedding ring.

He knew, though, that she was remembering.

'Raúl...'

He frowned when he saw Araminta walking towards him. She was wearing that slightly needy smile that Raúl recognised only too well and it made his early warning system react—because temporary distraction was his requirement tonight, not desperation.

'How are you?'

'Not bad,' she said, and then proceeded to tell him about her hellish divorce, how she was now single, how she'd thought about him often since the break-up, how she'd been looking forward to seeing him tonight, how she regretted the way things had worked out for them...

'I told you that you would at the time.' Raúl did not do sentiment. 'You'll have to excuse me. I have to make a call.'

'We'll catch up later, though?'

He could hear the hope in her voice and it irked him.

Was he good enough for her father now? Rich enough? Established enough?

'There's nothing to catch up on.'

Just like that he dismissed her, his black eyes not even watching her as she gave a small sob and walked off.

What on earth was he doing here? Raúl wondered. He should be getting ready to party on his yacht, or to hit the clubs—should be losing himself instead of getting reacquainted with his past. More to the point, there was hardly a limitless choice of women in this castle in the Scottish

Highlands. And after what Raúl had found out this morning his own company wasn't one he wanted to keep.

His hand tightened on the whisky glass he held. The full impact of what his father had told him was only now starting to hit him.

So black were his thoughts, so sideswiped was he by the revelations, Raúl actually considered leaving—just summoning his pilot and walking out. But then a tumble of dark hair and incredibly pale skin caught his eye and held it. She looked nervous and awkward—which was unusual for Gordon's tarts. They were normally brash and confident. But not this one.

He held her gaze when she caught his and now there was only one woman he wanted to walk towards him—except she was holding tightly to Gordon's arm.

She offered far more than distraction—she offered oblivion. Because for the first time since his conversation with his father he forgot about it.

Perhaps he would stay. At least for the service...

A deep Scottish voice filled the air and the guests were informed that the wedding would soon commence and they were to make their way to their seats.

'Come on.' Gordon took Estelle's hand. 'I love a good wedding.'

'And me.' Estelle smiled.

They walked through the mild night. The grounds were lit by torches and there were chairs set out. With the castle as a backdrop the scene looked completely stunning, and Estelle let go of her guilt, determined to enjoy herself. She'd been on a plane and, for the first time in her life, a helicopter, she was staying the night in a beautiful castle in the Scottish Highlands, and Gordon was an absolute delight. Despite having dreaded it, she was enjoying herself, Estelle realised as they took their seats and she made more small talk with Gordon.

'Donald says that Victoria's so nervous,' he told her. 'She's such a perfectionist, apparently, and she's been stressing over the details for months.'

'Well, it all seems to have paid off,' Estelle said. 'I can't wait to see what she's wearing.'

Just as she'd finally started to relax as the music changed and they all stood for the bride, just as she'd decided simply to enjoy herself, she turned to get a first glimpse of the bride—only to realise that Raúl was sitting behind her.

Directly behind her.

It should make no difference, Estelle told herself. It was a simple coincidence. But even coincidence was too big a word—after all, he had to sit *somewhere*. Estelle was just acutely aware that he was there.

She tried to concentrate on the bride as she made her way to Donald. Victoria really did look stunning. She was wearing a very simple white dress and carried a small posy of heather. The smile on Donald's face as his bride walked towards him had Estelle smiling too—but not for long. She could feel Raúl's eyes burning into her shoulder, and a little while later her scalp felt as if it were on fire. She was sure his eyes lingered there.

She did her best to focus on the service. It was incredibly romantic. So much so that when they got to the 'in sickness and in health' part it actually brought tears to her eyes as she remembered her brother Andrew's wedding, just over a year ago.

Who could have known then the hard blows fate had in store for him and his pregnant bride, Amanda?

Ever the gentleman, Gordon pressed a tissue into her hand.

'Thank you.' Estelle gave a watery smile and Gordon gave her hand a squeeze.

* * *

Please! Raúl thought. *Spare me the crocodile tears.* It had been the same with Gordon's previous girlfriend—what was her name? Raúl smiled to himself, as he had the day they were introduced.

Virginia.

This one, though, even if she wasn't to Raúl's usual taste, was stunning. Raven-haired women were far from a rarity where Raúl came from, and for that reason he certainly preferred a blonde—for variety, two blondes!

He wanted raven tonight.

Turn around, Raúl thought, for he wanted to meet those eyes again.

Turn around, he willed her, watching her shoulders stiffen, watching the slight tilt of her neck as if she was aware of but resisting his silent demand.

How she was resisting.

Estelle sat rigid and then stood in the same way after the service was over, when the bride and groom were letting doves fly. They fluttered high into the sky and the crowd murmured and pointed and turned to watch them in flight.

Reluctantly she also turned, and she must look up, Estelle thought helplessly as two black liquid pools invited her to dive in. She should, like everyone else, move her gaze upwards and watch the doves fly off into the distance.

Instead she faced him.

What the hell are you doing with him? Raúl wanted to ask. *What the hell are you doing with a man perhaps three times your age?*

Of course he knew the answer.

Money.

And Raúl knew then what to do—knew the answer to the dilemma that had been force-fed to him at breakfast-time.

His mouth moved into a smile and he watched as her head jerked away—watched as she stared, too late, up into the sky. And he saw her pale throat as her neck arched and he wanted his mouth there.

A piper led them back to the castle. He walked in front of her and Gordon. Estelle's heels kept sinking into the grass, but it was nothing compared to the feeling of drowning in quicksand when she had been caught in Raúl's gaze.

His kilt was greys and lilacs, his jacket a dark purple velvet, his posture and his stride exact and sensual. She wanted to run up to him, to tap him on the shoulder and tell him to please leave her alone. Yet he had done nothing. He wasn't even looking over his shoulder. He was just chatting with a fellow guest as they made their way back to the castle.

Very deliberately Raúl ignored her. He turned his back and chatted with Donald, asked a favour from a friend, and then flirted a little with a couple of old flames—but at all times he knew that her eyes more than occasionally searched out his.

Raúl knew exactly what he was doing and he knew exactly why.

Mixing business with pleasure had caused a few problems for Raúl in the past.

Tonight it was suddenly the solution.

CHAPTER FOUR

'EXCUSE ME, SIR.'

A waiter halted Estelle and Gordon as they made their way into the Grand Hall and to their table.

'There's been a change to the seating plan. Donald and Victoria didn't realise that you were seated so far back. It's all been rectified now. Please accept our apologies for the mistake.'

'*Oooh,* we're getting an upgrade,' Gordon said as they were led nearer to the front.

Estelle flushed when she saw that the rather teary woman she had seen earlier speaking with Raúl was being quietly shuffled back to the bowels of the hall. Estelle knew even before they arrived at the new table which one it would be.

Raúl did not look up as they made their way over. Not until they were being shown into their seats.

She smiled a greeting to Veronica and James, but could not even attempt one for Raúl—both seats either side of him were empty.

He had done this.

Estelle tried to tell herself she was imagining things, or overreacting, but somehow she knew she was right. Knew that those long, lingering stares had led to this.

The chair next to him was being held out. She wanted

to turn to Gordon, to ask if they could swap seats but she knew that would look ridiculous.

It was a simple change of seating, Estelle told herself.

She acknowledged to herself that she lied.

'Gordon.' Raúl shook his hand.

'Raúl.'

Gordon smiled as he took the seat next to Estelle, so she was sandwiched between them, and she leant back a little as they chatted.

'I haven't seen you since…' Gordon laughed. 'Since last wedding season. This is Estelle.'

'Estelle.' He raised one eyebrow as she took her seat beside him. 'In Spain you would be Estela.'

'We're in England.' She was aware of her brittle response, but her defences were up—though she did try to soften it with a brief smile.

'Of course.' Raúl shrugged. 'Though I must speak with my pilot. He was most insistent, when we landed, that this was *Scotland.*'

She tried so hard not to, but Estelle twitched her lips into a slight smile.

'This is Shona and Henry…' Raúl introduced them as a waiter poured some wine.

Estelle took a sip and then asked for water—for a draughty castle, it felt terribly warm.

There was brief conversation and more introductions taking place, and all would have been fine if Raúl were not there. But Estelle was aware, despite his nonchalant appearance, that he was carefully listening to her responses.

She laughed just a little too loudly at one of Gordon's jokes.

As she'd been told to do.

Gordon was busy speaking with James, and for something to do Estelle looked through the menu, squinting because Ginny had suggested that she leave her glasses at home.

Raúl misconstrued it as a frown.

'Vichyssoise,' came his low, deep voice. 'It is a soup. It's delicious.'

'I don't need hand-holding for the menu.' Estelle stopped herself, aware she was coming across as terribly rude, but her nerves were prickling in defensiveness. 'And you failed to mention it's served cold.'

'No.' He smiled. 'I was just about to tell you that.'

Soup was a terribly hard ask with Raúl sitting next to her, but she worked her way through it, even though her conversation with Gordon kept getting interrupted by his phone.

'I can't even get a night off.' He sighed.

'Important?' Estelle checked.

'It could be soon. I'll have to keep it on silent.'

The main course was served and it was the most gorgeous beef Estelle had ever tasted. Yet it stuck in her throat—especially when Veronica asked her a question.

'Do you work, Estelle?'

She took a drink of water before answering. 'I do a bit of modeling.' Estelle gave a small smile, remembering how Gordon had told her to respond to such a question. She just hadn't expected to be inhaling testosterone when she answered. 'Though, of course, taking care of Gordon is a full-time job...'

Estelle saw the pausing of Raúl's fork and then heard Gordon's stab of laughter. She was locked in a lie and there was no way out. It was an act, Estelle told herself. Just one night and she would never have to see these people again—and what did she care if Raúl thought her cheap?

'Could you pass me the pepper?' came the silk of his voice.

Was it the fact that it had been asked with a Spanish accent that made the question sound sexy, or was it that she was going mad?

She passed it, holding the heavy silver pot and releasing it to him, feeling the brief warmth of his fingertips as he took it. He immediately noticed her error. 'That's the salt,' Raúl said, and she had to go through it again.

It was bizarre. He had said hardly two words to her, had made no suggestions. There were no knees pressing into hers under the table and his hands had not lingered when she'd passed him the pepper, yet the air between them was thick with tension.

He declined dessert and spread cheese onto Scottish oatcakes. 'I'd forgotten how good these taste.'

She turned and watched as he took a bite and then ran his tongue over his lip, capturing a small sliver of quince paste.

'Now I remember.'

There was no implication. He was only making small talk.

It was Estelle's mind that searched every word.

She spread cheese on an oatcake herself and added quince.

'Fantastic?' Raúl asked.

'Yes.'

She knew he meant sex.

'Now the speeches.' Gordon sighed.

They were long. Terribly long. Especially when you had no idea who the couple were. Especially when you were supposed to be paying attention to the man on your right but your mind was on the one to your left.

First it was Victoria's father, who rambled on just a touch too long. Then it was the groom Donald's turn, and he was thankfully a bit quicker—and funnier too. He moved through the formalities and, on behalf of himself and his new wife, especially thanked all who had travelled from afar.

'I was hoping Raúl wouldn't make it, of course,' Donald said, looking over to Raúl, as did the whole room. 'I'm just thankful Victoria didn't see him in a kilt until *after* my ring was on her finger. Trust a Spaniard to wear a kilt so well.'

The whole room laughed. Raúl's shoulders moved in a light, good-natured laugh too. He wasn't remotely embarrassed—no doubt more than used to the attention and to having his beauty confirmed.

Then it was the best man's turn.

'In Spain there are no speeches at a wedding,' Raúl said, leaning across her a little to speak to Gordon.

She could smell his expensive cologne, and his arm was leaning slightly on her. Estelle watched her fingers around the stem of her glass tighten.

'We just have the wedding, a party, and then bed,' Raúl said.

It was the first hint of suggestion, but even so she could merely be reading into things too much. Except as he leant over her to hear Gordon's response Estelle wanted to put her hand up, wanted to ask for the lights to come on, for this assault on her senses to stop, to tell the room the inappropriateness of the man sitting beside her. Only not a single thing had he done—not a word or hand had he put wrong.

So why was her left breast aching, so close to where his arm was? Why were her two front teeth biting down on her lip at the sight of his cheek, inches away?

'Really?' Gordon checked. 'I might just have to move to Spain! In actual fact I was—'

Gordon was interrupted by the buzz of his phone and

Raúl moved back in his seat. Estelle sat watching the newly wed couple dancing.

'Darling, I am so sorry,' Gordon said as he read a message on his phone. 'I am going to have to find somewhere I can make some calls and use a computer.'

'Good luck getting internet access,' drawled Raúl. 'I have to go outside just to make a call.'

'I might be some time.'

'Trouble?' Estelle asked

'Always.' Gordon rolled his eyes. 'Though this is unexpected. But I'll deal with it as quickly as I can. I hate to leave you on your own.'

'She won't be on her own,' Raúl said. 'I can keep an eye.'

She rather wished that he wouldn't.

'Thanks so much,' Gordon said. 'In that dress she deserves to dance.' He turned to Estelle. 'I really am sorry to leave you…' For appearances' sake, he kissed her on the cheek.

What a waste of her mouth, Raúl thought.

Once Gordon had gone she turned to James and Veronica, on her right, desperately trying to feed into their conversation. But they were certainly not interested in Gordon's new date. Over and over they politely dismissed her, and then followed the other couples at their table and got up to dance—leaving her alone with Raúl.

'From the back you could be Spanish…'

She turned to the sound of his voice.

'But from the front…'

His eyes ran over her creamy complexion and she felt heat sear her face as his eyes bored into hers. And though they did not wander—he was far too suave for that—somehow he undressed her. Somehow she sat there on her seat beside him at the wedding as if they were a couple. And when he looked at her, she felt, for a bizarre second, as if she was completely naked.

He was as potent as that.

CHAPTER FIVE

'IRISH?' HE CHECKED, and Estelle hesitated for a moment before nodding.

She did not want to give any information to this man—did not even want to partake in conversation.

'Yet your accent is English?'

'My parents moved to England before I was born.' She gave a tight swallow and hoped her stilted response would halt the conversation. It did not.

'Where in England are they?'

'They're not,' Estelle answered, terribly reluctant to reveal *anything* of herself.

Raúl did not push. Instead he moved the conversation on.

'So, where did you and Gordon meet?'

'We met at Dario's.' Estelle answered the question as Gordon had told her to, trying to tell herself he was just being polite, but every sense in her body seemed set to high alert. 'It's a bar—'

'In Soho,' Raúl broke in. 'I have heard a lot about Dario's.'

Beneath her make-up her cheeks were scalding.

'Not that I have been,' Raúl said. 'As a male, I would perhaps be too young to get in there.' His lips rose in a slight smile and he watched the colour flood darker in her neck and to her ears. 'Maybe I should give it a try...'

He looked more closely at Estelle. She had eyes that were a very dark green and rounded cheeks—she really was astonishingly attractive. There was something rather sweet about her despite the clothes, despite the make-up, and there was an awkwardness that was as rare as it was refreshing. Raúl was not used to awkwardness in the women he dated.

'So, we both find ourselves alone at a wedding…'

'I'm not alone,' Estelle said. 'Gordon will be back soon.' She did not want to ask, but she found herself doing just that as she glanced to the empty chair beside him. 'How come…?' Her voice faded out. There was no polite way to address it.

'We broke up this morning.'

'I'm sorry.'

'Please don't be.' He thought for a moment before continuing. 'Really to say we broke up is perhaps an exaggeration. To break something would mean you had to have something, and we were only going out for a few weeks.'

'Even so…' Still she attempted to be polite. 'Breakups are hard.'

'I've never found them to be,' Raúl said. 'It's the bit before that I struggle with.'

'When it starts to go wrong?'

'No,' Raúl said. 'When it starts to go right.'

His eyes were looking right into hers, his voice was deep and low, and his words interesting—because despite herself she *did* want to know more about this fascinating man. So much so that she found herself leaning in a little to hear.

'When she starts asking what we are doing next weekend. When you hear her saying "Raúl said…" or "Raúl thinks…"' He paused for a second. 'I don't like to be told what I'm thinking.'

'I'm sure you don't.'

'Do you know what I'm thinking now?'

'I wouldn't presume to.' She could hardly breathe, because she was surely thinking the same.

'Would you like to dance?'

'No, thank you,' Estelle said, because it was far safer to stay seated than to self-combust in his arms. He was sinfully good-looking and, more worryingly, she had a sinking feeling as she realised he was pulling her in deeper with each measured word. 'I'll just wait here for Gordon.'

'Of course,' Raúl said. 'Have you met the bride or groom?'

'No.' Estelle felt as if she were being interviewed. 'You're friends with the groom?'

'I went to university with him.'

'In Spain?'

'No, here in Scotland.'

'Oh!' She wasn't sure why, but that surprised her.

'I was here for four years,' Raúl said. 'Then I moved back to Marbella. I still like to come here. Scotland is a very beautiful country.'

'It is,' Estelle said. 'Well, from the little I've seen.'

'It's your first time?'

She nodded.

'Have you ever been to Spain?'

'Last year,' Estelle said. 'Though only for a few days. Then there was a family emergency and I had to go home.'

'Raúl?'

He barely looked up as a woman came over. It was the same woman who had been moved from the table earlier.

'I thought we could dance.'

'I'm busy.'

'Raúl…'

'Araminta.' Now he turned and looked at her. 'If I wanted to dance with you then I would have asked.'

Estelle blinked, because despite the velvet of his voice his words were brutal.

'That was a bit harsh,' Estelle said as Araminta stumbled off.

'Far better to be harsh than to give mixed messages.'

'Perhaps.'

'So…' Raúl chose his words carefully. 'If taking care of Gordon is a full-time job, what do you do in your time off?'

'My time off?'

'When you're not *working*.'

She didn't frown this time. There was no mistake as to what he meant. Her green eyes flashed as she turned to him. 'I don't appreciate the implication.'

He was surprised by her challenge, liked that she met him head-on—it was rare that anyone did.

'Excuse me,' he said. 'Sometimes my English is not so good…'

When it suited him.

Estelle took a deep breath, her hand still toying with the stem of her glass as she wondered how to play this, deciding she would do her best to be polite.

'What work do you do?' She looked at him. She had absolutely no idea about this man. 'Are you in politics too?'

'Please!'

He watched the slight reluctant smile on her lips.

'I am a director for De La Fuente Holdings, which means I buy, improve or build, and then maybe I sell.' Still he watched her. 'Take this castle; if I owned it I would not have it exclusively as a wedding venue but also as a hotel. It is under-utilised. Mind you, it would need a lot of refurbishment. I have not shared a bathroom since my university days.'

She was far from impressed and tried not to show it. Raúl, of course, could not know that she was studying ancient architecture and that buildings were a passion of hers. The castle renovations she had seen were modest, the rooms cold and the bathrooms sparse—as it should be. The thought of this place being modernised and filled to capacity, no matter how tastefully, left her cold.

Unfortunately *he* didn't.

Not once in her twenty-five years had Estelle even come close to the reaction she was having to Raúl.

If they were anywhere else she would get up and leave.

Or, she conceded, if they were anywhere else she would lean forward and accept his mouth.

'So it's your father's business?' Estelle asked, trying to find a fault in him—trying to tell herself that it was his father's money that had eased his luxurious path to perfection.

'No, it was my mother's family business. My father bought into it when he married.' He saw her tiny frown.

'Sorry, you said De La Fuente, and I thought Fuente was *your* surname...'

For an occasional model who picked up men at Dario's she was rather perceptive, Raúl thought. 'In Spain it is different. You take your father's surname first and then your mother's...'

'I didn't know that.' She tried to fathom it. 'How does it work?'

'My father is Antonio Sanchez. My mother was Gabriella De La Fuente.'

'Was?'

'She passed away in a car accident...'

Normally he could just say it. Every other time he revealed it he just glossed over it, moved swiftly on—tonight, with all he had learnt this morning, suddenly he could not.

Every man except Raúl had struggled in the summer heat with full Scottish regalia. Supremely fit, and used to the sun, Raúl had not even broken a sweat. But now, when the castle was cool, when a draught swirled around the floor, he broke into one—except his face drained of colour.

He tried to right himself, reached for water; he had trained his mind not to linger. Of course he had not quite mastered his mind at night, but even then he had trained himself to wake up before he shouted out.

'Was it recent?' Estelle saw him struggle briefly, knew surely better than anyone how he must feel—for she had lost her parents the same way. She watched as he drained a glass of water and then blinked when he turned and the suave Raúl returned.

'Years ago,' he dismissed. 'When I was a child.' He got back to their discussion, refusing to linger on a deeply buried past. 'My actual name is Raúl Sanchez De La Fuente, but it gets a bit long during introductions.'

He smiled, and so too did Estelle.

'I can imagine.'

'But I don't want to lose my mother's name, and of course my father expects me to keep his.'

'It's nice that the woman's name passes on.'

'It doesn't, though,' Raúl said. 'Well, it does for one generation—it is still weighted to the man.' He saw her frown.

'So, if you had a baby…?'

'That's never going to happen.'

'But if you did?'

'God forbid.' He let out a small sigh. 'I will try to explain.'

He was very patient.

He took the salt and pepper she had so nervously passed to him and, heads together, they sat at the table while he made her a small family tree.

'What is your surname?'

'Connolly.'

'Okay, we have a baby and call her Jane…'

How he made her burn. Not at the baby part, but at the thought of the part to get to that.

'Her name would be Jane Sanchez Connolly.'

'I see.'

'And when Jane marries…' he lifted a hand and grabbed a fork as he plucked a name from the ether '…Harry Potter, her daughter…' he added a spoon '…who shall also be called Jane, would be Jane Sanchez Potter. Connolly would be gone!' He looked at her as she worked it out. 'It is simple. At least the name part is simple. It is the fifty years of marriage that might prove hard.' He glanced over to today's happy couple. 'I can't imagine being tied down to another, and I certainly don't believe in love.'

He always made that clear up-front.

'How can you sit at a wedding and say that?' Estelle challenged. 'Did you not see the smile on Donald's face when he saw his bride?'

'Of course I did,' Raúl said. 'I recognised it well—it was the same smile he gave at the last wedding of his I attended.'

She laughed. There was no choice but to. 'Are you serious?'

'Completely,' Raúl said.

Yet he was smiling, and when he did that she felt as if she should scrabble in her bag for sunglasses, because the force of his smile blinded her to all faults—and she was quite positive a man like Raúl had many.

'You're wrong, Raúl.' She refused to play his cynical game. 'My brother got married last year and he and his wife are deeply in love.'

'A year.' He gave a light shrug. 'It is still the honeymoon phase.'

'They've been through more in this year than most have been through in a lifetime.' And she'd never meant to but she found herself opening up to him. 'Andrew, my brother, was in an accident on their honeymoon—a jet ski…'

'Serious?'

Estelle nodded. 'He's now in a wheelchair.'

'That must take a lot of getting used to.' He thought for a moment. 'Is that the family emergency you had to fly home from your own holiday for?'

Estelle nodded. She didn't tell him it had been a trip around churches. No doubt he assumed she'd been hauled out of a club to hear the news. 'I raced home, and, really, since then things have been tough on them. Amanda was already pregnant when they got married…'

She didn't know why she was telling him. Perhaps it was safer to talk than to dance. Maybe it was easier to talk about her brother and the truth than make up stories about Dario's and seedy clubs in Soho. Or perhaps it was the black liquid eyes that invited conversation, the way he moved his chair a little closer so that he could hear.

'Their daughter was born four months ago. The prospect of being a dad was the main thing that kept Andrew motivated during his rehabilitation. Just when we thought things were turning around…'

Raúl watched her green eyes fill with tears, saw her rapid blink as she tried to stem them.

'She has a heart condition. They're waiting till she's a little bit bigger so they can operate.'

He watched pale hands go to her bag and Estelle took out a photo. He looked at her brother, Andrew, and his wife, and a small frail baby with a slight blue tinge to her skin, and he realised that they hadn't been crocodile tears he had witnessed during the wedding ceremony. He looked back to Estelle.

'What's her name?'

'Cecelia.'

Raúl looked at her as she gazed at the photo and he knew then the reason she was here with Gordon. 'Your brother?' Raúl asked, just to confirm things in his mind. 'Does he work?'

'No.' Estelle shook her head. 'He was self-employed. He…' She put away the photo, dragged in a breath, could not stand to think of all the problems her brother faced.

Exactly at that moment Raúl lightened things.

'My legs are cold.'

Estelle laughed, and as she did she blinked as a photographer's camera flashed in her face.

'Nice natural shot,' the photographer said.

'We're not…' Oh, what did it matter?

'I need to move.' He stood. 'And Gordon asked that I take care of you.' Raúl held out his hand to her. This dance was more important than she could ever know. This dance must ensure that tonight she was thinking only of *him*— that by the time he approached her with his suggestion it would not seem so unthinkable. But first he had to set the tone. First he had to make her aware that he knew the sort of business she was in. 'Would you like to dance?'

Estelle didn't really have a choice. Walking towards the dance floor, she had the futile hope that the band would break into something more frivolous than sensuous, but all hope was gone as his arms wrapped loosely around her.

'You are nervous?'

'No.'

'I would have thought you would enjoy dancing, given that you two met at Dario's.'

'I do love to dance.' Estelle forced a bright smile, remembered who she was supposed to be. 'It's just a bit early for me.'

'And me,' Raul said as he took her in his arms. 'About now I would only just be getting ready to go out.'

She couldn't read this man. Not in the least. He held her, he was skilled and graceful, but the eyes that looked down at her were not smiling.

'Relax.'

She tried to—except he'd said it into her ear, causing the sensitive skin there to tingle.

'Can I ask something?'

'Of course,' Estelle said, though she would rather he didn't. She just wanted this duty dance to end.

'What are you doing with Gordon?'

'Excuse me?' She could not believe he would ask that—could not think of anyone else who would be so direct. It was as if all pretence had gone—all tiny implications, all conversation left behind—and the truth was being revealed in his arms.

'There is a huge age difference...'

'That's none of your business.' She felt as if she was being attacked in broad daylight and everyone else was just carrying on, oblivious.

'You are twenty, yes?'

'Twenty-five.'

'He was ten years older than I am now when you were born.'

'They're just numbers.'

'We both work in numbers.'

Estelle went to walk off mid-dance, but his grip merely tightened. 'Of course...' He held her so she could feel the lean outline of his body, inhale the terribly masculine scent of him. 'You want him only for his money.'

'You're incredibly rude.'

'I'm incredibly honest,' Raúl corrected. 'I am not criticizing—there is nothing wrong with that.'

'*Vete al infierno!*' Estelle said, grateful for a Spanish schoolfriend and lunchtimes being taught by her how to curse. She watched his mouth curve as she told him in his own language to go to hell. 'Excuse me,' Estelle said. 'Sometimes my Spanish is not so good. What I mean to say is…'

He pressed a finger to her lips before she could tell him, in her own language and rather more crudely, exactly where he could go.

The contact with her mouth, the sensual pressure, the intimacy of the gesture, had the desired effect and silenced her.

'One more dance,' Raúl said. 'Then I return you to Gordon.' He removed his finger. 'I'm sorry if you thought I was being rude—believe me, that was not my intention. Accept my apology, please.'

Estelle's eyes narrowed in suspicious assessment. She was aware of the pulse in her lips from his mere touch. Logic told her to remove herself from this situation, yet the stir of first arousal won.

The music slowed and, ignoring brief resistance, he pulled her in tighter. If she thought he was judging her, she was right—only it was not harshly. Raúl admired a woman who could separate emotion from sex.

Raúl needed exactly such a woman if he were to see this through.

He did not think her cheap: on the contrary, he intended to pay her very well.

She should have gone then—back to the table, to be ignored by the other guests. Should have left this man at a safer point. But her naïve body was refusing to walk away; instead it was awakening in his arms.

He held her so that her head was resting on his chest. She could feel the soft velvet of his jacket on her cheek. But she was more aware of his hand resting lightly on the base of her spine.

A couple dancing, each in a world of their own.

Raúl's motives were temporarily suspended. He enjoyed the soft weight that leant against him, the quiet of his mind as he focused only on her. The hand on her shoulder crept beneath her hair, his fingers lightly stroking the back of her neck, and again he wanted his mouth there, wanted to lift the raven curtain and taste her.

His fingers told her so—they stroked in a soft probing and they circled and teased as she swayed in time to the music. Estelle felt the stirring between them, and though her head denied what was happening her body shifted a little to allow for him. Her nipples hurt against his chest. His hand pressed her in just a little tighter as again he broke all boundaries. Again he voiced what perhaps others would not.

'I always thought a sporran was for decorative purposes only...'

She could feel the heat of its fur against her stomach.

'Yet it is the only thing keeping me decent.'

'You're *so* far from decent,' Estelle rasped.

'I know.'

They danced—not much, just swaying in time. Except she was on fire.

He could feel the heat of her skin on his fingers, could feel her breath so shallow that he wanted to lower his head and breathe into her mouth for her. He thought of her dark hair on his pillow, of her pink nipples in his mouth at the same time. He wanted her more than he had wanted any other, though Raúl was not comfortable with that thought.

This was business, Raúl reminded himself as motive returned. Tonight she would think of *his* lean, aroused body. When she was bedded by Gordon it would be *his* lithe body she ached for. He must now make sure of that. It was a business decision, and he made business decisions well.

His hand slid from beneath her hair down to the side of her ribs, to the bare skin there.

She ached. She ached for his hand to move, to cup her breast. And again he confirmed what was happening.

'Soon I return you to Gordon,' Raúl said, 'but first you come to *me*.'

It was foreplay. So much so she felt that as if his fingers were inside her. So much so that she could feel, despite the sporran, the thick outline beneath his kilt. It was the most dangerous dance of her life. She wanted to turn. She wanted to run. Except her body wanted the feel of his arms. Her burning cheeks rested against purple velvet and she could hear the steady thud of his heart as hers tripped and galloped. No one around them had a clue about the fire in his arms.

He smelt exquisite, and his cheek near hers had her head wanting to turn, to seek the relief of his mouth. She did not know the range of *la petit mort* or that he was giving her a mere taste. Estelle was far too innocent to know that she was building up to doing exactly as instructed and coming to him.

Raúl knew exactly when he felt the tension in his arms slowly abate, felt her slip a little down his chest as for a brief moment she relaxed against him.

'Thank you for the dance.' Breathless, stunned, she went to step back.

But still he held her as he lifted her chin and offered his verdict. 'You know, I would like to see you *really* cuss in Spanish.'

He let her go then, and Estelle headed to the safety of the ladies' room and ran her wrists under the tap to cool them.

Careful, she told herself. *Be careful here, Estelle.*

There was a blaze of attraction more intense than any she had known. What Estelle *did* know, though, was that a man like Raúl would crush her in the palm of his hand.

She looked up into the mirror and took out her lipstick; she could not fathom what had just taken place—nor that she had allowed it.

That she had partaken in it.

And willingly at that.

'There you are.'

Gordon smiled as she headed back to the table and she could not feel more guilty: she'd even failed as an escort.

'I'm so sorry to have left you—some foreign minister wanted to speak urgently with me, but we couldn't get him on the line and when we did…' Gordon gave a weary smile. 'He had no idea what he wanted to speak to me about. I've been going around in circles.' Gordon drained his drink. 'Let's dance.'

It felt very different dancing with Gordon. They laughed and chatted as she tried not to think about the dance with Raúl.

Yes, she danced with Gordon—but it was the black eyes still on her that held her mind. Raúl sat at the table drinking whisky.

'I think you've made quite an impression. Raúl can't keep his eyes off you.'

She started in his arms. 'It's okay, Estelle.' Gordon smiled. 'I'm flattered—or rather my persona is. To have Raúl as competition is a compliment indeed.'

He kissed her cheek and she rested her head on his shoulder, and then her eyes fell to Raúl's black eyes that still watched and there was heat in her body, and she tried to look away but she could not. She watched his mouth move in a slow smile till Gordon danced her so that Raúl was out of her line of vision. Then, a moment later, her eyes scanned the room for him and prayed that the dangerous part of her night was now over.

Raúl was gone.

CHAPTER SIX

'SORRY!'

Gordon apologised profusely for scaring her, after Estelle had walked into the guest room much later that night to find a monster!

He whipped the mask off. 'It's for my breathing. I have sleep apnoea.'

Estelle had changed in a tiny bathroom along the draughty hall and was now wearing some very old, very tatty pale pink pyjamas that she only put on when she was sick or reading for an entire weekend. It was all she'd had at short notice, but Estelle was quite sure Gordon wasn't expecting cleavage and sexy nightdresses.

She offered to take the sofa bed—he was paying her, after all—but true to his word he insisted that she have the bed.

'Thank you so much for tonight, Estelle.'

'It's been fine,' Estelle said as she rubbed cold cream into her face and took her make-up off. 'It must be so hard on you, though,' she mused, trying to get off the last of her mascara. 'Having to hide your real life.'

'It certainly hasn't been easy, but six months from now I'll be able to be myself.'

'Can't you now?'

'If it was just about me then I probably would have by

now,' Gordon explained. 'Frank is so private, though—it would be awful for him to have our relationship discussed on the news, which it would be. Still, six months from now we'll be sunning it in Spain.'

'Is that where you're going to live?'

'And marry,' Gordon said. 'Gay marriage is legal there.'

Estelle was really tired now; she slipped into bed and they chatted a little while more.

'You know that Virginia has nearly finished her studies…?'

'I know.' Estelle sighed—not only because she would miss her housemate, but also because she would need to find someone else to share if she continued with *her* course. But then she realised what Gordon was referring to.

'She's starting work next month. I don't want to offend you by suggesting anything, but if you did want to accompany me to things for a few months…'

He didn't push, and for that Estelle was grateful.

'Have a think about it,' Gordon said, and wished her goodnight.

Estelle was soon drifting off, thinking not about Gordon's offer but about Raúl and his pursuit.

And it *had* been a pursuit.

From the moment their eyes had locked he had barely left her thoughts or her side, whether standing behind her at the wedding or sitting beside her at dinner. She still could not comprehend what had taken place on the dance floor; she had been searching for the bells and whistles and sirens of an orgasm, but how delicious and gentle that had been—how much more was there to know?

She didn't dare think too much about it now. Exhausted from a long and tiring day, Estelle was just about to drift off to sleep when Gordon turned on his ventilation machine.

Ginny hadn't told her about this part.

She lay there, head under pillow, at two a.m., still listening to the CPAP machine whirring and hissing. In the end she gave in.

She padded through the castle, her bare feet making not a sound on the stone floor. She headed to the small bathroom and took a drink from the tap, willing the night to be over.

Then she looked at her surroundings and regretted willing it over.

She stepped out onto a huge stone balcony, stared out to the loch. It was incredibly light for this time of the morning. She breathed in the warm summer night air and now her thoughts *did* turn to Gordon and his offer.

Estelle had already been coming to a reluctant decision to defer her studies and work full-time. It was all so big and scary—a future that was unknown.

She turned as the door opened, her eyes widening as Raúl stepped out.

He was wearing only his kilt.

Estelle would have preferred him with clothes on. Not because there was anything to disappoint—far from it—but the sight of olive skin, the light fan of hair on his chest and the way the kilt hung gave her eyes just one place to linger. There was nothing safe about meeting his gaze.

It was only then that she realised he had not followed her out here—that instead he was speaking on the phone.

He must have come out to get better reception. She gave him a brief smile and went to brush past, to get away from him without incident, but his hand caught her wrist and she stood there as he spoke into the phone.

'You don't need to know what room I am in…' He rolled his eyes. 'Araminta, I suggest that you go to bed.' He let out an irritated hiss. 'Alone!'

He ended the call and only then dropped Estelle's wrist. She stood as he examined her face.

'You know, without all the make-up you slather on...' His eyes searched her unmade-up skin. Her hair was tied in a low ponytail and she was dressed in a way he would not expect Gordon to find pleasing.

Raúl did.

She looked young—so much younger without all the make-up—and her baggy pyjamas left it all to Raúl's imagination. Which he was using now.

And then came his verdict.

'You look stunning,' Raúl said. 'I'm surprised Gordon has let you out of his sight.'

'I just needed some air.'

'I am hiding,' Raúl admitted.

'From Araminta?'

'Someone must have given her my phone number. I am going to have to change it.'

'She'll give in soon.' Estelle smiled, feeling a little sorry for the other woman. If Araminta had had a fling with him a few years ago and had known he would be here to-night—well, Estelle could see why her hopes might have been raised.

His phone rang again and he rolled his eyes and chose not to answer. 'So, what are you doing out here at this time of morning?'

'Just thinking.'

'About what?'

'Things.' She gave a wry smile, didn't add that far too many of her thoughts had been about him.

'And me,' Raúl admitted. 'It has been an interesting day.'

He looked out to the still, silent loch and felt a world away from where he had woken this morning. He didn't even know how he was feeling. He looked over to Estelle, who was gazing out into the night too, a woman who was comfortable with silence.

It was Raúl who was not—Raúl who made sure his days and nights were always filled to capacity so that exhaustion could claim him each night.

Here, for the first time in the longest time, he found himself alone with his thoughts—and that was not pleasant. But he refused to pick up to Araminta, knowing the chaos that might create.

It was Raúl who broke the silence. He wanted to hear her voice.

'When do you go back?'

'Late morning.' Estelle stared out ahead. 'You?'

'I will leave early.'

He walked to lean over the balcony, gazed into the night, and Estelle saw the huge scar that ran from his shoulder to his waist. He glanced around and saw the slight shock on her face. Usually he refused to offer an explanation for the scar—he did not need sympathy. Tonight he chose to explain it.

'It's from the car accident...'

'That killed your mother?'

He gave a curt nod and turned back to look into the night, breathing in the cool air. He was glad that she was here. For no other reason, Raúl realised, than he was glad. It was two a.m. in the second longest night of his life, and for the first one he had been alone.

'Can I ask again?' He had to know. 'What are you doing with Gordon?'

'He's nice.'

'So are many people. It doesn't mean we go around...' He did not complete his sentence yet he'd made his rather crude point. 'Are you here tonight for your brother?'

Estelle could not answer. She had agreed to be here for Gordon, yet she knew they both knew the truth.

'Do you have siblings?' Estelle asked.

There was a long stretch of silence. His father had asked that he not reveal anything just yet, but it would all be out in the open soon. Estelle came and stood beside him as she awaited his answer. Perhaps she would go straight to the press in the morning. Raúl actually did not care right now. He could not think about tomorrow. It was taking all his control to get through the night.

'Had you asked me that yesterday the answer would have been no.' He turned his head, saw her frown at his answer and was grateful that she did not push for more detail. Instead she stayed silent as Raúl admitted a little of the truth. 'This morning my father told me that I have a brother—Luka.' It felt strange to say his name. 'Luka Sanchez Garcia.'

From their little lesson earlier, Estelle knew they did not share the same mother. 'Have you met him?'

'Unwittingly.'

'How old is he?'

She asked the same question that he had asked his father, though the relevance of the answer she could not know.

'Twenty-five,' Raúl said. 'I walked into my father's office this morning, expecting my usual lecture—he insists it is time for me to settle down.' He gave a small mirthless laugh. 'I had no idea what was coming. My father is dying and he wants his affairs put in order. My affairs too. And so he told me he has another son...'

'It must have been the most terrible shock.'

'Skeletons in the closet are not unique,' Raúl said. 'But this was not some long-ago affair that has suddenly come to light. My father has kept another life. He sees his mistress in the north of Spain. I thought he went there so regularly for work. We have a hotel in San Sebastian. It is his main interest. Now I know why.'

Estelle tried to imagine what it was like, finding out something like this, and Raúl stood trying to comprehend that he had actually told another—how readily he had opened up to her. Then he reminded himself why. For his solution to come to fruition of *course* Estelle had to be told.

Some of it, at least.

He would never reveal all.

'His PA—Angela—she has always been...'

He gave a tight shrug. Angela had not been so much like a mother, but she had been a constant—a woman he trusted. Raúl closed his eyes, remembered walking out of his father's office and the words he had hurled to the one woman he had believed did not have an agenda.

'We have always got on. It turns out the son she speaks of often is in fact my half-brother.' He gave a wry smile. 'A lot of my childhood was spent with my aunt or uncle. I assumed my father was working at the hotel in San Sebastian. It turns out he was with his mistress and his son.' Black was the hiss that came from his mouth. 'It's all sorry and excuses now. I always prided myself on knowing what goes on, on being astute. It turns out I knew nothing.'

He had said enough. More than enough for one night.

'So, in answer to your question—yes. I have a brother.'

He shrugged naked shoulders and her fingers balled into her palms in an effort not to rest her hand on them.

'Unlike you, I care nothing for mine.'

'You might if you knew him.'

'That's not going to happen.'

She felt a small shiver, put it down to the night air. But his voice was so black with loathing it could have been that. 'I'm going to go in.'

'Please don't.'

Estelle had to get back—back to the safety of Gordon—yet she did not want to walk away from him.

She had to.

'Goodnight, Raúl...'

'Stay.'

She shook her head, grateful for the ringing of his phone—for the diversion it offered. But as she went to open the door she heard a woman's frantic voice coming down the corridor.

'Pick up Raúl. Where the hell are you?'

He had lightning reflexes. Quickly Raúl turned his phone off and pulled Estelle into the shadows.

'I need a favour.'

Before she knew what was happening she was in his arms, his tongue prising her lips open, his hand at her pyjama top. Estelle struggled against him before realising what was happening. She could hear Araminta calling out to Raúl, and if she saw the balcony any moment now she would come out.

But Araminta didn't. She stumbled past the balcony, the couple on it unseen.

He could stop now, Estelle thought. Except her pyjama top was completely open, her breasts splayed against his naked chest.

We *should* stop now, she thought as his tongue chased hers.

He made a low moan into her mouth; it was the sexiest thing she had ever heard or felt. He slid one hand over her bottom and his tongue was hot and moist.

Suddenly sending a message to Araminta was the last thing on Raúl's mind.

Estelle wanted his kiss to end, and yet she yearned for it to go on—like a forbidden path she was running down, wanting to get to the end, to glimpse again the woman he made her. It was a kiss that should not be happening, but it was one she did not want to end.

'Don't go back to him…' Raúl's mouth barely left hers as he voiced his command.

He had intended to speak with her at a later point, perhaps get her phone number, but having tasted her, having kissed her, he could not stand the thought of her in Gordon's bed. He would reveal his plan right now.

He peeled his mouth off hers, his breath coming hard on her lips. 'Come now with me.'

It was then that she fully realised her predicament. Raúl assumed this was the norm for her, that she readily gave her body.

As he moved in to kiss her again she slapped him. It was the only way she knew how to end this.

'You pay more, do you?' She was disgusted with his thought processes.

'I did not mean it like that.' Raúl felt the sting on his cheek and knew that it was merited—knew how his suggestion must have come across. But business had been the last thing on his mind. He had simply not wanted her going back to another man. 'I meant—'

'I know exactly what you meant.'

'Bastard!'

They both turned at the sight of a tear-streaked Araminta. 'You said you were tired, that you were in bed.'

'Can I suggest that you go back to your bed?' Raúl snapped to Araminta, clearly not welcoming the intrusion.

Estelle saw again just how brutal this man could be when he chose.

'How much clearer can I make it that I have absolutely no interest in you?'

He turned and came to help a mortified Estelle with her buttons, but her hand slapped him off.

'Don't touch me!'

She flew from the balcony and back to her room, stepped quietly in and slipped into bed, listened to the whirring of Gordon's machine, trying to forget the feel of Raúl's hands, his mouth.

Trying to deny that she lay there for the first time truly wanting.

CHAPTER SEVEN

'ESTELLE...'

Gordon was lovely when she told him what had happened. Well, not all of it. She didn't tell him about her conversation with Raúl, just that he had been trying to avoid a woman and had kissed her...

It was a terribly awkward conversation, but Gordon was writing her a cheque, so as not to embarrass her in front of his driver, and Estelle simply couldn't accept it and had to tell him why.

'Frank and I have three free passes.'

Estelle blinked as Gordon smiled and held out the cheque.

'We have three people each who, should something happen, wouldn't be construed as cheating with.' He gave her a smile. 'It's just a game, of course, and it's mainly movie stars, but Raúl could very easily make it to my list. No one can resist him when he sets his sights on them—especially someone as darling and innocent as you.'

'I feel awful.'

'Don't.' Gordon closed her hand around the cheque. 'My being in competition with Raúl Sanchez Fuente could only do wonders for my reputation, if word were ever to get out. It might even be the reason for our breaking up and me realising just how much I care for Virginia.'

'I'm sorry.'

'Don't be,' Gordon said, and gave her a kiss on the cheek. 'Just be careful.'

'I'll never see him again,' Estelle said. 'He doesn't know anything about me.'

'Mere details to a man like Raúl—and he takes care of them easily.'

Estelle felt the hairs on her arms stand up as she remembered that she had given him her name.

'Just do your hair and put on a ton of make-up and we'll head down for breakfast,' Gordon told her. 'If anyone says anything about last night just laugh and shrug it off.'

It was a relief to hide her blushes behind thick make-up. Estelle put on a skirt that was too short and some high wedges, and tied her hair in a high ponytail and then teased it with a comb and sprayed it.

'I feel like a clown,' she said to Gordon as she checked her reflection in the mirror.

'Well, you make *me* smile.'

Raúl had gone, and all Estelle had to endure were some daggers being thrown in her direction by Araminta as they ate a full Scottish breakfast. She was relieved not to see him, yet there was a curious disappointment at his absence which Estelle chose not to examine.

Finally they were on their way, but it was late afternoon before Gordon dropped her at her home.

'Think about what I said,' Gordon reminded Estelle as she climbed out.

'I think I've had my excitement for the year,' Estelle admitted as she farewelled him.

She let herself step into familiar surrounds and released a breath before calling out to Ginny that she was home.

'How are you feeling?' Estelle asked as she walked into the lounge.

'Awful!'

Ginny certainly looked it.

'I'm going to go home for a couple of days. My dad's coming to pick me up—I need Mum, soup and sympathy.'

'Sounds good.'

'How was it?

'It was fine,' Estelle said, really not in the mood to tell Ginny all that had happened.

Ginny would no doubt find out from Gordon, given how much the two of them discussed. Estelle was still irritated that Ginny told Gordon about her virginity but, seeing how sick Ginny was, Estelle chose to save that for later.

'Gordon was lovely.'

'I told you there was nothing to worry about.'

'I'm exhausted,' Estelle admitted. 'You didn't tell me about Gordon's sleep apnoea. I got the fright of my life when I walked in and he was strapped to a machine.'

Ginny laughed. 'I honestly forgot. Your brother's been calling you. A few times, actually.'

The phone rang then, and Estelle's heart lurched in hope when she saw that it was her brother. 'Maybe he's got that job.'

He hadn't.

'I found out on Friday,' Andrew said. 'I just couldn't face telling you.'

'Something will come up.'

'I'm not qualified for anything.'

Estelle could hear the hopelessness in his voice.

'I don't know what to do, Estelle. I've asked Amanda's parents if they can help—'

His voice broke then. Estelle knew the hell that would have paid with his pride.

'They can't.'

She could feel his mounting despair.

'Something will come up,' Estelle said, but she was finding it harder and harder to sound convincing. 'You've just got to keep applying for work.'

'I know.' He blew out a long breath in an effort to compose himself. 'Anyway, enough about me,' Andrew said, 'Ginny said you were in Scotland. How come?'

'I was at a wedding.'

'Whose?'

'I'll tell you all about it tomorrow.'

'Tomorrow?'

'I want to speak to you about something.' As a car tooted outside, Ginny stood. 'Andrew, I've got to go,' Estelle said. 'I'll call in tomorrow.'

Estelle didn't know how to tell Andrew she had some money for him, but anyway she knew that one month's mortgage payment would only be a Band-Aid solution. She was relieved that Ginny would be out for a few days because she really wanted some time to go over what she was considering.

The library was offering her more hours. Perhaps she could defer her studies and move in with Andrew and Amanda for a year, pay them rent, help out with little Cecelia, maybe even take Gordon up on his offer… Yes, she was glad Ginny would be away, because she needed to think properly.

'Your dad's here,' Estelle said.

'Thanks so much for last night, Estelle,' Ginny said, grabbing her bag and heading out of the door, waving to her father, who had climbed back into the car when he saw her.

Ginny was too dosed up on flu medication even to notice the expensive car a little further down the road.

Raúl noticed *her*, though—and a frown appeared on his face as he saw Virginia, Gordon's regular date, disappearing into a car driven by another older male. After Raúl's father's revelations he was past being surprised by anything, but there was a curious feeling of disappointment as he thought of Estelle and Virginia together with Gordon.

No.

He did not like the images that conjured, so he settled for the slightly more palatable version—that Estelle hadn't picked him up at Dario's; instead Estelle and Virginia must both work for the same escort agency.

He needed someone tough, Raúl told himself. He needed a woman who could separate sex from emotion, who could see what he was about to propose as a financial opportunity rather than a romantic proposition.

Except his knuckles were white as he clutched the steering wheel. Since last night there had been an incessant gnawing in his stomach when he thought of Estelle with Gordon. Now that gnawing had upgraded to a burn in the lining of his gut.

Estelle would be far better with him.

Was he arrogant to think so? Raúl pondered briefly as he walked up her garden path.

Perhaps, he conceded, but he was also assured enough to know that he was right.

'What did you forget...?' Estelle's voice trailed off when she saw that it wasn't Ginny.

Raúl preferred the way she'd looked last night on the balcony, but her appearance now—the short skirt, the heavy make-up, the lacquered hair—actually made things easier.

'What do you want?'

'I wanted to apologise for what I said last night. I think it was misconstrued.'

'I think you made things perfectly clear.' She drew in

a breath and then gave a small nod. 'Apology accepted. Now, if you'll excuse me?'

Her hand was ready to close the door on him. There was just a moment and Raúl knew he had to use it wisely. There was no time for mixed messages. He knew he had better reveal the truth up-front.

'You were right—I didn't want you to go back to Gordon, but not just because…' The door was closing on him so Raúl told her exactly what he was here for. 'I wanted to ask you to marry me.'

Estelle laughed.

After the tension of the last twenty-four hours, then her brother's tears on the phone, and now Raúl, standing absolutely immaculate in black jeans and a shirt at her door with his ridiculous proposal, all she could do was throw her head back and laugh.

'I'm serious.'

'Of course you are,' Estelle answered. 'Just as you were serious last night when you told me just how much you don't want to marry—ever.'

'I don't want to marry for love,' Raúl said, 'but I do need a bride. One with a level head. One who knows what she wants and goes for it.'

There was that implication again, Estelle realised. She was about to close the door, but then she looked down to the cheque Raul was holding—one with her name on it—and she saw the ridiculous amount he was offering. He surely wasn't serious. She looked up at him and realised that possibly he was—that he could pay for her services. As Gordon had.

Estelle gave a nervous swallow, reminding herself that whatever happened, whatever Raúl thought, she must not betray Gordon's confidence.

'Look—whatever you think, Gordon and I…'

'Should that be, Gordon, *Virginia* and I?' He watched her flaming cheeks pale. 'I just saw her leave. Are you both dating him?'

'I don't have to explain anything to you.'

'You're right,' Raúl conceded.

'How did you know where I lived?'

'I checked your bag when you were dancing with Gordon.'

Estelle blinked. He was honest, brutally honest—and, yes, she couldn't help herself. She was curious.

'Are you going to ask me in or do I stand and speak here?'

'I don't think so.' Common sense told her to close the door on him, but as she stared into black eyes curiosity was starting to win. Things like this—conversations like this—simply didn't happen to Estelle. But, more than that, she wanted to find out more about this man who had been on her mind from the second their eyes had locked.

'I ask for ten minutes,' Raúl said. 'If you want me to leave then, I shall, and I will never bother you again.'

He spoke in such a matter-of-fact voice. This was business to him, Estelle realised, and he assumed it was the same for her. She chose to keep it that way.

'Ten minutes,' Estelle said, and opened the door.

He looked around the small house. It was typical student accommodation, yet she was not your typical student.

'You are studying?'

'Yes.'

'Can I ask what?'

Estelle hesitated, not keen on revealing anything to him, but surely it could do no harm. 'Ancient architecture.'

'Really?' Raul frowned. Her response was not the one he'd been expecting.

She offered him a seat and Raúl took it. Estelle chose a

chair on the opposite side of the room to him. He wasted
no time getting to the point.

'I have told you that my father is sick?' Raúl said, and
Estelle nodded. 'And that for a long time he has wanted
to see me settled? Now, with his death nearing, more and
more he wishes to see his wish fulfilled—he has convinced
himself that a wife will tame my ways.'

Estelle said nothing. She just looked at this man she
doubted would ever be tamed; she had tasted his passion,
had heard about his appalling reputation. A ring on his
finger certainly wouldn't have stopped what had taken
place last night.

'You might remember I told you my father revealed he
has another son?'

Again Estelle nodded.

'He has said that if I do not comply, if I do not settle
down, then he will leave his share of the business to my...'
He could not bring himself to call Luka his brother. 'I refuse to allow that to happen.'

She could see the determination in his eyes.

'Which is why I have come this evening to speak with
you.'

'Why aren't you having this conversation with Araminta? I'm sure she'd be delighted to marry you.'

'I did briefly consider it,' Raúl admitted, 'but there are
several reasons. The main one being she would not be able
to reconcile the fact that this is a business transaction. She
would agree, I think, but it would be with hope that love
would grow, that perhaps a baby might change my mind.
It will not,' Raúl said. His voice was definite. 'Which is
why I come to speak with you. A woman who understands
a certain business.'

'I really think you have the wrong idea about me.'

'I am not here to judge you. On the contrary, I admire a woman who can separate love from sex.'

He did not understand the wry smile on her face. If only he knew. It faded as he continued.

'We are attracted to each other.' Raúl said it as a fact. 'Surely for you that can only be a bonus?'

Estelle blew out a breath; he was practically calling her a hooker and yet she was in a poor position to deny it.

'We both like to party,' Raúl said. 'And we like to live life in the fast lane—even if we know how to take things seriously at times.'

He was wrong about the fast lane, and Estelle knew if she admitted the truth he'd be gone. But, yes, she *was* undeniably attracted to him. Her skin was tingling just from his presence. Her mind was still begging for a moment of peace just to process the dance and the kiss they had shared last night.

He interrupted her wandering thoughts

'Estelle. I have spoken with my father's doctor; it is a matter of weeks rather than months. You would only be away for a short while.'

'Away?'

'I live in Marbella.'

Now she definitely shook her head. 'Raúl, I have a life here. My niece is sick. I am studying…'

'You can return to your studies a wealthy woman—and naturally you will have regular trips home.'

He looked at her, with her gaudy make-up and teased hair. He chose to remember her fresh-faced on the balcony, recalled the comfort she had given even before they had kissed. He should not care, but he did not like the life she was leading. Suddenly it was imperative for reasons other than appeasing his father that she take this chance.

'I do not judge you, Estelle, but you could come back

and start over. You can live the life you want to without ever having to worry about the rent.'

Estelle stood and walked to the window, not wanting him to see the tears that sprang in her eyes because for a moment there he had sounded as if he actually cared.

'You certainly won't have to host dinner parties or cook for me. I work hard all day. You can shop. We'll eat out every night. And there are many clubs to choose from, parties to attend. You would never be bored.'

He had no idea about her at all.

'After my father's death, after a suitable pause, we will admit our whirlwind marriage cannot deal with the grief— that with regret we are to part. No one will ever know you married for money. That would be written into the contract.'

'Contract?'

'Of course,' Raúl said. 'One that will protect both of us, that will lay down all the rules. I have asked my lawyer to fly in for a meeting at midday tomorrow. Naturally it will be a lengthy meeting. We will have to go over terms.'

'I won't be there.'

He didn't look in the least deterred.

'Raúl, my brother would never believe me.'

'I will come with you and speak to him.'

'Oh, and he'll believe *you*? He'll believe we met yesterday and fell madly in love? He'll have me certified insane before he lets me fly off with a stranger—'

'We met last year.' Raúl interrupted her tirade. It was clear he had thought it all through. 'When you were in Spain. It was then that we fell madly in love, but of course with your brother's accident it was not the time to say so, or to make plans to move, so we put it down to a holiday romance. We met again a few weeks ago and this time around I had no intention of letting you go.'

'I don't want to lie to him.'

'You are always truthful?' Raúl checked. 'Does he know about Gordon, then? Does he know—?'

'Okay,' she interrupted. Because of course there were things her brother didn't know. She was actually considering it—so much so that she turned to him with a question. 'Would *your* family believe it?'

'Before I found out about my father's other life I chose to let him think I was serious about someone I used to date. It was not you I had in mind, but they do not know that.'

It could work.

The frown that was on her brow was smoothed, the impossibility of it all was fading, and Raúl knew it was time to leave.

'Sleep on it,' Raúl said. 'Naturally there is more that I have to tell you, but I am not prepared to discuss certain things until after the marriage.'

'What sort of things?'

'Nothing that impacts on you now—just things that a loving wife would know all about. It is something I would not reveal to anyone I did not trust or love.'

'Or pay for?'

'Yes.' He placed the cheque on the coffee table and handed her two business cards.

'That is the hotel my lawyer will be staying at. I have booked an office there. The other card contains my contact details—for now.'

'For now?'

'I am changing my phone number tomorrow,' Raúl said. 'One other thing…' He ran a finger along her cheek, looked at the full mouth he had so enjoyed kissing last night. 'There will be no one else for the duration of our contract…'

'It's not going to happen.'

'Well, in case you change your mind—' he handed her an envelope '—you might need this.'

She opened it, stared at the photo that had been taken last night. His arm was on the chair behind her, she was laughing, and there was Raúl—smiling, absolutely beautiful, his eyes on her, staring at her as if he was entranced.

He must have known the photographer was on his way, Estelle realised. He had been considering this even last night.

Raúl *had* rearranged the seating—she was certain of it now.

She realised then the lengths he would go to to get his way.

'Did you arrange for Gordon to be called away?'

'Of course.'

'You don't even try to deny it?'

He heard her anger.

'You'd prefer that I lie?' Raúl checked.

She looked to the mantelpiece, to the photo of her brother and Amanda holding a tiny, frail Cecelia. She was so tired of struggling. But she could not believe that she was considering his offer. She had considered Gordon's, though, Estelle told herself. Tomorrow she had been going to tell her brother she was deferring her studies and moving in with them.

She had already made the decision to up-end her life.

This would certainly up-end it—but in a rather more spectacular way.

She went into the kitchen with the excuse of making coffee, but really it was to gather her thoughts.

Bought by Raúl.

Estelle closed her eyes. It was against everything she believed in, yet it wasn't just the money that tempted her. It was something more base than that.

A man as beautiful as Raúl, for her first lover. The thought of sharing his bed, his life—even for a little while—was as tempting as the cheque he had written. Estelle blew out a breath, her skin on fire, aroused just at the thought of lying beside him. Yet she knew that if Raúl knew she was a virgin the deal would be off.

'Not for me.'

He was standing at the kitchen door, watching as she spooned instant coffee into two mugs.

'I'll leave you to think about it. If you do not arrive at the appointment then I will accept your decision and stop the cheque. As I said, tomorrow my phone number will be changing. It will be too late to change your mind.'

It really was, Estelle knew, a once-in-a-lifetime offer.

CHAPTER EIGHT

'I WILL FLY your family out for the wedding...'

They were sitting in Raúl's lawyer's office, going over details that made Estelle burn, but it was all being dealt with in a cool, precise manner.

'I will speak with your parents and brother.'

'My parents are both deceased.' Estelle said it in a matter-of-fact way. She was not after sympathy from Raúl and this was not a tender conversation. 'And my brother and his wife won't be able to attend—Cecelia is too sick to travel.'

'You should have *someone* there for you.'

'Won't your family believe us otherwise?' There was a slight sneer to her voice, which she fought to check. She had chosen to be here, after all. It was just the mention of her parents, of Cecelia, that had her throat tightening—the realisation that everything in this marriage bar love would be real and she would be going through it all alone.

'It has nothing to do with that,' Raúl said. 'It is your wedding day. You might find it overwhelming to be alone.'

'Oh, please,' Estelle responded, determined not to let him see her fear. 'I'll be fine.'

'Very well.' Raúl nodded. 'It will be a small wedding, but traditional. The press will go wild—they have been waiting a long time for me to marry—but we will not let them know we are married till after.'

They had been talking for hours; every detail from wardrobe allowance to hair and make-up had been discussed.

Estelle had insisted she could choose her own clothes.

'I have a reputation to think of,' had been Raúl's tart response.

Estelle was entitled to one week every month to come back to the UK and visit her family for the duration of the contract.

'I am sure we will both need the space,' had been Raúl's explanation. 'I am not used to having someone permanently around.'

There was now an extremely uncomfortable conversation—for Estelle, in any case—about the regularity of sex, and also about birth control and health checks. Raúl didn't appear in the least bit fazed.

'In the event of a pregnancy—' the lawyer started.

Raúl was quick to interrupt. Only now did he seem concerned by the subject matter being discussed. 'There is to be no pregnancy.' There was a low menace to his voice. 'I don't think my bride-to-be would be foolish enough to try and trap me in *that* way.'

'It still needs to be addressed.' The lawyer was very calm.

'I have no intention of getting pregnant.' Estelle gave a small nervous laugh, truly horrified at the prospect. She had seen the stress Cecelia had placed on Andrew and Amanda, and they were head over heels in love.

'You might change your mind,' Raúl said, for he trusted no one. 'You might decide that you like the lifestyle and don't want to give it up.' He looked to his lawyer. 'We need to make contingency plans.'

'Absolutely,' the lawyer said.

It could not be made clearer that this was all business.

Estelle sat as with clinical detachment he ensured that he would provide for any child they might have on the condition that the child resided in Spain.

If she moved back to England, Estelle would have to fight against his might just to make the rent.

'I think that covers it,' the lawyer said.

'Not quite.' Estelle cleared her throat. 'I'd like us to agree that we won't sleep with each other till after the wedding.'

'There's no need for quaint.'

'I've agreed to all your terms.' She looked coolly at him. It was the only way for this to work. If he knew she was a virgin this meeting would close now. 'You can surely agree to one of mine? I'd like some time off before I start *working*.' She watched his jaw tighten slightly as she made it clear that this *was* work.

'Very well.' Raúl did not like to be told that sleeping with him would be a chore. 'You may well change your mind.'

'I shan't.'

'You will be flown in a couple of days before the wedding. I will be on my yacht, partying as grooms do before their marriage. You shall have the apartment to yourself.' He had no intention of holding hands and playing coy for a week. He waited for her nod and then turned to his lawyer. 'Draft it.'

They waited in a sumptuous lounge as the lawyer got to work, but Estelle couldn't relax.

'You are tense.'

'It's not every day you get offered a million dollars.' She could at least be honest about that. 'Nor move to Marbella…'

'You will love it,' Raúl said. 'The night-life is fantastic…'

He just didn't know her at all, Estelle realised yet again.

'How did your parents die?' Raúl asked, watching as her shoulders stiffened. 'My family are bound to ask.'

'In a car accident,' Estelle said, turning to him. 'The same as your mother.'

He opened his mouth to speak and then changed his mind.

'I just hope everyone believes us,' Estelle said.

'Why wouldn't they? Even when we divorce we'll maintain the lie. You understand the confidentiality clause?' Raúl checked. 'No one is ever to know that this is a marriage of convenience only.'

'No one will ever hear it from me,' she assured him. The prospect of being found out was abhorrent to Estelle. 'Just a whirlwind romance and a marriage that didn't work out.'

'Good,' Raúl said, 'And, Estelle—even if we do get on…even if you do like—'

'Don't worry, Raúl,' she interrupted. 'I'm not going to be falling in love with you.' She gave him a tight smile. 'I'll be out of your life, as per the contract.'

CHAPTER NINE

RAÚL HAD BEEN RIGHT.

Estelle stood on the balcony of his luxurious apartment, looking out at the marina, on the morning of her
wedding day, and was, as Raúl had predicted, utterly and
completely overwhelmed.

She had arrived in Marbella two days ago and had
barely stopped for air since. Stepping into this vast apartment, she had fully glimpsed his wealth. Every room bar
the movie screening room was angled to take in the stunning view of the Mediterranean, and every whim was catered for from Jacuzzi to sauna. There was a whole new
wardrobe waiting for her too. The only thing lacking was
that the kitchen cupboards and fridge were empty.

'Call Sol's if you don't want to go out,' Raúl had said.
'They will bring whatever you want straight over.'

The only vaguely familiar thing had been the photo of
them both, taken at Donald's wedding, beautifully framed
and on a wall. But even that had been dealt with by Raúl.
It had been manipulated so that her make-up was softer,
her cleavage less revealing.

It had been a sharp reminder that he thought her a tart.

Raúl knew the woman he wanted to marry, and it wasn't
the woman he had met, so there had been trips to a beauty
salon for hair treatments and make-up lessons.

'I don't *need* make-up lessons,' Estelle had said.

'Oh, baby, you do,' had been his response. 'Subtle is best.'

Constantly she had to remind herself to be the woman he thought he had met. A woman who acted as if delighted by her new designer wardrobe, who didn't mind at all when he told her to wear factor fifty-plus because he liked her pale skin.

But it wasn't that which concerned Estelle this morning as she looked out at the glittering sea and the luxurious yachts, wondering which one was Raúl's.

Tonight she would be on his yacht.

This night they would be sharing a bed.

Estelle wasn't sure if she was more terrified of losing her virginity, or of him finding out that she had never slept with anyone before.

Maybe he wouldn't notice, she thought helplessly. But she knew she didn't have a hope of delivering to his bed the sexually experienced woman that Raúl was expecting. Last night, before heading off with his sponsors for his final night as a single man, Raúl had kissed her slowly and deeply. The message his tongue had delivered had been an explicit one.

'Why do you make me wait?'

Tonight he would find out why.

'You have a phone call.' Rosa, his housekeeper, brought the phone up to the balcony. It was Amanda on the line.

'How are you doing?' Amanda asked.

'I'm petrified.' It was nice to be honest.

'All brides are,' Amanda said. 'But Raúl will take good care of you.'

He had utterly and completely charmed Amanda, but had not quite won over Andrew.

'I am not letting her go again.' He had looked Andrew

straight in the eye as he said it. 'If I move Estelle to Spain I want to make a proper commitment. That is why she will come to be my wife.'

So easily he had lied.

Estelle knew she must remember that fact.

'How did the dress turn out?' Amanda asked.

'It's beautiful,' Estelle said. 'Even better than I imagined it would be.'

It was the only thing Estelle had been allowed to organise. It had all be done online and by phone, and the final adjustments made when she had arrived.

'How is Cecelia?' Estelle asked, desperate for news of her niece.

'She's still asleep.'

It was nine a.m. in Spain, which meant it was eight a.m. in the UK. Cecelia had always been an early riser. More and more she slept these days, though Amanda always did her best to be upbeat.

'I'm going to dress her up for the wedding and take a photo and send it. Even if we can't be there today, know that we're thinking of you.'

'I know.'

'And I'm not your sister, but I do think of you as one.'

'Thank you,' Estelle said, her eyes welling up. 'I think of you as a sister too.'

They weren't idle words; many hours had been spent in hospital waiting rooms this past year.

'Is that the door?' Amanda asked.

'Yes. Don't worry, someone else will get it.'

'Do you have a butler?'

'No!' Estelle laughed, swallowing down her tears. 'Just Raúl's housekeeper. Though it's going to start to get busy soon, with the hairdresser...' She turned around as she heard her name being called, and Estelle's jaw dropped as she saw her brother coming through the door.

'Andrew!'

'Is that where he's got to?' Amanda laughed, and then she was serious. 'I'm so sorry that I couldn't be with you today—I'd have given anything. But with Cecelia…'

'Thank you,' Estelle said, and promptly burst into tears, all her pent-up nerves released.

'I think she's pleased to see me,' Andrew said, taking the phone and chatting to Amanda briefly before hanging up.

'I can't believe you're here,' Estelle admitted.

'Raúl said he thought you might need someone today, and of course I wanted to give you away. If anything happens with Cecelia he's assured me I'll be able to get straight back.'

She couldn't believe that Raúl would do this for her. Until now she hadn't fully realised how terrifying today was, how real it felt.

Raúl had.

'When did you get in?'

'Last night,' Andrew said. 'We went to Sol's.'

'You were out with Raúl?'

'He certainly knows how to party.' Andrew smiled. 'I'd forgotten how.'

Even if she was doing all this for her brother and his wife, of the many benefits of marrying Raúl, this was one Estelle had not even considered—that her brother, who was still having trouble accepting the diagnosis that he would never walk again, who had, apart from job interviews and hospital appointments, become almost reclusive, would fly not just to Spain but so far out of his comfort zone.

It was a huge and important step, and it was thanks to Raúl that he was here.

'I've got something for you.'

Estelle bit her lip, hoping they hadn't spent money they didn't have on a gift for a wedding that wasn't real.

'Remember these?' Andrew said as she opened the box. 'These' were small diamond studs that had belonged to her mother. 'Dad bought them for her for their wedding day.'

She had never felt more of a fraud.

'Enough tears,' Andrew said. 'Let's get this wedding underway.'

Raúl was rarely nervous, but as he stood at the altar and waited for Estelle, to his own surprise, he was.

His father had almost bought their story, and Raul's future with the company was secure, but instead of a gloating satisfaction that his plans were falling into place today he thought only of the reasons he had had to go to these lengths.

His head turned briefly and he caught a glimpse of Angela in the middle of the church. She was seated with his father, as ever-present PA. His mother's family were still unaware of the real role she played in his father's life—and the role she had played in his mother's death.

He stared ahead, anger churning in his gut that Angela had the gall to be here. He wouldn't put it past her to bring her bastard son.

Then he heard the murmur of the congregation and Raúl turned around. The churning faded. Just one thought was now in his mind.

She looked beautiful.

He had wondered how Estelle might look—had worried that, left to her own devices, a powder-puff ball would be wobbling towards him on glittery platform shoes, smiling from ruby-red lips.

He had not—could not have—imagined this.

Her dress was cream and made of intricate Spanish lace. It was fitted, and showing her curves, but in the most elegant of ways. The neckline was a simple halter neck. She carried orange blossom, as was the tradition for Spanish brides, and her lipstick was a pale coral.

'*Te ves bella.*' He told her that she looked beautiful as she joined him, and he meant every word. Not one thing would he change, from her black hair, piled high up on her head, to the simple diamond earrings and elegant cream shoes. She was visibly shaking, and he made a small joke to relax her. 'Your sewing is terrible.'

She glanced at his shirt and they shared a smile. With so little history, still they found a piece now, at the altar—as per tradition, the bride-to-be must embroider her groom's shirt.

'I'm not marrying a billionaire to sit sewing!' she had said teasingly, and Raúl had laughed, explaining that most women did not embroider all of the front of the shirt these days. Only a small area would be left for her, and Estelle could put on it whatever she wanted.

He had half expected a € but had frowned this morning when he had put on his shirt to find a small pineapple. Raúl still couldn't work out what it meant, but it was nice to see her relax and smile as the service started.

They knelt together, and as the service moved along he explained things in his low, deep voice, heard only by her.

'*El lazo,*' he said as a loop of satin decorated with orange blossom was placed over his shoulders and then another loop from the same piece was placed over hers. The priest spoke then for a moment, in broken English, and Estelle's cheeks burnt red as he told them that the rope that bound them showed that they shared the responsibility for this marriage. It would remain for the rest of the ceremony.

But not for life.

She felt like a fraud. She *was* a fraud, Estelle thought, panic starting to build. But Raúl took her hand and she looked into his black eyes. He seemed to sense that she was suddenly struggling.

'He asks now that you hand him the Arras,' Raúl said and she handed over the small purse he had given her on arrival. It contained thirteen coins, he had explained, and it showed his financial commitment to her.

It was the only honest part of the service, Estelle thought as the priest blessed them and handed it back to her.

Except it felt real.

'It's okay,' he said to her. 'We are here in this together.'

It felt far safer than being in it alone.

The service ended and an attendant removed the satin rope and presented it to Estelle; then they walked out to cheers and petals and rice being thrown at them. Raúl's hand was hot on her waist, and he gripped her tighter when she nearly shot out of her dress at the sound of an explosion.

'It's firecrackers,' Raúl said. 'Sorry I forgot to warn you.'

And there would be firecrackers later too, Estelle thought, when they got to bed and she told him the truth! But it was far too late now to warn him.

It really was a wonderful wedding.

As Raúl had told her on the night they had met, there were no speeches; instead it was an endless feast, with dancing and celebration and congratulations from all.

She met Paola and Carlos, Raúl's aunt and uncle, and they spoke of Raúl's mother, Gabriella.

'She would be so proud to be here today,' Paola said. 'Wouldn't she, Antonio?'

Estelle saw how friendly they were with Raúl's father,

and also with Angela, who was naturally seated with them. No longer were they names, but faces, and a shiver went down her arms as she imagined their reaction when the truth came out.

'My son has excellent taste.' Antonio kissed her on the cheek.

Estelle had met him very briefly the day before, and Raúl had handled most of the questions—though both had seen the doubt in his eyes as to whether this union was real.

It was slowly fading.

'It is good to see my son looking so happy.'

He *did* look happy.

Raúl smiled at her as they danced their first dance as husband and wife, with the room watching on.

'Remember our first dance?' Raúl smiled.

'Well, we shan't be repeating *that* tonight.'

'Not till later.' Raúl gazed down, saw her burning cheeks, and mistook it for arousal.

He could never have guessed her fear.

'I ache to be inside you.'

Other couples had joined them. The music was low and sensual and it seemed to beat low in her stomach. His hand dusted her bare arm and she shivered at the thought of what was to come, wondered if those eyes, soft now with lust and affection, would darken in anger.

'Raúl…' Surely here was not the place to tell him, but it felt better with people around them rather than being alone. 'I'm nervous about tonight.'

'Why would you be nervous?' he asked. 'I will take good care of you.'

He would, Raúl decided. He was rarely excited at the thought of monogamy but he actually wanted to take care of her, could not stand to think of what she might have put her body through. There was a surge of protectiveness that shot through him then, and his arms tightened around her. He could feel her tension and nervousness and again he wanted to make her smile.

'Can I ask why,' he whispered into her ear as they danced, 'you embroidered a pineapple on my shirt?'

'It's a thistle!'

A smile spread on her lips and he felt her relax a little in his arms.

'For Scotland.'

Raúl found himself smiling too. 'All day I have been trying to work out the significance of a pineapple.'

She started to laugh and Raúl found himself laughing a little too.

He lowered his head and kissed her lightly.

It was expected, of course. What groom would *not* kiss his bride?

Many times since he had put his proposition to her Estelle had had doubts—the morality of it, the feasibility of it, the logistics—but as he kissed her, as she felt his warm lips and the soft caress of his hand near the base of her spine, true doubt as to her ability to go through with the deal surfaced. For once it had nothing to do with her hymen. She was suddenly more worried about her heart.

It was the music. It was the moment. It was having her brother here. It was Raúl's kiss. All these things, she told herself, were the reasons she felt as she did—as if this were real…as if this were love.

Estelle excused herself a little while later and went to the bathroom, just so she might collect herself, but brides could not easily hide on their wedding day.

'Estelle?' She turned at the sound of a woman's voice. 'I am Angela—Raúl's father's PA.'

'Raúl has spoken about you,' Estelle responded carefully.

'I'm sure what he had to say was not very flattering.' There were tears in the older woman's eyes. 'Estelle, I don't know what to believe...'

'Excuse me?'

'About this sudden marriage.' Angela was being as upfront with Estelle as she was with Raúl. 'I do know, though, that Raúl seems the happiest I have seen him. If you *do* love your husband...'

'If?'

'I apologise,' Angela said. 'Given that you surely love your husband, I ask this not for me, and not even for Antonio's sake. Whatever Raúl thinks of me, I care for him. I want him to come and visit us. I want us to be a family, even for a little while.'

'You could have had that years ago.' Estelle answered as she hoped Raúl would expect his loyal wife to.

'I want him to make peace with his father while there is still time. I don't want him to have any guilt when his father passes. I know how much guilt he has over his mother.'

Estelle blinked, unsure how to respond because there was so much she didn't know about Raúl. What did he have to feel guilty about? Raúl had been a child, after all. He had agreed to tell her more on their honeymoon—had said that he would be the one to deal with any questions tonight.

'I have always loved Raúl. I have always thought of him as a son.'

'So why did you leave it so late to tell him?' Perhaps it was the emotion of the day, but the tears that flashed in Estelle's eyes were real. 'If you cared so much for him—'

Estelle halted. It wasn't her place to ask, and Raúl certainly wouldn't thank her for delving. She was here to ensure his father left his share of the business to him, that was all. She would do well to remember that.

'I *do* care,' Angela responded. 'Whatever Raúl thinks of me, from a distance I have loved him as a son.'

'From a distance?' Estelle repeated, making the bitter point.

Turning on her heel, she walked out and straight into Raúl's arms.

'She wanted to speak about you,' Estelle told him. 'I don't know how well I handled it.'

'We'll discuss it later,' Raúl said, for he had seen Angela follow her in. 'Now we have to hand out the favours.'

It really was an amazing party, and for reasons of her own Estelle didn't particularly want it to end.

As per tradition, the bride and groom had to see off all their guests and be the last to leave. Antonio tired first, and she felt the grip of Raúl's hand tighten on hers as his father left with his loyal PA.

'It's been great,' Andrew said as he prepared to head back to the hotel he was staying in. 'Once Cecelia is well, and I'm working, I'm going to bring Amanda and Cecelia here for a holiday, to visit you.'

'You do that,' Estelle said, and bent down and gave her brother a cuddle, then stood as Raúl shook his hand.

'Look after my sister.'

'You do not have to worry about that.'

'Have a great honeymoon.'

A driver sorted out the wheelchair and they waved Andrew off and then headed back inside.

Apart from the staff it was just Raúl and Estelle now, and still the music went on as they danced their last dance of the night.

'It really helped having Andrew here.' Her hands were round the back of his neck, he held her hips, and she would give anything not to disappoint him tonight—anything to be the experienced lover he assumed she was.

'I thought it might.'

'It didn't just help me,' Estelle admitted, and started to tell him about how Andrew's confidence had been lacking.

But he dropped a kiss on her shoulder. 'Enough about others.'

Estelle swallowed. She could feel his fingers exploring the halter neck, his other hand running down the row of tiny buttons that ran to the base of her spine, and she knew he was planning his movements, undressing her slowly in his mind as they danced.

'Raúl...' His mouth was working over her bare shoulder, kissing it deeply; she could feel the soft suction, feel the heat of his tongue and his ardour building. 'I've never slept with anyone before.'

He moaned into her shoulder and pulled her tighter into him, so she could feel every inch of the turn-on he thought she was giving him.

'I mean it.' Her voice was shaking. 'You'll be my first.'

'Come on, then.' His mouth was now at her ear. 'Let's go and play virgins.'

CHAPTER TEN

THEY WERE DRIVEN the short distance to the marina, but for Estelle it just passed in a blur.

It was almost morning, yet despite the hour the celebrations continued.

Alberto, the skipper, welcomed them, and briefly introduced the staff—but Estelle barely took in the names, let alone her surroundings. All she could think of was what was soon to come as the crew toasted them and then Raúl dismissed them.

'Tomorrow I will show you around properly,' Raúl said, taking her champagne glass. 'But for now...'

There was no escaping. He pulled her towards him, his tongue back on her neck, at the crease between her neck and shoulder. He *had* been mentally undressing her before, for now his hands moved straight to the halter neck and expertly unravelled the carefully tied bow.

He had been expecting a basque, had anticipated another contraption to disable, but the dress had an inbuilt bra and he gave a low growl of approval as one of the breasts that had filled his private visions in recent days fell heavy and ripe into his palm.

'Raúl, someone might come...'

'That would be *you*,' he said, but she did not relax. 'No one will disturb us.'

Raúl lowered his head and licked around the pale areola, flicked a nipple that had been crushed all day by fabric back into rapid life, surprised that she was concerned that someone might come in. The staff on his yacht had seen many a decadent party—a husband and wife on their wedding night paled in comparison with what usually took place. He took the breast he craved in his mouth again, felt her hand try to push him back. He was at first surprised by her reticence—but then he remembered their game.

'Of course.' He smiled. 'You are nervous.'

He lifted her up and carried her down to the master stateroom, kissing her the entire way. He lowered her to the ground, turning her around so he could work on the tiny buttons from behind. It did not halt his mouth; his tongue kissed every inch of newly exposed flesh till her spine felt as if it were on fire.

He peeled off her dress, then her shoes and stockings. As his tongue licked and nibbled her sex through her silk panties the sensations his mouth delivered drove her wild. He only removed her panties when the moisture his mouth had made matched the dampening silk.

'Raúl…' Her hands were on his head—contrary hands that tried to halt him, while her moans of mounting desire urged him on.

'I want you so bad.' He peeled off her panties and, kneeling, parted her lips, his tongue darting to the swelling bud over and over as her hands knotted in his hair.

'Raúl…' she whimpered, lost between bliss and fear. 'I'm serious. I really haven't slept with anyone before.'

He simply didn't believe her. As she came under his mouth she had a hopeless thought that maybe he wouldn't guess, maybe he wouldn't know. Because despite her naïveté her body responded with ease. She throbbed against his mouth, more aroused than sated as he softly kissed the lingering orgasm.

He relished her taste, was assured she was moist. He was desperate now to take her.

He rose to his full height then, and shrugged his jacket off.

Breathless, aroused, moving on instinct, her hands shaking with want, she undid the buttons of his shirt. He was so dark and sultry, and he wore it well. His lips parted as her hands roamed his chest and she licked at his nipples as she undid his belt.

Raúl wanted her fingers at his zipper, and he wished she would hurry, but she lingered instead, feeling his thick heat through the fabric, her fingers lightly exploring. His already aching erection hardened further beneath her fingers. 'Estelle…' He could barely get the word out, but thankfully she read the urgency and slid the zipper down, and he let out a breath as she freed him.

He was delicious to her hands. She ran her fingers along his length, felt the soft skin that belied the strength beneath. She was petrified at the thought of him inside her, but wanting him just the same. She could see a trickle of silver and caught it with her finger, then swirled it around the head, entranced by its beauty.

Raúl closed his eyes in a mixture of frustration and bliss, for he wanted her hand to grip him tight, yet conversely he liked the tentative tease and exploration, liked the feel of her other hand gently weighing him.

Deeply they kissed, his tongue urging her to move faster, his erection twitching at the pleasure of her teasing, till he could take it no more.

'*Te quiero.*'

He told her he wanted her in Spanish as he pushed her

onto the bed. *'Tengo que usted tiene.'* He told her he had
to have her as he parted her legs.

'Be gentle.' She was writhing and hot beneath him, her
words contrary to the wanton woman in his arms. Her sex
was slippery and warm and engorged as his hand stroked
her there. She was as close to coming as Raúl, and his
answer to her final plea was delivered as he nudged her
entrance.

'It's way too late for gentle, baby.'

How he regretted those words as he seared and tore
into her.

Raúl heard her sob, heard her bite back a scream.

Estelle knew then she had been a fool to think he might
somehow not notice. He tore through her barrier but the
pain did not end there. His fierce erection drove through
tight muscles full of resistance. Too late to halt, too late
to be tender, he froze—just not quickly enough. He leant
on his elbows above her as she tried to work out how to
breathe with Raúl inside her.

He attempted slow withdrawal. She begged that he did
not. She lay there, trying to accommodate him, waiting for
the heat and pain to subside, her muscles clamped around
him.

'I take it out slowly,' Raúl said. He felt sick—appalled
by his own brutality—and guilty too at the pleasure of her,
hot and tight around him. He was so close to coming and
trying to hold on. 'I'll just—'

'Don't.'

Her eyes were screwed tight as he moved a fraction
backwards, but when he halted, when he stilled, her body
relaxed a little. Estelle tried to release herself. She moved
to slide away from him. Yet the pain was subsiding to a
throbbing heat so she moved again, warming to the sensation of him inside her.

It was a different type of command she gave next. 'Don't stop.'

'Estelle?' He did not want to stop, and yet he did not want to hurt her; he moved slowly a little within her, his breath shallow, panting as if he had already come.

Her hands moved to his buttocks and she felt them tauten beneath her fingers. It was Estelle who pressed and dictated the tempo and, rarely for Raúl, he let her. Rarely for Raúl, he was humbled. He did not think of the questions he must ask her, just focused on the tight grip and the heat of her on his unsheathed skin, and all he could do was kiss her. Every inch of him held back, resisting the beckoning of oiled muscles that gripped as he slid past them, that urged him now to move faster, to take her deeper.

Estelle's breath was quickening. He felt the somewhat impatient rise of her groin, the press of her hands in his buttocks, and he could hold back no more.

Still he had not taken her fully, but now he thrust in. Estelle's neck arched as he probed and located fresh virgin flesh with each deepening thrust, and when he had filled her, when every part of her was consumed, he moved out and did it again, angling his hips, hitting her deep inside till she was moaning.

He was moving fast now, and she wrapped her legs around him, could not believe how her body had just taken over. For she lifted to him, was building to him, working with him, both heading to the same mutual goal.

No longer naïve, her body shattered in an orgasm like nothing she had ever given herself—for there she could stop, there she could halt. And it was nothing like the teasing he had given her either, for here in Raúl's bed he urged her on further, broke all limits, ensured that she screamed.

She pulsed around the head of him. He was stroking her deep inside—one spot that had her sobbing, one tender spot that he hit over and over—till she sobbed, and then he released himself into her. Her thighs were in spasm as a fresh wave of orgasm crashed through her body—and, yes, just as he had warned her, she cussed him in Spanish till he kissed her, till she was lying beneath him no longer a virgin.

She looked up at him, expecting a barrage of questions, a demand for an explanation, but instead he moved onto his side and put his arm around her, pulling her into him.

'I should have known' was his reprimand.

'I tried to tell you.'

'Estelle…' he warned.

She gave a small nod, conceding that tonight might have been rather too late.

'We will speak about it in the morning.'

For now, they held each other, lay in each other's arms, tired and sated and both in a place they had never thought they might be.

Estelle a bought bride; Raúl a man who had married and made love to a virgin.

CHAPTER ELEVEN

ESTELLE WOKE AND had no idea where she was for a moment.

Her body was bruised and sore. She could hear a shower.

She rolled over in bed and saw the evidence of their union, and moved the top sheet to cover it.

'Hiding the evidence?'

Estelle turned and was shocked at the sight of him. There was a towel round his hips, but his chest was covered in the bruises she now remembered her mouth making. He turned and took a drink from the breakfast table that had presumably been delivered and she saw the scratches on his back, remembered the wanton place he had taken her to.

'I need to have a shower.'

'We need to talk.' But then he conceded, 'Have some lunch and a shower. Then we will talk.'

'*Lunch?*'

'Late lunch,' Raúl said. 'It is nearly two.'

Estelle quickly gulped down some grapefruit juice and then headed to the bathroom. When she had found out they would be honeymooning on a yacht she had expected basic bathroom facilities; instead it was like a five-star hotel. The bathroom was marble, the taps and lighting incredible, yet she barely noticed. Her only thought was getting to her make-up bag.

The doctor had told her how important it was to take her pill on time every day. She was still getting used to it. Her breasts felt sore and tender, as if she were getting her period, and she still felt a little bit queasy from the new medication.

Estelle swallowed down the pill, making a mental note to change the alarm on her phone to two p.m.—or should she take it at seven tomorrow?

Her mind felt dizzy. She had seen that Raúl was less than impressed with her this morning and no doubt he would want a thorough explanation. She still hadn't worked out what to say.

Estelle showered and put on the factor fifty he insisted on, then sorted out her hair and make-up, relieved when she headed back into the bedroom and Raúl wasn't there. She selected a bikini from the many he had bought her, and also a pale lilac sarong. Her head was splitting from too much champagne and too much Raúl. She sat on the bed and put on espadrilles. Then, dressed—or rather barely dressed, as Raúl would want her to be—she stood. But her eyes did not go to the mirror—instead they went to the bed.

Mortified at the thought of a maid seeing the stained sheets, Estelle started to strip the bed.

'What are you doing?'

'I'm just making up the bed.'

'If I had a thing for maids then it would have been stipulated in the contract,' Raúl said. 'And if I had a thing for virgins,' he added, 'that would have been stipulated too.'

Estelle said nothing.

'Just leave it.' His voice was dark. 'The crew will take care of that. I will show you around.'

'I'll just wander…' She went to walk past.

'You can't hide from me here,' he warned, taking her wrist. 'But we will discuss it later. I don't want the staff getting even a hint that this is anything but a normal honeymoon.'

'Don't you trust your staff?' It was meant as a small dig—because surely a man in his position could easily pay for his privacy?

'I don't trust anyone,' Raúl said, watching the fire mount on her cheeks as his words sank in. 'And with good reason.'

She followed him up onto the deck. The sun blinded her for a moment.

'Where are your sunglasses?'

'I forgot to bring them.' She turned to head back down, but Raúl halted her, calling out to one of the crew. 'I can get them myself.'

'Why would you?'

Sometimes she forgot just how rich and spoilt he was. This was not one of those times. Despite the fact there were some of the crew around, he pulled her into his arms and very slowly kissed her.

'Raúl....' She was embarrassed by his passion. She looked into his black eyes and knew he was making a point.

'We are here for two days, darling. The plan is for us to fully enjoy them.'

His words were soft, the message not.

'I'll show you around now.'

A maid handed her her sunglasses and then Raúl showed her their abode for the next few days. The lounge that she had barely noticed last night was huge, littered with low sofas; another maid was plumping the cushions. There was a huge screen and, though nervous around him, Estelle did her best to be enthusiastic. 'This will be lovely for watching a movie.'

Raúl swallowed and caught the maid's eyes, and as Estelle went over to look at his DVD collection he quickly led her away.

'Here is the gym.' He opened a door and they stepped in. 'Not that you'll need it. I will ensure that you get plenty of exercise.'

Only there, with the door safely closed, did he let his true frustration slip out. He closed the door and gave her a glimpse of what was to come.

'If you think we are going to be sitting around watching movies and holding hands—'

'I know what I'm here for.'

'Make sure that you do.'

Raúl had woken at lunchtime from his first decent sleep in days, from his first night without nightmares. For a moment he had glimpsed peace—but then she had stirred in his arms and he had looked down to a curtain of raven hair and felt the weight of her breast on his chest. The sheet had tumbled from them; he'd seen her soft pale stomach and the evidence of their coupling on her inner thigh.

He had gone to move the sheet to cover them, but the movement had disturbed her a little and he had lain still, willing her back to sleep, fighting the urge to roll over and kiss her awake, make love to her again. He had felt the heat from her palm on his stomach and had physically ached for that hand to move down. His erection had been uncomfortable.

He'd fought the bliss of the memories of last night as his hand had moved down—and then halted when he'd realised his own thought-processes.

Sex Raúl could manage—and often.

Making love—no.

Last night had been but one concession, and he reminded himself she had lied.

He had removed her hand from him then and spent a

full ten minutes examining her face—from the freckles dusting her nose to the full lips that had deceived him.

He stood in the well-equipped gym and looked at them now. Absolutely he would make things clear.

'We have several weeks of this,' Raúl said. 'I wanted a woman who could handle my life, who knew how to have fun.' He did not mince words. 'Who was good in bed.'

He watched her cheeks burn.

'I'm sure I'll soon learn. I'll keep up my end of the deal—I don't need hand-holding.'

'There will be no holding hands.' He took her hand and placed it exactly where it had been agreed it would visit regularly. 'You knew what you were signing up for...'

He had to hold her back; he had to be at his poisonous worst. He could not simply dump her, as he usually did when a woman fell too hard. They had weeks of this and he could not risk her heart.

Instead he would put her to work.

'Let's have a spa.'

She saw the challenge in his eyes, knew that he was testing her, and smiled sweetly. 'Let's!'

She followed him up onto the deck, trying to ignore the fact that he had fully stripped off as she took off her espadrilles and dropped her sarong.

'Take off your top.'

'In a moment...'

He could sense rather than see that she was upset, and it made him furious. He was actually wishing his father dead, just so this might end.

'Take off your top,' he said again. Because if she thought she was here to discuss the passing scenery, or for them to get to know each other better, then she was about to find out she was wrong.

Estelle might have taken him for a fool.

He wasn't one.

Her face was one burning blush as her shaking hands undid the clasp, and she sank beneath the water as she removed it and placed the bikini top on the edge.

'Good morning!' The skipper made his way over. Naked breasts were commonplace on the Costa Del Sol—and especially on Raúl Sanchez Fuante's boat. He had no trouble at all looking Estelle in the eye as he greeted her. She, though, Raúl noted, was close to tears as she attempted to smile back.

'We are heading towards Acantilados de Maro-Cerro Gordo,' Alberto said, and then turned to Raúl. 'Would you like us to stop there tonight? The chef is looking forward to preparing your dinner and he wondered if you would like us to set up for you to eat on the bay?'

'We'll eat on the boat,' Raúl said. 'We might take a couple of jet skis out a little later and take a walk.'

'Of course,' Alberto said, then turned to Estelle.

'Do you have any preferences for dinner? Any food choices you would like the chef to know about?'

'Anything.'

Raul heard her try to squeeze the word out through breathless lips.

'It's a beautiful bay we are stopping at.' Albert happily chatted on. 'It's not far at all from the more built-up areas, but soon we will start to come into the most stunning virgin terrain.'

He wished them a pleasant afternoon and headed off.

'I've already explored the virgin terrain...' Raúl drawled, once he was out of earshot.

Estelle said nothing.

'Here.' Annoyed with himself for giving in, but hating her discomfort, he threw her the bikini top. 'Put it on if you want.'

She really was shaken, Raúl thought with a stab of guilt as he watched her trembling hands trying to put the damp garment on. Going topless was nothing here—nothing at all—but then he remembered last night: her shaking, her asking him to be gentle. Pleas he had ignored.

He strode through the water and turned her around, helping her with the clasp of her bikini top. Then, and he didn't know why, he pulled her into his arms and held her till she had stopped shaking—held her till the blush had seeped from her skin.

And then he made her burn again as he dropped a kiss on her shoulder and admitted a truth to her about that virgin terrain.

'...and it was stunning.'

CHAPTER TWELVE

NORMALLY RAÚL'S YACHT sailed into the busiest port, often with a party underway.

This early evening, though, they sailed slowly into Acantilados de Maro-Cerro Gordo. The sky was an amazing pink, the cliffs sparkling as they dropped anchor near a secluded bay.

'The beaches are stunning here,' Alberto said, 'and the tourists know it. But this one has no road access.' He turned to Raúl. 'The jet skis are ready for you both.'

Only as they were about to be launched did Raúl remember. He turned and saw her pale face, saw that she was biting on her lip as she went to climb on the machine, and his apology was genuine.

'Estelle, I'm sorry. I forgot about your brother's accident.'

'It's fine,' she said through chattering teeth. 'He was showing off...mucking around...' She was trying to pretend that the machine she was about to climb on *didn't* petrify her. 'I know we'll be sensible.'

Raúl had had no intention of being sensible. He loved the exhilaration of being on a jet ski and had wanted to share it with her—had wanted to race and to chase.

Instead he was taking her hand. 'It's not fine. You don't have to pretend.'

Oh, but she did. At every turn she had to pretend, if she was to be the temporary woman he wanted.

'Come on this one with me,' Raúl said. 'Alberto, take her hand and help her on.'

They rode towards the bay in a rather more subdued fashion than Raúl was used to.

The maid who was setting up the dinner table caught Alberto's eye when he came to check on her progress and they shared a brief smile.

His bride and the effect she was having on Raúl was certainly not one they had been expecting.

'I think I might go and reorganise his DVD collection,' the maid suggested and Alberto nodded.

'I think that might be wise.'

Estelle held tightly onto Raul's waist as the jet ski chopped through the waves, and because her head kept knocking into his back in the end she gave in and rested it there, not sure if her rapid heart-rate was because she was scared by the vehicle, by the questions she would no doubt soon be facing, or just by the exhilaration.

Making love with Raúl had been amazing. She was sore and tender but now, feeling his skin beneath her cheek, feeling the ocean water sting her and the wind whip her hair, she could not regret a moment. Even her lie. Feeling his passion as he had seared into her was a memory she would be frequently revisiting. For now, though, Estelle knew she had to play it tough—had to convince him better than she had so far that she was up to the job he had paid her for.

He skidded into the shallows and she unpeeled herself from him and stepped down.

'It's amazing…' She looked up at the cliffs, shielding her eyes. 'Look how high it is.'

He did, but only briefly. Estelle was too busy admiring the stunning view to notice his pallor.

'What did Angela say to you at the wedding?' Raúl asked.

She had been expecting a barrage of questions about her lack of experience, and was momentarily sideswiped at his choice of topic for conversation, but then she reminded herself his interest in her was limited.

'She wasn't sure whether or not we were a true couple,' Estelle said.

'You corrected her?'

'Of course,' Estelle said. 'She seems to think that *if* I love my husband, then I should encourage you to make peace with your father while there is still time.' She glanced over to him as they walked. 'She wants us to go there and visit.'

'It is too late to play happy families.'

'Angela said that she doesn't want you to suffer any guilt, as you did over your mother's death...'

'Misplaced guilt,' Raúl said, but didn't elaborate any more.

He stopped and they sat on the beach, looking out to the yacht. She could see the lights were on, the staff on deck were preparing their meal. It was hard to believe such luxury even existed, let alone that for now it was hers to experience. It was the luxury of *him* she wanted, though; there was more about Raúl that she needed to know.

'I didn't know how to answer her,' Estelle admitted. 'You said there was more you would tell me. I have no real idea about your family, nor about you.'

'So I will tell you what you need to know.' He pondered for a moment on how best to explain it. 'My grandfather—my mother's father—ran a small hotel. It did well and he built another, and then he purchased some land in the north,' Raúl explained.

'In San Sebastian?' Estelle asked.

He nodded. 'On his death the business was left to his three children—De La Fuente Holdings. My father and mother married, and my father started to work in the family business. But he was always an outsider—or felt that he was, even though he oversaw the building of the San Sebastian hotel. When I was born my mother became unwell. In hindsight I would say she was depressed. It was then he started to sleep with Angela. Apparently Angela felt too much guilt and left work, moved back to her family, but they started seeing each other again...'

'How do you know all this?'

'My father told me the morning I met you.'

It was only then that Estelle fully realised this was almost as new to him as it was to her.

'Angela got pregnant, the guilt ate away at him, and he told my mother the truth. He wanted to know if she could forgive him. She cried and wailed and screamed. She told him to get out and he went to Angela—the baby was almost due. He assumed my mother would tell her family, that she would turn to them. Except she did not. When she had the car accident and died my father returned and soon realised no one knew he had another son. Instead they welcomed him back into the company.' He was silent for a moment. 'Soon they will find out the truth.'

'Angela said that you blamed yourself for your mother's death?'

'That is all you need to know.' He looked over to her. 'Your turn.'

'I don't know what to tell you.'

'Why you lied?'

'I didn't lie.'

'The same way my father didn't lie when he didn't tell me had another son? The same way Angela didn't lie when she failed to tell mention her son, Luka, was my brother?' He did not want to think about that. 'Okay, if you didn't outright lie, you *did* deceive.'

He watched her swallow, watched as her face jerked away to look out to the ocean.

'I wanted an experienced woman.'

'Sorry I don't know enough tricks—'

'I wasn't talking about *sex*!' Raúl hurled. 'I wanted a woman who could handle things. Who could keep to a deal. Who wasn't going to fall in love...'

'Again you assume!' Estelle flared. 'Why would I fall in love with some cold bastard who thinks only in money— who has no desire for true affection? A man who tells me what to wear and whether or not I can tan.'

Her eyes flashed as she let out some of the anger she had suppressed over the past few days while every decision apart from her wedding dress had been made by him.

'Raúl, I would not have a man choose my clothes or dictate to the hairdresser the style of my hair, or the beautician the colour of my nails. You're getting what you paid for—what you wanted—what you demanded. Consider my virginity a bonus!'

She dug her heels deep into the sand and almost believed her own words. Tried to ignore that last night, as she'd been falling asleep in his arms, foolish thoughts had invaded. Raúl's doubts about her ability to see this through perhaps had merit, for he would be terribly easy to love...

She turned around and faced him.

'I'm here for the money, Raúl.' And not for a single second more would she allow herself to forget it. 'I'm here with you for the same reason I was with Gordon.'

He could not stand the thought of her in bed with him—

could not bear to think about it. But when he did, Raúl frowned.

'If you were with Gordon for money, how come you were trying to change the sheets before the maid got in.'

'I was never with Gordon in that way. I just stood in for Ginny.'

'You shared his bed,' Raúl said. 'And we all know his reputation…'

'Unlike you, Gordon didn't feel comfortable going to a wedding alone,' Estelle said carefully.

'So he paid you to look like his tart?' Raúl checked. 'What about Dario's…?' His voice trailed off and he frowned as he realised the lengths Gordon had gone to, then frowned a little more as realisation hit. 'Is Gordon…?' He didn't finish the question—knew it was none of his business. 'You needed the money to help out your brother?'

She conceded with a nod.

'Estelle, it is not for me to question your reasons—'

'Then don't.'

Her warning did not stop him.

'Andrew would not want it.'

'Which is why he will never find out.'

'I know that if I had a sister I would not want her—'

'Don't compare yourself to my brother. You don't even have a sister, and the brother you *do* have you don't want to know.'

'What's that got to do with it?'

'We're two very different people, Raúl. If I discovered that I had a brother or sister somewhere I'd be doing everything I could to find out about them, to meet them—not plotting to bring them down.'

'I'm not plotting anything. I just don't want him taking what is rightfully mine. Neither do I want to end up working alongside him.'

She looked at the seductive eyes that invited you only to bed, at the mouth that kissed so easily but insisted you did not get close.

'You miss out on so much, Raúl.'

'I miss out on nothing,' Raúl said. 'I have everything I want.'

'You have everything money can buy,' Estelle said, remembering the reason she was here. 'Including me.'

When he kissed her it tasted of nothing. It tasted empty. It was a pale comparison to the kiss he had been the recipient of last night. And when he took her top off he knew she was faking it, knew she was thinking of the boat and of people watching, knew she was trying not to cry.

'Not here,' Raúl said for her.

'Please, Raúl…'

Her mouth sought his. She was still playing the part, too inexperienced to understand that he knew her body lied.

He wanted it back, the intimacy of last night, which meant taking care of her.

For now.

Surely for a couple of days he could take care of her. They could just enjoy each other and break her in properly. The last thing he wanted was her tense and teary, feeling exposed.

He had glimpsed her toughness, admired the lengths she would go to for her family, and he believed her now— she did not want his love

'Later.' Raúl pulled his head back from her mouth. 'I'm starving.'

He helped her with her bikini, used his chest as a shield as he did up the clasp, just in case any passing fish were having a peek, or telescopes were trained on them. But rather than making him feel irritated, her coyness now made him smile.

Especially when he thought of her unleashed.

'Come on,' Raúl said, despite the ache in his groin. 'Let's head back.'

CHAPTER THIRTEEN

'WE WILL GO and shower and get dressed for dinner,' Raúl said as they boarded and Alberto took the jet ski. 'Do you want me to ask Rita to come down and do your hair?'

'Rita?'

'She is a masseuse and a beautician. If you want her to come and help just ask Alberto,' Raúl said, heading off to the stateroom.

Estelle called him back. She could smell the food and was honestly starving. 'Why do we have to get dressed for dinner?' Estelle did not notice the twitch of his lips, though Alberto did. 'It's only us.'

'On a yacht such as this one, when the chef...' Raúl began. But he was torn, because etiquette often had no place on board and it seemed petty to put her right. 'Very well.' He turned to Alberto, who was already on to it.

'I'll let the chef know.'

They rinsed off under the shower on deck and then took their seats.

Raúl was rather more used to a well-made-up blonde in a revealing dress sitting opposite him, but there was something incredibly appealing about sitting for dinner half-naked and scooping up the delicacies the waiters were bringing.

'I could get far too used to this,' Estelle started, and

then stopped herself, remembering his words at the lawyer's. 'I meant...'

'I know what you meant.'

She was relieved to see he was smiling.

'The food really is amazing,' Raúl agreed. 'They chef is marvellous. Chefs on yachts generally are—that is why we keep coming back for more.'

They chatted as they ate, far more naturally than they had before, and it wasn't just for the benefit of the staff.

It was simply a blissful night.

They danced.

On the deck of his yacht they danced when the music came on.

'I understand now why we should have changed for dinner,' Estelle admitted. 'Do you think I've offended anyone?'

'I don't think you could if you tried.'

The sky was darkening and Raúl looked out to the cliffs, and rather than remembering hell he buried his face in her hair. It took only the smell of the ocean in her hair for him to escape.

'And for the record,' Raúl said, 'although you accuse me being a controlling bastard, I was worried about you burning. I have never seen paler skin.'

'I think I *am* a bit sunburnt.'

'I know.'

They moved down to the lounge room. Estelle was starting to relax—so much so that she didn't spring from his arms when some dessert wine was brought through to them.

'Let's go to bed...' His hand was in her bikini top, trying to free her breast.

'Not yet,' she breathed into his mouth. 'I'll never sleep.'

'I have no intention of letting you sleep.'

'Let's watch a movie,' Estelle said, unwrapping herself from him and heading over to his collection.

'Estelle—no!'

'Oh, sorry.' She'd forgotten what he'd told her in the gym, about no hand-holding and movies, and she turned and attempted a smile. 'Sure—let's go to bed.'

'I didn't mean that,' Raúl said through gritted teeth, wondering how he'd ended up with the one hooker to whom he'd have to apologise for his DVDs. 'I just don't think there will be anything there to your taste.'

He braced himself for the rapid demise of a pleasant night as Estelle flicked through his collection.

'I love this one.'

'Really?' Raúl was very pleasantly surprised.

'Actually…' She skimmed through a couple more. 'This one's my favourite.' She held up the cover to him and didn't understand his smile.

'Of course it is,' Raúl said, pulling her down beside him, smiling into her hair. One day he would tell her how funny that was—one day when it wouldn't offend, when she knew him better. He would laugh about it with her.

But there would not *be* that day, he reminded himself.

This was just for now.

He had not lain on a sofa and watched a movie—not one with a plot, anyway—since he couldn't remember when.

Estelle shivered. The doors were open and the air was cooling. He pulled down a rug from the back of the sofa and covered them, felt her bottom curving into him.

'Sore?' He kissed her pink shoulders as he made light work of her bikini top.

'A bit.'

Estelle concentrated on the movie as Raúl concentrated on Estelle. He kissed her neck and shoulders for ages, then played with her breasts, massaging them with his palms, taking her nipples between thumb and fingers. Then slowly, when he knew there would be no qualms from Estelle, moved one hand down and untied her bikini bottoms.

His question, when repeated, was a far more personal one as his fingers crept in.

'Sore?'

'A bit,' she said again, but he was so gentle, and it felt so sublime.

She could feel the motion of the boat, and him huge and hard behind her; she could feel the urging of his mouth to turn to him and growing insistence from behind.

'Turn around, Estelle.' His breathing was ragged.

'In a minute.' She wasn't even watching the film. Her eyes were closed. She was just loving the feel of him playing with her and longing for it to go on. 'It's coming to the best bit.'

He pulled her up a little further, so that her naked bum was against his stomach, and he angled her perfectly. She felt the long, slow slide of him where he had stabbed into her last night. She was still bruised and swollen and hot down below, and yet she closed around him in relief.

'*This* is the best bit,' Raúl's low voice corrected her.

He pressed slowly into her, his fingers playing with her clitoris, slid slowly and deeply, with none of the haste of last night, and it was Estelle who was fighting to hold back.

'I'm going to come.'

'Not yet,' he told her, teasing her harder with his fingers, thrusting himself deeper inside.

'I am.' She was trembling and trying to hold on.

'Not yet.'

He stroked her somewhere so deep, the feeling so intense that she let out a small squeal.

'There?' he asked.

Estelle didn't know what he meant, but then he stroked her there again and she sobbed. 'There!' She was begging as over and over he massaged her deep, hitting her somewhere she hadn't even known existed. 'There…'

She was starting to cry, but with intense pleasure, and then she could no longer hold it. There was no point even trying.

There was a flood of release as she pulsed around him, and Raúl moaned as she tightened over and over around his thick length. He felt the rush of her orgasm flowing into him and he shot back in instant response, spilling deep into her, loving her abandon, loving the Estelle his body revealed.

Loving too the tinge of embarrassment that crept in as she struggled to get her breath back.

'What was that?'

'Us,' he said, still inside her. And it was not the cliffs he feared now, but the perfume of the ocean in her hair as he inhaled it—a fear that was almost overwhelming as he realised how much he had enjoyed this night.

Not just the sex, not just the talking, not just dinner.

But *now*.

'We should head back.'

They had been snorkelling. It had all started off innocently, but had turned into a slightly more grown-up activity. Raúl did not know if it was her laughter, or the feel of her legs wrapped around him, or just that he was simply enjoying her too much, but he kissed her cheek and unwrapped her legs from his waist.

'Is it dinner-time?'

'I meant we should head back for Marbella…'

It had been two nights and two amazing days, and more of a honeymoon than Raúl had ever intended for it to be.

They *were* dressing for dinner tonight, because they wouldn't be dawdling on their return. Which meant this would be their last night on the yacht.

She missed it already.

Even as Rita did her hair and make-up she missed the yacht, because it had been the most magical time. As if they had suspended the rules of the contract, their time had been spent talking, laughing, eating, making love—but Raúl had made it clear that things would be different when they returned to Marbella.

She felt as if they were approaching that already as Rita pushed the last pin into Estelle's hair. Raúl's expression was tense as he picked up his ringing phone.

'I will tell the chef you will be up soon,' Rita said, and Estelle thanked her and started to put on her dress.

She didn't understand what was being said on the phone, but given the terse words, she guessed it wasn't pleasant.

'They are getting married.' Raúl hung up and was silent.

By the time he told her what the call had been about he was doing up his tie, but kept getting the knot wrong.

'Oh.' She didn't know what else to say, just went on struggling with her zip.

'Come here.' He found the side zipper. 'It's stuck.'

She stood still as he tried to undo it.

'My father says he wants to do the right thing by Angela—wants to give her the dignity of being his wife and his widow. He wants her to have a say in decisions by the medical staff.'

'What did you say?'

'That it was the first decent thing I had heard on the subject.'

'Are you going to attend?'

He didn't answer her question; instead he hurried her

along. 'Come on. They will be serving up soon. It is not fair to keep the chef waiting.'

Since when was Raúl thoughtful about his staff? Estelle thought, but said nothing.

It was an amazing dinner. The chef had made his own paella, and even Raúl agreed, it was the best he had tasted.

Yet he barely touched it.

He looked at Estelle; she looked exquisite. Her hair was up, as it had been on their wedding day, her black dress looked stunning, and he told himself he could do it—that it wasn't a problem after all.

'What would you think if we did not turn around for Marbella?'

Estelle swallowed the food she was relishing and took a drink of water, nervous for the same reasons as Raúl.

'We could head to the islands, extend our trip…'

'So that you miss your father's wedding?'

'He has chosen to marry when I am on my honeymoon. He doesn't know we were to be on our way back.'

'You'll have to face him at some point.'

'You don't tell me what I have to do!' he snapped, and then righted himself, trying to explain things a little better. 'He wants a wedding—one happy memory with his wife. I doubt that will be manageable with me there. Especially if Luka attends.' He took a breath. 'So how about a few more days?' He made it sound so simple. 'I have not had a proper holiday in years…'

'I thought your life was one big holiday?'

'No,' Raúl said. 'My life is one big party. We will return to that in a few days.' He issued it as a warning, telling her without saying as much that what happened at sea stayed at sea.

He was waiting for her decision. But then Raúl remem-

bered the decision was entirely his. He was paying for her
company—not her say in their location.

'I will let the staff know.'

'Now?'

'They have to plot the route, inform...'

He didn't finish, just headed off to let the crew know,
and Estelle sat there, suddenly nervous.

She wanted to be back on safe water—because living
with Raúl like this, seeing this side of him, she was struggling to remember the rules.

Their 'couple of days' turned into two weeks.

They sailed around Menorca and took their time exploring its many bays. Estelle's skin turned from pale to pink,
from freckles to brown. He watched her get bolder, loved
seeing her stretch out on a lounger wearing only bikini
bottoms, not even a little embarrassed now. Her sexuality
was blossoming to his touch, before his eyes.

Finally they sailed back into Marbella. Normally the
sight of it was the one he loved best in the world, yet there
was a moment when he wanted to tell the skipper to keep
sailing, to bypass Marbella and head to Gibraltar, take the
yacht to Morocco, just to prolong their time. Except he was
growing far too fond of her.

She put a hand on his shoulder, joined him to watch
the splendid sight, but she felt his shoulder tense beneath
her touch.

Raúl turned. She was wearing espadrilles and bikini
bottoms, his own wedding shirt knotted beneath her now
rosy bust, her cheeks flushed and her lips still swollen
from their recent lovemaking.

'You'd better get dressed.'

Usually Raúl was telling her she was *over*dressed.

'The press may be there. The cream dress,' he told her. 'And have Rita do your make-up.'

As easily at that he demoted her, reminded her of her place.

Back on dry land he took her hand. But it was just for the cameras that he put his shoulders around his new wife.

It was in case of a long lens that he picked up her and carried her into his apartment, back to the reality of his life.

CHAPTER FOURTEEN

IT WAS A life she could never have imagined.

Raúl worked harder than anyone she knew.

His punishing day started at six, but rather than coming in drained at the end of it he would have a quick swim in the pool, or they'd make love—or rather they'd have sex. Because the Raúl from the yacht was gone now. A quick shower after that and then they'd get changed for dinner. Meals were always eaten out, and then they would hit the pulsing nightlife, dancing and partying into the early hours.

Estelle couldn't believe this was the toned-down version of Raúl.

'I can cook,' Estelle said, and smiled one night as they sat at Sol's and waited for their dishes to be served. 'It might be a novelty…'

'Why would you cook when a few steps away you can have whatever you choose?'

It was how he lived: life was a smorgasbord of pleasure. But six weeks married to Raúl, even with a week off to visit her family, was proving exhausting for Estelle—and she wasn't the one working. Or rather, she corrected herself as the waiter brought her a drink, she *was* working, twenty-four-seven, because no way would she be dining out every night, no way would she be wandering along streets that still pumped with music well after midnight on a Tuesday.

It had been Cecelia's cardiology appointment today, and Estelle was worried sick and doing her best not to show it. But she kept glancing at her phone, willing it to ring, wondering when she'd hear.

'How's your new PA?' Estelle asked as she bit into the most gorgeous braised beef, which had been cooked over an open fire.

'Okay.' Raúl shrugged. 'Angela trained her well...'

He looked down at her plate, stabbed a piece of beef with a fork and helped himself. Estelle was getting used to the way they shared their meals; it was the norm here.

'It *is* much more difficult without Angela,' Raúl admitted. 'Only now she is gone are we seeing how much she did around the place.'

'When will she be back?'

'She won't,' Raúl said. 'She is taking long service leave to nurse my father. Once he dies and it gets out about her she won't be welcome there.'

'Oh, well, you'll only have to see her at the funeral, then.'

Raúl glanced up. He could never be sure if she was being flip or serious. 'When are you going to see your father?' she asked him.

She was being serious, Raúl quickly found out.

'He chose to live in the north—he chose to end his days with his other family. Why should I....?' He closed his tense lips. 'I do not want to discuss it.'

'Angela called again today.'

'I told you not answer to her.'

'I was waiting for my brother to ring,' Estelle said. 'It was Cecelia's cardiology appointment today. I didn't think to look when I picked up.' Estelle could not finish her dinner and pushed the plate away.

'You're not hungry?'

'Just full.'

'I was thinking...' Raúl said. 'There is a show premiering in Barcelona at the weekend. I think it might be something we would enjoy.'

'Raúl...' She just could not sit and say nothing—could not lie beside him at night and sleep with him without caring even a bit, without having an opinion. Surely he could understand that? 'I was riddled with guilt when my parents died.'

'Why?'

'For every row, for every argument—for all the things we beat ourselves up about when someone dies. Guilt happens whatever you do. Why not make it about something you couldn't have changed, instead of something you can?' On instinct she went to take his hand, but he pulled it back.

'You're starting to sound like a wife.'

She looked at him.

'Believe me, I don't feel like one.'

Estelle pounced on her phone when it rang.

'I need to take this.'

'Of course.'

It was Amanda, doing her best, as always, to sound upbeat. 'They're going to keep Cecelia in for a few nights. She's a bit dehydrated...'

'Any idea when she's going to have surgery?'

'She's too small,' Amanda said. 'They've put a tube in, and we're going to be feeding her through that. She might come home on oxygen...'

Raúl watched Estelle's eyes filling with tears but she turned her shoulders and hunched into the phone in an effort to hide them. He heard her attempt to be positive even while she was twisting her hair around and around her finger.

'She's a fighter,' Estelle said, but as she did so she closed her eyes.

'How is your niece?' Raúl asked as she rang off.

'Much the same.' She didn't want to discuss it for fear she might break down—Raúl would be horrified! Seeing that he'd finished eating, Estelle gave him a bright smile. 'Where do you want to go next?'

'Where do *you* want to go?' Raúl offered.

Home, her body begged as they walked along the crowded street. But that wasn't what she was here for. She'd been transferring money over to Andrew since he'd gone back to England. The first time she'd told Andrew it was money she'd been saving to get a car. The second time she'd said it was a loan. Now she'd just given him a decent sum that would see them through the next few months, telling Andrew that she and Raúl simply wanted to help.

It was time to earn her keep.

They passed a club that was incredibly loud and very difficult to get into. It was a particular favourite of Raúl's. 'How about here?'

Estelle woke to silence. It was ten past ten and Raúl would long since have gone to work.

She sat up in bed and then, feeling dizzy, lay back down.

How the hell he lived like this on a permanent basis, Estelle had no idea. All she knew was she was not going out tonight.

He could, she decided, dressing and heading out not for the trendy boutiques but for the markets. She just wanted a night at home—or rather a night in Raúl's home—and something simple for dinner. There must be some subclause in the contract that allowed for the occasional night off?

Marbella was rarely humid, the mountains usually shielded it, but it struggled today. The air was thick and oppressive and the markets were very busy. Estelle had bought the ripest, plumpest vine tomatoes, and was deciding between lamb and steak when she passed a fish stall and gave a small retch. She tried to carry on, to continue walking, tried to focus on a flower stall ahead instead of the appalling thought she had just had.

She couldn't be pregnant.

Estelle took her pill at the same time every day.

Or she had tried to.

All too often Raúl would come home at lunchtime, or they'd be in a helicopter flying anywhere rather than to his father's—the one place he needed to be.

She couldn't be pregnant.

'Watch where you're going!' someone scolded in Spanish as she bumped into them.

'Lo sierto,' Estelle said, changing direction and heading for the *Pfarmacia*, doing the maths in her head and praying she was wrong.

Less that half an hour later she found out she was right.

Raúl didn't get home from work till seven, and when he did it was to the scent of bread baking and the sight of Estelle in his underutilised kitchen, actually cooking.

'Are we taking the wife thing a bit far?' Raúl checked tentatively. 'You don't have to cook.'

'I want to,' Estelle said. She was chopping up a salad. 'I just want to have a night in, Raúl.'

'Why?'

'Because.' She frowned at him. 'Do you ever stop?'

'No,' he admitted, then came over and give her a kiss. 'Are you okay?'

'I'm fine. Why?'

'You didn't wake up when I left this morning. You seem tense.'

'I'm worried about my niece,' Estelle said, removing herself from him and adding two steaks to the grill.

She was curiously numb. Since she'd done the test Estelle had been operating on autopilot and baking bread, which she sometimes did when she didn't want to think.

She just couldn't play the part tonight.

They carried their food out to the balcony and ate steak and tomato salad, with the herb bread she had made, watching a dark storm rolling in.

Estelle wanted to go home, wanted this over. Though she knew there was no getting out of their deal. But she needed a timeframe more than ever now. She wanted to be far away from him before the pregnancy started showing.

She could never tell him.

Not face to face, anyway.

Estelle could not bear to watch his face twist, to hear the accusations he would hurl, for him to find another reason not to trust.

'I spoke with my father today.'

She tore her eyes from the storm to Raúl. 'How is he?'

'Not good,' Raúl said. 'He asks that I go and see him soon.'

'Surely you can manage to be civil for a couple of days?' She was through worrying about saying the wrong thing. 'Yes, your father had an affair, but clearly it meant something. They're together all this time later...'

'An affair that led to my mother's death.' He stabbed at his steak. 'Their lies left the guilt with *me*.' He pushed his plate away.

The eyes that lifted to hers swirled with grief and confusion and now, when all she wanted was to be away from him, when she must guard her heart properly, when she needed it least, Raúl confided in her.

'I had an argument with my mother the night she died. She had missed my performance at the Christmas play—as she missed many things. When I came home she was crying and she said sorry. My response? *Te odio.* I told her I hated her. That night she lifted me from my sleep and put me in a car. The mountains are a different place in a storm,' Raúl explained. 'I had no idea what was happening; I thought I had upset her by shouting. I told her I was sorry. I told her to slow down...'

Estelle could not imagine the terror.

'The car skidded and came off the mountain, went down the cliffside. My father returned from his so-called work trip to be told his wife was dead and his son was in hospital. He chose not to tell anyone the reason he'd been gone.'

'Did they never suspect he and Angela?'

'Not for a moment. He just seemed to be devoting more and more time to the hotel in San Sebastian. Angela was from the north and she resumed working for him again. Over the years, clearly when Luka was older, she started to come to Marbella more often with my father. We had a flat for her, which she stayed in during the working week.'

'He had two sons to support,' Estelle said. 'Maybe it was the only way he could see how.'

'Please!' Raúl scoffed. 'He was with Angela every chance he could get, leaving me with my aunt and uncle. Had he wanted one family he could have had it. Perhaps it would have been a struggle, but his family would have been together. He chose this life, and those choices caused my mother's death.'

'Instead of you?'

'I blamed myself for years for her death. I thought the terrible things I said...'

'You were a child.'

'Yes,' he said. 'I see that now. The night she died was two days after Luka's birth. I realise now that she was on her way to confront them.'

'In a storm, with a five-year-old in the back of her car,' Estelle pointed out.

'I thought she was trying to kill me.'

'She was ill, Raúl.'

He nodded. 'It would have been nice to know that she was,' Raúl said. 'It would have been nice to know that it was not my words that had her fleeing into the night.'

'It sounds as though she was sick for a long time, and I would imagine it was a very tough time for your father...' Estelle did not want involvement. She wanted to remove herself as much as she could before she told him. Yet she could not sit back and watch his pain. 'He just wants to know you're happy, that you're settled. He just wants peace.'

'We all want peace.' He was a moment away from telling her the rest, but instead he stood and headed through the balcony door. 'I'm going out.'

Estelle sat still.

'Don't wait up.'

'I won't.'

She didn't want him going out in this mood, and she followed him into the lounge while knowing he wouldn't welcome her advice. 'Raúl, I don't think—'

'I don't pay you to think.'

'You're upset.'

'Now she tells me what I'm *feeling*!'

'Now *she* reminds you that she read that contract before she signed it. If you think you're going to go out clubbing and carrying on in your usual way I'll be on the next plane home…' she watched his shoulders stiffen '…with every last cent you agreed to pay me.'

He headed for the door.

'Hope the music's loud enough for you, Raúl!' she called out to him.

'It could never be loud enough.'

There was a crack from the storm and the balcony doors flew wide open. He turned then, and she glimpsed hell in his eyes. There was more than he was telling her, she knew that, and yet she did not need to know at this moment.

He was striding towards her and she understood for a moment his need for constant distraction, for *she* was craving distraction now. She was pregnant by the man she loved, who was incapable of loving her. How badly she didn't want to think about it. How nice it would be for a moment to forget.

His mouth was, perhaps for the last time, welcome. The crush of his lips was so fierce he might have drawn blood. Yet it was still not enough. He wrestled her to the floor and it was still too slow.

Here beneath him there were no problems—just the weight of him on her.

He was pulling at his zipper and pressing up her skirt. She was kissing him as if his lips could save them both. The balcony doors were still wide open. It was raining on the inside, raining on them, yet it did not douse them.

He had taught her so much about her body, but she learned something new now—how fast her arousal could be.

He was coming even before he was inside her; she could feel the hot splash on her sex. Estelle was sobbing as he thrust inside her, holding onto him for dear life. Each thrust of his hips met with her own desperation. It was fast and it was brutal, and yet it was the closest they had ever been.

He was at her ear and breathing hard when he lifted his face. She opened her eyes to a different man.

'Come with me to see them?'

He was asking, not telling.

'Yes.'

'Tomorrow?'

'Yes.'

It felt terribly close to love.

CHAPTER FIFTEEN

THEY FLEW EARLY the next morning, over the lush hills of Spain to the north, and even as his jet made light work of the miles there was a mounting tension. Had they run out of time?

Far from anger from Raúl, there was relief when Angela came out of the door to greet them, a wary smile on her face.

'Come in,' she said. 'Welcome.'

She gave Estelle a kiss on the cheek, and gave one too to Raúl. 'We can do this,' she said to him, even as he pulled back. 'For your father. For one day...'

Raúl nodded and they headed through to the lounge.

If Estelle was shocked at the change in his father, it must be hell for Raúl.

'Hey,' he greeted his son. 'You took your time.'

'I'm here now,' Raúl said. 'Congratulations on your wedding.' He handed Antonio a bottle of champagne as he kissed him on the cheek. 'I thought we could have a toast to you both later.'

'I finally make an honest woman of her,' Antonio said.

Estelle watched as Raúl bit back a smart response. There really was no time for barbs.

'Your brother is flying in from Bilbao tonight. Will you stay for dinner?' Antonio's eyes held a challenge.

'I'm not sure that we can stay…'

'A meeting between the two of you is inevitable,' Antonio said. 'Unless you boycott my funeral. I am to be buried here,' he added.

She watched Raúl's jaw tighten as he told his son that this was the home he loved. Yet he had denied his first son the chance of having a real home.

'I will make a drink,' Angela said to Estelle. 'Perhaps you could help me?'

Estelle went into the kitchen with her. It was large and homely, and even though she was hoping to keep things calm for Raúl, Estelle was angry on his behalf.

'We will leave them to it,' Angela said as Estelle sat at the table. 'You look tired.'

'Raúl doesn't live a very quiet life.'

'I know.' Angela smiled and handed her a cup of hot chocolate and a plate of croissants.

Estelle took a sip of her chocolate, but it was far too sickly and she put the cup back down.

'I can make you honey tea,' Angela offered. 'That is what I had when…' Her voice trailed off as she saw the panic in Estelle's eyes and realised she must not want anyone to know yet. To Angela it was obvious—she hadn't seen Estelle since her wedding day, and despite the suntan her face was pale, and there were subtle changes that only a woman might notice. 'Perhaps your stomach is upset from flying.'

'I'm fine,' Estelle said, deliberately taking another sip.

'I am worried that when Antonio dies I will see no more of Raúl…'

Estelle bit her lip. Frankly she wouldn't blame him. Because being here, seeing first-hand evidence of years of lies and deceit, she understood a little better the darkness of his pain.

'He is like a son to me.'

Estelle simply couldn't stay quiet. 'From a distance?'
She repeated Angela's own words from the wedding day
and then looked around. There were pictures of Luka, who
looked like a younger Raúl.

'Raúl is here too.' Angela pointed to a photo.

'He wasn't, though.' Estelle could not stand the pretence. 'You had a home here—whereas Raúl was being
shuffled between his aunt and uncle, occasionally seeing
his dad.'

'It was more complicated than that.'

'Not really.' Estelle simply could not see it. 'You say
you think of him as a son, and yet…'

'We did everything the doctor said,' Angela wrung her
hands. 'I need to tell you this—because if Raúl refuses
to speak with me ever again, then this much I would like
you to know. The first two years of Luka's life Antonio
hardly saw him. He did everything to help Raúl get well,
and that included keeping Luka a secret. The doctor said
Raul needed his home, needed familiarity. How could we
rip him away from his family and his house? How could
we move him to a new town when the doctor insisted on
keeping things as close to normal as possible?'

Estelle gave a small shrug. 'It would have been hard
on him, but surely no harder than losing his mother. He
thought it was because of something he had said to her.'

'How could we have known that?'

'You could have spoken to him. You could have asked
him about what happened. Instead you were up here, with
his dad.'

There was a long stretch of silence, finally broken by
Angela. 'Raúl hasn't told you, has he?'

'He's told me everything.'

'Did Raúl tell you that he was silent for a year?' She

watched as Estelle's already pale face drained of colour. 'We did not know what happened that day, for Raúl could not tell us. The trauma of being trapped with his dead mother...'

'How long were they trapped for?'

'For the night,' Angela said. 'They went over a cliff. It would seem Gabriella died on impact. When the *médicos* got there he was still begging her to wake up. He kept telling her he was sorry. Once they released him he said nothing for more than a year. How could we take him from his home, from his bed? How could we tell him there was a brother?'

'Excuse me—'

Estelle retched and cried into the toilet, and then tried to hold it together. Raúl did not need her drama today. So she rinsed her mouth and combed her hair, then headed back just as Raúl was coming out from the lounge.

'Are you okay?'

'Of course.'

'My father is going to have a rest. As you heard, my brother is coming for dinner tonight. I have agreed that we will stay.'

Estelle nodded.

'Somehow we will get through dinner without killing each other, and then,' Raúl said, 'as my reward for behaving...' He smiled and pulled her in, whispered something crude in her ear.

Far from being offended, Estelle smiled and then whispered into *his* ear. 'I can do it now if you want.'

She felt him smile on her cheek, a little shocked by her response.

'It can wait.' He kissed her cheek. 'Thank you for today. Without you I would not be here.'

'How is he?'

'Frail…sick…'

'He loves you.'

'I know,' Raúl said. 'And because I love him also, we will get through tonight.'

She wasn't so sure they'd get through it when she met Luka. He was clearly going through the motions just for the sake of his parents. Angela was setting up dinner in the garden and Antonio was sitting in the lounge. It was Estelle who got there first, and opened the door as Raúl walked down the hall.

The camera did not lie: he was a younger version of Raúl—and an angrier one too.

Luka barely offered a greeting, just walked into his family home where it seemed there were now two bulls in the same paddock. He refused Raúl's hand when he held it out to him and cussed and then spoke in rapid Spanish.

'What did he say?' Estelle asked as Luka strode through.

'Something about the prodigal son's homecoming and to save the acting for in front of his father.'

'Come on,' Estelle said. There would be time for dwelling on it later.

He caught her wrist. 'You're earning your keep tonight.'

He saw the grit of her teeth and the flash of her eyes.

'Do you do it deliberately, Raúl?' she asked 'Does it help to remind me of my place on a night like tonight?'

'I am sorry. What I meant was that things are particularly strained. When I asked you I never anticipated bringing you here. Certainly I never thought I would set foot in this house.'

They could not discuss it properly here, so for now she gave him the benefit of the doubt. They went out to the garden, where Luka was talking with his father, and they all sat at the table for what should have been a most difficult dinner. Instead, for the most part, it was nice. It was little uncomfortable at first, but soon conversation was flowing as Estelle helped Angela to bring out the food.

'I never thought I would see this day,' Antonio said. 'My family all at the same table…'

Antonio would never see it again.

He was so frail and weak it was clear this would be the last time. It was for that reason, perhaps, that Luka and Raúl attempted to be amicable.

'You work in Bilbao?' Raúl asked.

'I do,' Luka said. 'Investment banking.'

'I had heard of you even before this,' Raúl said. 'You are making a name for yourself.'

'And you.' Luka smiled but it did not meet his eyes. 'I hear about your many acquisitions…'

Thank God for morphine, Estelle thought, because Antonio just smiled and did not pick up on the tension.

The food was amazing—a mixture of dishes from the north and south of Spain. There was *pringá*, an Andalusian dish that was a slow-cooked mixture of meats and had been Raúl's favourite as a child. And there was *marmitako* too, a dish from the Basque Country, which was full of potatoes and pimientos and, Antonio said, had kept him going for so long.

'So you study?' Antonio said to Estelle.

'Ancient architecture.' Estelle nodded. 'Although, I haven't been doing much lately.'

'Yes, what happened to your online studies?' Raúl teased.

'Sol's happened.' Estelle smiled.

Raúl laughed. 'Being married to me is a full-time job…'

Raúl used the words she had used about Gordon. It was a gentle tease, a joke that caused a ripple of laughter—

except their eyes met for a brief moment and it hurt her that he was speaking the truth.

It *was* a job, Estelle reminded herself. A job that would soon be over. But then she thought of the life that grew inside her, the baby that must have the two most mismatched parents in the world.

Not that Raúl knew it.

He thought she loved the clubs and the parties, whereas sitting and eating with his family, as difficult as it was, was where she would rather be. This night, for Estelle, was one of the best.

'You would love San Sebastian.' Antonio carried on speaking to her. 'The architecture is amazing. Raúl, you should take Estelle and explore with her. Take her to the Basilica of Santa Maria—there is so much she would love to see…'

'Estelle would prefer to go out dancing at night. Anyway,' Raúl quipped, 'I haven't been inside a church for years.'

'You will be inside one soon,' his father warned. 'And you should share in your wife's interests.'

Estelle watched thankfully as Raúl took a drink rather than delivering a smart response to his father's marital advice.

And, as much as she'd love to explore the amazing city, she and Raúl were simply too different. And the most bizarre thing was Raúl didn't even know that they were.

She tried to imagine a future: Raúl coming home from a night out to a crying baby, or to nannies, or having access weekends. And she tried to picture the life she would have to live in Spain if she wanted his support.

Estelle remembered the menace in his voice when he had warned that he didn't want children and decided then that she would never tell him while this contract was between them. When she was back home in England and there was distance, when she could tell him without breaking down, or hang up on him if she was about to, *then* she would confess.

And there would be no apology either. Estelle surged in sudden defensiveness for her child—she wasn't going to start its life by apologising for its existence. However Raúl dealt with the news was up to him.

'So…' Still Antonio was focused on Estelle. 'You met last year?'

'We did.' Estelle smiled.

'When he said he was seeing an ex, I thought it was that…' Antonio snapped his fingers. 'The one with the strange name. The one he really liked.'

'Antonio.' Angela chided, but he was too doped up on morphine for inhibition.

'Araminta!' Antonio said suddenly.

'Ah, yes, Araminta.' Estelle smiled sweetly to her husband. 'Was that the one making a play for you at Donald's wedding?'

'That's the one.' Raúl actually looked uncomfortable.

'You were serious for a long time,' Antonio commented.

Estelle glanced up, saw a black smile on Luka's face.

'Weren't you engaged to her?' he asked. 'I remember my mother saying that she thought there might soon be a wedding.'

'Luka,' Angela warned. 'Raúl's wife is here.'

'It's fine,' Estelle attempted—except her cheeks were on fire. She was as jealous as if she had just found out about a bit of her husband's past she'd neither known of nor particularly liked. 'If I'd needed to know about all of Raúl's past before I married him we'd barely have got to his twenties by now.'

She should have left it there, but there was a white-hot

feeling tearing up her throat when she thought of how he'd so cruelly dismissed Araminta—and that was someone he'd once cared about.

It was for that reason her words were tart when she shot Raúl a look. 'Though you failed to mention you'd ever been engaged.'

'We were never engaged.'

'Please!'

Antonio's crack of laughter caught them all by surprise and he raised a glass to Estelle. 'Finally you have met your match.'

It wasn't a long night. Antonio soon tired, and as they headed inside Luka farewelled his father fondly. But the look he gave to Estelle and Raúl told them both he didn't need him to see him to the door in *his* home.

They headed for bed. Estelle was a bit embarrassed by her earlier outburst, especially as everyone else seemed to have managed to behave well tonight.

'I'm sorry about earlier,' she said as she undressed and climbed into bed. 'I shouldn't have said anything about Araminta.'

'You did well,' Raúl said. 'My father actually believes us now.'

He thought she had been acting, Estelle realised. But she hadn't been.

It felt very different sleeping in his father's home from sleeping in Raúl's apartment or on his yacht. Even Raúl's ardour was tempered, and for the first time since she had married him Estelle put on her glasses and pulled out a book. It was the same book she had been reading the day she had met him, about the mausoleum of the First Qin Emperor.

She was still on the same page.

As soon as this was over she was going to focus on

her studies. It had been impossible even to attempt online learning with Raúl around.

'Read me the dirty bits,' Raúl said, and when she didn't comment he took the book from her and looked at the title. 'Well, that will keep it down.'

For his effort he got a half smile.

'You really like all that stuff?'

'I do.'

His hand was on her hip, stroking slowly down. 'They should hear us arguing now,' he teased lightly. 'You demanding details about my past.'

'I don't need to know.'

'My time in Scotland was amazing.' Raúl spoke on regardless. 'I shared a house with Donald and a couple of others. For the first time since my mother died I had one bedroom, one home, a group of friends. We had wild times but it was all good. Then I met Araminta, we started going out, and I guess it was as close to love as I have ever come. But, no, we were never engaged.'

'I really don't need to hear about it.' She turned to him angrily. 'Do you remember the way you spoke to her?' She struggled to keep her voice down. 'The way you treated her?' She looked at his black eyes, imagined running into him a few years from now and being flicked away like an annoying fly. She wasn't hurting for Araminta, Estelle realised. She was hurting for herself—for a time in her future without him.

'So, should I have slept with her as she requested?'

'No!'

'Should I have danced with her when she asked?'

Estelle hated that he was right.

'Anyway, we were never engaged. Her father looked down on me because I didn't come with some inherited title, so I ended things.'

'You dumped her for that?'

'She was lucky I gave a reason,' Raúl said.

Estelle let out a tense breath—he could be so arrogant and cold at times.

'Normally I don't.'

She returned to her book, tried to pick up where she had left off. Just as she would try to pick up her life in a few weeks' time. Except now everything had changed.

'Put down the book,' Raúl said.

'I'm reading.'

'You are the slowest reader I have ever met,' Raúl teased. 'If we ever watch a movie with subtitles we will have to pause every frame.'

She gave up pretending to read, and as she took off her glasses and put down the book he was suddenly serious.

'Not that we will be watching many more movies.'

She lay on her pillow and faced him.

'I could not have done this without you,' Raúl said. 'I nearly didn't come here in time.' He brushed her hair back from his face with her hand.

'You made it, though.'

'It will be over soon.' He looked into her eyes and didn't know if he was dreading his father dying or that soon she would be gone. 'You'll be back to your studies…'

'And you'll be back on your yacht, partying along the coastline.'

'We could maybe go out on the yacht this weekend?' Was he starting to think of her in ways that he had sworn not to? Or was he simply not thinking straight, given that he was here? 'We had a good time.'

'We did have a good time,' Estelle said, but then she shook her head, because she was tired of running away from the world with Raúl. 'But can we just leave it at that?'

She did not want to taint the memory—didn't want to

return to the yacht with hope, only to find out that what they had found there no longer existed.

But for one more night it did.

He held her face and kissed her—a very slow kiss that tasted tender. She felt as if they were back on the boat, could almost hear the lap of the water as he pulled her closer to him and wrapped her in his arms, urged her to join him in one final escape.

Estelle did.

She kissed him as though she were his wife in more than name. She kissed him as though they were really the family they were pretending to be, sharing and loving each other through difficult times.

He had never known a kiss like it; her hands were in his hair, her mouth was one with his, their bodies were meshing, so familiar with each other now. And he wanted her in his bed for ever.

'Estelle….' He was on the edge of saying something he must not, so he made love to her instead.

His hands roamed her body; he kissed her hard as he slid inside her. Side on, they faced each other as he moved and neither closed their eyes.

'Estelle?'

He said it again. It was a question now—a demand to know how she felt. She could feel him building inside her but she was holding back—not on her orgasm. She was holding back on telling him how she felt. They were making love and they both knew it, though neither dared to admit it.

She stared at this man who had her heart. She didn't even need to kiss him to feel his mouth, because deep inside he consumed her. She was pressing her hips into him, her orgasm so low and intense that he moaned as she gripped him. He closed his eyes as he joined her, then forced them open just to watch the blush on her cheeks, the grimace on her face, just to see the face he loved come to him.

She knew he would turn away from her afterwards. Knew they had taken things too far, that there had been true tenderness.

She looked at the scar on his back and waited till dawn for his breathing to quicken, for Raúl to awake abruptly and take her as he did most mornings.

It never happened.

CHAPTER SIXTEEN

HE WOKE AND he waited for reason.

For relief to flood in because he had held back his words last night.

It never came.

He turned and watched her awaken. He should be bored by now. She should annoy him by now.

'What am I thinking?' he asked when she opened her eyes and smiled at him.

'I wouldn't presume to know.'

'I *did* meet you that night,' he said. 'Despite the dress and the make-up, it *was* Estelle.'

He was getting too close for comfort. Raúl had never been anything other than himself. She, on the other hand, changed at every turn—he didn't actually know her at all. Sex was their only true form of communication.

Estelle could hear noises from the kitchen and was relieved to have a reason to leave. 'I'll go and give Angela a hand.' She went to climb out of bed, wondering if she should say anything about what Angela had told her last night. 'I spoke to her yesterday…'

'Later,' Raúl said, and she nodded.

Today was already going to be painful enough.

* * *

'Buenos días,' Raúl greeted Angela.

'Buenos días.' Angela smiled. 'I was just making your father his breakfast. What would you like?'

'Don't worry about us,' Raúl said. 'We'll have some coffee and then Estelle and I might go for a walk.'

'What time are you going back?'

'I'm not sure,' Raúl said. 'Maybe we might stay a bit longer?'

'That would be good,' Angela said. 'Why don't you take your father's tray in and tell him?'

He was in there for ages, and Angela and Estelle shared a look when at one point they heard laughter.

'I am so glad that they have had this time,' Angela said, and then Raúl came out, and he and Estelle headed off for a walk along the sweeping hillsides on his father's property.

'Have you been here before?' Estelle asked. 'To San Sebastian, I mean?'

'A couple of times,' Raúl said. 'Would you like to explore?'

'We're here to spend time with your father,' Estelle said, nervous about letting her façade down, admitting just how much she would like to.

'I guess,' Raúl said. 'But, depending on how long we stay, I am sure the newlyweds would like some private time too.'

'Wouldn't you be bored?'

'If I am I can wait in the gift shop.' Raúl smiled, and so did she, and then he told her some of what he had been talking about with his father. 'He has told my aunt and uncle about Angela and Luka.'

'When?'

'Yesterday. When he knew I was on my way,' Raúl said. 'He didn't want to leave it to me to tell them.'

'How did they take it?'

'He asked if we heard any shouting while we were fly-ing up.' Raúl gave a small mirthless laugh. 'They want him dead, of course. He told them they wouldn't have long to wait.'

They walked for ages, hardly talking, and Raúl was comfortable with silence, because he was trying to think—trying to work out if she even wanted to hear what he was about to ask her.

'You miss England?'

'I do,' Estelle said. 'Well, I miss my family.'

'Will you miss me?' He stopped walking.

She turned to him and didn't know how to respond. 'I won't miss the clubs and the restaurants...'

'Will you miss *us*?'

'I can't give the right answer here.'

'You can.' He took her in his arms. 'You were right. I miss out on so much...'

It was a fragile admission, she could feel that, and she was scared to grasp it in case somehow it dispersed. But she could not deny her feelings any longer. 'You don't have to.'

His mouth was on hers and they were kissing as if for the first time—a teenage kiss as they paused in the hills, a kiss that had nothing to do with business; a kiss that had nothing to do with sex. His fingers were moving into her hair, touching her face as if he were blind, and she was a whisper away from telling him, from confessing the truth. Just so they could tell his father—just so there might be one less regret.

'Raúl...'

He looked into her eyes and she thought she could tell him anything when he looked at her like that. But for the moment she held back. Because a child was something far bigger than this relationship they were almost exploring. She remembered her vow to do this well away from their contract.

'Let's get back.'

They walked down the hill hand in hand, talking about nothing in particular—about France, so close, and the drive they could maybe take tomorrow, or the next day. They were just a couple walking, heading back home to their family—and then she felt his hand tighten on hers.

'It's the *médico*.'

They ran the remaining distance, though he paused for just a moment to collect himself before they pushed open the front door. Because even from there they could hear the sound of Angela sobbing.

'Your father...' Angela stumbled down the hall and Raúl held her as she wept into his arms. 'He has passed away.'

CHAPTER SEVENTEEN

ESTELLE COULDN'T BELIEVE how quickly things happened.

Luka arrived soon after, and spent time with his father. But it was clear he did not appreciate having Raúl and Estelle in his home.

'Stay,' Angela said.

'We'll go to a hotel.'

'Please, Raúl…'

Estelle's heart went out to her, but it was clear that Luka did not want them there and so they spent the night in a small hotel. Raúl was pensive and silent.

The next morning they stood in the small church to say farewell. The two brothers stood side by side, but they were not united in their grief.

'I used to think Luka was the chosen one,' Raúl said as they flew late that afternoon back to Marbella for the will to be read, as per his father's wishes. 'When I found out—when my father said he wanted to die there—I felt his other family were the real ones.' His eyes met hers. 'Luka sees things differently. He was a secret—his father's shame. I got to work alongside him. I was the reason he did not see much of his father when he was small. His hatred runs deep.'

'Does yours?'

'I don't know,' Raúl admitted. 'I don't know how I feel.
I just want to get the reading of the will over with.'

It wasn't a pleasant gathering. Paola and Carlos were
there, and the look they gave Angela as she walked in
was pure filth.

'She doesn't need this—' Estelle started, but Raúl shot
her a look.

'It was never going to be nice,' he said.

Estelle bit her lip, and tried to remember her opinion
on his family was not what she was here for. But she kept
remembering the night they had made love, their walk on
the hill the next morning, and tried to hold on to a love
that had almost been there—she was sure of it.

She sat silent beside him as the will was read, heard the
low murmurs as the lawyer spoke with Angela. From her
limited Spanish, Estelle could make out that she was keeping the home in San Sebastian and there were also some
investments that had been made in her name.

And then he addressed Luka.

Estelle heard a shocked gasp from Paola and Carlos and
then a furious protest started. But Raúl sat still and silent
and said nothing.

'What's happening?'

He didn't answer her.

As the room finally settled the lawyer addressed Raúl.
He gave a curt nod, then stood.

'Come on.'

He took her by the arm and they walked out.

Angela followed, calling to him. 'Raúl…'

'Don't.' He shrugged her off. 'You got what you wanted.'

Estelle had to run to keep up with his long strides, but
finally he told her what was happening.

'His share of the business goes to Luka.' His face was
grey when he turned and faced her. 'Even dying still he

plays games, still he lies.' He shook his head. 'I get a vine-yard…'

'Raúl,' Angela had caught up with them. 'He saw how happy you two were the night before he died.'

'He did not change his will.'

'No, but it was his dream that his two sons would work side by side together.'

'He should have thought about that twenty-five years ago.'

'Raúl…'

But Raúl was having none of it. He strode away from Angela and all too soon they were back in his apartment and rapid decisions were being made.

'I'll sell my share,' he said. 'I will start again.' He would. Raúl had no qualms about starting again. 'And I will sell that vineyard too…'

'Why?'

'Because I don't want it,' he said. 'I don't want anything from *him*. I don't want to build bridges with my brother.' *His* mother's business was being handed over to her husband's illegitimate son—it would kill her if she wasn't dead already.

Raúl was back in the mountains—could hear her furious shouts and screams, the storm raging; he could hear the screech of tyres and the scrape of metal. He was over the cliff again. But that part he could manage—that part he could deal with. It was next part he dreaded.

It was the silence after that, and he would do anything never to hear it again.

'You don't have to make any decisions tonight. We can talk about it—'

'We?' His lips tore into a savage smile. '*We* will talk about *my* future? Estelle, I think *you* are forgetting your place.'

'No.' She refused to deny it any longer. 'The morning your father died, when were talking, we were *both* choosing to forget my place. If you want a relationship you can't pick and choose the times!'

'A relationship?' He stared at her for the longest time.

'Yes,' Estelle said, and she was the bravest she had ever been. 'A relationship. I think that's what you want.'

'Now she tells me what I want? You *love* me, do you? You *care* about me, do you? Have you any idea how boring that is to hear? I *bought* you so we could avoid this very conversation. You'd do well to remember that.'

Estelle just stood there as he stormed out of the apartment. She didn't waste her breath warning him this time.

She refused to be his keeper.

CHAPTER EIGHTEEN

RAÚL SAT IN Sol's with the music pumping and stared at the heaving dance floor.

A vineyard.

A vineyard which, if he sold it, wouldn't even pay for his yacht for a year—would Estelle stick around then?

Yes.

He had never doubted his ability to start again, but he doubted it now—could not bear the thought of letting her down.

'Te odio.' He could hear his five-year-old voice hurling the words at his mother, telling her he hated her for missing his play.

He'd been a child, a five-year-old having a row, yet for most of his life he had thought those words had driven his mother to despair that day.

Could he do it?

Whisk Estelle away from a family that loved her to live in the hills with a man who surely wasn't capable of love?

Except he did love her.

And she loved him.

He had done everything he could think of to ensure it would not happen, had put so many rules in place, and yet here it was—staring at him, wrapping around him like a blanket on a stifling day.

He did not want her love, did not want the weight of it. Did not want to be responsible for another's heart.

She would stand by him, Raúl knew, but the fallout was going to be huge. The empire was divided. He could smell the slash and burn that would take place and he did not want her exposed to it.

His phone buzzed in his pocket but he refused to look at it, because if he saw her name he would weaken.

Raúl looked across the dance floor, saw an upper-class hooker, ordered her a drink and gestured her over.

He took out some money and as she opened her bag made his request.

'Lápiz de labios,' Raúl said, and pointed to his neck.

He did not have to explain himself to her. She delivered his request—put her mouth to his neck and did as he asked.

'Perfume,' he ordered next, and she took out her cheap scent and sprayed him.

'Gracias.'

It was done now.

Raúl stood and headed for home.

CHAPTER NINETEEN

'AMANDA.' ESTELLE ATTEMPTED to sound normal when she answered the landline. She was staring at the picture of them on Donald's wedding night, trying to fathom the man who simply refused to love.

'I tried your mobile.'

'Sorry…' Estelle had started to talk about the charger she'd left in San Sebastian, started to talk about little things that weren't important at all, when she realised that for once Amanda wasn't being upbeat. 'What's happened?'

'I tried to ring Raúl—I wanted him to break the news to you.'

Estelle felt her heart turn to ice.

'We're at the hospital and the doctors say that they're going to operate tomorrow.'

'Has she put on any weight?'

'She's lost some,' Amanda said. 'But if they don't operate we're going to lose her anyway.'

'I'm coming home.'

'Please…'

'How's Andrew?'

'He's with her now. He's actually been really good. He's sure she's going to make it through.'

'She will.'

'I don't think so,' Amanda admitted, and her sister-in-law who was always so strong, always so positive, finally broke down.

Estelle said everything she could to comfort her, but knew they were only words, that she needed to be there.

'I'm going to hang up now and book a flight,' Estelle told her. 'And I'll try and sort out my phone.'

'Don't worry about the phone,' Amanda said. 'Just get here.'

Estelle grabbed her case and started piling clothes in. Getting to the airport and onto a flight was her aim, but the thought of Cecelia, so small and so weak, undergoing something so major was just too overwhelming and it made Estelle suddenly fold over. She sobbed as she never had before—knew that she had to get the tears out now, so she could be strong for Amanda and Andrew.

Raúl heard her tears as he walked through the apartment and could not stand how much he had hurt her—could not bear that *he* had done this.

'Estelle...' He saw the case and knew that she was leaving.

'Don't worry.' She didn't even look at him. 'The tears aren't for you. Cecelia has been taken back into hospital. They can't wait for the surgery any longer...' She thought of her again, so tiny, and of what would happen to her parents if they lost her. The tears started again. 'I need to get back to them.'

'I'll fix it now.'

He couldn't *not* hold her.

Could not stand the thought of her facing this on her own, not being there beside her.

He held her in his arms and she wept.

And he could not fight it any more for he loved her.

'We'll go now.'

'No.' She was trying to remember that she was angry, but it felt so good to be held.

'Estelle, I've messed up, but I know what I want now. *I know...*'

She smelt it then—the cheap musky scent; she felt it creep into her nostrils. She moved out of his arms and looked at him properly, smelt the whisky on his breath and saw the lipstick on his neck.

'It's not what you think,' Raúl said.

'You're telling me what I think, are you?' Oh, she didn't need him to teach her to cuss in Spanish! 'You win, Raúl!' Her expression revealed her disgust. 'I'm out of here!'

The tears stopped. They weren't for him anyway. She just turned and went on filling her case.

'Estelle—'

'I don't want to hear it, Raúl.' She didn't even raise her voice.

'Okay, not now. We will speak about it on the plane.'

'You're not coming with me, Raúl.'

'Your brother will think it strange if I do not support you.'

'I'm sure my brother has other things on his mind.' She looked at him, dishevelled and unshaven, and scorned him with her eyes. 'Don't make this worse for me, Raúl.'

He went to grab her arm, to stop her.

'Don't touch me!'

He heard her shout, heard the pain—not just for what was going on with her niece, but for the agony of the betrayal she perceived.

'You can't leave like this. You're upset...'

'I'm upset about my niece!' She looked at him. 'I would *never* cry like this over a man who doesn't love me.' She didn't care how much she hurt him now. 'I'm not your mother, Raúl, I'm not going fall apart, or drive over a cliff-edge because the man I'm married to is a cheat. I'm far stronger than that.'

She was.

'All I want now is to get home to my niece.'

He'd lost her. Raúl knew that. Arguing would be worse than futile, for she needed to be with her family urgently.

'I will call my driver and organise a plane.'

'I can sort out transport myself.' Tears for him were starting now, and she didn't want Raúl to see—love was not quite so black and white.

'If you take my plane it will get you there sooner,' Raúl said.

And it would get her away from him before she broke down—before she told him about the baby...before she weakened.

It was the only reason she said yes.

CHAPTER TWENTY

RAÚL STOOD IN the silence.

It was the sound he hated most in the world.

It was his nightmare.

Only this was one *he* had created.

The scent that filled his nostrils was not leaking fuel and death but the scent of cheap perfume and the absence of *her*.

He wanted to chase Estelle—except he was not foolish enough to get in a car, and he could not follow her as his driver was taking her to the airport.

Raúl called a taxi, but even as he climbed in he knew she would not want him with her on the flight. Knew he would be simply delaying her in getting to where she needed to be. They passed De La Fuente Holdings and he looked up, trying to imagine it without his father and Angela, and with Luka working there. Trying to fathom a future that right now he could not see.

Noticing a light on, he asked the driver to stop…

'Raúl!'

Angela tried not to raise her eyes as a very dishevelled Raúl appeared from the elevator.

He was unshaven, his eyes bloodshot. His hair was a mess, and there was lipstick on his collar…

It was the Raúl she knew well.

'What are you doing here at this time, Raúl?'

'I saw the light on,' Raúl said. 'Estelle's niece is sick.'

'I am sorry to hear that. Where is Estelle?'

'Flying back to London.'

'You should be with her, then.' Angela refused to mince her words. He might not want to hear what she had to say to him—he could leave if that were the case.

'She didn't want me to go.'

'So you hit the clubs and picked up a *puta*?'

'No.'

'Don't lie to me, Raúl,' Angela said. 'Your wife would never wear cheap perfume like that.'

'I wouldn't cheat on her. I couldn't.'

Angela paused. Really, the evidence was clear—and yet she knew Raúl better than most and he did not lie. Raúl never attempted to defend the inexcusable.

'So what happened?' Angela asked.

He closed his eyes in shame.

'You know, when you live as a mistress apparently you lose the right to an opinion on others—but of course you have them.' Harsh was the look she gave Raúl. 'Over and over I question your morals.'

'Over and over I do too,' Raúl admitted. 'She got too close.'

'That's what couples do.'

'I did not cheat. I wanted her to think that I had.'

'So now she does.' Angela looked at him. 'So now she's on her own, dealing with her family.'

Angela watched his eyes fill with tears and she tried not to love him as a son, tried not to forgive when she should not. But when he told her what had happened, told her what he had done, the filthy place his head had been, she believed him.

'You push away everyone who loves you. What are you scared of, Raúl?'

'This,' Raúl admitted. 'Hurting another, being responsible for another...'

'We are responsible for ourselves,' Angela said. 'I have made mistakes. Now I pay for them. Now I have till the morning to clear out my office. Now your aunt and uncle turn their backs on me. I would do it all again, though, for the love I had with your father. Some things I would do differently, of course, but I would do it all again.'

'What would you do differently?'

'I would have insisted you were told far sooner about your father and I. I would have told you about your brother,' she said. 'We were going to before you went to university, but your father decided not to at the last moment. I regret that. I should have stood up to him. I should have told you myself. I did not. And I have to live with that. What would *you* have done differently, Raúl?'

'Not have gone to Sol's.' He gave a small smile. 'And many, many other things. But that is the main one now.'

'You need to go to her. You need to tell her what happened—why you did what you did.'

'She doesn't want to hear it,' Raúl said. 'There are more important things on her mind.'

He could not bring himself to tell Angela that their marriage was a fake. If this was fake, then it hurt too much.

And if it was not fake, then it was real.

'If you are not there for her now, with her niece so ill, then it might be too late.'

Raúl nodded. 'She has my plane.'

'I will book you on a commercial flight,' Angela said. 'You need to freshen up.'

He headed to his office, stared in the mirror and picked

up his razor. He called his thanks as she brought him in coffee and a fresh shirt.

'This is the last time I do this for you.'

'Maybe not,' Raúl said. 'Maybe your sons might have a say in that.'

Angela's eyes welled up for a moment as finally he acknowledged the place she had in his heart. But then she met his eyes and told him, 'I meant this is the last time I help you cover up a mistake. Estelle deserves more.'

'She will get it.'

'Your father was so pleased to see how you two were together,' Angela said. 'He was the most peaceful I have ever seen him. He knew he had not allowed time for you and Luka to sort things out, but you are brothers and he believes that will happen. The morning he passed away we were watching you and Estelle walking in the hills. We saw you stop and kiss.'

Raúl closed his eyes as he remembered that day, when for the first time in his life he had been on the edge of admitting love.

'He knew you were happy. I am so glad that I told him about the baby.'

Raúl froze.

'Baby?'

There was no mistaking his bewilderment.

'She has not told you?'

'No!' Raúl could not take it in. 'She told *you*?'

'No,' Angela said. 'I just knew. She did not have any wine; she was sick in the morning…'

Yes, Estelle was tough.

Yes, she could do this without him.

He did not want her to.

'Book the flight.'

CHAPTER TWENTY-ONE

'RAÚL!'

The only possible advantage to being in the midst of a family crisis was that no one noticed the snap to her voice or the tension on Estelle's features when a clean-shaven, lipstick-free Raúl walked in.

'I'm sorry I couldn't get here sooner.' He shook Andrew's hand.

'No, we're grateful to you for getting Estelle here,' Andrew said. 'We're very sorry about your father.'

It was strange, but in a crisis it was Andrew who was the strong one. Amanda barely looked up.

'Is she in surgery?' Raúl sat down next to Estelle and put his arm around her. He felt her shoulders stiffen.

'An hour ago.' Her words were stilted. 'It could be several hours yet.'

The clock ticked on.

Raúl read every poster on the wall and every pamphlet that was laid out. She could hear the turning of the pages and it only served to irritate her. Why on earth had he come? Why couldn't she attempt to get over him with him still far away?

'Why won't they give us an update?' asked Amanda's mother. 'It's ridiculous that they don't let us know what's going on.'

'They will soon,' Andrew said, and Raúl watched as Andrew put his arm around his wife and comforted her, saw how she leant on him, how much she needed him.

Despite everything.

Because of everything, Raúl realised.

'Why don't you wait in the hotel?' Estelle suggested when she could not stand him being in the room a moment longer. 'I've got a room there.'

'I want to wait with you.'

He headed out to the vending machine and she followed him. 'I need some change,' he said. 'I haven't got any pounds.'

'Why would you make this worse for me?'

'I'm not trying to make it worse for you,' Raúl said. 'I know this is neither the time nor the place, but you need to know that nothing happened except my asking a woman to kiss my neck and spray me with her perfume.' He looked her right in the eye. 'I wanted you gone.'

'Well, it worked.'

'I made a mistake,' Raúl said. 'The most foolish of mistakes. I did not want to put you through what was to come.'

'Shouldn't that be *my* choice?' She looked at him.

'Yes,' he said simply. 'As it should be mine.'

Estelle didn't understand his response, was in no mood for cryptic games, and she shook her head in frustration. She wanted him gone and yet she wanted him here— wanted to forgive, to believe.

'I can't do this now,' Estelle said. 'Right now I have to concentrate on my niece.'

As much as Raúl longed to be there for her, that much he understood. 'Do you want me to wait in the hotel or stay with you here?'

'The hotel,' Estelle said—because she could not think straight with him around, could not keep her thoughts where they needed to be with Raúl by her side. She wanted his arms around her, wanted the comfort only he could give, and yet she could not stand what he had done.

'Could I get a coffee as well?' Andrew wheeled himself over.

'Of course,' Raúl said as Estelle handed him some change.

'Estelle, could you take Amanda for a walk?' Andrew asked. 'Just get her away from the waiting room. Her parents are driving her crazy, asking how much longer it will be.'

'Sure.'

Estelle's eyes briefly met Raúl's, warning him to be gone by the time she returned, and Raúl knew the fight he had on his hands. He watched as Estelle suggested a walk to Amanda and he saw a family in motion, supporting each other, a family that was there for each other. A family who helped, who fixed—or tried to.

He looked to Andrew. 'You have the best sister in the world.'

'I know,' Andrew said. 'I'd do anything for her.'

As would Estelle for him, Raúl thought. She'd sold her soul to the devil for her family, but now he understood why.

'I am going to wait in the hotel,' Raúl said. 'I didn't sleep at all last night.'

'I know.' Andrew nodded. 'I'm sure Estelle will keep you up to date.'

'What hotel is she staying at?'

'Over the road,' Andrew told him. 'Good luck—I'm sure it's not at all what you're used to.'

'It will be fine.'

'You just wait.' Andrew gave a pale smile. 'I had to wait fifteen minutes just for them to find a ramp.'

They chatted on for a while—Andrew trying to keep

his mind out of the surgery, Raúl simply because Andrew wanted to talk.

'I had my reservations about the two of you at first,' Andrew admitted. 'You're so opposite.'

And then Raúl found out from his wife's brother just how much Estelle hated clubs and bars, found out exactly the lengths she had gone to for her family.

There was one length she would not go to, though. Raúl was certain of that now.

He walked alongside Andrew's chair, down long corridors, past the operating theatres and Intensive Care, and back again a few times over—until he saw Estelle returning and knew it was better for her that he leave.

He paced the small hotel room, waiting for news—because surely it was taking too long. It was now nine p.m., and he was sick to his stomach for a baby he had never met and a family he wanted to be a part of.

'She made it through surgery.'

Raúl could hear both the relief and the strain in Estelle's voice when the door opened.

'When did she get out of Theatre?'

'About six.' She glanced over to him. 'Was I supposed to ring and inform you?'

He could hear the sarcasm in her voice. 'I just thought it was taking too long. I thought...'

'I'm sorry.' Estelle regretted her sarcastic response— she could see the concern on his face was genuine. 'It was just a long wait till they let Andrew and Amanda in to see her. They've only just been allowed.'

'How is she?'

'Still here.' Estelle peeled off her clothes. 'I've lost my phone charger. I gave Andrew your number in case anything happens overnight.'

It was, though she would never admit it, a relief to have him here, to know that if the phone rang in the night he would be the one to answer it. It was a relief, too, to sink into bed and close her eyes, but there was something that needed to be dealt with before the bliss of sleep.

'I'm not going to tell them we're over yet,' Estelle said. 'It would be too much for them to deal with now. But after we visit in the morning can you make your excuses and leave.'

'I want to be here.'

'I don't want you here, though, and given what's happened you don't own me any more.' She stared into the dark. 'Exclusive, remember?'

'I've told you—nothing happened,' Raúl said. 'Which means I do still own you.'

'No,' Estelle said, 'you don't. Because whatever went on I've decided that I don't want your money. It costs too much.'

'Then pay me back.'

'I will…' she attempted, but of course a considerable amount had already been spent. 'I fully intend to pay you back. It just might take some time.'

'Whatever you choose. But it changes nothing now, Estelle…' He reached for her, wanted to speak with her, but she shrugged him off and turned to her side.

'I'd like the night off.'

'Granted.'

She woke in his arms and wriggled away from them, and then rang her brother. Raúl watched as she went to climb out of bed, saw the extra heaviness to her breasts and the darkening pink of her areolae, and he loved her all the more for not telling him, for guarding their child from the contract that had once bound them. It was the only leverage he had.

'You'll leave after visiting?' Estelle checked.

'Why would I leave my wife at a time like this?' Raúl asked. 'I'm not going anywhere, Estelle.'

'I don't want you here.'

'I don't believe you,' Raúl said. 'I believe you love me as much as I love you.'

'Love you!' Estelle said. 'I'd be mad to love you.' She shook her head. 'You might have almost sent me crazy once, Raúl, but if I possibly did love you then it's gone. My love has conditions too, and you didn't adhere to them. I don't care about technicalities, Raúl. Even if you didn't sleep with someone else, what you did was wrong.'

'Then we go back to the contract.' He caught her wrist. 'Which means I dictate the terms.'

'Your father's dead. Surely it's over?'

'We agreed on a suitable pause. You should read things more closely before you sign them, Estelle.' He watched her shoulders rise and fall. 'But I agree it has proved more complicated than either of us could have anticipated. For that reason, I will agree that the contract expires tomorrow.'

'Tomorrow?' Estelle asked. 'Why not now?'

'I just want one more night. And if I have to exercise the terms of the contract to speak with you—believe me, I shall.'

CHAPTER TWENTY-TWO

'SHE'S PINK!'

Estelle couldn't believe the little pink fingers that wrapped around hers. Even Cecelia's nails were pink—it was suddenly her favourite colour in the world.

'That's the first thing we said.' Andrew was holding Cecelia's other hand. 'She's been fighting so much since the day she was born.' Andrew smiled down at his daughter.

All were too entranced by the miracle that was Cecelia to notice how much Raúl was struggling.

Raúl looked down at the infant, who resembled Estelle, and could hardly believe what he had almost turned his back on.

'I have to go and do some work,' Raúl said. 'Do you want to get lunch later?'

Estelle looked up, about to say no, but he was talking to Andrew.

'Just at the canteen,' he added.

'That would be great.' Andrew smiled. 'Estelle, could you take Amanda for some breakfast? She wants one of us with Cecelia all the time but she needs to get out of the unit and get some fresh air.'

'Sure.' Estelle stood.

'I thought we could go for dinner tonight.'

This time Raúl *was* speaking to Estelle.

'I'm here to be with my niece.'

'Andrew and Amanda are with her. As long as she continues to improve I am sure they expect you to eat.'

'Of course we do,' Andrew said. 'Go out tonight, Estelle. You need a break from the hospital too!'

It was a long day. The doctors were in and out with Cecelia, and talked about taking her breathing tube out if she continued to hold her own. Amanda's parents went home, to return at the weekend, and after they had gone Estelle finally persuaded Amanda to have a sleep in one of the parents' rooms.

It was exhausting.

As she closed the door and went to head back to Cecelia she wondered if she had, after all, grown far too used to Raúl's lifestyle—she would have given anything to be back on his yacht, just drifting along, with nothing to think about other than what the next meal might be and how long it would be till they made love again.

Being Raúl's tart hadn't all been bad, Estelle thought with a wry smile as she returned to Cecelia.

It was being his wife that was hell.

'Amanda's asleep,' Estelle said. 'Well, for a little while.'

'Thanks for being here for us,' Andrew said. 'Both of you. Raúl's great. I admit I wasn't sure at first, but you can see how much he cares for you.'

She felt tears prick her eyes,

'Did you ask him to offer me a job?'

'A job?'

She couldn't lie easily to her brother, but instantly he knew that Estelle's surprised response was real, that she'd had no idea.

'Raúl said that when things are sorted with Cecelia there will be a job waiting for me. He wants me to check out his hotels, work on adjustments for the disabled. There will be a lot of travel, and it will be tough being away at first. But once Cecelia's better he says we can broaden things so it's not just about travelling with disabilities but with a young child as well.'

It was a dream job. She could see it in her brother's eyes. Soon he would be earning, travelling, and more than that his self-respect and confidence would start to return.

'It sounds wonderful.' Estelle gave him a hug, but though she smiled and said the right thing she was furious with Raúl—his company was about to implode, and she and Raúl were soon to divorce quietly.

How dared he enmesh himself further? How dared he involve Andrew in the chaos they had made?

She wanted it to be tomorrow, she wanted Raúl gone so she could sort out how she felt, sort out her life, sort out how to tell him that the temporary contract they had signed would, however tentatively, bind them for life.

There was a note from Raúl waiting for her when she reached the hotel, telling her that he was tied up in a meeting but would see her at the restaurant at eight.

'You signed up for this,' Estelle told herself aloud as she put on her eye make-up. She wondered if it would be just dinner, or perhaps a club after, or…

Estelle closed her eyes so sharply that she almost scratched her eyeball with her mascara wand. He surely wouldn't expect them to sleep together?

He surely wouldn't insist?

Then again, Estelle told herself as she took a taxi to the restaurant, this was Raúl.

Of course he would insist.

Worse, though, she knew she must comply—no matter the toll on heart.

* * *

He turned heads. He just did.

He was waiting for her at the bar, and when they walked into the smartest of restaurants he might as well have being stepping out of a helicopter in a kilt—because everybody was looking at him.

'You look beautiful,' Raúl told her as they sat down.

'Thank you,' she said.

He could feel the anger hissing and spitting inside her, guessed that she must have spoken to Andrew since lunchtime.

'It's a lovely dress,' he commented. 'New?'

'I chose it.'

'It suits you.'

'I know.'

He ordered wine. She declined.

He suggested seafood, which he knew she loved, but he had read in one of the many leaflets he perused in the hospital waiting room that pregnant woman were advised not to eat it.

'I thought you loved seafood?' Raúl commented when she refused it, wondering what her excuse would be.

'I've had enough of it.'

She ordered steak, and he watched her slice it angrily before she voiced one of the many things that were on her mind.

'Did you offer my brother a job?'

'I did.'

'Why would you do that? Why would you do that when you're about to walk away? When you know the company's heading for trouble?'

'We're not heading for trouble,' Raúl said. 'I have been speaking with Luka at length today, and Carlos and Paola too. There is to be a name-change. To Sanchez De La

Fuente... Anyway, if there is trouble ahead it will only be in the office. Your brother will not be dealing with it.'

'What about when we divorce? Will you use him as a pawn then?'

'Never. I tell you this: it is a proper offer, and as long as your brother does well he will have a job.'

'You say that now...'

'I always keep my word.' He looked at her. 'I don't lie,' Raúl said. 'From the start I have only been myself.' He watched the colour spread up her cheeks. 'You get the truth, whether you like or not. I think we both know that much about me.'

Reluctantly she nodded.

'It is only wives that I employ on a whim. I am successful because I choose my employees carefully and I don't give out sympathy jobs. Your brother pointed out a few things that could be changed at the hotel. He would like the menu outside the restaurant to be displayed lower too. He said he would not like to find out about the menu and the prices from a woman he was perhaps dating with.'

Estelle gave a reluctant smile. It was the sort of thing Andrew *would* say.

'He said that a lower table at Reception would be a nice touch, so that anyone in a wheelchair could check in there. That means I do not have to refurbish our reception areas. He has saved me more than his year's wage already.'

'Okay.'

'I don't want my hotels to be good, I want them to be the best—and by the best I mean the best for everyone: businessmen, people with families, the disabled. Your brother, as I told him, will soon be all three.' He looked at her for a long moment, wondering if now she might tell him. 'It is good to see Cecelia improving,' Raúl said. 'It must be a huge relief.'

'It is,' Estelle admitted. 'I think we're only now realising just how scary the last few months have been.'

'Does seeing your niece make you consider ever having a baby?'

She gave a cynical laugh.

'It's just about put me off for life, seeing all that they have had to go through.'

'But they've made it.'

She wasn't going to tell him about the baby, Raúl realised. But, far from angering him, it actually made him smile as he sat opposite the strongest woman he knew.

'Here…' At the end of the meal he smeared cream cheese on a cracker, added a dollop of quince paste and handed it to her.

'No, thanks. I'm full.'

'But remember the night we met…'

'I'd rather not.'

He saw tears prick her eyes and went to take her hand. He could not believe all that they had been through in recent weeks. As she pulled her hand away Raúl wasn't so sure they'd survived it.

'I'm sorry for hurting you. I overreacted—thought I was going to lose everything, thought I might not be able to give you the lifestyle—'

'Like I need your yacht,' Estelle spat. 'Like I need to eat out at posh restaurants seven nights a week, or wear the clothes you chose.'

'So if you don't want all that,' Raúl pointed out, 'what *do* you want?'

'Nothing,' Estelle said. 'I want nothing from you.'

He called for the bill and paid, and as they headed out of the restaurant he took her hand and held it tightly. He turned her to him and kissed her.

It tasted of nothing.

He kissed her harder.

She wanted to spit him out. Not because she loathed his mouth but because she wanted to sink into it for ever—wanted to believe his lies, wanted to think for a moment that she could hold him, that he'd want their baby as much as she did, that he'd want the real her if he knew who she was.

'Where now?' Raúl asked. 'I know…' He held her by the hips. 'You could show me Dario's…'

'I didn't meet Gordon at Dario's,' Estelle said. 'I told you that.'

'We could go anyway,' Raúl said. 'It's our last night together, and it sounds like fun.'

He saw the conflict in her eyes, saw her take a breath to force another lie. He would not put her through it, so he kissed her instead.

'Let's get back to the hotel.'

'Raúl…' She just couldn't go through with it—could not keep up the pretence a moment longer, could not bear to be made love to just to have her heart ripped apart again.

'What?' He took her by the hand again, led her to a taxi.

'Come on, Estelle…' He undressed speedily. 'It's been a hell of a day. I would like to come.'

'You can be *so* romantic.'

'But you keep insisting this is not about romance,' Raúl pointed out.

Her face burnt.

'I don't understand what has suddenly changed. We have been having sex for a couple of months now…' He was undoing her zipper, undressing her. He was down on one knee, removing her shoes. 'Tomorrow we are finished. Tonight we celebrate.'

'I don't want you.'

'So you did the other times?' he checked.

At every exit he blocked her. At every turn he made her see it had never been paid sex for her—not for one single second, not for one shared kiss. She had been lying from the very start. For she had loved him from the start.

'Estelle, after tonight you have the rest of the century off where we are concerned.'

He laid her on the bed and kissed her, felt her cold in his arms. His mouth was on her nipple and he swirled it with his tongue then blew on it, watching it stiffen and ripen. Then he took it deep in his mouth, his fingers intimately stroking her. He filled her mouth with his tongue and she just lay there.

This was what she had signed up for, Estelle reminded herself. She didn't have to enjoy it. Except she was.

It was like a guilty secret—a *filthy* guilty secret. Because she wanted him so—wanted him deep inside her. She turned her cheek away but he turned it back and kissed her. She did not respond—or her mouth did its best not to.

He felt the shift in her…kissed her back to him.

He felt the motion of her tongue on his, felt *her*.

'Tell me to stop and I will,' Raúl said.

She just stared at him.

'Tell me…'

She couldn't

'You can't stop this any more than I can…'

He moved up onto his elbows and she tried not to look at him, looked at his shoulder, which moved back and forth over her.

'Tell me…' he said.

She held on.

'Tell me how you feel…'

In a moment she would. In a moment she'd be sobbing

and begging in his arms. She lifted her hips, and then lifted them again, just so she could hurry him along.

'I'm going to come...' she moaned.

'Liar.'

He pushed deeper within her, hit that spot she would rather tonight he did not, for her face was burning, and her hands were roaming, and her hips were lifting with a life of their own as she let out a low, suppressed moan.

She felt a flood of warmth to her groin, felt the insistence of him inside her, the demand that she match his want.

'You couldn't pay for this...' He was stroking her deep inside and seducing her with his words. 'You could never fake this...'

He slipped into Spanish as she left the planet; he toppled onto her and bucked rapidly inside her as she sobbed out her orgasm. She didn't know where she started or ended, didn't know how to handle the love in her heart and the child in her belly. All belonged to the man holding her in his arms.

'You want me just as much as I want you.'

'So?' She stared back at him. 'What does that prove? That you're good in bed?' She turned away from him and curled up like a ball. 'I think you already knew that.'

'It proves that I am right to trust you. That it is nothing to do with contracts or money. That you *do* love me as much as I love you.'

'You don't know me, though.' She started to cry. 'I've been lying all along.'

'I know you far more than you think,' Raúl said.

'You don't. Your father was right. I like churches and reading...'

'I know that.'

'And I hate clubs.'

'I know that too.'

'I'm nothing like the woman you thought you met.'

'Do you not think I'd long ago worked that out?' Raúl kissed her cheek. 'My virgin hooker.'

He heard her gurgle of laughter, born from exhausted tears.

'I don't get how you're the one with no morals, yet I'm the one who's lied.'

'Because you're complicated,' Raúl said. 'Because you're female.' He kissed her mouth. 'Because you loved me from the start.'

She went to object, but he was telling the truth.

'Do you know when I fell in love with you?' Raúl said. 'When I saw you in those tatty pyjamas and I did not want you in Gordon's bed. It had nothing to do with me paying you. I deserved that slap, but you really did misinterpret my words.'

She was so scared to love him, so scared to tell him about the baby. But if they were to survive, if they were to start to trust, then she had to. It never entered her head that he already knew.

'When were you going to tell me you're pregnant, Estelle?'

She felt his hand move to her stomach, felt his kiss on the back of her neck. All she could be was honest now. 'When I was too pregnant to fly.'

'So the baby would be English?'

'Yes.'

'And you would support it how?'

'The same way that billions of non-billionaires do.'

'Would you have told me?'

'Yes.' She needed the truth from him now and she turned in his arms. 'Are you still here because of the baby?'

'No,' Raúl said. 'I am here because of you.'

She knew he was telling her the truth—not just because he always did, but because of what he said.

'I have had three hellish nights in my life. The first I struggle to speak about, but with you I am starting to. The second was the night after I'd found out about my brother and you were there. I went to bed not thinking about revenge or hate, but about a kiss that went too far and a slap to my cheek. I guess I loved you then, but it felt safer not to admit that.'

'And the third?'

'Finding myself in a nightmare—but not the one I am used to,' Raúl said. 'I was not in a car calling out to my mother. I was not begging her to slow down, and nor was I pleading with her to wake...'

Tears filled her eyes as she imagined it, but she held onto them, knew she would only ever get glimpses of that time and she must piece them together in the quiet of her mind.

'Instead I realised, again, that a woman I loved was gone because of my harsh actions and words. Worse, though. This time it *was* my fault.'

She heard him forgive what his five-year-old self had said as the past was looked at through more mature eyes.

'I went to Angela. She was always the one I went to when I messed up, and I had messed up again. I asked her what to do. I was already on my way to you. It was then that she told me that at least my father had known about the baby... It would seem I was the last to know.'

'I never told her.'

'I'm glad that she guessed. She told my father that morning. I'm glad that he knew, even if I did not.' He looked at her and smiled. 'Opposites attract, Estelle.' He kissed her nose. 'It's law. You can't argue with that.'

'I'm not arguing.'

'Did you hate every dance?' he asked.

She shook her head. 'Of course not.'

'We'll have to get babysitters when we want to go out soon.'

He blew out a breath at the thought of the changes that were to come and she saw that he was smiling.

'Who'd have thought?'

'Not me,' Estelle admitted.

'So, how do you tell your wife you want to marry her all over again?'

'We don't need to get married again,' Estelle said. 'Though a second honeymoon might be nice.'

'Where?'

He was going to make her say it.

'Where?'

'On the yacht.'

Yes, she could get used to that—especially when he made love to her all over again. Especially when he made her laugh about the maid's secret swapping of his DVDs.

No, he had never lied. But he'd never been more honest—and it felt so good.

'Do you think your family will notice a change in us?'

'No.' Estelle smiled. 'They think we met and fell head over heels in love.'

'They were right.' Raúl pulled her to him and then kissed her again. 'We were the only ones who couldn't quite believe it.'

EPILOGUE

IT WAS A beautiful wedding, held on the yacht, which had dropped anchor in Acantilados de Maro-Cerro.

It was Raúl's wedding gift to Gordon for bringing Estelle to him.

The grooms wore white and, contrary to Spanish tradition, there *were* speeches.

'I never thought I'd be standing declaring my love amongst my closest family and friends...' Gordon smiled, and then the dancing started.

Estelle leant against Raúl, feeling the kicks of their baby inside her.

'Is that Gordon's son Ginny is dancing with?' Estelle asked.

'They've been going out for a while.'

'Really?' Estelle smothered a smile. Raúl noticed everything. 'Gordon was once married before—ages ago, apparently.'

'How will they say they met? She can hardly admit she was his father's...' He stopped as Estelle dug him in the ribs. 'Sorry,' Raúl said. 'Sometimes I forget your other life.'

She didn't laugh this time, because the feeling was starting again—like a tight belt pulling around her stomach.

'Do you remember when we stopped here?' Raúl asked.

'When we took out a jet ski and you were scared and trying not to show it.'

'Of course I do.' Estelle attempted to answer normally. 'And I remember when we went snorkeling, and I—'

'Estelle?' He heard her voice break off mid-sentence.

Estelle had been trying to ignore the tightenings, but this one she could not ignore. Raúl's hand moved to her stomach, felt it taut and hard beneath his hands.

'I'll organise a speedboat to take us back to Marbella.'

'It might be ages yet. I don't want to make a fuss.'

'I think it would be a bit more awkward for Gordon if you have the baby here.' He glanced around at the guests and then went to have a word with Alberto, who soon organised transport.

'We are going to head off,' Raúl said when Gordon cornered them. 'Estelle is tired…' But then he couldn't lie— because Estelle was bent over.

'Oh, my!' Gordon was beaming.

'Please,' Estelle begged. 'I don't want everyone to know.'

There was no chance of keeping it quiet as she was helped down to the swimming platform, from where she was guided onto a speedboat. They sped off to the cheers and whistles of the wedding party.

'I wanted to have it in England…'

'I know.' They were supposed to have been flying there the next morning. 'But you wanted to be at the wedding too,' he reminded her.

'I know.'

'You can't have everything,' he teased. 'That's only me.'

She groaned with another pain and buried her face in his neck, wondering how much worse the pains would get, grateful that Raúl was so calm.

He *was* calm—he had everything he wanted right here on this small boat.

He looked up at the cliffs. He had long ago let go of that night, but there was a brief moment of memory just then. It didn't panic him. For a minute he thought of his mother and prayed for her peace.

It was the longest night, and her labour went on well into the next day.

Estelle pushed and dug her nails into his arms, and just when she was sure she could not go on any longer, finally the end was in sight.

'No empujen!'

'Don't push,' Raúl translated.

He had been incredibly composed throughout, but he was starting to worry now, watching the black hair of his infant and realising that soon he would be a father for real.

And then he saw her.

Red, angry, with black hair and fat cheeks.

And as he held her he was more than willing to be completely responsible for this little heart.

The midwife asked if they had a name as she went to write on the wristband and he looked at Estelle. They had chosen a few names, but had opted to wait till the baby was here before they decided. There was one name that had not been suggested till now.

'Gabriella?' Estelle said, and he nodded, unable to speak for a moment. The name that had once meant so much pain was wrapped now in love, and his mother's name would go on.

'Gabriella Sanchez Connolly,' Raúl said.

'She needs a middle name,' Estelle said.

'What about your mother's?' Raúl said, but Estelle already had her mother's name, and thanks to Spanish tradition Connolly was there, too.

Together they held and gazed at their very new daughter, quietly deciding what her full name would be.

'I want to ring Andrew and tell him he's an uncle,' Estelle said, her eyes filling with selfish tears—because though she could not be happier still she wanted to share the news. She wanted her brother to see Gabriella, as she had held Cecelia the day she was born.

'Why would you ring?' Raúl asked. 'They are waiting outside. I will go and bring them in now.'

Raúl stepped out into the waiting room.

His eyes were bloodshot, his hair unkempt, he was unshaven and there was lipstick on his collar—only this time Angela was smiling.

'It's a girl,' Raúl said. 'Both are doing really well,' he said.

Amanda burst into tears and Andrew shook his hand.

'Baby!' Cecelia said, pointing to her little cousin as Estelle showed off the newest arrival to the Connolly clan and thought that Raúl had somehow made an already perfect day even better.

'Come and see,' Raúl said to Angela, who was standing back at the door.

'She's beautiful.' Angela looked down and smiled at the chubby cheeks, seeing the eyes of Luka and Raúl. 'Just perfect—does she have a name?'

'Gabriella,' Raúl said, and looked at the woman who had been like a mother to him, even if it had been from a distance. 'Gabriella Angela Sanchez Connolly.'

Yes, Spanish names could be complicated at times, but they were very simple too.

It was a perfect day, and later came a blissful night, with

Estelle sharing a drink of champagne with her family till
Cecelia was drooping in Andrew's arms.

'We're going to get back to the hotel,' Andrew said,
looking down at Gabriella. He gave Estelle's hand a
squeeze. 'Mum and Dad would have been really proud.'

'I know.'

And then it was just the two of them, lying in bed together, on their first night with Gabriella here.

'There is a text from Luka.' Raúl gave a brief eye-roll
as he read the message. 'I have a feeling Angela may have
hijacked his phone and typed it.' Raúl's voice was wry.
Things were still terribly strained with Luka, but Raúl,
very new to being a brother, was trying to work through it.

Not that Luka wanted to.

'You'll get there,' said Estelle.

'Perhaps,' Raúl said.

'Thank you for today.'

Gabriella, who was snuggled up in her cot beside them,
made a small noise, and Raúl thought his heart might burst
with pride and love as he gazed at his sleeping daughter.

'Thank *you*,' he said. 'I never thought I could feel so
much happiness.'

'I meant for bringing my family over. It means so much
to me to have them here.'

'I know it does.' He turned his gaze from his daughter to his wife. 'I know, thanks to you, the importance of
family—even a difficult one.' He kissed her tired mouth.
'And no matter what happens I am never going to forget it.'

* * * * *

A GAME OF VOWS

MAISEY YATES

Maisey Yates is a *USA Today* bestselling author of more than thirty romance novels. She has a coffee habit she has no interest in kicking, and a slight *Pinterest* addiction. She lives with her husband and children in the Pacific Northwest. When Maisey isn't writing she can be found singing in the grocery store, shopping for shoes online, and probably not doing dishes. Check out her website, www.maiseyyates.com.

CHAPTER ONE

HANNAH WESTON swore as she tripped over the hem of her wedding dress, her focus diverted by the scrolling numbers on the screen of her smart phone. She'd said she wouldn't work today. She'd lied.

The exchange was closed today, but she had a lead and she needed to chase it up before she made her vows. She had clients depending on her. And he would never know.

She dropped into the limo, her eyes still trained on her phone as she gathered her dress up into a satin ball and pulled it inside, slamming the door behind her.

"Going to the chapel?"

Hannah froze, her blood turning to ice as the limo pulled away from the curb and headed into the San Francisco traffic. That voice. She knew that voice.

She couldn't look up, her eyes still set on her phone. She curled her fingers more tightly around the heavy fabric of her wedding gown, as she took a breath and raised her gaze, locking with the dark, intense eyes in the rearview mirror.

She knew those eyes, too. No one had eyes like him. They seemed to cut through you, possessing the ability to read your innermost secrets. Able to mock and flirt in a single glance. She still saw those eyes in her dreams. And sometimes her nightmares.

Eduardo Vega. One of the many skeletons in her closet. Except, he wasn't staying put.

"And I'm going to get married," she said tightly. She didn't get intimidated. She did the intimidating. Back in NY she'd had more guts than any man on the trading room floor. She'd had Wall Street by the balls. And now, she was a force to be reckoned with in the world of finance. She didn't do fear.

"Oh, I don't think so, Hannah. Not today. Unless you're interested in getting arrested for bigamy."

She sucked in a sharp breath. "I am not a bigamist."

"You aren't single."

"Yes, I am. The paperwork was…"

"Never filed. If you don't believe me, do some research on the matter."

Her stomach squeezed tight, the world tilting to the side. "What did you do, Eduardo?" His name tasted so strange on her tongue. But then, it had never been familiar. He was a stranger, essentially, her ex-husband. She had never known him, not really.

They had lived together, sort of. She'd inhabited the spare room in his luxury penthouse for six months. They hadn't shared meals, except on weekends when they'd gone to his parents' home. They hadn't shared a bed. Hadn't shared more than the odd hello when they were in his massive home. It was only in public that he'd ever really talked to her. That he'd ever touched her.

He had been quick, blessed with money, a strategic mind and a total lack of caring in regards to propriety. She'd never met a man like him. Before or since. Of course, she hadn't been blackmailed into marriage before or since, either.

"Me?" His eyes met hers in the mirror again, a smile curving his lips, a flash of white teeth against dark skin. "Nothing."

She laughed. "That's funny. I don't believe you. I signed the papers. I remember it very clearly."

"And you might have known they were never finalized if you had left a forwarding address for your mail. But that's not the way you do things, is it? Tell me, are you still running, Hannah?"

"What did you do?" she asked, refusing to let his last barb stick in its target. She didn't have to answer to Eduardo. She didn't have to answer to anyone. And she most definitely didn't have to run.

She met his eyes in the mirror and felt a sharp pang of emotion that mocked her previous thought. Why was this happening now? She was getting married in an hour. To Zack Parsons, the best man she'd ever known. He was respectful, and honorable. Distant. Able to help give her a career boost. He was everything she wanted, everything she needed.

"It's a complicated process," he said, his accent as charming as ever, even as his words made her blood boil. "Something perhaps...went amiss?"

"You bastard! You utter bastard!" She shut the web browser on her phone and pulled up the number pad, poised to dial.

"What are you doing, Hannah?"

"Calling...the police. The national guard."

"Your fiancé?"

Her stomach tightened down on itself. "No. Zack doesn't need to know...."

"You mean you didn't tell your lover about your husband? Not a great foundation for a marriage."

She couldn't call Zack. She couldn't let Eduardo anywhere near the wedding. It would topple everything she'd spent the past nine years building. She hated that he had the power to do that. Hated facing the truth that he'd had power over her from the moment she'd met him.

She gritted her teeth. "Neither is blackmail."

"We traded, *mi tesoro*. And you know it. Blackmail makes it sound sordid."

"It was. It continues to be."

"And your past is so clean you can't stand getting your hands dirty? We both know that's not true."

A very rude word hovered on the edge of her lips. But freaking out at Eduardo wasn't going to solve her problem. The very pressing problem that she needed to get to the hotel and take vows. "I'm going to ask you again, before I open the door and roll out into midday traffic and completely destroy this gown: What do you want? How do I give it to you? Will it make you go away?"

He shook his head. "I'm afraid not. I'm taking you back to my hotel. And I'm not going away."

Her lip curled. "Have you got a thing for women in wedding dresses? Because you got me into one quickly last time we met, and now you seem interested in me again...and here I am in a wedding dress."

"It's not the dress."

"Give me one good reason not to call the police and tell them I've been kidnapped."

"Hannah Mae Hackett."

Her real name sounded so unfamiliar now. Even more so coming from him instead of being spoken with a Southern twang. Even still, a lead weight settled in her stomach when he said it.

"Don't even say it," she bit out.

"You don't like your name? Well, I imagine not. You *did* change it."

"Legally. I am *legally* not that name anymore. My name is Hannah Weston now."

"And you *illegally* gained scholarships, and entrance, to the university in Barcelona by falsifying your school records."

She clenched her teeth, her pulse pounding hard. She was so very screwed. And he knew it. "This sounds like a conversation we had five years ago. If you recall, I already married you to keep you from spreading it around."

"Unfinished business."

"The only thing unfinished, apparently, is our divorce."

"Oh, no, there is so much more than that." He pulled the

limo against a curb in front of one of the famous boutique hotels in San Francisco. Marble, gold trimming and sharply dressed valets signaled the luxury of the place to everyone in the area. It was the sort of thing that had drawn her from the time she was young. The sort of thing she'd really started hungering for when she realized she had the power to change her circumstances.

Every time she checked into a hotel, as soon as the door was closed and she was isolated from the world, she would twirl in a circle and fall onto the bed, reveling in the softness. The cleanliness. The space and solitude. Even now that she had her own penthouse with thousand thread count sheets, she still did it.

The hotel wasn't evoking those kinds of feelings in her today. Not with Eduardo present.

The valet took the keys and Eduardo came to Hannah's door, opening it. "Wait…did you steal this?" she asked, looking at the limo.

As Eduardo bent down, Hannah fought the urge to shrink back. "I bought it from the chauffeur. Told him to go buy one that was newer. Nicer."

"And he didn't seem to care that he was supposed to pick me up?"

"Not when I gave him enough money for two new limousines. No."

"He was going to leave a bride stranded on her wedding day?"

Eduardo shrugged. "The world is filled with dishonest and self-serving people. You, my dear, should know all about that."

She snorted and rucked her dress up over her knees, climbing out of the car without touching Eduardo. She straightened and let her dress fall neatly into place. Then she tugged on her veil, fanning it over her shoulders. "Don't say it like you aren't one of the self-serving, my darling husband."

She looked at him fully. He was still everything he'd been five years ago. Tall, broad, arresting, a vision of perfect male beauty in his well-cut suit. His bronzed skin was highlighted perfectly by his white dress shirt; his dark hair reached the collar of his jacket.

He'd always made her feel like someone had put both hands on her shoulders and shaken her. He'd always had the power to disrupt the order of her life, to make her feel like she was dangerously close to losing the control she'd worked so hard to cultivate over the years.

It was the thing she'd always hated most about him. That he was so darned magnetic. That he always had the power to make her tremble when nothing else could.

It wasn't just that he was good-looking. There were a lot of good-looking men in the world, and she was too much in control of herself to let that affect her. It was the fact that he exuded a kind of power that she could never hope to achieve. And that he had power over her.

She breezed past him, ignoring the scent of his cologne and skin, ignoring the way it made her stomach tighten. She strode into the hotel lobby, well aware that she was making a spectacle and not caring at all. She breathed in deep. She needed focus. She needed to find out what he wanted so she could leave, as quickly as possible.

"Mrs. Vega, Mr. Vega." A woman that Hannah assumed was a manager, rounded the check-in desk with a wide, money-motivated grin on her face. "So lovely to have you here. Mr. Vega told me he would be bringing his bride when he came to stay this time. So romantic."

She had to bite back a tart curse.

Eduardo closed the distance between them and curled his arm around her waist. Her breath rushed from her body. For a moment, just one crazy moment, she wanted to lean against him. To draw closer to his masculine strength. But only for a moment.

"Very," he said.

"Is there liquor in the room?" she asked, wiggling away from him.

The manager, whose name tag identified her as Maria, frowned slightly. "There is champagne waiting for you."

"We'll need three," she said.

Maria's frown deepened. "I…"

"She's kidding," Eduardo said.

Hannah shook her head. "I've been hammered since I took my vows. I intend to spend the rest of the day that way."

"We'll just go upstairs."

"Send champagne," Hannah said as Eduardo attempted to drag her from the desk in what she imagined he thought was a loving, husbandly manner.

He ushered her into a gilded elevator, a smile pasted on his darkly handsome face until the door closed behind them.

"That was not cute, Hannah," he said.

She put her hand on her hip and gave him her sassiest smile. She didn't feel sassy, or in control, but she could fake it with the best of them. "Are you kidding me? I think I'm ready for my close-up. That was fine acting."

He shot her a bland look. "Your entire life has been acting. Don't expect accolades now."

Her smile faltered for a moment. "Look, I am on edge here."

"You aren't crying. No gnashing of teeth over leaving your fiancé at the altar."

She bit the inside of her cheek. "You don't know anything about my relationship with Zack, so don't pretend you do. I care about him. I don't want to leave him at the altar. I want you to come to your senses and give me the keys to your ill-gotten limo so I can drive myself to the hotel and marry him." The image of Zack, in that black, custom tux, standing in front of all of their friends and coworkers…it made her feel sick. She'd never, ever intended to put him through that kind of humiliation. The idea of it being reversed made her skin crawl.

"Whether I drive you there or not, your marriage won't be legal. I explained that already."

"They gave me a marriage license," she said, her voice sounding distant, echoey. Her hands were starting to shake. Why was she reacting this way? Why was she being so weak? Was she in shock?

"And we were married, and attempted to divorce out of your home country. Things get missed."

"How could something this important just get missed?" she said, exploding. "I don't believe for one second you... *forgot* to file the papers."

His smile turned dark. "Stranger things have happened, *tesoro.*"

For the first time she noticed that he wasn't exactly the same. She'd thought his eyes the same, but she saw now they weren't. He used to sparkle. His brown eyes glittering with mischief. He'd been so amused at finding out her secret, that she wasn't who she'd claimed to be. He'd been even more amused at the thought of marrying an American girl to gall his father, when he'd mandated his son take a wife to gain leadership of their company. To prove he was a family man. It had been the best joke to him, to marry a college student with no money, no connections and no cooking skills.

The sparkle was gone now. Replaced with a kind of black glitter that seemed to suck the light from the room, that seemed to absorb any kind of brightness and kill it. It did something strange to her. Pulled at her like the sparkle never had.

"Like getting kidnapped on your wedding day?"

"Coerced away, perhaps. But don't tell me you haven't got pepper spray somewhere in your purse. You could have stopped me. You could have called the police. You could have called your Zack. You didn't. And you still aren't doing it.

You could turn and walk out of this room right now and get a cab. I wouldn't stop you. And you know that."

"But you *know*. You know everything. And I…"

"And it would ruin your reputation with your clients. No one wants to hear their financial adviser is a high school drop-out who committed fraud to get her college degree."

"You're right, that kind of information does make client meetings awkward," she said, her voice flat, a sick feeling settling in her stomach.

"I imagine so. Just remember how awkward it made our meeting back when you were my intern."

"I think the real awkwardness came when you blackmailed me into marrying you."

"You keep using that word. Was it really blackmail?"

"According to Webster's Dictionary? Yes."

He shrugged. "Either way, had you not had something for me to hold over your head…it wouldn't have worked."

"You're so smug about it," she said, seething now. The clock on the nightstand read five minutes to her wedding and she was standing in an opulent hotel suite, in her wedding gown, with another man. "But you've had everything handed to you in your life, Eduardo. You work because your daddy gave you an office. I had to make my own destiny, and maybe…maybe the way I went about it was a little bit shady."

"The United States government calls it fraud. But *shady* is fine."

"You have no idea what it's like," she said.

"No, you're right. I can hardly speak around the silver spoon in my mouth. What would I know about hardship?" His lip curled, his expression hard, cynical. A new look for Eduardo.

"Your only hardship was that your father demanded you give up your life as a partying man whore and find a wife. So what did you do? You twisted my arm, because you thought a *gringa* wife, especially one who wasn't Catholic and couldn't cook, would be a funny way to follow your father's orders without actually following them. And I went along with it, because it was better than losing my job. Better than getting kicked out of university. Everything was a game to you, but to me, it was life."

"You're acting like I hurt you in some way, Hannah, but we both know that isn't true. I gave you your own room. Your own wing of the penthouse. I never intruded on you, never once took advantage of you. I kept to our agreement and released you from our bargain after six months, and you left. With all the money I promised you," he said. "You keep forgetting the money I gave you."

She clenched her teeth. "Because I didn't spend it." She hadn't been able to. Leaving him, or more to the point, his family and the city that had started to feel like home, had felt too awful. And she'd felt, for the first time, every inch the dishonorable person she was. "If you want your ten thousand dollars, it's in a bank account. And frankly, it's pennies as far as I'm concerned at this point."

"Oh, yes, you are very successful now, aren't you?"

She didn't feel it at the moment. "Yes. I am."

Eduardo advanced toward her. "You are good with finances, investments."

"Financial planning, strategies, picking stocks. You name it, I'm good at it."

"That's what I want from you."

"What? Financial advice?"

"Not exactly." He looked out the window, his expression inscrutable. "My father died two years ago."

An image of the hard, formidable, amazing man that Eduardo had been blessed enough to call his father swam before her eyes. Miguel Vega had been demanding. A taskmaster. A leader. He had cared. About his business, about his children. About his oldest son, who wasn't taking life seriously enough. Cared enough to back him into a corner and force him to marry. It was a heavy-handed version of caring, but it was more than Hannah had ever gotten from her own father.

Eventually, that man, his wife, Eduardo's sister, had come to mean something to her. She'd loved them.

"I'm so sorry," she said, her voice muted now, a strange kind of grief filling her heart. Not that Miguel would have missed or cared about her. And she didn't deserve it. She'd lied to him. And as far as he was concerned, she'd left his son.

"As am I," Eduardo said. "But he left me in charge of Vega Communications."

"And things aren't going well?"

"Not exactly." A muscle in his jaw ticked. "No, not exactly."

"Do you need me to look at your books? Because I can do that after I marry Zack."

He shook his head, his dark eyes blazing. "That can't happen, *tesoro*."

"But it can," she said, desperation filling her again. It was past bridal-march time. She could just picture the hotel, all decked out in pink ribbon and tulle. Her beautiful pink wedding cake. It was her dream wedding, the dream she'd had since she was a little girl. Not some traditional wedding in a cathedral, conducted entirely in Latin. A wedding that was a show for the groom's family. A wedding that had nothing to do with her.

It was a wedding with a groom who didn't love her, but at least liked her. A groom who didn't find the idea of taking vows with her to be a joke. He at least wanted her around. Being wanted on a personal level was new for her. She liked the way it felt.

"Sorry, Hannah. I need you to come back to Spain with me." He looked out the window. "It's time I brought my wife back home."

"No is the same in both of our languages, so there should

be nothing lost in translation when I say no." Hannah took a step back; her calf connected with the soft edge of the mattress, her dress rustling with the motion.

"Sorry, but this isn't a negotiation. Either you come with me now, or I march you down the aisle at the hotel myself, and you can explain, in front of your guests, and your groom, exactly why you can't marry him today. How you were about to involve him in an illegal marriage."

"Not on purpose! I would never have done this to him if I would have known."

"Once the extent of your past history is revealed, he may not believe you. Or, even if he did, he may not want you." His lips curved up into a smile, his eyes absent of any humor. And that was when she had the very stark, frightening impression that she was looking at a stranger.

He was nothing like the Eduardo she'd once known. She didn't know how she'd missed it. How it hadn't been obvious from the moment she'd seen his eyes in the rearview mirror. Yes, he had the same perfectly curved lips, the same sharply angled jaw. The same bullheaded stubbornness. But he no longer had that carefree air he'd always conducted himself with. There were lines by his eyes, bracketing his mouth. A mouth that looked like it had forgotten how to smile.

Maybe the death of his father had taken a serious toll on him. But she didn't care. She couldn't afford to care. She had to look out for herself, just as she'd been doing all of her life. No one else would. No one else ever had.

"Bastard," she spat.

"You're getting repetitive," he said dryly.

"So what? You expect me to come back to Spain and just... be your wife?"

"Not exactly. I expect you to come back and continue to act as my wife in name only while you help me fix the issues I'm having with Vega Communications."

"Why?"

"Because I don't need anyone to know there are issues. Not my competitors, I don't need them smelling blood in the water. Not my mother, she has no need to worry. My sister… I don't want to worry her, either. No one can know." There was an edge to his voice, evidence of fraying control. She could work with that. She could definitely work with that.

The pieces started falling into place in her mind. "So you think it can look like a reconciliation five years in the making. Your wife is suddenly back in Barcelona and hanging on your arm. Rather than letting anyone in on the fact that you needed to bring in outside consultation to help straighten up your finances?"

"That's the sum of it," he ground out.

It made sense now. All fine and good for him to sweep in like a marauder and demand her cooperation. But all that sweeping was hiding very real problems.

And those problems meant she had a lot more power than she'd thought she'd possessed thirty seconds earlier.

Her lips curved into a smile, the heated adrenaline she always felt when presented with a battle spreading through her chest, her limbs. "You need me. Say it."

"Hannah…"

"No. If I'm going to even consider doing this, you admit it. To me, and to yourself. You never would back then, but now…now I'm not a scared college student trying to hold on to my position at school." She met his eyes without flinching. "Admit that you need me."

"You were never a scared college student," he bit out. "You were an angry one. Angry you'd been caught out and desperate to do anything to keep it secret."

"Well, now you're sounding a little desperate." She crossed her arms beneath her breasts and cocked her hip to the side. "So, at least say please."

His lip curled into a sneer, a muscle in his jaw ticking. He was weighing his options. "Please."

She tilted her chin up and smiled, the sort of smile she knew would make his blood boil. "Good boy."

The feral light in his eyes let her know that she'd just about gone too far. She didn't care. He couldn't screw up her day any more than he already had.

He didn't move for a beat. She could see him, calculating, making decisions. For a moment she thought he might reach out and grab her. Take her in his arms and…strike her? Certainly not. No matter what Eduardo was, he wasn't a monster. Kiss her?

That he might do. The thought made her stomach tighten, made her heart beat faster.

She saw him visibly relax. "A lot of confidence and attitude coming from a woman who could face criminal charges if the right words were spoken into the wrong ears."

She put her hands on her hips. "But you showed your hand, darling," she said, turning his use of endearments back at him. "I may be over a barrel, but you're tied to me. If I go over the cliff, you're coming, too. I might be stuck, but you're just as stuck. So, let's be civil, you and I, huh?"

"Let's not forget who stands to lose the most," he said, his voice hard.

She examined his face, the hard lines etched into it. Brackets around his mouth, creases in his forehead. Lines that had appeared sometime in the past five years, for they hadn't been there back when she'd first met him. "I have a feeling you might have a bit more to lose than you're letting on."

"What about you? At the least you stand to lose clients, your reputation. At the most?"

He didn't have to finish the sentence. It was possible she could lose…so much. Everything. That she could face criminal charges. That she could find herself with her degree revoked. That she could find herself back in Arkansas in a single-wide mobile home that had a lawn with more pink plastic flamingos than it had grass.

She couldn't go back to that. To that endless, blank hell that had no end. No beginning. No defining moments. Just an eternity of uncomfortable monotony that most people she'd lived around had tried to dull with the haze of alcohol or the high of drugs.

No. She wasn't taking any chances on returning to that life. Not ever.

"Your point is taken," she said. "Anyway…I can't go and marry Zack now, no matter what, can I?"

"Not unless you want to extend your list of criminal activity."

"I didn't hurt anyone, Eduardo," she said stiffly.

Eduardo surveyed the slim, cool blonde standing in front of him, arms crossed over the ornate bodice of her wedding dress. His wife. Hannah. One of the images in his mind that had remained bright and clear, no matter how thick the fog was surrounding other details, other memories.

His vision of her as a skinny college student with a sharp mind and more guts than any person he'd ever met, had stayed with him. And when he'd realized just how much of a struggle things were becoming with Vega Communications, it had been her image he'd seen in his mind. And he'd known that he had to get his wife back.

His wife. The wife who had never truly been his wife beyond her signature on the marriage certificate. But she was a link. To his past. To the man he'd been. To those images that were splintered now, like gazing into a shattered mirror. He had wondered if seeing her could magically put him back there. If she could make the mirror whole. Reverse things, somehow.

Foolish, perhaps. But he couldn't get her out of his mind, and there had to be a reason. Had to be a reason she was so clear, when other things simply weren't.

Thankfully, he'd managed to get his timing just right. And

in his new world, one of migraines and half-remembered conversations, good timing was a rarity he savored.

"Does that make falsifying school records all right, then?" he said, watching her gray-blue eyes turn a bit more gray. A bit more stormy, as she narrowed them in his direction.

He personally didn't care what she'd done to get into university. Back then, he'd selected her to be his intern based on her impeccable performance in college, and not on anything else. Clearly she'd been up to the task, and in his mind, that was all that mattered.

But he'd use every bit of leverage he had now, and he wouldn't let his conscience prick him over it. Hannah knew all about doing what had to be done. And that's what he was doing now.

"I don't suppose it does," she said tightly. "But I don't dwell on that. I gave myself a do-over in life, and I've never once regretted it. I've never once looked back. I messed up when I was too young to understand what that might mean to my future, and when I did realize it…when it was too late…"

"You acted. Disregarding the traditional ideas of right and wrong, disregarding who it might hurt. And that's what I'm doing now. So I hope you'll forgive me," he said, aware that no sincerity was evident in his voice. He felt none.

She was testing him, needling him, trying to make him angry. It had worked, but it wouldn't divert his focus. She was his focus.

"So you think that makes it okay?" Her full lips turned down.

"I'm not overly concerned with questions of morality at the moment. I need to drag Vega back up to where it belongs."

"How is it you've managed to let it get so bad?" she said, again, not hesitating to throw her own barbs out.

There was no way in hell he was talking about his shortcomings. Not now. Maybe not ever. It wasn't her concern.

"We all have strengths," he said tightly. "It's the budget I'm having an issue with. Investments. Taxes. I am not an expert."

"Hire someone."

"I did. He didn't do his job."

"Basically, you didn't notice that he was screwing up?"

The thought of it, of trying to keep track of that, plus the day-to-day running of Vega, made his head swim, made his temples pound. His breath shortened, became harder to take in. Panic was a metallic taste on his tongue.

Would he ever feel normal? Or was this normal now? Such a disturbing thought. One he didn't have time to dwell on.

"I didn't have time," he gritted.

"Too busy sleeping around?" she asked.

"Different heiress every night," he said, almost laughing out loud at his own lie.

"Better than toying with the domestic staff, I suppose. Or blackmailing interns into marriage."

"Ours was a special case," he said.

"Oh, yes, indeed. I suppose that's why I feel suffused with a warm glow of specialness."

He chuckled, gratified when Hannah looked stymied by the reaction. She wanted to make him angry. He wouldn't allow it. One of the gifts of his head injury, one of the few. It had cooled his passions, and while that had been inconvenient in some ways, in others, it had proven valuable. He was no longer hotheaded. Usually. No longer impulsive. According to some, he was no longer fun. But he didn't know how to fix that. He found he didn't care anymore. Another gift.

"Well, it is your big day. Shouldn't a bride feel special?"

She uttered a truly foul word and sat on the edge of the bed, the white skirt of her dress billowing out around her. Like an angry, fallen, snow angel. "Low."

"Do you love this man? The one you were meant to marry today?" He found that did trouble his conscience, even if it was only a bit of trouble.

She shook her head slowly. "No."

He shook his head. "Using someone else?"

"Hardly using him. Zack doesn't love me, either. Neither of us have time for some all-consuming passionate affair. But we *like* each other. I like him. I don't like the idea of him being stood up. I don't like the idea of humiliating him."

"More humiliating, I think, if he finds out his almost-wife has been lying to him. About so many things."

She looked down at her fingernails. "Zack has his secrets. He doesn't think anyone realizes it…but he has them. I can tell. And I know better than to ask about them."

"And that means…"

"He would have accepted that I had mine. We didn't share everything."

"I doubt he intended to share you with another husband."

"Well, it's not going to happen now." A brief expression of vulnerability, sadness, crossed Hannah's features. And as quickly as he'd glimpsed it, it disappeared. Clearly, she had some amount of feeling for her lover, no matter what she said.

"Plans change." As he knew all too well.

"I have to call…someone," she said, her heart twisting.

"It's too late to salvage the day."

"I'm aware," she snapped. "Just…give me a minute."

She pulled her phone from her purse.

"Who are you calling?"

"My assistant. She's in the office minding things since I'm away. Shelby?" Her tone turned authoritative.

She paused for a moment, her cheeks turning a dull pink. "I know. I can't…I can't go through with it. It's complicated. And I can't get to the hotel." She gave him a pointed look. "Can you drive over and…and tell Zack?"

"Tell him what?" Eduardo heard her assistant's shriek from where he was standing.

"That I'm sorry. That I wish I had been brave enough to do

it differently but I can't. I know it's rush hour and it's going to take forever, but please?" Hannah paused again.

"Thank you. I...I have to go." She hit the end call button and rounded on him. "I hope you're pleased with yourself."

He wasn't, not then. But this wasn't about how he felt. This was about what had to be done. This was about trying to fix Vega. Trying to fix himself.

"Not really. But I promise you in the end you will be."

"I doubt that."

"Once everything is resolved I will give you permission to speak of your part in the resurrection of my family's company."

He hadn't intended on giving her that much. The offer shocked him. He wasn't usually spontaneous anymore.

"Really?" she asked, her expression guarded, but the interest in her eyes too keen for her to conceal entirely.

"Really. I promise, in the end, I'll divorce you and you can crow your achievements. What I don't want is anyone undercutting the business while it's vulnerable. But afterward, say whatever you like, drag me through the mud, talk about my inadequacies. It's only pride," he said. Pride he'd had to give up a long time ago. He clung to what he could, but it was limited.

"You'll really divorce me this time? Forgive me for not trusting you."

"If you don't move around like a gypsy, then you should get papers letting you know when everything is final." The first aborted divorce hadn't been intentional. Another side effect of the accident that had changed everything. But, this side effect happened to be a very fortunate one indeed.

"Fine. We have a deal." Hannah extended her slender hand and he grasped it in his. She was so petite, so fine-boned. It gave the illusion of delicacy when he knew full well she possessed none. She was steel beneath that pale skin.

A smile curved his lips, satisfaction burning in his chest. "Good girl."

CHAPTER TWO

"You made me buy my own ticket." Hannah stood in the doorway of Eduardo's penthouse, exhausted and wrinkled from travel, still angry at the way everything had transpired. She'd had short notice, and limited options. She'd had to fly economy.

An infuriating smile curved Eduardo's lips. "I did. But I knew you could afford it."

"Doesn't chivalry dictate you buy your blackmailed wife's plane ticket?" Hannah dropped her suitcase next to her feet and crossed her arms. The most shocking thing about Eduardo's appearance had been his departure, with a demand that she meet him in Barcelona in twenty-four hours. And she could get there herself.

It had been a blow to her pride, and he knew it. Because she'd been forced to get herself to Spain. She'd been the one to board the plane. If he'd tied her up and thrown her into cargo she could have pretended he'd truly forced her. That she was a slave to him, rather than to the mistakes of her past and her intense need to keep them secret.

But there was nothing more important than her image. Than the success she'd earned. Than never, ever going back to that dark place she'd come from.

Because of that, she was a slave to Eduardo, and a coward where Zack was concerned. More than a day since their almost-wedding and she hadn't called him. Of course, he hadn't called her, which spoke volumes about the quality and nature of their relationship.

"I checked and there was no specific entry in the handbook about the most chivalrous way to force one's estranged bride to come and do their bidding."

"What's the point of even having a handbook, then?" She let out a long breath and looked pointedly at the doorway Eduardo was blocking with his broad frame. "Aren't you going to invite me into our home?"

"Of course," he said.

They'd shared the penthouse for six months five years ago. They'd been the most bizarre six months of her life. Sharing a home with a man who hardly acknowledged her presence, unless he needed her for a gala or to make a show of togetherness at a family dinner.

It was a six months she'd done a very good job of scrubbing from her mind. Like every other inconvenient detail in her past, it had been chucked into her mental closet, the door locked tight. It was where every juicy secret belonged. Behind closed, difficult-to-access doors.

But now it was all coming back. Her fourth year in Spain, when she'd been accepted into a coveted internship at Vega Communications. Everything had been going so well. She'd started making connections, learning how things worked at a massive corporation.

Then one day, the boss's son had called her into his office and closed the door.

Then he'd told her he'd done a little digging and found out her real name. That she wasn't Hannah Weston from Manhattan, but that she was Hannah Hackett from Arkansas. That she hadn't graduated top of her class, but that she had no diploma at all.

And then, with supreme, enraging arrogance he had leaned back in his chair; hands behind his head; humor, mocking, glittering in his eyes, and he'd told her that her secret would be safe.

If she would marry him.

That sickening, surreal moment when she'd agreed, because there was nothing in the world that could compel her to lose the ground she'd gained.

Eduardo stepped aside and she breezed past him, leaving her suitcase for him to handle. Things were rearranged. His furniture new, but still black and sleek. The appliances in his kitchen were new, too, as was the dining set.

But the view was the same. Cathedral spires rising above gray brick buildings, touching the clear sky. She'd always loved the city.

She'd hated Eduardo for forcing her into marriage. Had hated herself nearly as much for being vulnerable to him, for needing to keep her secrets so badly.

And then she'd moved into his home, and she'd started to think the forced marriage wasn't so bad after all. It was so expansive, plush, and refined. Like nothing she'd ever experienced.

Secretly, shamefully, she'd loved it. As long as she could ignore the big Spaniard that lived there, too, everything was wonderful. Comfortable.

She'd made it into school, but she was still living on a meager budget. And Eduardo had shown her luxury she'd never seen before. She'd thought she'd known. She hadn't. Her imagination hadn't even scratched the surface of what true wealth meant. Not until she'd met the Vega family.

It had given her something to aspire to.

"Everything looks…great." Surreal. She'd never gone back to a place before. When she left, she left. Her childhood home, Spain, her place in New York.

"Updated a bit. But your room is still available."

"Haven't had any other temporary wives in my absence?"

"No, unlike some people I think having more than one spouse at a time is a bit too ambitious."

"Yes, well, you know it wasn't my intention to have more than one," she bit out, a sour feeling settling in her stomach. "Zack was decent, you know." She eyed the open door, and her suitcase, still occupying their position in the hall. "He was one of the few truly good people I've ever met. I hate that I did this to him."

"Have you been in contact?"

"No."

"Perhaps you should...?"

She clenched her teeth. "I don't know if that's such a good idea. Anyway, he hasn't called me, and he didn't come by my house, so, maybe he doesn't care." That actually hurt a little.

"If he thinks you're missing, he may send out a search party. I didn't think you wanted to publicize our marriage. Or rather, why you ran out on your wedding. It doesn't matter either way to me."

She swore and took her phone from her purse. "Fine. But Shelby did go and speak to him." She bit her lip and looked down at the screen. Still no calls from him, and she'd been sort of hoping there would have at least been one. There was a text from Shelby.

"And have you heard from him?"

"No." Strange. But she couldn't really imagine Zack playing the part of desperate, jilted groom. Decent he was, but the man had pride. She opened the text from Shelby and her heart plummeted. "Zack wasn't at the hotel when she arrived."

"So he still hasn't heard from you at all."

She clutched the phone tightly against her chest. Eduardo was watching her far too closely. She needed a moment. Just a moment.

"Why don't you bring my bags in?" she asked.

Dark eyes narrowed, but he walked over to the entry and pulled her bags just inside the door, shutting it behind him.

She bit her lip and looked back down at her phone.

"Scared?" he asked.

"No," she muttered. She opened up the message screen and typed in Zack's name, her fingers hovering over the letters on the touch screen as she watched the cursor blink. She really didn't know what to say to him. "Nothing about this in the chivalry handbook?" she asked.

Eduardo crossed his arms over his broad chest and leaned against the back of the couch. "I think we both have to accept that we're on the wrong side of honor at this point in time."

"Good thing I never gave honor much thought," she said.

Except she was now. Or at least giving thought to what a mess she'd made out of Zack's life. She growled low in her chest and shot Eduardo one last evil glare.

I'm so sorry about the wedding, Zack.

She let her thumb hover over the send button and then hit it on a groan.

"What did you tell him?"

"Nothing really yet." She pulled up another text window.

I met someone else. I— She paused for a moment and looked at Eduardo. If she'd been speaking, she would have gagged on the next word. —love him.

She closed her eyes and hit Send. Let him think that emotion had been in charge. She and Zack were both so cynical about love…he might even find it funny. That had been the foundation of their relationship really. Zack had wanted a wife, the stability marriage would bring. But he wanted a wife who wouldn't bother him about his long working hours, and who didn't want children. Or love.

They'd been so well suited.

"There. I hope you're happy. I just ruined things with my best bet for a happy ending."

"You said you didn't love him," Eduardo said.

"I know. But I like him. I respect him. How often do you get that in a marriage?"

"I don't know. I've only ever had separate bedrooms and blackmail in my marriage. What excuse did you give him?"

"I told him how much I loved you, dearest," she bit out.

He chuckled. "You always were an accomplished little liar."

"Well, I don't feel good about this one."

"You felt good about the others?"

She truly didn't know the answer. "I…I never thought about how I felt about it. Just about whether or not it was necessary. Anyway, I don't lie as a matter of course."

"You just lie about really big things infrequently?"

"Every job application has started with questions about college. Didn't I get near-perfect grades at university? Didn't I have a prestigious internship at Vega Communications? No lies. No one wants to know about high school, not once you've been through university."

"And your fiancé?"

"Never asked many questions. He liked what he knew about me." And neither of them knew all that much. Something she was realizing now that she was being haunted by her past. She and Zack had never even slept together. Not for lack of attraction. She'd been quite attracted to him, impossible not to be, but until things were legal and permanent between them she'd felt the need to hang on to that bit of control.

It was so much easier to deny her sex drive than to end up back where she'd been nine years ago. Being that girl, that was unacceptable. She never would be again.

"Lies by omission are still lies, *querida*."

"Then we're all liars."

"Now, that's true enough."

"Show me to my room," she said, affecting her commanding, imperious tone. The one she had gotten so good at over the years. "I'm tired."

A slow smile curved his lips and she fought the urge to punch him.

"Of course, darling."

This time, he picked up her bags without incident and she followed him into her room. Her room. Her throat tightened. Her first experience with homecoming. Why should it mean anything? He had replaced the bedding. A new dark-colored comforter, new sable throw pillows, new satin curtains on the windows to match. The solid desk she'd loved to work at was still in its corner. Unmoved. There was no dust on it, but then, Eduardo had always had a great housekeeper.

"This is...perfect," she said.

"I'm glad you still like it. I remember you being...giddy over it back when we were first married."

"It was the nicest room I'd ever been in," she said, opting to give him some honesty, a rare thing from her. "The sheets were...heaven."

"The sheets?"

She cleared her throat. "I have a thing for high-quality sheets. And you definitely have them here."

"Well, now you get to live here again. And reap the benefits of the sheets."

She arched a brow. "My fiancé was a billionaire, you know."

"Yes, I know. I would expect you to find nothing less," he said.

"I'm not sure how I feel about your assessment of my character, Eduardo. You express no shock over Zack's financial status, or over the fact that we weren't in love."

"You're mercenary. I know it...you know it. It's not shocking."

She *was* mercenary. If being mercenary meant she did what she had to to ensure her own success. Her own survival. She'd needed to be. To move up from the life she'd been born into. To overcome the devastating consequences of her youthful actions. And she'd never lost a wink of sleep over it. But for some reason, the fact that it was so obvious to Eduardo was a little bit unsettling.

"Is it mercenary to try and improve the quality of your life?" she asked.

"It depends on the route you take."

"And the resources available to you are a major factor in deciding which route to take," she said.

"I'm not judging you, Hannah, believe it or not."

She planted her hands on her hips. "No, you're just using me."

"As you said, you do what you must to improve the quality of your life." His expression was strange, tense. Dark.

She looked away. "I have to do something."

"What is that?"

She looked down at her left hand, at the massive, sparkly engagement ring Zack had given her a few months earlier. She tugged it off her finger, a strange sensation moving through her like a strong wind. Sadness. Regret. Relief.

"I have to send this to Zack." She held it up and realized her hands were shaking. She couldn't keep it. Not for another second. Because mercenary she might be. But she wasn't a thief. She wouldn't take from Zack. Wouldn't do any more damage than she'd already done.

"I can have someone do that for you. Do you know where he is?"

"Thailand," she said, without missing a beat. "We were supposed to honeymoon there."

"And you think he went?" he asked, dark eyebrows raised.

She smiled. "Zack had business in Thailand, so yes, I think he went. No, I know he went. He's not the kind of man to let a little thing like an interrupted marriage keep him from accomplishing his goals."

Eduardo studied her, dark eyes intense. "Perhaps he was perfect for you."

"Yeah, well, I'm trying not to dwell on that." She held the ring out and Eduardo opened his hand. She dropped it into his palm. "I have the address of the place we were meant to stay at."

"*Bien.* I'll call a courier and have it rushed." He closed his hand around the ring, the glittering gem disappearing. All she could think of was that he held her future in his hand. The future that might have been. The one that was not eclipsed by Eduardo.

She looked up, their eyes clashing. Her throat tightened, halting her breath.

"Good," she said, barely able to force out the words. She turned to the desk and saw a pad and pen slotted into the wooden slats built into it for organization. It was where she'd kept them when she'd lived here. She bent and scribbled the address for the house she should be in now, with Zack.

Her fingers felt stiff and cold around the pen. She straightened and handed him the note. "There. That should do it."

"I'm surprised you don't want to keep the ring."

"Why? I didn't keep the one you gave me, either."

"We had a prior agreement. I get the feeling you didn't have an agreement like that with him."

"Separate beds, separate lives, unless a public appearance is needed? No. We were meant to be married for real." She swallowed hard. "And all things considered, I don't feel right keeping his ring. I was the one who wronged him."

"Careful, Hannah, I might start thinking you grew a conscience in our time apart."

"I've always had one," she said. "It's been inconvenient sometimes."

"Not too inconvenient."

"Oh, what would you know about a conscience, Eduardo?"

"Very little. Only that it occasionally takes the form of a cricket."

A reluctant laugh escaped her lips. "That sounds about

right. So…if you could mail my ring to him, that would be great."

"I'll call now." He turned and walked out of the room, leaving her alone.

She sat on the edge of the bed, her emotions a blank. She wasn't sure what she was supposed to feel. Why she suddenly felt more relieved than upset about leaving Zack behind. Marriage to him would have been good.

And yet, when she thought of the honeymoon, when she thought of sharing his bed…she couldn't make the man in her vision Zack.

The man she saw was darker, more intense. The man she saw was Eduardo. His hands on her skin, his lips on her throat…

She flopped backward and covered her face with her hands. "Stop it," she admonished herself. She rolled onto her side and grabbed a pillow, hugging it tightly to her chest. She hadn't done that since high school. Comforting then, even when the world was crumbling around her, and just as comforting now.

Eduardo had always been handsome. He'd always appealed to her. That was nothing new. But she'd never once been tempted to act on any kind of attraction while they'd lived together. It hadn't been part of her plan. And she didn't deviate from her plans. Plans, control, being the one in charge of her life, that was everything. The most important thing.

Not Eduardo's handsome face and sexy physique.

"Feeling all right?" Eduardo asked from the doorway.

She snapped back into a sitting position, pillow still locked tightly against her breasts. "Fine."

Eduardo couldn't hold back the smile that tugged at the corner of his lips. Hannah Weston, flopped on her bed like a teenage girl. A show of softness, a show of humanity, he hadn't expected from an ice queen like her. Like her reaction when he mentioned her fiancé. Like when she'd given back the other man's ring.

It suited him to think of Hannah as being above human emotion. It always had. He needed her. He didn't know all the reasons why, but he did. And that meant it was easier to believe that she would simply go with the option that benefited her most and feel no regret over leaving the inferior choice behind.

But that wasn't how she was behaving. And it gave him a strange twinge in his chest that seemed completely foreign.

Hannah stood up from the bed and put the pillow gingerly back in its place. She cleared her throat and straightened. She looked…soft for a moment. Different than he'd ever seen her before. She was beautiful, no question, more so now than she'd been as a too-thin college student.

She was still thin, but her angles had softened into curves, her cheekbones less sharp, her breasts small but round.

Instantly, an image of him pushing her on the bed, tugging her shirt up, filled his mind. He could take those breasts into his hands…suck her nipple between his lips, his teeth…

A rush of blood roared through his body, south of his belt. How long had it been since that had happened? Since he'd been aroused by an actual woman. In solitude, with a fantasy, he could certainly find release. But with a woman? One he had to somehow seduce and charm when he had no more seduction and charm left in him? That had been beyond him for quite some time.

"I can see that. You epitomize 'fine.'"

"I'm ready to find out what your game plan is, Vega," she said, crossing her arms beneath those small, gorgeous breasts.

"My game plan?"

"Yes. I don't like not knowing the score. I want to know exactly what you have planned and why."

"Tomorrow, I plan to take you to the office, to let you look at things and get a feel for the state of the company."

"All right. What else?"

He felt the need to goad her. To shake her icy composure. As she was shaking his. He took a step forward, extended his hand and brushed his knuckles over her cheek. Her skin was like a rose petal, soft and delicate. "Well, tonight, my darling bride, we dine out." Her eyes darkened, blush-pink lips parting. She was not unaffected by him. His body celebrated the victory even as his mind reminded him that this had no place in their arrangement. "I intend to show all of Barcelona that Señora Vega has returned to her husband."

CHAPTER THREE

GLAMOROUS events and upscale restaurants had become typical in Hannah's world over the past five years. But going with Eduardo wasn't.

The car ride to La Playa had been awkward. She'd dressed impeccably for the evening, as she always did, her blond hair twisted into a bun, her lips and dress a deep berry color, perfect for her complexion.

Eduardo was perfectly pressed as always in a dark suit he'd left unbuttoned and a white shirt with an unfastened collar.

All of that was as it should be. The thing that bothered her was the tension between them. It wasn't just anger, and heaven knew she should feel a whole lot of anger, but there was something else. Something darker and infinitely more powerful.

Something that had changed. It was directly linked to the change in Eduardo, the dark, enticing intensity that lived in him now. The thing she couldn't define.

The thing that made her shake inside.

Eduardo maneuvered the car up the curb and killed the engine. She opened the door and was out and halfway around the car when she nearly ran into him. Her heart stalled, her breath rushing out of her.

"I would have opened your door for you," he said.

She inhaled sharply, trying to collect herself. "And I didn't need you to."

"You're my wife, *querida,* here to reconcile with me. Don't you think I would show you some chivalry?"

"Again with the chivalry. I thought you and I established that honor wasn't our strong point."

"But it will be as far as the press is concerned. Or, more to the point, our relationship needs to seem like a strength." He leaned forward and brushed his knuckles gently over her cheekbone, just as he'd done back in the penthouse.

And just as it had done back at the penthouse, her blood pressure spiked, her heartbeat raging out of control.

She'd had a connection with Zack, and certainly physical attraction. They hadn't slept together, but they'd kissed. Quite a bit. Enough to know that they had chemistry. Now the idea of what she'd shared with Zack being chemistry seemed like a joke.

It had been easy to kiss Zack and say good-night. To walk away. His lips on hers only made her lips burn.

A look from Eduardo made her burn. Everywhere.

She'd lived with him before, though, and nothing had happened between them. There was no reason to think she couldn't keep a handle on it this time.

She turned her face away from him, the night air hitting her cheek, feeling especially cold with the loss of his skin against hers.

He cupped her chin with his thumb and forefinger, turning her face so that she had to look at him. "You can't act like my touch offends you."

"I'm not," she said, holding her breath as she took a step closer to him, as she slid her hand down his arm and laced her fingers with his. "See?"

She was sure he could hear her heart pounding, was certain he knew just how he was affecting her. Except…he wasn't gloating. He wasn't poised to give her a witty comeback, or make fun of her.

"You seem so different," she said, following him to where

the valet was standing. He ignored her statement and gave his keys to the young man in the black vest, speaking to him in Spanish, his focus determinedly off Hannah, even while he held on to her hand.

He tightened his grip on her as they walked on the cobblestones, to the front of the restaurant. It was an old building, brick, the exterior showing the age and character of Barcelona. But inside, it had been transformed. Sleek, sophisticated and smelling nearly as strongly of money as it did of paella, it was exactly the kind of place she'd imagined Eduardo would like.

It was exactly the kind of place *she* liked.

A man dressed all in black was waiting at the front. His face lit with recognition when Eduardo walked in. "Señor Vega, a table for you and your guest?"

"Sí," he said. "This is Señora Vega, my wife. She's come back to Barcelona. I'm very…pleased to see her." He turned to the side, brushing her hair off her face. Heat sparked, from there down through her body. She tried to keep smiling.

The man cocked his head to the side, clearly pleased to be let in on such exclusive news. *"Bienvenido a Barcelona, señora.* We're glad to have you back."

She could feel Eduardo's gaze on her, feel his hold tighten on her waist. She forced her smile wider. "I'm very glad to be back."

"Bien. Right this way."

He led them to a table in the back of the room, white and glossy, with bright red bench seats on either side of it. There was a stark white curtain shielding part of the seating area from view, giving an air of seclusion and luxury.

Eduardo spoke to their host in Spanish for a moment before the other man left and Eduardo swept the curtain aside, holding it open for her. She looked at him, the smile still glued on her face. "Thank you."

Back when they'd been married, they might have gone to a

place like this late on a Saturday night. And everyone inside would know Eduardo. Would clamor for his attention. And she would play her part, smiling and nodding while mentally trying to decide what appetizer to get.

There was none of that tonight. If people had looked at them, it had been subtle. And no one spoke to Eduardo. No one stopped to ask about business. Or where the next big party was. Or which nightclub was opening soon.

She looked behind them and saw that people were staring. Trying to be covert, but not doing a good job. Their expressions weren't welcoming. They looked... They looked either afraid or like they were looking at a car crash and she couldn't figure out why.

"You play your part very well," Eduardo said, not paying any attention to the other diners, "but then, you always did."

"I know," she said. She played every part well. A girl from the Southern United States with bad grades, a thick-as-molasses accent and a total lack of sophistication had to work hard to fit in with the university crowd in Barcelona. But she'd done it.

She'd dropped most of her accent, studied twice as hard as anyone else, and perfected an expression of boredom that carried her through posh events and busy cities without ever looking like the country mouse she was.

It was only when she was alone that she gave herself freedom to luxuriate in comfortable sheets and room service, and all of the other things her new life had opened up to her.

"And you're never modest, which, I confess, I quite like," he said. "Why should you be? You've achieved a great a deal. And you've done it on your own."

"Is this the part where you try and make friends with me?" she asked.

He laughed, a sort of strained, forced sound, nothing like the laugh he'd once had. It had been joyous, easy. Now he sounded out of practice. "Don't be silly, why would I do that?"

"No reason, I suppose. You never did try to be my friend. Just my fake husband."

"Your real husband," he corrected. "Ours just hasn't been a traditional marriage."

"Uh, no. Starting with you calling me into your office one day and telling me you knew all my secrets and that, unless I wanted them spilled, I would do just as you asked me."

A waiter came by and Eduardo ordered a *pre fixe* meal. Hannah read the description in the gilded menu and her stomach cramped with hunger. She was thin—she always had been—but it had more to do with her metabolism than watching her diet. Food was very important to her.

When the waiter had gone, she studied Eduardo's face again. "Why did you do that? Why did you think it would be so...funny to marry me?"

He shook his head. "Very hard to say at this point in time. Everything was a joke to me. And I felt manipulated. I resented my father's heavy hand in my life and I thought I would play his game against him."

"And you used me."

He met her eyes, unflinching. "I did."

"Why?"

He looked down, a strange expression on his face. "Because I could. Because I was Eduardo Vega. Everything, and everyone, in my life existed to please me. My father wanted to see me be a man. He wanted to see me assume control. Find a wife, a family to care for. To give of myself instead of just take. I thought him a foolish, backward old man."

"So you married someone you knew he would find unsuitable."

"I did." He looked up at her. "I would not do so now."

She studied him more closely, the hardened lines on his face, the weariness in his eyes. "You seem different," she said, finally voicing it.

"How so?" he asked.

"Older."

"I am older."

"But more than five years older," she said, looking at the lines around his mouth. Mostly though, it was the endless darkness in his eyes.

"You flatter me."

"You know I would never flatter you, Eduardo. I would never flatter anyone."

A strange expression crossed his face. "No, you wouldn't. But I suppose, ironically, that proves you an honest person in your way."

"I suppose." She looked down at the table. "Has your father's death been hard on you?"

"Of course. And for my mother it has been…nearly unendurable. She has loved him, only him, since she was a teenager. She's heartbroken."

Hannah frowned, picturing Carmela Vega. She had been such a sweet, solid presence. She'd invited Eduardo and Hannah to dinner every Sunday night during their marriage. She'd forced Hannah to know them. To love them.

More people that Hannah had hurt in order to protect herself.

"I'm very sorry about that."

"As am I." He hesitated a moment. "I am doing my best to take care of things. To take care of her. There is something you should know. Something you *will* know if you're going to spend any amount of time around me."

Anticipation, trepidation, crept over her. He sounded grave, intense, two things Eduardo had never been when she'd known him. "And that is?" she asked, trying to keep her tone casual.

Eduardo wished the waiter had poured them wine. He would have a word with the manager about the server after their meal.

Before he could answer Hannah's question, their waiter

appeared, with wine and mussels in clarified butter. He set them on the table and Eduardo picked up the glass, taking a long drink.

When the waiter left again, he set it on the table, his focus back on Hannah, his resolve strengthened.

"I was involved in an accident, very soon after you left."

"An accident?"

"At my family's stables. I was jumping my horse in a course I had ridden hundreds of times. The horse came to a jump he'd done before, but he balked. I was thrown." That much, he had been told by others later. It was strange how vividly he remembered the moments leading up to the accident. The smell of the dirt, grass and the sweat of the horses. He could remember mounting his horse and coaxing him into a trot, then a canter. He could remember nothing after that. Nothing for days and days after. They were gone. "I wasn't wearing a helmet. My head hit the edge of the jump, then the ground." The regret of that burned in him still. It had been a simple thing, a commonplace activity, and it had changed his life forever. "It's funny, because you see, I did forget to file the divorce papers."

Hannah looked pale, her cheeks the color of wax, her lips holding barely a blush of rose. For the first time since he'd known her, she looked truly shaken. "It doesn't sound funny."

"You can laugh at it, *querida.* I don't mind."

"I do. I mind, Eduardo. How badly were you hurt?"

He shook his head. "Badly enough. There has been…damage." He hated to speak of it. Hated to voice the lasting problems the accident had caused. It made them seem real. Final. He didn't want them. Five years later and he couldn't believe he was trapped with a mind that betrayed him as his did.

"I have issues with my memory," he said. "My attention span. Frequent migraines. And I have had some changes in my personality. At least I've been told so. It's hard for me to truly…remember or understand the man I was before."

He looked at her face, stricken, pained. Strange to see her that way. She had always been as cool and steady as a block of ice. Even when he'd called her into his office all those years ago to tell her he'd discovered she'd faked her paperwork to get into college, she'd been stoic. Angry, but poised.

With a calm that women twice her age couldn't have affected, she'd agreed to his foolish marriage scheme. It seemed foolish to him now, anyway. He'd been such a stupid boy, full of his own importance, laughing at life.

Yes, he certainly had changed.

Even now, sitting across from Hannah, as he had done that day he'd coerced her into marriage, he couldn't understand the man that he'd been. Couldn't understand why it had been so amusing. Why he had felt entitled to drag her into his game.

He had been convinced that being near her would...

"I noticed," she said, her voice soft.

"I suppose you did." He lifted his wineglass to his lips again, trying to ignore the defeat that came when the crisp flavor hit his tongue. Wine didn't even make him feel the same. It used to make him feel lighter, a bit happier. Now it just made him tired. "It is of no consequence. With the changes came no desire for me to change back." It wasn't true, not entirely, but he was hardly going to give her reason to pity him. He could take a great many things, but not pity.

"Is this why you're having problems with Vega?" she asked.

"Essentially." The word burned. "I had someone hired to..." He chose his words carefully. He disliked the word *help* almost as much as he disliked saying he couldn't do something. Of course, the verbal avoidance game was empty, because it didn't change reality. "To oversee the duties of managing finances and budgets. Someone else to do taxes. Neither did an adequate job, and now I find myself with some issues to work out, and no one that I trust to handle it."

"And you trust me?" Her tone was incredulous, blue eyes round.

"I don't know that I trust you, but I do know your deepest and darkest secrets. In the absence of trust, I consider it a fairly hefty insurance policy."

She took another sip of her wine. "There are some things about you that are still the same," she said.

"What things?" he asked, desperate to know.

For a moment, she felt like the lifeline he'd built her up to be. No one else seemed to see anything in him from before. They saw him as either diminished in some way, or frightening. His mother and sister, loving as ever, seemed to pity him. He felt smothered in it.

"You're still incredibly amused by what you perceive to be your own brilliance."

Unbidden, a laugh escaped his lips. "If a man can't find amusement with himself, life could become boring."

"A double entendre?" She arched her brow.

"No, I'm afraid not. Further evidence of the changes in me, I suppose." And yet with Hannah, sometimes he felt normal. Something akin to what and who he had been. It felt good to exchange banter, to have her face him, an almost-friendly adversary. For the moment.

"You're also still a stubborn, arrogant autocrat." She seemed almost determined to prove to herself that he was the same.

"As ever."

"And your father's business? Vega Communications? Is it all still a joke to you?"

"Is that what you thought? That it was a joke to me?"

She looked down. "You taking me as a wife was certainly a joke. A joke you used to convince him to pass Vega into your hands then."

"Evidence that nothing about Vega Communications was ever a joke to me."

"Because providing mobile phone service to an ever-increasing number of countries is your passion?"

"Because it's my birthright. It's part of my family legacy." And because if he failed at that, he had nothing to strive for. "Like you, I did very well at university. I earned a degree… I earned my position. Yes, I had connections, but you managed to get into Vega as an intern. You've managed to make your own connections. Why be disdainful simply because my course was more set than yours?"

She looked thoughtful as she took a mussel on the half shell between her thumb and forefinger. "I was disdainful because I never thought you cared about it. Or even wanted it. Not really."

"I expected it. I suppose, given that it seemed a certainty, I lacked the blatant desperation you possessed."

She put the mussel between her lips and sucked out the flesh. It wasn't a sexy action. Not really. And yet, when she did it, it was oddly compelling. It was because her lips managed to look sensual, inviting and soft, all while her eyes told him she'd happily bite his tongue if he dared follow the impulse that originated south of his belt.

"Desperation?" she asked, taking the white linen napkin from her lap and dabbing the side of her mouth. "Drive, maybe."

"If it makes you feel better."

"It does. Humor me."

He inclined his head. "If you wish. Anyway, I may sympathize with you a bit more now. I have to fix this. Vega is my family. My life."

The glee she'd seemed to take from her initial thought of his being desperate had diminished. "You used to like other things better."

"I did."

"Parties. Loose women."

"I was faithful to you during our marriage." A statement

more true than she realized. But the fallout from the head injury had been extensive. He'd lost his passion for everything. Had lost friends. He'd had a hunger for life once. For fun and pleasure, for laughter.

He had nothing more than a white-knuckled grip on existence now. A human, biological need to keep breathing. And with that, came the need to save Vega.

It gave him a reason to go on, anyway, and that was, at this point in his life, more valuable than passion.

"Prince Charming in the flesh," she said lightly.

The waiter returned and set a fish course before them, Spanish rice and spiced greens on the side. Hannah wasted no time in helping herself. She had always liked eating. He'd been fascinated by it. When they would go to his family's house for dinner, she'd always eaten as much as he did, if not more. Still, she'd always looked thin. Hungry. But he'd suspected, even then, that her hunger wasn't for food.

She'd been hungry for money. Status. Success.

She still was. It was why she was here with him. Why he'd been able to demand she return to Spain.

"Not entirely," he said, his tone heavier than he intended it to be.

"So tell me then," she said, blue eyes glittering with mischief. "Will you be faithful to me during our reconciliation?" Her lips closed around her fork and his gut tightened.

"That all depends, Hannah," he said, words forming before thought, his body leading the proceedings.

"On?"

"On whether or not you intend to share my bed this time."

Hannah nearly choked on her rice. "What?"

Eduardo leaned back in his chair, a dark glint in his eye, a lean, hungry look to his features. "You heard me, *querida*. Will I need to seek my amusement elsewhere? Or will you share my bed?"

"I am not sleeping with you," she said, the very idea of the invasion, the intimacy, the loss of utter and complete control, making her feel shivery and panicky. Hot.

"Then I suppose the answer to the question is not your concern."

"No," she bit out.

She didn't truly care who he slept with. She'd been trying to goad him, nothing else. They did that. They always had. Verbal sparring had been the only level they'd ever truly connected on.

They shared a love of arguing, which, in some ways, made them the perfect married couple for the public. For all she knew of married couples.

"At least we're on the same page," he said, returning his focus to his dinner.

What did that mean? That he didn't want her? That made her…mad. And it shouldn't. She shouldn't care. Men, attraction, sex, none of it fit into her life. She'd been about to make room for Zack, and of course she'd intended to sleep with him eventually. But she'd been in control of it, no question. She'd been able to wait, and so had he. She and Zack were both all about control, about keeping things in order, in their neat little boxes.

Eduardo would never fit into a box. She would never be able to shove him to one side of her life and ignore him unless she wanted to open him up and indulge. Nope. That wasn't possible. He was too much. Too…present. He was impossible to simply ignore.

She didn't want to sleep with him anyway. She'd denied her sex drive, rightly, necessarily, for the past nine years. Sure, she'd been about to end the dry spell with marriage. But it hadn't been the attractor to marrying Zack. It had never been that important. It wasn't all-consuming.

It wouldn't be with Eduardo, either. She could keep on ignoring it, no question. And Eduardo wouldn't change that.

So his lack of desire for her shouldn't matter. Her ego was just feeling bruised.

"Good thing. So," she said, "what's your plan for tomorrow? Just waltzing into the office and announcing we're reconciling?"

A smile curved his lips. An unsettling, dark smile that made her stomach tighten and her heart pound. "Why don't we just see what happens?"

CHAPTER FOUR

WHY don't we just see what happens?

Even getting out of the car the next morning, business armor in the form of a sleek-fitting pair of slacks and a dark blue button-up shirt, she heard his words playing through her head. They'd sounded like a double entendre. Like he'd disregarded the previous portion of the conversation where she'd said she wouldn't sleep with him.

Smug-ass Spaniard.

She tightened her hold on her laptop bag and chanced a glance at him out of the corner of her eye. He was looking sexier than he ever had, at least to her, in a navy suit, his dark hair left slightly disheveled, as if theirs was a reconciliation made in the bedroom.

He paused in front of the heavy glass door of the tall, modern building and held it open for her, his dark eyes never leaving hers.

She made eye contact as she walked in. She wasn't about to let him intimidate her. Nope. Not going to happen.

Her gaze was steely. She was sure of it. And his was... amused. It was the first time she'd seen him amused, really amused, in a way that reminded her of the old Eduardo, since he'd hijacked a limo and disrupted her wedding.

A leaden weight dropped into her stomach. A sudden reminder of why he'd changed.

She tossed her hair and continued into the building. She

knew it well. She'd interned there for months and then she'd become the boss's daughter-in-law. She'd learned about the way a big business ran here, had faced down Eduardo for the first time.

Another strange wave of homecoming melancholy washed over her. She tried to clear her tightened throat.

"*Buenos días,* Paola." Eduardo greeted the woman sitting behind the reception desk.

"*Buenos días, Señor Vega.*" She looked up for the first time, her eyes rounding when she saw Hannah. "Hannah," she said.

Hannah's heart beat against her breastbone. She remembered her? She'd never wondered much if people remembered her. She'd never been back to a place to find out.

"Hi, Paola." She'd always like Paola. The other woman had always been nice to her, not laughing at her mangled Spanish, always offering her a smile when she'd come in for work after classes.

She wondered what Paola had thought when she'd suddenly "abandoned" Eduardo and their six-month union.

"You're…back?" she asked, her focus darting from Eduardo and back to Hannah.

"Yes," Eduardo said, turning to her, his expression soft, the hard glint in his eye telling her the expression was a lie. "She is." He lifted his hand and brushed his finger lightly over her cheek.

A shiver wound through her, tightening her stomach, her lungs, her nipples. She'd tried to forget this part of being near him. Had tried, and failed, so many times to forget what it had felt like on their wedding day when his lips had touched hers.

To forget that he brought out a beast in her. One that was normally asleep, or at least dormant, kept mollified by the occasional fantasy and gratuitous amounts of cop shows with men in tight uniforms.

This was different than those contained, allowed moments

of desire. This was different even than the attraction she'd felt for him back when they'd first married. This wasn't something she had a grasp on; it was nothing she could control or shut off.

The wedding kiss, and feelings it had created in her, had lingered. But she'd been able to keep it where it belonged. Stored for her convenient use late at night, never invading her body or thoughts during the day. Never when it wasn't appropriate.

It was invading now.

She swallowed hard and worked at composing her face. She wasn't going to break; she wasn't going to show nerves. Or arousal. "That's right," she said. "I am."

Then, just to prove to him that he wasn't the only one who could play the game, she leaned in, pausing for a moment as his scent hit her. Sandalwood and skin. She couldn't remember ever noticing the way he smelled before. It was foreign. Sexy. Piquing her curiosity, her need to draw closer.

So she did, because that had been her intent. Not for any other reason. Her eyes met his as her lips connected with his cheek. Smooth still, clean, a hint of aftershave lingering. She closed her eyes, just for a moment, and let the feel of him beneath her lips fully wash over.

Then she pulled back, quickly, her head swimming, her heart pounding.

"Yes, I'm back," she said, blowing out a breath and smiling at Paola, trying to ignore the intense quivering in her stomach.

"Good," she said. "Very good. We're glad to have you."

"As am I," Eduardo said, his eyes never leaving Hannah. "Come, *querida,* I want to show you some of the changes I've made."

She offered Paola another smile and a stilted nod before following Eduardo into the first elevator on the right. She let out a breath when the platinum doors closed.

"Very convincing," Eduardo said, a strange smile curving his lips. It was almost predatory.

"I know, right?" she snapped. "I'm a great actress, remember?"

"Why didn't you just head to Hollywood instead of pursuing a career in finance? You wouldn't have had to fake school transcripts."

She cleared her throat and tightened her hold on her bag. "Too much chance involved. I don't do chance. I do certainty. Control. Something I could work hard enough to achieve. Luck has never really been on my side—" she swept a hand up and down in Eduardo's direction "—obviously. So I didn't figure I should make a plan that included lucking into anything."

"Are you saying our association has been unlucky for you?"

She gritted her teeth, thinking of the letter of recommendation that had happened to find the firm she'd wanted so badly to get a job at in New York. A letter from the HR department at Vega. "Not entirely, but you have to admit, getting kidnapped on your wedding day isn't good luck."

He chuckled as the elevator stopped. "Now, that depends."

The doors slid open and he stepped out; she followed. "On what?"

"On how you feel about the person you're marrying."

The floor was quiet, essentially vacant. The highest offices in the building were reserved for the big dogs of the company, and at this point, Eduardo was the biggest dog.

He opened the door to what had been his father's office, and Hannah's throat constricted. More emotion. She wasn't used to it. She didn't like it, either.

"You don't have to open doors for me, you know," she said, sweeping into the room. "I know you aren't a gentleman."

He arched a brow and closed the door behind them. "I'm hardly trying to convince you otherwise."

"Obviously."

"All right, Hannah," he said, moving to his desk, his demeanor changing. He sat down and hit a few keys on his keyboard, waking up the flat-screen monitor. "This is what we're looking at."

"What's this?"

"Financial records for the past few years."

"I need to sit," she said.

He stood from the computer chair and she slid past him, trying to ignore the little jolt of pleasure she felt when she brushed against him. "So, what exactly do you think is going on?"

He blew out a breath. "Certain things in particular are problematic for me. Remembering numbers and dates are among them. But it wouldn't be as big of an issue had I not hired someone to handle it that didn't do his job."

"On purpose or…criminally?" she asked, opening the report for the previous years' finances.

"I'm not entirely certain."

"Well, incompetence should be criminal," she said, skimming the numbers. "And please hold all comments on how I should be an expert on the matter. I am in here saving your butt, after all."

"You are so very charming, Hannah."

She gritted her teeth and leaned in closer to the computer screen, trying to close him out of her range of focus. "Yeah, well, had I gone to charm school I probably would have failed there just as spectacularly as I flunked out of high school."

"Why did you fail high school? Because we both know you're capable of doing the work."

Her stomach dipped and she tried to will away the gut-tearing pain that always came with this set of memories. Tried to put herself firmly in the present, as Hannah Weston. Not as the Hannah she had been. "I didn't try."

"That doesn't sound like you, either."

"Yeah, well, making stupid financial decisions doesn't sound like you, and yet here we are."

She chanced a look at his face. His expression was hard, his lips set into a grim line. She'd gone too far again. She knew that. But she wasn't opening the door on her past. She just wasn't. She couldn't.

He gripped the arms of the chair and turned her so that she was facing him. "Stupid? Stupid decisions? Is that what you call them?"

"I was making a point." She slid the chair back and stood. The idea was to bring her up to his level. But since her eyes only met his chest, the only point it served to make was that, even in three-inch heels, she was a whole lot smaller than he was.

"Then you won't mind if I make one of my own." He wrapped his arm around her waist and tugged her against him, her breasts coming into contact with his chest. He raised his hand, brushing his shaking thumb over her lip, the gesture shockingly gentle given the heat and anger visible in his eyes.

The rage in him was palpable, satisfying in a way. She'd brought him to the brink with her words. His muscles trembled as he held her. She waited. For his lips to crash down on hers. Rough and painful. The way it often was with men when they lacked control or were just too turned on to think straight. The way it most certainly would be with him so angry.

But there was no crash.

He dipped his head, his lips a breath from hers. The breath fled her body, all her focus diverting to him. He was so close. So tempting. She found her face tilting so that her mouth could meet his, found herself giving in. Giving up.

His lips were hot, firm. And suddenly, he wasn't holding her to him anymore. She'd melted against him. His tongue slid against the seam of her mouth and she opened, heat flooding her, making her core tighten, her breasts feel heavy. He wrapped his other arm around her and she lifted her hands, pressing them on his hard chest.

He angled his head, deepening the kiss, tightening his hold on her. She whimpered and freed her hands, sighing when her breasts met his chest. She wrapped her arms around his neck, threading her fingers through his hair, holding him to her.

He devoured her, and she returned the favor. Never, not in their six months of marriage, had they kissed like this. Nothing more than proprietary pecks for public displays. A slightly more intimate kiss on their wedding day, since they'd had an audience.

But this was just them. Alone. And there was no control. No thought. She hadn't even tried to maintain her hold on either, she'd simply released them, and drowned in his kiss.

Then, just as suddenly as he'd embraced her, he released her, his eyes dark black pits that seemed to draw her in and repel her at the same time. And she realized she didn't have half the hold over him as he did over her.

"The point I was making," he bit out, his tone rough, strained, "is that you might not like me, and you might want to think that I'm somehow stupid, but we both know that I have the power here."

She took in a shaking breath. "You…bastard."

"Don't forget it. I'm not a boy you can manipulate. I'm not the foolish idiot I once was who might have been distracted by a pretty face." He turned away from her, heading out the door. "Let me know what you find."

She didn't answer. She couldn't. As soon as he exited the office she pounded her fist on the desk, letting the sting alleviate the burn of humiliation that had taken over.

She wouldn't let him make a fool of her like that. Never again.

Eduardo drew a shaking hand over his face. He had not meant to do that. He had not meant to touch her, or kiss her. He hadn't meant to lose control.

Rage had been a feral beast inside of him, pushing him,

driving him. Rage, and then, the hot surge of lust that had tipped him over the edge.

His body burned. He'd been so close to pushing her on the surface of the desk and…

He laughed into the empty room and gave thanks for the mostly private floor.

He hadn't touched a woman in five years. Five years of celibacy that he hadn't minded in the least. Now it seemed to be crushing him, five years all added together and suddenly very, very apparent.

It was more than that, though. It was this thing in him that he didn't know. This strain of unpredictability that he couldn't control or anticipate.

He didn't understand the man he'd been. He didn't know, or like, the man he was.

This wasn't how it was supposed to work. She wasn't supposed to appeal to the new, darker side of him. She was supposed to remind him of that light, easy time. Was supposed to bring those feelings back.

Beyond that, he did need her to help straighten out the company's finances, and he could not afford to be distracted. He had to see this through, and he could not afford a distraction. He couldn't afford to divert his focus any more than it already was. He had no control over the effects of his injury. No control over the forgetfulness or the migraines. But he would damn well control his body's reaction to her.

He gritted his teeth and walked back into the office. Hannah jumped and turned.

"Knock for heaven's sake," she growled, turning back to the screen.

"It's my office."

"Well…you left."

"And now I am back."

"Yes, you are," she said, her shoulders rolled forward, her expression intense, focused on the screen. She let out a short breath. "It's not that bad." She turned the chair so that she was facing him, a guarded expression on her face.

"You don't think?"

"No. The fees you incurred for late taxes…I can't help you with that. That was the work of a very sucky employee and I'm glad he's been fired. The rest is manageable. I could recommend some investment and savings strategies and, actually, you're missing a few tax breaks you could take advantage of while making sure your employees get better benefits."

"You make it sound…easy."

"It is," she said. "When it's your area of expertise. Can you explain to me exactly what isn't working for you? I need to know so I can help you get a system in place."

He hated that word. *Help.* He had thought nothing of it before his accident. But then, he hadn't needed it. He was supposed to be the one who provided help, the one people went to. He was the man of the Vega family. He wasn't supposed to need so much.

"Numbers and dates get reversed when I read them. And I have a very hard time remembering them. And my attention span has…shortened. It's hard to sit down and read something for a long time. Harder to retain it."

"Do they think it will ever change?"

He shrugged, like it didn't matter. "Probably not, but it's impossible to know, really."

"You're okay with it?"

A chuckle escaped his lips, not because he felt there was anything funny, but because it seemed the only response he was capable of for a moment. "Would you be okay if you woke up with a brain that wasn't yours? That's how I feel. All the time."

She looked down, her complexion pale. "I've been trying to be someone else for the past nine or ten years. I might not mind."

"Trust me, *querida,* you would. But, either way, I cannot

change what is. So I only concern myself with what can be changed."

She planted both hands on his desk and pushed herself into a standing position. She seemed to have forgotten the kiss, her expression as icy and composed as ever. He still shook inside.

"What I would like to do, is work on implementing a system that will be easier for you to track. Then I want to make sure you find some good, trustworthy financial managers. Not until everything is corrected, you understand."

"You always did think quickly on your feet. Or in an office chair."

Her lips curved into a smile. A real smile, not a smirk or a forced expression. "This is what I do. I'm good at it."

"You always have been. That's why I came to you."

"That and the leverage."

"A man can't go into battle unarmed."

A flicker of heat sparked in her eyes and he knew that she was replaying the kiss. So, she wasn't unaffected. She hadn't brushed it off. But she was right, she was an accomplished actress. She'd gotten even better, even harder to read since the beginning of their sham marriage. He had worried about her breaking character then. Even now, with the little spark visible in the depths of her eyes, he doubted anyone else would see anything beyond the cool, composed beauty she seemed to project. It would keep most people from looking deeper.

She was a petite blonde, well dressed, perfectly coiffed. She had a look that could easily become generic, and might be to some. It was her eyes that showed how different she was. That showed her intelligence, her steel.

She cleared her throat, tilted her chin up. "Well, I doubt anyone would accuse you of that."

"I'm flattered by the assessment."

"Don't be, or I'll have to punch you in the ego again."

"I see, so you're trying to knock me down a couple of pegs in an attempt to gain the upper hand. It won't work. I'm happily absent an ego, in many ways. Social status means little to me. I haven't tried to impress friends or women in so many years I can hardly remember why I ever bothered in the first place. Though, the forgetting could also be a side effect of my head injury."

She shifted, her lips bunching together.

"You don't like it when I joke about my accident?" he asked.

She shrugged. "It's your trauma, man. Deal with it however you want."

"I've dealt with it," he said, his words coming out harsher than intended. Lies. "I've dealt with my father's death, with trying to ensure my mother and sister are happy, well taken care of. And now, I'm dealing with fixing what has fallen into disrepair here at the company."

"And I'm here to help you do it." She arched her pale eyebrows. "Under sufferance, you understand, but I am here. And I am helping."

For some reason, his entire body didn't seize in response to the use of the word.

"You are."

CHAPTER FIVE

HANNAH leaned against the railing on the penthouse terrace and looked down at the city. The sky was dark, stars piercing holes in the blackness, and below, Barcelona was lit. Cars still crowded the road, people headed to restaurants and clubs.

She breathed in deep—warm air filling her lungs. She smelled salt, the sea, but it wasn't the same as it was in San Francisco or New York. Here it seemed spicier, richer. It always had. It had always called to her in a different way. Begged her to strip off her control and let herself go free.

And she had always denied it.

"Having trouble sleeping?"

She turned, her heart catching when she saw Eduardo leaning in the doorway. He'd traded in his work attire for casual black pants and a tight T-shirt that hugged his muscular physique almost as tightly as she'd hugged him earlier in his office.

Don't think about that.

She wouldn't. Not again. That was over. Done. No more kissing. Not in private anyway.

"I'm still a little off. Jet lag and all."

"Tell me, Hannah."

Her throat tightened, strange, irrational fear assaulting her. "Tell you what?"

"Tell me what you've been doing with yourself these past five years."

She almost sighed in relief. Five years she could do. "Working. I was in New York for about three years, working on Wall Street, of all things, then I relocated to San Francisco. I started to get a good client base at the firm I was with, doing personal financial management and investments. I hit a bit of a wall, though, because male bosses, coworkers and clients always seemed to think single meant available. So when I met Zack a year ago, it seemed perfect. I could get married, and I could do my job without so much sexual harassment."

"And that's the only reason you were going to marry him? I hate to be the one to tell you, but men who are inclined to behave that way sexually harass women with wedding rings, too."

"Sure they do, but Zack is influential. Wealthy. It would be a brave man who attempted to poach on his territory."

Eduardo chuckled, dark and enticing. "Like me?"

"Yes. Brave or stupid."

His eyes locked with hers. "Do you remember what happened last time you used that word?"

Heat and regret assaulted her. Heat from the memory of the kiss, regret because she'd insulted him. She wished she felt more regret in regards to the actual kissing.

"I won't do it again."

"Good." He walked to the railing, resting his forearms on the metal surface. He was barefoot. Strange that she noticed. He seemed slightly more human than usual in that moment. "Were you going to have a family with him? Children?"

A shiver started in her stomach, working its way through her. "No. No children."

"You don't want them?"

"No. Never. What would I do with a baby, anyway?" She laughed, as though it were the most ridiculous thing in the world. And she fought hard against the tight, clenching pain in her womb. Against the memories.

"Raise it, I suppose. But then, wearing a baby in a sling

while you're cursing and trading stocks is maybe not that practical."

She swallowed the bile that was rising in her throat. "You want children?"

"No," he said. Just no. Good. She didn't want to talk about her aversion to children, either. Didn't want to open up that box. It held so much fear, and regret and guilt. She just couldn't look in it at the moment. She did her best to never, ever look in it. To never remember.

"Not practical for people like us," she said. She and Zack had had a very similar conversation once. And in his response she'd sensed the same dark grief that she felt hovering around the edges of his answers. Another reason she'd never pressed him for his secrets. She was certain they shared something too similar, too painful. She knew it was why he'd never pressed for hers.

"Of course not."

"We were going to be partners. Help each other out. It's good to have a partner in life."

"I suppose so," he said slowly. "But that isn't how I want to live."

"No?"

"No. I would rather be able to do things independently. If I ever had a wife…I would have wanted to take care of her."

"Not every woman wants to be taken care of." But for a moment she wondered what it would be like. To have someone shoulder some of the pain. To have someone who knew every secret. Who shared every fear. Someone who would cover her, shield her.

A silly thought. She didn't want that. She was the only person she could trust. The only person she could depend on.

"It's how I think things should be done. That's how my parents did things. They were happy."

"How is your mom?"

"Grieving. Still. She spent more than thirty years with my father. His death has been hard for her."

"I'm sorry. Your parents were… They're the only place I've ever seen love, let's put it that way."

"The only place? What about your parents?"

What was the harm in giving him a little? He knew more about her than anyone else. "I don't know. I don't think they ever married. When I was three my mom left me at my dad's single-wide and never came back. She had all my stuff tied up in a little plastic bag. Anyway, he didn't know what to do with a kid. He…he tried I guess. But he was kind of a mess."

He frowned. "Your mother left you?"

"Not every family is perfect. But I don't dwell on it."

"You don't even acknowledge it."

"I lived in this dirty, dusty mobile home. The park it was in had a dirt road and when trucks would drive by, the dirt was like a cloud. It settled on everything. Everything was always dirty. I actually felt lucky to only have one parent. There was no fighting in my house. I could always hear the neighbors screaming at each other. My father never yelled. He just barely ever said hi, either."

She could stay out all night and he'd hardly ever raise an eyebrow when she'd come in at breakfast. She could still see him, sitting in his chair with a bowl of cereal in his lap and a beer already in his hand.

"How were the sheets?" he asked.

"I didn't have any. Just a mattress on the floor and a blanket. We didn't have a washer and dryer so…I used to hitchhike to the Laundromat sometimes so I could clean my blankets and clothes."

She shook her head. "I mean…would you want to talk about that? Who wants that life?"

He frowned. "No one. Is that why you erased your past?"

She swallowed. "One of the many whys. But let's not even get into that." It was one thing to talk about her parents, such as they were. To talk about the things that had been out of her control. The poverty, the neglect. She could handle that.

But she'd made her own mistakes. Those were the ones that stayed closest to her, like a layer over her skin, protective and confining at the same time, impossible to remove. A part of her she wished away every day, and one she depended on to move forward.

"Fine by me." He looked out at the view. "Tell me, Hannah, what is it like to walk away from everything?" His tone was husky, sincere. Surprising.

"I… It's like walking out of prison," she said. "Like I imagine it might be, anyway. You spend all this time in a place you know isn't right, and yet, you have to stay. Until one day, you just walk out into the sunlight. You'd never go back, even though going forward is frightening. Because there's so much possibility when before that…there was nothing."

"How did you end up in Spain? Why Spain?"

Admitting she'd sort of put her finger on the globe in a random place would seem silly. As silly as the fact that she'd chosen her new last name from an upscale department store she'd seen on TV. But that was the truth. She'd been so desperate then, to shed who she was, to try and be someone else. To make something else of herself. "I wanted to get very far away. I wanted out of the country because…"

"It would be easier for you to get away with false transcripts."

"Yes. Of course they were very good, and I had changed my name legally by that point." She didn't know why she was telling him all of this. Only that with him determinedly keeping his focus on the street below, the darkness surrounding them, it seemed easy.

"And where did you get the money for it?"

The fifteen thousand dollars she never wanted to talk about. Fifteen thousand dollars she did her best to *never* think about. It had bought documents; it had supplied her with her plane ticket and passport, ID that carried her new name.

A gift. The money had been a gift, not payment, because how could a price be put on what she'd given? At least, that was what they'd told her. The Johnsons, from somewhere in New Hampshire. The couple she'd given her baby to. Oh, they'd paid all the legal adoption fees, and her hospital bill, but in the end, they'd wanted to do more. To get her on her feet. Provide her with a new start so she didn't end up back in the same place.

They had. They truly had. She should be grateful. She was.

But thinking about it was like drawing her skin off slowly. It still made her feel raw, freshly wounded and bleeding. Still made her ache with guilt. Guilt over everything. That it had ever happened. That she'd made the choice she had. And then there was the guilt that came along with the occasional, sharp sweep of relief that she'd chosen to give the baby up. That she hadn't kept him. That she hadn't spent their lives repeating the cycle her parents had been a part of.

"From a friend," she said. It was a lie. But it was the kind of lie she was used to. The kind of lie that kept all the events from her past glossed over. The kind that kept it hidden away. Kept it from being drawn out into the light and tearing her apart.

"Good friend."

"Oh, yeah. Great friend." She cleared her throat and blinked hard. "And you, Eduardo, what's it like to have a place you can call yours? What's it like to feel at home?" She wished she hadn't asked. It was too revealing. The ache in her voice was so obvious, at least to her own ears.

"I have never thought very much about it, or rather, I never had. Not before. I always took it as my due. Vega was to be mine, my position in both society and my family always sure and set. Now that I know what it's like to feel like a stranger to myself? Well, now I wish I would have appreciated the ease a bit more."

Silence fell between them and she closed her eyes, listening to the traffic below, music coming from somewhere nearby.

"Did we just have a moment?" she asked.

"A what?"

"A moment. Like, a human moment where we talked without fighting or snarking or trying to put each other down."

"I think we did. But we need never speak of it again."

She opened her eyes and looked into his. Even in the dim light, she could see a glimmer of mischief there, something like the old Eduardo.

"It's a deal," she said.

For one moment, her mind went blank of everything. Everything but his face, and what it had been like to be in his arms earlier. What it had been like to kiss him. And in that moment, she couldn't remember why kissing him wasn't a great idea. But just for that one moment.

Then that blank simplicity got crowded out by reality, by the reason why she couldn't kiss him. Not now, not ever.

She wasn't building a life here with him. When this was over, she had to go back home. To her clients, to her job. Assuming Zack wasn't having her blacklisted.

"I'm tired now," she lied. She didn't think she would ever be able to sleep right while she was here. While she knew he was right across the penthouse from her, sleeping. Possibly naked. It hadn't bothered her five years ago. She didn't know what had changed in her since then.

That was a lie. She did know. Eduardo had changed. And there was something about him now that called to her.

She really had to get a grip on herself. And the weak, mushy emotion she seemed to be tempted to wallow in the past few days. She didn't have time, she didn't need to, she didn't want to.

She was Hannah Weston. She was her own invention, her own woman. And she could do this.

"Good night, Eduardo," she said, bringing a little steel back into her tone. "See you at the office tomorrow."

CHAPTER SIX

"Your wife is back and you didn't tell your mother?"

Eduardo turned to face Hannah, who was sitting at his desk, holding his phone more tightly to his ear as his mother's voice rang through loudly.

"*Lo siento, Mama.* It happened very suddenly. I have been working at…making amends." Bringing his mother into the charade wasn't ideal, but he would do what had to be done. He'd been avoiding her for weeks. That period of avoidance had clearly ended.

"You've been making amends? For what, Eduardo? She was the one who left you without a word. After six months of marriage. Divorced." She said the word like it was something truly foul.

"Ah, yes, but we were not divorced. We never have been. Hannah and I are as married today as we were that day in the cathedral."

Hannah's focus snapped up from the computer, her blue eyes trained on him, her expression hard. *"What?"* she mouthed.

He covered the mouthpiece on the phone. *"My mother,"* he mouthed back to her.

Then her lips formed a soundless version of a truly filthy word. He chuckled and uncovered the phone.

"We will come to see you this weekend. In fact, let's make it a long weekend at the *rancho*. Bring Selena, of course."

Hannah threw her hands in the air, her eyes round. He offered her a half smile and she put her hands on her throat like she was choking herself, then pointed at him. He suppressed a laugh and listened to his mother's response.

"See you then," he said, cutting off any last protests. She would be there. She would never disappoint him.

"What did you do that for?" Hannah exploded.

"Because, it's what I would do if we were really reconciling, which means it's what we should do in order to make it look like we're reconciling. *Entiende?*"

"No. *No entiendo.* I don't understand at all. Why bother bringing your mom and Selena into this? It's not...fair."

"To them or to you?"

"Either one," she said. "Look, I liked your family—a lot—when I was here. They were really good to me and I hated lying to them. I don't want to do it again."

"You're sparing my mother from the possibility of losing Vega. I think she'll forgive you."

"I'll be honest with you, Eduardo. I don't think you're in danger of losing Vega. Things aren't quite as good as they were a few years ago, but that's true for a lot of companies. And anyway, your personal assets are quite healthy. Once you get your financial manager in place—"

"But if I don't figure out a system..."

"We will," she said, moving into a standing position and grasping her hands behind her back, arching forward, stretching, a short little kitten sound escaping as she did. His body kicked into gear, a hard and serious reminder of the power she seemed to command over him.

Her breasts were perfect. Small and round. He ached to have them in his palms. In his mouth.

"We had better," he bit out, averting his eyes. He had to get a grip. He had other things to worry about, things much more important than his neglected sex drive.

"I'm confident that we can figure something out," she said,

rounding the desk, her hips dipping with each step. She was still angry. Her hips moved more when she was angry, her lips pulled tight. "Now," she breathed out, "do we really have to spend the weekend with your family?"

"Yes. My mother will not let it go…you know it as well as I do. And I think it would do us both good to get out of the city."

"It's only been a few weeks. And anyway, I like the city, so I feel no such need."

"Ah, but you do." He started to circle her. Her head swiveled as far as it possibly could as she tried to track his movement. He put his hands on her shoulders, savoring the heat of her body coming through her thin top. "You're very tense." He moved his thumb into her muscle and discovered that tense was an understatement.

"Ow," she groused.

"You will feel better in a moment." He moved his thumb on the other side, digging deeper. She arched back, whimpering.

"It doesn't feel better yet."

"Your muscles are like rocks. It doesn't help that you hunch at the computer."

"Shut up, I do not hunch."

"You do." He worked both of her shoulders until he felt some of the tightness ease, until she stopped fidgeting and started melting into his touch. He swept her blond hair to the side and slid his thumb up the back of her neck. This time, the sound she made was decidedly pleased, and more than a little bit sexy.

"Yes, just like that," she said, arching into his touch, instead of trying to escape it.

"I do like to hear you say that," he said. He tilted his head to the side and pressed a kiss just beneath her earlobe. She stiffened, then pulled away from him.

"I'm still mad at you," she said, turning to face him, her eyes looking a little glazed, her cheeks flushed.

"That's okay. It doesn't mean you can't kiss me. You were mad at me last time, too."

She drew her plump lower lip between her teeth and shook her head. "Nope. Not kissing you."

"Why not?"

"Because it's not what we're here to do."

She was right. He knew it. And until he'd touched her again, he'd firmly believed it. There was too much at stake for him in so many ways. And yet he couldn't find it in him to suppress the desire. "That's true. But mixing a little pleasure in with business doesn't have to be detrimental."

"Maybe not, but it usually is."

"Speaking from experience."

"No, I'm way too smart for that. I keep business and personal very, very separate. And you, my dear, are business. Always have been."

She was lying. He extended his hand and drew his finger along the curve of her cheek, felt her tremble beneath his touch. Now *she* knew she was lying, too.

"We'll finish up work for the day, and when we get back to the penthouse, we'll get ready to drive to the *rancho* first thing in the morning."

Eduardo owned a Jeep, which surprised her almost as much as his insistence they make the drive out of Barcelona and into the countryside with the top down.

But the air was warm and the scenery was beautiful, so she wasn't going to complain. Even though her hair was whipping around so violently she nearly swallowed a chunk of it. She tugged the strands from her lips and shook her head, hoping to get it somewhat back into place.

"I don't think I ever came out here with you…before, I mean," she said, competing with the wind and the engine.

"No. This is new. I bought it after my accident. I liked

going to a place where I could think. Somewhere away from the city and…people."

"You have horses?"

He nodded, his eyes never leaving the road. "Yes. I don't ride them."

"You don't?"

"No."

"I assume you have staff that do?"

"Of course. And you know Selena is really into horses."

"I remember. She must be…not a teenager anymore." She remembered Eduardo's younger sister, all long skinny limbs, round eyes and glossy hair. She'd been fifteen when Hannah had seen her last, but she would be twenty now. A woman, not a girl.

"No, she's not."

"Strange because it doesn't feel like it's been that long since… Well, in some ways. There are times when it feels like this was part of another lifetime. And like I'm in an alternate dimension now."

"It's very possible, I suppose. Maybe I'm in one, too, and I'll wake up with a throbbing headache and my memory fully restored."

"Click your heels together and say 'there's no place like home.'"

"Qué?"

"Dorothy. *The Wizard of Oz.* You don't know that movie? Everyone knows that movie."

He shook his head. "I've seen it. I…didn't remember the reference."

An uneasy silence fell between them, her stomach tightening as the meaning of his statement settled in. "If I clicked my heels together," she said, "and said that, I wonder where I would end up? Maybe in the middle of nowhere."

"You don't have a home?"

"Right now I have an apartment in San Francisco. But is

it home? I don't know about that." She looked down at her hands. "Sometimes I think it would be a blessing to have a little memory loss."

"Was it that bad?"

Unbidden, she thought about what it had felt like to have her baby move inside of her. Of the moment he'd been delivered. Of having to turn away as the nurse carried him from the room so that she wouldn't have time to memorize his tiny, perfect face.

She had it memorized anyway. One moment was enough. And not enough.

She tried to breathe past the tightness in her chest. "Some things really are that bad."

"I've forgotten a great many things that didn't matter. But I don't know they don't matter. And that's the worst part. You're not sure if you've forgotten something trivial, or vital. A lot of the time I'm unsure if I've forgotten anything at all. I could neglect an important document and never once have that nagging feeling you count on having to keep you on track."

She redirected her thoughts, pulling the door closed on her memories, on her emotions, locking it tight. "Have you set up alerts?"

"What kind?"

"You could have them on your phone, your computer. We could sync them up so you could be reminded at different times of the day that certain things need doing."

"I don't forget everything," he said, his tone rough.

"I know that. But you don't always know what will slip your mind, do you? So you have to be willing to put down your pride for a little bit and cover your bases. This isn't about hanging on to your manly image."

"The hell it's not," he grumbled.

"Eduardo." She sighed. "Get over yourself."

"Why would I want to do that? I am so wonderful." He tossed her a smile and for a moment, the heaviness in her lightened. For the rest of the trip, they kept the topics neutral, choosing to avoid anything real or personal.

When they pulled off the main road and onto a winding, single-lane paved road that wound up the mountain, Hannah tried not to show any nerves.

"You're bothered by heights?" he asked.

"Oh, only a little," she said. She hated to show fear, of any kind. Especially a silly fear of heights. "I mean, if another car came around the corner our only options are the side of the mountain and plummeting to our doom."

"I promise to keep the plummeting to a minimum."

"Appreciated," she said tightly.

She breathed a sigh of relief when the road curved in, away from the drop and through a thick grove of trees. It was cool, green and lush, shaded from the heat of the day.

The trees thinned and faded until they were surrounded by green fields, stretching to the mountains on one side, and to the edge of a cliff on the other, overlooking the brilliant, jewel-bright sea.

Large iron gates secluded the property from the rest of the world. Eduardo used an application on his phone to enter in the code and the gates swung open.

"I use letters in my security code," he said as they drove on. "They're easier for me to remember. I'm not sure why."

"I'm not, either. I would have to do some reading on the subject."

The house was set back into the property, nearer to the sea, bold floor-to-ceiling windows reflecting the sun. It was an angular, modern house with traditional white stucco and a red ceramic tile roof. A mix of the old and new, very like its owner.

"This is beautiful," she said. "Quiet, too."

"Away from the noise," he said. "For a while I badly needed that. Things are better now than they were."

"I'm glad to hear that."

"I still prefer to be here. Alone."

"That's very unlike you. You used to drag me to parties all the time. Parties with music so loud we rarely had to talk to anyone. And if I didn't go, you went by yourself."

"I used to like that sort of thing. I don't now." He pressed another button on his phone and a door to the large garage opened, and he pulled the car inside.

"Very techie," she said.

"It makes my life easier."

"And I'm sure we can come up with even more ways to make it easier on you. Why haven't you seen anyone about this before?"

His body tensed. "I saw doctors."

"I know, but have you ever gone to programmers or anything with a list of your specific issues? I'm almost certain there are some simple…"

"No. I'm not spreading this around for the world to see. I'll not be made to look like a fool. Or stupid," he said, his dark gaze pointed on hers. He looked down at his hands. "Tell me something, Hannah."

"What?"

"Why did I like going to all those parties?"

"What?" she asked.

"Why did I like them? The idea of going to parties…now it seems like it would be loud and…confusing. I can't imagine what it was that made me like them before and sometimes I think if I could just remember…then I could make myself feel it again."

Hannah's stomach tightened. "Eduardo…I…" She took a breath. "You liked to be around people. To have them see you. You always commanded the room and you…thrived on that."

He rested his head on the back of the seat. "I still can't…" He let out a long breath. "I can't feel it now."

He killed the engine and slammed the driver's-side door shut, skipping the chivalry and walking straight into the house alone. She unbuckled and followed him out of the Jeep and into the house.

Yet again, the luxury available to the Vega family floored her. She was no slouch, and she made a darn decent income, but this was beyond the everyday version of luxury.

Sweeping vistas of the sea, intensely green fields and mountains, marble floors and a grand, curving staircase. Light poured in, light everywhere, making it feel like she was still outdoors, bringing the natural beauty into the man-made extravagance.

She pulled her lips tight, doing her very best not to look impressed. "Eduardo...I'm going to get lost in this palace without a guide." She was determined to change the subject. Determined to ignore the pain in her chest. His pain.

He came into the entryway, his expression neutral. So she wasn't the only one trying to play a game, trying to hide her feelings. "I will happily give you the tour." There was a glimmer in his eyes, one she didn't like at all. She had a feeling he was about to do something to make her angry, since that seemed to be the only thing that made him laugh these days.

"What?" she asked, following him up the curving staircase. "And shouldn't I go get my bags?"

"I don't know what you mean, and one of my staff will have your bags delivered to the room later."

"You know what I mean. You look amused, and that never bodes well for me. And *the* room?"

"Yes. The room. Our room."

So that was the cause of the glitter. "Our room? I do hope you're having a malfunction with your English, darling."

"No malfunction, I speak English as well as you do. But we're selling a reconciliation here, and we can hardly sleep across the hall from each other."

She sputtered. "You...you..."

"Relax, *querida,* I'm giving us rooms that connect to each other. I'm not so base as to try and force you to share a bed with me. Still, we will have to be careful that it's not suspected you aren't sleeping with me."

She made a face at him. "You did that just to make me mad."

"I have to confess, it is one of my few joys in life. To watch the color rise in your cheeks." He paused at the top of the stairs and turned to face her, his eyes dark, assessing. Far too assessing. "I love to watch you lose control."

"I did not lose control. You couldn't make me lose control," she said, realizing she sounded childish and very much on the edge of control. Unable to stop it.

He chuckled and turned away from her. "If you say so."

"I do," she muttered, crossing her arms beneath her breasts and trailing behind him, down the expansive half floor, open to the living area below. There were two dark double doors at the end of the hall, and he opened them to an impressive luxury suite.

"I trust you will find this suitable. This is, of course, my room. And that is the door to yours." He indicated a door on the far end of the room. She passed him, her eyes resting longingly on the massive king-size bed piled high with silk pillows, and went to the other door.

She turned the knob and opened it, revealing a smaller, but no less impressive suite.

The bed wasn't as grand, the linen white with pink ribbon edging the bottom of the bedspread, and tied around the throw pillows, making them look like little gifts.

The walls were white, the floors a pale marble, decorated with fuzzy-looking pink carpets.

"It's so pink," she breathed, hating in some ways how perfect it was.

"It's not quite as edgy as you are, I confess."

She turned and saw Eduardo leaning in the door. A giggle bubbled in her throat when she realized that he'd probably imagined she would hate it. But he hadn't seen her very,

very pink wedding cake, or the pink bows she'd selected to go on all of the chairs. He'd never seen her pink dishes in her kitchen, or the pink bed set in her room.

"I happen to love pink," she said, smiling sweetly. "My room when I was a teenager was very…" Dirty. Dark. Depressing. "It wasn't to my taste and I used to dream of decorating my own place as feminine and frilly and bright as I liked. So as soon as I could, I did. It's something I've never grown out of, alas."

One dark brow shot up. "I never would have guessed that about you."

"No, I doubt anyone would. But my life is not an open book."

"I have noticed that."

"Now you know my deep, dark secret. Beneath my ass-kicking facade, I have a thing for ruffles." She liked that she'd caught him off guard. It was a small thing, but she took more than a little pleasure in it.

He shook his head. "Now that is interesting."

"I live to interest."

"I seriously doubt that."

"You're right. I don't care enough about what people think." That wasn't true, either. She wished it was. "What's the thread count on the sheets?"

"I can't remember *The Wizard of Oz*. You think I'll remember that?"

The corner of her mouth tugged up in a reluctant half smile. "Fine, I'll read the tags when you leave."

"I think my mother and Selena will be here soon. If you'd like to dress for dinner."

"Is there something wrong with the way I'm dressed?"

"Do you own anything that's not designed to fit into a boardroom environment?"

"Pink pajamas."

"And now that no longer surprises me, but you can't wear that for dinner, either."

"Yes, I have some other clothes."

"Good. Then I'll have your things sent up." He turned away, then stopped. "Hannah, try to relax. You can think of this as a vacation."

CHAPTER SEVEN

"I DON'T take vacations."

Eduardo turned at the sound of Hannah's voice.

She was at the foot of the stairs, wrapped tightly in a black, knee-length dress, her blond hair loose for once, cascading over her shoulders in an elegant wave. She shifted, her expression tight, painted red lips pulled into a pucker.

"Why does that not surprise me?"

"I hear you don't take them anymore, either."

He shook his head. "I've no inclination to. I often work from here."

"Is it easier? Less distraction?"

He nodded slowly. He'd never really thought of it in those terms. He'd just thought he liked the quiet now, when before he'd thrived in the frenetic pace of the city. He'd enjoyed staying up late and getting up for work the next day. Had liked being surrounded by constant motion and high energy.

He didn't now. He liked solace. Privacy. Order. When there was no order his brain was utter chaos. He'd realized and adjusted for that early on.

"I suppose so. Plus, it's nice to avoid the stares. I'm the accident people can't help but gawk at, after all. Rich playboy, victim of a horrible, unfortunate incident. The public very often enjoy seeing people brought down."

"I don't see you as being brought down. Things are just different, that's all."

Her words, spoken from tight lips, with stilted, stubborn confidence, did something to him. To his chest. His heart. It was strange. Hannah wasn't looking at him with pity, far from it. She seemed to disdain him, but she also believed in him. Not out of obligation or caring, but because she simply did.

It was more valuable in some ways than the confidence shown him by his mother and sister. More valuable than he cared to acknowledge.

Are you so weak you need validation from a woman who would happily spit on you?

No. He wasn't. He was Eduardo Vega, and someday, all of him would remember that. And what that meant.

He heard an engine, tires on gravel. "They're here. Time to play loving couple."

"And dodge verbal barbs," Hannah grumbled, moving to stand next to him. She kept a thin line of space between their bodies. She didn't want to touch him, and that bothered him.

Because she needed to, needed to be comfortable with him if they were to look like a reconciling couple.

He slid his arm around her waist and she stiffened for a moment before relaxing beneath his touch. "They still think our marriage was real, and they need to think it's real now. Remember, we are deliriously happy to be back together."

"We should write that down," she whispered. "It keeps slipping my mind."

"We can't both start forgetting things, Hannah. We'll be in serious trouble if neither one of us can remember what's going on."

He felt her frame jolt with shocked laughter.

"That's better," he said.

Hannah steeled herself for the invasion of Eduardo's family. It wasn't going to be easy, and why should it be? She'd lied to them. So had Eduardo. They both deserved a little contempt. Of course, she was the only one who would get any.

The door opened and Carmela walked in, followed by

Selena. Both women were dressed in a flamboyant yet so-phisticated manner, complete with gloves that extended to their elbows and hats with wide brims.

"*Hola,* Eduardo," Selena said, striding forward. Eduardo released Hannah and leaned forward, embracing his sister.

When they parted, Selena eyed Hannah as if unsure of how to receive her or what to say. Hannah very much felt the same unease.

Carmela hung back.

"Hello," Hannah said, calling on all of her nerve, wondering why it was hard. Why she cared. Normally, she could turn off fear, and embrace control. Could put on an easy, charming persona that made everyone feel at ease. Just like she could turn into a pit bull in business negotiations. She swallowed. "It's good to see you again. I'm…pleased to be back. Pleased to be here with Eduardo and…both of you."

Carmela nodded stiffly. "If he is happy to have you, then so are we. No more must be said on the subject. There will be no anger. Come, I am hungry." She led the way into the dining area and Selena followed. Eduardo held back, and Hannah followed his lead.

"If she says she's not going to be angry, she won't be. You can unclench."

Hannah let out a breath. "I'm sorry, I feel like a jerk. I can't believe you're making me do this to your family. Again. How do you look in the mirror?"

For a moment, Eduardo's expression was unguarded, his dark eyes stripped of their shields. It was an expression of cold, deep fear. It was one she could relate to. The kind of fear that lived deep in her, waiting to wrap its icy hands around her throat at the first opportunity. The kind she ran from every day.

"It helps that I hardly recognize the man looking back at me," he said, his voice rough. "I am doing what I must. I cannot fail."

And she knew then, that this wasn't about the media, but

about him. About proving he was still who he used to be, even though it was so clear he wasn't. The question he'd asked her in the car swam through her mind, made her stomach twist. His desire to understand who he'd been, to try and take himself back there.

To make himself something else.

But it echoed in her. She knew it. Understood it. Lived it every day. The need to be more than who she was. Although, while she was terrified she'd someday morph back into who she'd been, he was afraid he would never be the same.

"I will make sure you don't," she said, the vow coming from deep inside of her, from a core of emotion she hadn't realized she still possessed.

He nodded once, wrapped his arm around her waist and guided her into the dining room.

Hannah sank slowly into the warm water of the in-ground hot tub, her knotted muscles protesting the attempt at forced release.

She was stressed. Stressed was a normal state for her so she was rarely aware of it, but she darn well was now. Dinner with Eduardo's family had been difficult. Going to their room, knowing there would be much speculation had been even worse. Which was why, at eleven o'clock, she'd given up any hope of sleeping, even in her princess bed, and had dug in her bags until she'd produced her black, one-piece swimsuit.

She did need a vacation. But not here. Not with Eduardo. Not for the first time, she wondered about Zack. It was weird how much she didn't miss him. She was starting to be thankful, really thankful, they hadn't gotten married.

Still, she felt bad. She draped her arm over the edge of the hot tub and grabbed her phone, which was close by, as always. She fired off a quick message to him before she could think better of it.

It only took a few minutes for a message to ping back.

Fine. I'm with Clara.

Clara was Zack's best friend and business partner. Hannah had been, on a couple of occasions, slightly jealous of the other woman. She'd had a piece of Zack Hannah had never been able to tap into. A piece of him she hadn't wanted to try and tap into, truth be told. Well, he'd taken Clara on their honeymoon, which was proof of how special she was to him.

Maybe...maybe it had turned into something more? She wasn't usually a squishy romantic, but it really helped to think of Zack finding someone else. Someone better.

Are you having a good time?

It was inane and stupid to ask, but she did care.
His reply came a moment later.

Better than I imagined.

She found herself smiling.

I hope you're happy. Happier than you would have been with me.

She hesitated before hitting Send, then took a breath and pressed it.
A reply pinged back.

You be happy, too.

She laughed.

Okay.

She hit Send one last time and put the phone down. Happy. What was that anyway? She'd always thought of it as something she'd reach the farther away she got from Arkansas. The further away she got from the moment the nurses had whisked her baby from the room and handed him to another woman. That the more she made, the more status she gained, the closer it would bring her there. None of it ever seemed to be enough, though. She never seemed closer to happy.

"Do you ever sleep?"

Hannah turned to see Eduardo standing there, dressed in black swim shorts, his chest bare. She almost swallowed her tongue. He was the single most beautiful man she'd ever seen. Well-defined pecs, covered with a fine dusting of dark hair. His abs…she had the completely unbidden thought that it would be heaven to run her fingers over the ripple of muscle. Not just her fingers. Maybe her tongue, too.

Gah! Where had that come from?

"I don't sleep much," she said. Her thighs trembled a little bit when he took a step toward her and she realized, stupidly late, that he was probably planning on getting into the hot tub with her.

"Neither do I." He rounded the hot tub and descended the steps, the water covering his muscular thighs, lean hips, up to his belly button. Not that she was watching with rapt attention. No.

She edged away, trying to put some distance between them, trying to do it subtly. "Yeah, well, I'm always on red alert. Thinking about all the things I have to do at work, stuff like that."

"About your ex-fiancé?"

"Uh, funny you should mention him. I just texted him. He took another woman on our honeymoon so hopefully he's doing all right."

"That doesn't bother you?"

"I actually know her. She's a friend of his, so it could be platonic. But if not…well, I sort of hope it's not. I want him to be happy."

"And the idea of your ex-lover with another woman doesn't...doesn't make you angry?"

Hannah cleared her throat. "Zack was never my lover."

To his credit, Eduardo's face remained unreadable. "I find that hard to believe."

"Yeah, I figured you would. That was why I never corrected you before. Frankly, I don't really care what you think of it, but it is true."

"Why is that?"

"Why weren't we lovers?"

"Yes."

"We weren't in love. I didn't want him to use me. So I figured if we waited on that until after the wedding...no danger." It wasn't entirely true, but she was hardly giving him the whole truth about her sex life. It wasn't his business anyway.

"I don't believe that, Hannah. You don't seem like the sort of woman who could be used. You're far too hard and savvy for that."

She shrugged, her shoulders rising from the warm water, the night air biting them. "All right then, why do you suppose I didn't sleep with him?"

"You like control too much. So making him wait gave you control."

She rolled her eyes and leaned her head back. "You make it sound like I was leading him around by the—" She popped her head back up and met Eduardo's mocking gaze. "I wasn't. That wasn't why. But yeah, maybe control a little bit. Just not like you mean it."

"I understand control, Hannah, wanting it, going to great lengths to keep it. You hardly have to justify yourself to me."

"I feel like I do when you look at me like that. It's your superpower. I never justify myself to anyone. But with you, I do, a little bit."

"Too bad it's a superpower that's of no use to me."

"Thanks," she said, smiling at him. A big fake smile.

He sighed and sat down, draping his arms over the back of the hot tub. She was across the tub from him and she still felt hotter. Felt like she was way too close to him.

"So," she said. "Did your mom say terrible things about me in those few minutes you hung back in the dining room with her?"

"No. She said she wants me to be happy. Just like she said in front of you."

Hannah sighed. "She's a better person than I am. I would hate me."

"If someone did that to your son?"

Hannah's heart dropped into her stomach. "I...I'll never know. I don't have a son. I don't want children." It sounded slightly panicked, and not the least bit cool. But she didn't want to think about it. Didn't want to get anywhere near the topic.

"So you've said."

"Yes, well, I'm saying again." And now she sounded defensive.

"Who hurt you, Hannah?" he asked, pushing off from the wall and walking to the middle of the tub. His chest gleamed in the light from the house, bronzed and muscular. He looked like the angel of death, trying to confront her with the thing she feared most.

"I already told you. My parents sucked."

"But that's not it, I think."

He drew closer, knelt down in front of her, his eyes level with hers. "What happened?"

She couldn't stand it. The concern on his face, in his tone. Couldn't deal with the slow ache it caused in her heart. "Why the hell do you care? You won't remember it twenty minutes after I tell you."

His hand shot out, gripping the back of the hot tub; his eyes blazed with heat. Anger, certainly, and something else. The anger she could handle; it was the else that scared her.

He lifted his other hand, cupped her chin. "Why do you do that?"

"Do what?" she asked, jerking her face away.

"Why do you lash out? Is it when I get too close?"

"What? What does that mean?"

"You can be so pleasant, I've seen it. And then you can put all your shields up and go on attack. I think it's when I start to get close to the truth. And it scares you."

Yes, it scared her to her soul. She wanted to deny it, and she couldn't, because she was trembling inside. But being angry was so much easier than being afraid. And pushing someone away was so much easier when she was being mean.

She pressed her back against the wall, trying to put some more distance between them. "Maybe I'm just not a nice person. Did you ever consider that?"

"I don't think that's the case. I've been accused of being a terrible, boring bastard the past few years. But I don't think that's your problem."

"Maybe you just aren't very good at reading people."

He shook his head. "An interesting gift, or rather, strange side effect, of my injury. I do not surround myself with so much noise, so it seems I have more time, more of an ability to look closely at the people who are around me. You aren't mean, Hannah. You're afraid. The question is, what are you afraid of?"

Her heart was pounding, her body hyperaware of his nearness. She took a breath and pushed off from the wall, standing so that he was slightly beneath her. She put her hand on the back of his neck.

"I'm not afraid of anything," she said, lying. Boldly. Her hands were shaking, her body was shaking. But she couldn't let him win. Couldn't let him see any weakness. Couldn't let him see her.

He took his hand off the wall and put it on the small of

her back, his fingers rough, hot against her skin. Steam rose
between them and stirred when she breathed out.

"Is that so?" he asked.

In response she dipped her head, brushing his lips with
hers. A hard zip of attraction punched her, deep in her core.
He wrapped his other arm around her, his hand splayed between her shoulder blades. She wrapped her arms around his
neck and leaned down, deepening the kiss as much as she
could in her position.

Her brain was screaming that she was making a mistake.
Walking into danger.

Her body was complaining that she wasn't walking fast
enough.

She'd been out to prove a point, but everything, the previous conversation, the reason behind her action, was shrouded
in the mist that curled between them, that seemed to have
wrapped itself around her mind, shielding her in a blessed
haze where all that mattered was the feel of his hard body
against hers, the feel of his mouth covering hers.

He lowered his hand slowly, cupping the curve of her butt,
down to her thigh, tugging gently. She followed his lead, lowering herself so she was straddling his legs, the hard ridge
of his arousal apparent, thick and tempting between them.

He pulled her hard against him and she let her head fall
back as he kissed her neck, her collarbone. His mouth so hot
on her wet skin, warming her where the night air had left
her cold.

"Oh, yes," she said, rocking against him, seeking out the
pleasure she knew he could provide. Pleasure she knew would
far surpass any sexual experience she'd had before.

She tightened her hold on him, claimed his mouth again,
her tongue delving deep, his returning the favor, exploring,
creating a delicious friction that made her internal muscles
tighten.

She could lose herself in him. In this. Close out everything and embrace the passion. The moment. The need to have him deep inside of her, thrusting hard and deep, mirroring the action of his tongue.

She wanted to surrender. To her feelings. Her body's needs. To him.

She wanted to give him her control.

Panic hit her, hard in the breast and she pushed at his chest, trying to free herself from his embrace. He slowly released his hold on her, his expression confused, hazy. She stumbled back, splashing water up around them, and climbed up the side of the hot tub, not bothering to get around him by using the stairs.

"No, this isn't happening," she said, panic clawing at her. Mocking her. Reminding her that she wasn't brave, that she wasn't different. That if she let go, all of the trappings, everything she'd built for herself, would fall away and reveal who she really was. The stupid girl, needy girl. Ready to give it all up so someone would just pay attention to her for a minute. For a few hours. So that she could have someone look at her like she mattered. Forget what she wanted. Forget self-esteem, self-respect. Control.

"I think it is. It has," he said. "It seems to keep happening."

She shook her head. "No. I'm not sleeping with you."

"Oh, so what was that then? Another effort on your part to keep a man controlled? To lead him around by his balls?"

"If you didn't think with them, it wouldn't work so well," she shot back, dying inside. She felt like her defenses were crumbling, like all of her armor was melting from the heat of Eduardo's touch. And she couldn't allow that.

"Perhaps I was wrong, Hannah. Perhaps I was looking for more where more did not exist."

"I told you." She turned and grabbed a towel from one of the lounge chairs, wrapping it around her body. A physical barrier in the absence of a much-needed emotional one.

"You did. Understand this, though—unlike your ex, I will not be a part of your games. You will not play with me."

"You just let me." She turned on her heel and walked out of the courtyard, leaving a trail of wet footprints behind her.

She climbed up the stairs, towel clutched tightly to her chest. She opened the door to her room and closed it firmly behind her, leaning against it. Then she put her hand over her mouth and muffled a sob.

She slid down to her knees, her body shaking as she gave in to tears for the first time in more years than she could count.

Eduardo knocked on the door that connected his room to Hannah's. He had a feeling he would regret checking on her. He shouldn't care what she was feeling. She'd played him. She'd tried to use her body to control him; she'd insulted him.

And yet, he found he still didn't believe it was her. Still didn't believe she was being genuine. She had been afraid. Not just when he'd asked her about her past, she'd been afraid when they'd kissed. Of the passion that had flared up between them.

He felt wild. He didn't feel like himself, whoever the hell that was. And looking at Hannah, touching Hannah, didn't take him back. It took him somewhere else entirely. He had no idea what to do with that.

He knew what he wanted. And for now, wanting something, needing, that was enough.

She didn't answer. He let out a growl and opened the door without waiting for a response.

He saw her, sitting against the wall, her knees drawn up to her chest, her head down. She looked like a broken doll.

"Hannah?" he asked, a pang hitting him hard in the chest.

She raised her head, and he saw tears shining on her cheeks, illuminated by the moonlight. She wiped her cheek with her arm. "Go away."

He took a step toward her. He didn't know what it was that

compelled him when it came to this woman. He didn't know why she felt so imbedded in him, and yet, she did. A part of him he couldn't escape, a part he couldn't forget.

He hadn't wanted to pursue anyone since his accident. He'd had no focused sexual desire.

But Hannah, tough as nails Hannah, who liked pink, who was sitting on the floor now, wet, still in her bathing suit, all her armor stripped, looking like she would shatter if he touched her, she drew him.

She had fascinated him back when they'd first met. A scrappy, low-class, determined girl who had clawed her way up from nothing, just to get an education. To try and change her life. But the fascination had changed. It was different now. Deeper. As though she'd burrowed beneath his skin.

"Are you all right?" he asked.

She pushed up from the floor and stood. He expected her to yell at him. To insult him. Because he'd caught her feeling vulnerable, and that was what she did when he spotted a crack in her armor.

Instead she just straightened, blond hair flicking over her shoulders like a silvery wave, her chin tilted upward. She was like a proud queen, one who would never acknowledge what he'd just witnessed. She would pretend to be above it, above him, if she had to, in order to protect herself. To keep herself securely locked in her ivory tower.

"Of course."

She would never take sympathy from him, and he didn't like seeing her broken. "You owe me an apology, Hannah," he said, changing tactics, hardening his tone.

She tipped her chin up. "For?"

A smile curved his lips, heat pooling in his gut as he stepped toward her. "You insulted me. Good manners dictate you tell me you're sorry."

"But I'm not."

It was a bad idea to push her. It had been a bad idea to

come to her room in the first place. "Perhaps I can change your mind."

She took a step toward him. "I doubt it."

"I don't."

Hannah sucked in a deep breath, tried to erect a barrier between herself and the dark sensuality radiating from Eduardo.

She hated how she shook when she was near him. How much her body ached for his. She hadn't had sex in nine years. Pathetic, but true. All because of fear. All because she was afraid that if she ever let herself lose control, she would find out that she had never changed. It was why she lashed out at him, it was why she ran from him.

She hated fear. Hated how much of it lived inside of her. She'd bought into her own lie of strength. Had done for years. She'd found someone who hadn't challenged her, who hadn't tapped into any sort of deep sexuality, who hadn't worked at uncovering her secrets, and she'd been able to pretend. Pretend that nothing had ever happened to her, that she had never been Hannah Mae Hackett. High school dropout, pregnant teenager, fraud.

With Eduardo, she couldn't pretend.

With Eduardo she couldn't hide the fear, not from him, not from herself. He stripped her with one look. And his touch…

It had to stop. She wouldn't be afraid. She could still have control, even in this. She had to.

She took another step toward him and put her hand on his face. He reached up, wrapped his fingers around her wrist. "Do not test me, Hannah, not again. I am not playing games. If you kiss me, you had better intend to follow through."

"Or what?"

He chuckled. "I would never hurt you. Would never force myself on you. But I will never allow you to touch me again, either. I do not play. If you turn back now, nothing will happen between us."

"I don't intend to turn back," she said.

"Then why did you earlier?"

"Because this is a very, very bad idea. I thought I would turn back while I still could." Now if she turned back she would be doing it because of fear, and she would know that was why. But if she kissed him… She could do it now. While she had him off guard. While she was in command.

He turned her hand and pressed a kiss to the underside of her wrist, his dark eyes never leaving hers.

"Why don't you kiss me?" she asked.

"Why don't you apologize?"

A laugh escaped, nervous. Strange sounding. "I might feel more sorry if you just give me what I ask for."

He hesitated for a moment, dark eyes glittering. Then he dipped his head, his mouth claiming her quickly, fiercely. She didn't want anything intruding, no thoughts, no emotions; she only wanted what he made her feel. The intense ache that he brought to her core, the desire to have him, over her, in her.

She ran her hands down his bare chest, relishing the feel of his muscles beneath her palms. She'd never touched a man who looked like him, had never been with a real man, truly. Fumbling teenage boys who didn't know what foreplay meant hardly counted as comprehensive sexual experiences.

They hadn't been the complete sensual playground that Eduardo was. He was so masculine, so perfectly formed.

She felt her breath getting short, choppy, and she slowed it, taking a few steadying breaths to help reset the rhythm. To keep herself from losing her mind.

She had the control here. He wanted her; she could see the hunger in his lean face. She held the power.

He moved his hands up her waist, kissing her deeply, thoroughly, his thumbs skimming the undersides of her breasts. She moaned into his mouth and an answering sound of pleasure reverberated in his chest.

He slid his hands higher, cupping her, teasing her nipples. A shot of pure, liquid heat poured into her core. She put her hands on his butt and drew him tighter against her, his erection pressing hard against her hip.

He gripped one of the straps on her swimsuit and tugged it down, dropping a kiss onto her shoulder, peeling the Lycra away from her skin, exposing her breast. "Oh, yes. So beautiful," he said, his voice rough, pained.

He lowered his head, his tongue caressing her nipple, circling it before he sucked it deeply into his mouth. She raised one hand quickly, fisting his hair, holding him to her. He lowered her other strap, baring her other breast. He moved his attention there, lavishing it with the same, very thorough attentions.

She closed her eyes, the sheer intensity of the desire rocketing through her making it impossible to move. Impossible to breathe. Impossible to do anything but stand there and just let him have his way with her body.

When he gripped her swimsuit and pulled it down the rest of the way, a flash of panic hit her. But it was dark. He wouldn't be able to see. Wouldn't notice the silvery lines that trailed over her stomach.

Even if he did, it didn't mean he would know what they were.

He sucked harder on her breast while he teased the other one with his thumb and that last conscious thought fled.

He raised his head and kissed her mouth again, his hair-roughened chest providing the stimulation now.

"Yes, yes," she repeated, over and over, mindlessly as he backed her to the bed and lowered her onto the soft surface.

Dimly, she remembered that she was supposed to take control, that this was about proving that she wasn't afraid, that she could master her need for him, and hold him in the palm of her hand.

The only part that registered was the last one.

She reached down between them and touched at the apex

of his thighs with her hand, moving her palm over the hard ridge of his shaft.

A little tremor of fear shot through her. Fear of pain. It had been a long time. And it had never been with a man like him.

"I… Do you have condoms?" she asked, a trickle of panic hitting her. She shook it off. She wasn't going to let fear have anything in her anymore. Wouldn't let it have anything in this.

He swore. "Just a moment."

He rose from the bed and walked out of the room. She scooted to the center of the mattress, reclining against the pillows. Some of the arousal fog cleared without him there, touching her and kissing her.

It was too late to turn back now. If she did, it would be because of fear, and she wasn't going to let fear have a foothold anymore.

But she was taking the control back. She wasn't letting him turn her into a mindless pleasure zombie. That was her job.

He returned a few moments later, a box in hand. "It was in the bathroom. What conscientious staff I have."

"You didn't know if they were in there?"

"I have not needed them." He set the box down on the nightstand and tore it open, taking out a condom packet. And then she forgot to ask him why he hadn't needed them.

He handed the condom to her and she got up onto her knees, scooting to the edge of the bed. She swallowed hard and hooked her fingers in the waistband of his swim trunks, the damp fabric clinging to his body and she dragged it downward.

When she'd gotten the shorts off, she took him into her hand, reveling in the hot, silky skin, the hardness of him. She squeezed him lightly and he groaned, the sound deep and satisfying.

"You are certainly no ordinary man," she said. He let his head fall back, a raw groan coming from deep inside of him.

"That's right, Eduardo," she whispered. "Let me." A straight shot of power coursed through her, making her feel fearless.

She lowered her head and flicked the tip of her tongue over his shaft, her stomach tightening with desire as his hand came up to her head, his fingers tangling in her hair. She explored him with her tongue and he tightened his hold on her, halting her movements.

"I can't," he rasped. "I'm too close."

She lifted her head, satisfied that she was in his power. That she was going to do this her way.

She tore open the packet and rolled the condom onto him, then straightened and wrapped her arms around his neck, kissing him, drawing him down onto her.

"Not yet," he said, lowering his head again, kissing her breasts, her ribs, her stomach. Her breath caught when he lingered at the tender skin beneath her belly button. Then he parted her thighs gently, his tongue hot and unexpected against her core.

She arched off the bed, scrambling for something to hold on to, finding his shoulders and clinging tight. "Eduardo…"

His breath was hot on her sensitive skin, his lips hovering just above her. "Now tell me you're sorry, Hannah." Another light touch of his tongue sent a flash of brief pleasure through her.

She put one hand over her face, her cheeks burning, her body begging for release.

"Tell me, Hannah." He kissed her inner thigh and her body shook.

"No."

The tip of his tongue blazed a trail from where he'd kissed her, straight to her clitoris. Just a tease. Nothing more. "Do you want to come or not?"

"You…bastard," she panted.

He chuckled. "That doesn't sound like an apology."

"It wasn't."

He moved his hand between her thighs, his thumb sliding over her slick flesh. She gripped both his shoulders, hard, her teeth locked together. Her hips moved in rhythm with his touch. His fleeting, too-light touch.

"Touch me, dammit," she said.

"Not until you tell me you're sorry."

Her muscles were shaking, her body begging her tongue to simply say the words. She needed release. She needed him. To hell with control. "I'm sorry."

He gave her a wicked grin, then lowered his head, his tongue working magic on her as he slid one finger inside her tight body.

"Oh, yes," she breathed. It had been worth it. No amount of pride was valuable enough to hold on to, and miss this.

He lavished attention on her, fully, completely, with his mouth and hands. Something started tightening inside of her. Tension she was afraid might break her.

A second finger joined the first and the tension in her broke, shattering through her like a million glittering stars. There was no thought; there was nothing but the blinding intensity of her release.

When she returned to earth, he was there, poised above her, dark eyes intent on hers. He pushed her hair off her damp forehead, his hand shaking. Evidence that he didn't have the control he'd appeared to have. "Now," he said.

He put his hand on her thigh and lifted it so her leg hooked over his hip. The thick head of his erection pressed against her body and she arched into him. He slid in easily, filling her, stretching her in the best way.

She gripped his shoulders, her nails digging into his skin. He began to move, his thrusts hard, controlled and perfect. She moved against him, met his every move. Each time their bodies connected a sharp, white-hot sensation of pleasure struck her. She didn't think it was possible to be so turned on so quickly again.

But she was. She was craving release, needing more of the heady rush he'd always given her.

His breath was hot on her neck, quick and harsh. She turned her head and kissed his cheek, and he turned, catching her mouth, a shudder rolling through his body as she slid her tongue against his.

"*Dios,* yes," he ground out.

The controlled nature of his thrusts frayed; his movements turning choppy, desperate, keeping time with the manic need that was rolling through her, demanding release again.

He thrust into her one last time, his muscles going stiff, his entire body freezing as he found his release on a feral groan. She flexed against him and her own orgasm washed over her, waves of pleasure coursing through her as her body tightened around his. He was so deep in her, so connected with her, and in that moment, it was all that mattered.

He collapsed onto his forearms, his breathing harsh, his muscles trembling. Then he separated from her body and gathered her close to him, her backside curving into his body, his hand resting on her stomach.

They didn't speak for a long moment; the only sounds in the room were their broken, uneven breaths. He curled a lock of her hair around his finger, the touch comforting, almost as intimate as sex in a strange way.

Her brain felt foggy. Events from only moments ago running together, reduced to points of aching need and sweeping, powerful release. Sometime soon, she might feel humiliation at the fact that she'd given him so much, so quickly.

But not now.

"I didn't forget how to do it," he said finally, still out of breath.

She laughed. "What does that mean?"

"You are the first woman I've been with since my accident. I suppose I've been true to our marriage vows all this time," he said, a strange note in his voice.

It was her instinct to try and ruin the moment. To break the spell of closeness that seemed woven around them. But she couldn't. She didn't want to. She just wanted a moment. Then tomorrow, she could go back to holding him at a distance. Things could go back to the way they'd been. Mystery solved. Sexual tension broken.

But now, just now, she wouldn't ruin it.

"So have I," she said softly.

"You have what?" he asked.

"Been true to our marriage vows. I haven't…I haven't been with anyone since our wedding."

"And you didn't even know we were still married," he said.

"No. But I imagine both of us had reasons other than that for staying out of physical relationships." A stupid thing to say, because she didn't want to get into her reasons.

"There's never been time." He paused. "Or desire. I haven't truly wanted anyone since it happened. I've been too busy licking my wounds."

"And tonight you licked me," she said, injecting some completely inappropriate levity, trying to draw the topic away from where it was.

He laughed and rolled her beneath him, kissing her lips. "I have to go take care of things."

He got out of bed and she watched him walk to the bathroom. Watched the masculine, perfect shape of his backside. He was gorgeous, no question.

He returned a moment later, his expression stormy. "We have a problem."

CHAPTER EIGHT

"WHAT?" Hannah tugged the covers up over her breasts and even with the current issue hammering away in his head, he felt a pang of regret.

"The condom broke." Something that had never happened to him before. He knew it was possible, but what the hell was the point of them if they were so fragile? "Are you on birth control?"

She hesitated. "No?"

"What's that supposed to mean? Why did you say it like you don't know?"

"I...I do know. I'm not. I mean...I didn't need to be. I mean...but things happen. These things do. The odds are so low. And I mean, a little leak will hardly..."

"Release millions of sperm?"

She cringed. "Well, okay, when you put it that way. But..."

"But it's enough to cause an accident."

Her expression turned dark. "I know how all that works, but thank you for educating me."

"I'm being realistic. We may have a situation."

"We won't," she bit out. "No one is that unlucky."

Anger boiled in his stomach. Of course it would be unlucky to be pregnant; it would be unlucky for both of them. But it struck a blow to his pride. All he could think was that she wouldn't want to be shackled to a *stupid* man for the rest of her life.

"Well," he said, his tone soft, deadly, "if you are so unlucky as to be carrying my child, be sure to let me know."

"I'll deliver the message by rock through your office window," she spat.

"Appreciated." He turned toward his room, his broad back filling the door. She'd pushed him away again. But she had to. She really had to.

It was the only way she could protect herself.

"Don't think you're going to force an apology out of me this time," she said.

He froze, his shoulders rising slightly before he turned, his eyebrows drawn together. "Don't play like I forced you, Hannah, when we both know you were begging."

She curled her fingers around the bedding. "Go away, Eduardo."

"Running again?" She opened her mouth and he cut her off. "Oh, yes, Hannah, you're running, even if you are staying in your bed. You have to do it by making a bitchy comment or whatever you think it will take to push me, or anyone else in your life, away. You don't fool me. You aren't hiding your fear from me. I will leave, only because I have no desire to spend another moment in your company tonight. But understand, you're not pushing me away if I don't want to be pushed."

He turned and walked out, shutting the door firmly behind him.

Hannah sat in the middle of the big bed, naked, physically and emotionally. She picked up one of the silken pink pillows and threw it in the direction of the closed door. It was safer to be angry than to cry again. She wasn't going to cry. She wasn't going to think about the torn condom. What that might mean.

She wasn't going to think about how it had felt to have him inside of her. Connected with her.

She really wasn't going to think about how it had been

the first time she'd felt close to someone in her entire life. And she wasn't going to think about how much she wanted to do it again.

When Hannah appeared at breakfast she didn't look much like a corporate barracuda who spat venom at unwitting victims with little warning. She looked nervous. Her blond hair was tousled and there were dark circles under her eyes. Her skinny-cut black pants and fitted, black short-sleeved shirt enhanced the thinness of her frame, and the paleness of her skin.

Eduardo leaned back in his chair and raised his coffee mug to his lips. His mother and sisters both nodded in greeting.

"Morning," Hannah said, not making eye contact with him as she took her seat at the table.

"Good morning," he said, setting his mug down on the table, taking no satisfaction in the shudder of her shoulders when his mug clattered against the glass tabletop. "Did you sleep well?"

She forced a smile. "Not really. You hogged the covers all night."

"My apologies, *querida*."

"None needed. Some coffee might be nice, though."

His mother reached out and rang a bell that sat at the center of the table. Eduardo cringed. He hated that thing. He was far too modern-minded to ring for his servants. But Carmela Vega insisted. She was old money and old class. Although, perhaps that had little to do with it, because he could easily imagine Hannah ringing for servants.

"Thank you," Hannah said to his mother.

"De nada."

Rafael came in and Hannah ordered her coffee to her specifications. She really did look exhausted. Pity he hadn't been able to keep her up all night in the way he'd like to have kept her up all night. But the fact that he'd irritated the sleep out of her was a close second as far as his personal satisfaction went.

"What are your plans for the day, Mama?" he asked.

"I thought Selena and I might go down to the shops."

Only his mother would leave Barcelona and shop in a small, seaside town. "That sounds like fun."

Selena turned her attention to Hannah. "You can join us, if you like, Hannah."

Hannah looked like a large-eyed woodland creature caught in the pull of headlights. "I...I..."

"Hannah and I have work today." He didn't want to let her out of his sight for the day. She might run. "She's helping me implement some new systems at Vega. Hannah is something of a financial genius."

"Is that right?" Carmela asked, eyebrows raised.

"I've been busy the past five years," Hannah said, her tone soft. She was so subdued. It was very unlike her and he found he didn't care for it.

"Yes, well, that is commendable," his mother said. "We'll leave you two."

"*Adiós,* Eduardo. Bye, Hannah," Selena said, standing with her mother and exiting the room.

"Your mother hates me," Hannah said when the women disappeared.

He shrugged. "Maybe."

Rafael returned with a fresh cup of coffee and a half-filled French press. *"Gracias,"* Hannah said, taking a sip of her already-prepared coffee. Rafael left again and Hannah set her mug down. "I would rather if she didn't hate me, but I suppose it doesn't do any good for her to like me since I'm leaving again...whenever. As soon as we get these systems in place and you feel comfortable."

"I suppose not." He found his body rebelled at the idea of her leaving. He felt possessive of her now. Stupid because before his accident he'd slept with any number of women and he'd never felt possessive of them. Quite the opposite, he'd felt ready to bolt out of bed, call them a cab and see they were safely delivered home so that he could sleep. Alone.

He frowned. The memories pricked his conscience and he realized that he didn't like the way he'd treated women then. He wondered if that had to do with the accident, with the changes in him, or just being older.

Interesting, since he normally envied the man he'd once been to a certain extent. But not in that area. He'd been a playboy, happily seeking release with any willing woman. Now the emptiness of that echoed in him.

With Hannah it had been more. More than release. More than amusement. It had been something serious, something that made him feel different in the bright light of day. He was angry with her, for the way she'd acted after, and still, he felt a connection with her that hadn't been there before.

As if, when he'd parted from her last night, he'd left a piece of himself behind.

"What is the work plan for the day?" she asked, her expression projecting extreme annoyance and boredom at the same time.

"Bring your coffee up to my office."

She stood and waited for him, then followed him out of the room and up the curving staircase, down to the end of the hall. His home office faced the sea, large expansive windows letting in plenty of natural light. And all easily covered with blinds that dropped at the push of a button. Just in case he got hit with a particularly bad migraine.

Fortunately, he felt fine. Which meant the only headache he would have to contend with was Hannah.

"Did you have anything more to show me?" she asked.

"No. I was hoping you would start presenting some solutions."

She shifted her weight to the balls of her feet. She looked like she was ready to sprint away if need be. "Actually, I do have some solutions. Well, thoughts mainly."

"Do you?"

"Yes. You prefer to work here now?"

"It's noisy in the office. I don't care for it."

"Right, which is why you have your floor essentially vacant," she said slowly.

"Yes. I can't handle the noise of all the people talking all the time. Even without people working on the floor, the interruptions, the traffic, it can start to…"

"It wears on you."

An understatement. The lowest moment in his memory was of throwing a mug at the wall in front of his secretary when she'd come in talking and he'd been in the throes of a migraine. It hadn't been aimed at her, and it hadn't come anywhere near her, but the blinding pain and anger…the fact he'd had no control over it in that moment. That he'd frightened her. It lived with him.

She'd quit soon after and he couldn't blame her.

"I find things easier here," he said, looking at his hands.

Hannah frowned. "Did you have trouble working around people before?"

"I just don't like noise," he said.

"What about it?"

He looked out at the sea, frowning. He'd been through some of this with a doctor years ago, and had since given up. He didn't like talking about how nothing had changed. There was no point. "It makes my head hurt."

"Anything else?"

"And I get irritable."

"Yeah, I've noticed," she said dryly. "What else?"

"I can't concentrate," he bit out.

"And numbers, finances, they give you the most trouble."

"I can't…I can't hang on to a thought about it for long enough to make decisions."

"And it's high pressure," she said, pushing.

"Yes."

"I think it might have less to do with you having trouble understanding the financial side of things and more to do with you having a harder time focusing on things that stress you out."

An uncomfortable tightness invaded his stomach. "It does not stress me out. I just… The answers are there in my brain but I can't seem to make a fast decision. I can't find the answer in time. Or at all." And the more he thought about it, the less able he was to reach out and grasp onto a thought firmly. It slipped away from him, hiding deep in the dark corners of his brain that seemed unknowable to him now.

"It does stress you out. Why haven't you talked to a doctor about this? I'm sure…"

"I don't need to talk to a doctor," he said, something exploding inside of him. "Not again. I don't need to go and sit there, and outline the same problems and have some old man look at me with pity in his eyes as he tells me, again, that they may never go away. That I will never be the man I was. That I won't have all the answers, or a witty joke on hand. That I will never be able to take the reins of Vega as I should have been able to, because I will never be able to make snap decisions, or keep meticulous records."

He planted his hands on his desk and leaned in so that his face was a breath from hers. "I can't concentrate long enough to fill out a damn report. How am I supposed to keep track of intricate financial details? Do you know the answer?" He pushed off and straightened, running his hand through his hair. "Do you?" he asked again, his voice sounding rougher this time, desperate. He loathed it. Despised himself in that moment. He was shaking. With anger. Fear.

"I…I just don't know," she said softly. "But we can figure it out."

He swallowed hard, his chest seizing up tight. "Or maybe I should just concede to the fact that I can't."

She stood and slapped her palms down on his desk before

rounding to the front, her blue eyes blazing. "No. That's... that's just wrong, Eduardo. You can do this. You aren't stupid. What I said...that was wrong, too. And I'll apologize for that willingly, with no...coercion." Her face turned pink when she said that last part. "It's just a matter of figuring out loopholes. Shortcuts."

Anger burned in him. At her. At the world. "I shouldn't need them," he growled.

"But we all do sometimes," she said, her tone rising with his.

"Maybe you do, Hannah Weston, but I don't. I am Eduardo Vega, son of one of the greatest business minds that ever lived, and I sure as hell should not need a shortcut."

"Then it's your pride keeping you from succeeding. Not your injury. Keep that in mind if you start losing a handle on things again. I can't help you if you won't accept help."

"I am accepting help," he shouted, well beyond his limits now. Beyond the point of sublimating his rage. "Why do you think I asked you here?"

Hannah came closer, not cowed by his outburst. "You didn't ask me here. You all but forced me and you know it. And you aren't accepting help. Did you think I would come in, take a look at things, make some investments and leave you?"

"Yes," he said, realizing as he spoke the word that it was true.

"Just leave you without solving the problem?"

"Yes," he said again. Because he hadn't wanted to admit there was a real problem. A reset. He'd been after a reset. To get everything back to a golden point so he could move forward, steering the ship, on course again.

That he would see Hannah, and remember who he was. Not just remember, but feel those same feelings. That amusement, that desire and ability to simply flip his middle finger at the world, enjoying his position of success, feeling invincible. Untouchable.

Far from that, he felt like he was drowning, reaching blindly for a hand. Hannah's hand. Praying she would be able to hold him above water.

Such weakness. Such horrifying, unendurable weakness.

"That can't happen, Eduardo," she said.

"Why not?" he asked, drained now, the anger, the fight, leaving him in a rush. Leaving him defeated.

He looked so bleak. Hannah had never seen that expression on his face before. Had never seen him look so tired. And in spite of the fact that she'd been determined to hang on to anger where he was concerned, she found in that moment she couldn't.

It had been easy to fight him, to rage at him while he was raging at her. But she saw beneath it now. Saw it for what it was.

"Because things have changed. You've changed." She wasn't telling him anything he didn't know. But she wondered if she was the first person, other than doctors, who'd been brave enough to tell the almighty Eduardo Vega the real and absolute truth he didn't want to hear. "And all you can do is work with what you have. Not what you wish you had, not what you once had, but what you have, here and now."

He shook his head. "I don't want to." It didn't sound petulant like it might have, it simply sounded dry. Resigned.

"Eduardo, you were always fun in your way. A bit of an ass, I mean, enough of one that you blackmailed me into marrying you as a way to goad your father. But you were easygoing, outgoing. And you never would have taken the responsibility of running Vega seriously. You used to kill me with your smug smile and your dismissal of your duties. Everything was a game to you. And now…now it's not. Now I believe you have it in you to do it. So yeah, maybe there are some other issues, but you can work around those. We can work around those."

He let out a slow, shaking breath. "So I am forced to confront the fact that I would never have chosen to live up to my full potential before, and now that I would…now that I would, my potential is greatly diminished."

"That's not it at all." Her stomach tightened, that fierce feeling of empathy, of connection, she'd felt with him that day his mother had arrived at the house intensified. Until that moment she hadn't felt closer to him since they'd slept together. If anything, she'd felt like any connection they might have had had been severed. But now it was back, and it was stronger.

He laughed. "It's not? Enlighten me then, Hannah."

"It will only be that if you insist on beating your head against a brick wall you could walk around if you weren't so stubborn. If you weren't letting your pride have control."

He raised his head, dark eyes glittering. "Pride is the one thing I still have."

She shook her head. "It's not. Trust me."

"It's myself I don't trust," he said, his eyes blank. "I don't know my own mind."

"Then learn it. When you're ready." She walked past him and out the door of the office. She was feeling…too much. Feeling in general. Tomorrow they would go back to Barcelona. She could get back to the business of seeing him as business. She could forget that this weekend ever happened.

She had to.

CHAPTER NINE

EDUARDO drew a hand over his face, fighting the anger, the frustration that was mounting inside of him. Then he gave up, giving it free rein as he pushed every piece of paper off his desk in a broad sweep and watched them all flutter to the floor.

He took a sharp breath, trying to gain a hold on himself. Trying to satisfy the dark, uncontrollable feelings that were firing through his veins. He put his head down and pushed his fingers through his hair, trying, desperately to think of what he'd just read.

Nothing. There was nothing. A void. A blank void that the information had fallen into and no matter how hard he tried, he couldn't get it back.

He let out a growl of frustration and picked his paperweight up from his desk, hurling it at the wall. Not even that helped. Nothing helped.

He pushed back from his desk and put his hands on his head as he paced.

The door to his office opened and Hannah walked in, the corners of her lips turned down. "Are you okay?"

Something in him shifted when he saw Hannah. It had been three weeks since they'd been back from his ranch. Three weeks of living together like strangers. Of pretending they'd never touched each other. That he'd never been inside her.

It was slowly driving him crazy. The financial reports from his retail stores were finishing the job. Quickly.

"Do I look okay?" he asked, moving his hand in a broad stroke in front of him, indicating the papers on the floor.

"No," she said, closing the door behind her. "What's up?"

"I can't do it, Hannah." The words burned his throat. "I can't remember. I can't..."

"Hey, take a breath."

"I did take a breath," he said through clenched teeth. "Then I realized it didn't fix anything so I destroyed my office instead."

"Productive."

In spite of himself, he snorted a laugh. "I thought so. Just as productive as me attempting to comprehend anything in these reports."

"Eduardo..."

He turned away from her, from the pained expression in her eyes and looked out at the city. "Do you have any idea how...frustrating it is, to have such a lack of control. To... I can't make it work. I can't make my mind what it was. I can't make it what I want." A dagger of pain pierced his temple and he winced.

"Maybe you should take a break."

He turned back to her. "I don't have time for a break."

"Then maybe ask for help instead of being so stubborn!"

The anger drained from him, as sudden and as uncontrollable as it had come on. And now he just felt exhausted. Down to his bones. "Help me, Hannah."

Something in her expression softened. If she tried to touch him...if she said she was sorry...he couldn't handle that.

Then, just as suddenly as the softness had appeared, it was replaced by her mask of hard efficiency. A mask he needed her to wear.

"What do you need help with?"

"In general. Help. All the help you can give me. I can't

focus on this." He indicated the papers again. "I can't retain it. I can barely read it. The words just keep…moving. I don't know why. Today it's like everything is moving too fast. I can't…"

She bent and gathered up the papers, glancing at the page numbers and, with a speed that made him vaguely jealous, put them in order.

"Close your eyes." He frowned. "Do it," she said.

He complied and felt a rush of calm go through him. All of the light and busy surroundings shut out, and he felt like he could think a bit better.

She started reading. Out loud. To him. Like he was a child who needed a bedtime story. About the amount of returns over the Christmas shopping season.

He straightened in his chair, his eyes popping open. "I'm not a child."

"I know. I'm not treating you like one. What I'm curious to know is how it is for you to listen to things rather than read them. Some people are auditory learners rather than visual."

"I never had a problem with visual…"

"Before. I know. But that was before."

"How do you know so much about this?"

"About learning? I had to teach myself how to learn when I decided I wanted to go to college. So, I researched every studying trick imaginable. Every way I could think of to do well on tests. I had to take an entrance exam, you know? And I only went to two years of high school. I had to study more than anyone else going into those tests, and I wasn't a natural intellectual. But I needed to be. So I learned to be."

"What kinds of things did you do?"

"Well, sometimes I would record my notes, and then play them back in headphones before going to sleep. I would write things out dozens of times. Drink coffee while I was study-ing, and again while I was taking the test. Taste is a really powerful memory trigger it turns out. Anyway, I don't see why we can't try to apply the principles to you."

A strange feeling moved through him. Respect? Yes, respect for Hannah. Intense and strong. And with that, the feelings of attraction he'd been working so hard to repress over the past few weeks.

Every time he'd passed her as she went into her office on his otherwise secluded floor. Every time he passed her in the hall in his home. Every time he closed his eyes at night and thought of her, so near, and yet so unobtainable.

"You are very clever, Hannah. Smart."

"No less for needing to use those tricks?"

"More so, perhaps. You found ways to make it work for you."

"And that's what you'll do, Eduardo." She lifted the stack of papers again. "Now, close your eyes."

This time he let her read and he found he had an easier time grasping meaning. Holding on to details that had passed through his mind before like water through a sieve. And when she quizzed him at the end, he could remember most of what he'd heard. Not all, but much more than he would have remembered had he read through it, and in much less time.

Now, when he spoke to his managers he wouldn't sound completely ignorant. Would sound more like a man who was equipped to hold his position.

"Better," he said, rising from his chair and rounding the desk.

"Yes," she agreed, a smile on her beautiful face. Was she happy for him? Or was it her own success that had her beaming from ear to ear in such an uncharacteristic way? "Now this is an easy one. You just need phone calls. They can fax you the reports so you can have them on file, but you can get a verbal briefing on the phone."

"You are truly a genius, Hannah," he said. And impulsively, he leaned forward and kissed her on the cheek. "Thank you."

She put her hand up to her cheek, her eyes round. "You're welcome."

He realized it was the first time he'd touched her since their night together. Unbidden, images of her hands on his body, his mouth on her breasts, came into his mind. He'd been without sex for five years until recently, largely of his own accord, and now three weeks without seemed a hellish eternity.

"Hannah…"

She backed away. "No. Not… I'm glad that that's helping. I want to keep helping. I'm really close to being able to give you some nice projected stats on how well we could do if we bought out Bach Wireless. But…no."

He hadn't realized that the hunger inside of him had been projected so clearly. And of course she'd said no. Of course she had. She should. Being with her had been like being thrown into a fire. It had been all-consuming, a flame that would ravage and devour everything in its path. He didn't have the kind of time needed to devote to something like that.

He had to focus on Vega. He had to keep things moving forward. They both needed to be fully engaged in business for that. Not fully engaged in bedroom games.

"Back to work then," he said.

She nodded curtly and walked out of the room. He tried to ignore the ache that started in his groin and seemed to spread to his entire body. Hannah was off-limits. If he said it enough times, he might start to believe it.

She was late. She was late, late, late. And her shady, private detour was making her late for work, and not just for her period. She wanted to crawl under the potted plant in the lobby of Vega Communications and cry. But she didn't have time.

She had to go pee on a stick, see one line instead of two and get to work.

Eduardo was already in his office on the top floor. She walked past, trying to keep her steps quick but quiet, trying to keep from disturbing him as she made her way to the private bathroom at the end of the floor. She closed herself in and locked it, unwrapping the box that contained the test with shaking fingers.

The test itself was wrapped in some sort of heinous, indestructible foil. Keys. She did have the keys from home in her purse. She grabbed one and jabbed at the packaging until she worked the slim, innocuous-looking white test free.

Actually taking the test was easy. It was the wait that was hard.

She'd never imagined she'd be back in this position again. Except, instead of huddling in a cramped, filthy bathroom in her childhood home, shaking and on the verge of vomiting, she was huddled in a gorgeous, spotlessly clean bathroom on the highest floor of one of the world's largest and most prestigious companies. Shaking and on the verge of vomiting.

She paced while she waited. And counted. And closed her eyes. And considered throwing up.

"Just one," she whispered. "Just one line." She opened her eyes slowly and looked down at the white test lying on the white counter. All that stark white made it impossible to miss the two glaring pink lines that had bled into the test.

And then she did throw up.

"Hannah?" The door behind her shook as Eduardo knocked on it heavily. "Are you okay? Are you sick?"

"Yes," she called back. She shifted so that she was sitting inelegantly by the toilet, a cold sweat had broken out across her forehead, down her back.

"You're okay or you're sick?"

"I'm sick," she called back.

"Do you need help?"

"No." She pulled into a sitting position and took the test

off the counter, wrapping it four times over in toilet paper
before throwing it into the garbage.

Why was this happening to her? Why was she being pun-
ished for sex? Was she just extremely fertile? Or extremely
unlucky.

Everything started hitting her. The test she'd taken at sixteen. All the options she'd weighed then. Going to the clinic.
Leaving the clinic, on a dead run, unable to go through with
ending the pregnancy. Going to the adoption agency. The first
time she'd felt the baby move. How strange, miraculous and
heartbreaking it had been.

Labor and delivery. That brief flash of pink, wrinkled
skin. Her baby squalling as he was taken from the room and
to his parents.

He wasn't her baby. He belonged to Steve and Carol
Johnson. He was their son. But he still felt like part of her.
Part of her she couldn't get back. Part of her she'd had to give
up. And with him, she gave up so much more.

And then she'd made a promise. That she would do everything to be the best she could be. That she wouldn't waste
her life. Through extreme pain, physically and emotionally,
she'd been given a wake-up call and she had vowed she would
make the absolute most of it.

And she had. She'd done it. She'd made a success of herself. She'd let go of the girl she'd been. At least she thought
she had. She didn't feel like it now. She just felt scared.

She couldn't do it again. She couldn't. It would break her.

Loss, a deep, unending sense of loss filled her and she
put her hands on her stomach to try and stop the pain from
spreading.

"Hannah? Do I have to break the door in?"

She shook off the pain, tried to find her strength. Tried
to find Hannah Weston, so she wouldn't drown in Hannah
Hackett. "You'll do yourself another head injury, Ed, so
maybe don't."

"Hannah," he growled.

She turned on the sink and ran cold water over her hands, dragging them over her face, not caring if she smeared her makeup. Then she jerked the door open and came face-to-face with Eduardo. She had no idea what to say to him.

"Hi."

"You look terrible," he said.

"Thanks"

"You're pale," he said. "And you look like…well, you look sick."

"I am," she snapped.

"Do you need anything?"

A time machine. So she could go back to four weeks earlier when she'd decided having sex with him would be a way to regain control. It hadn't worked. Not in the least. And it certainly wasn't worth the consequence.

"I don't think there's anything you could do for me at the moment. Let's go in your office."

One thing she wasn't, was a coward. She wasn't going to hide it from him. It was implausible at best. So she would tell him. But she didn't know what she would tell him. She was the world's worst candidate to be a mother. But she honestly didn't know if she could go through giving up another child.

But she wasn't sure if she could be a mother, either. She knew nothing about it. She'd never had one. She didn't know if she had a nurturing bone in her body. She was insensitive. She swore. She was a workaholic. She had a criminal history. The list went on.

"Sit down," she said.

"Hannah, what is it?"

"You remember how we had sex?"

One of his dark eyebrows shot up. "Yes, I seem to remember something about that."

"Right, well…also, remember the condom broke."

"I do remember," he said, his tone turning heavy, wooden.

"Well, I…we…that is…you…"

"You're pregnant."

"Well, when you say it like that you make it sound like it's all my fault. But you know I didn't get that way on my own."

"Hannah, I am well aware of how it happened and I am not fobbing the blame off onto you, so stop panicking for a second," he growled.

"Stop? Stop panicking? Eduardo, I have barely started panicking. There is an entire repertoire of panic for me to work through before I can even begin to wind down the panicking."

"There's no need to panic."

"Why is there no need to panic?"

"Because we're more than capable of handling this situation."

"Are we?" she asked, her throat almost completely constricted. "Do you have any idea… I mean. Do you? And what will we do with a baby, Eduardo, what? Will you strap him to your chest and bring him to work? You can't concentrate as it is. And me…what? I'm going to put on an apron and turn into Susie Homemaker?"

"We'll get nannies," he said.

"What kind of life is that for a child?"

"A life. There doesn't seem to be an alternative."

"Adoption," she said. The word sounded flat and cold in the room.

"I'm not giving away my child."

His words hurt. They cut her deep, tapped into a wound still raw and bleeding, covered, but never healed. "That's not what adoption is. It's giving your child the best chance possible. That's what it is. Wouldn't…wouldn't I have been better off? If my mother had given me up instead of neglecting me for three years of my life and then dropping me off with a father who didn't want me?" She couldn't voice the rest. Couldn't say anything about how this had happened before. It all just stuck in her throat. Painful. Horrendous. "Do you understand what it's like? To live with someone who just doesn't give a damn about what you do? Who doesn't even worry about you if you stay out all night? I was doing everything you should be afraid your child is out doing. Drinking, and having sex and he never… He didn't care. So tell me, Eduardo, what kind of life was that? Why should a child, anyone, ever live where they aren't wanted?"

"Are you saying you don't want the baby?"

"No. That's not it…that's not…"

"We could take care of a child, Hannah. It's different. We both have money."

"Money isn't enough."

"It's a start, at least."

She took a shaky breath. "Nothing has to be decided now," she said finally. "It's early. There's no need to—" she laughed "—well, to panic."

Eduardo felt like he'd been hit in the chest. He couldn't breathe. He could hardly think. Hannah was pregnant. The only time he'd ever thought about children had been in terms of preventing them. He'd vaguely assumed, prior to his injury, that he would settle down for real one day and in that scenario, there had been a hazy assumption of children, but he'd never truly thought about it in a real sense.

And since his accident…well, he'd avoided women. Avoided all kinds of relationships. The thought of having a child when everything was so much harder than it had once been… Hannah was right in many ways. He wasn't sure he could handle being a father and running Vega. He could scarcely run Vega, and Hannah knew it better than most.

Knew what sorts of limitations she was dealing with when it came to the father of her baby.

"Right," he said, as if having decided that maybe they could just put it out of their minds for a while, but he doubted he would think of anything else. He wasn't sure how he ever could.

"Right," she said, looking as unconvinced as he felt.

"Let's go back to the *rancho*," he said. He needed solitude. Quiet. He needed to not be here, in this place that reminded him of his shortcomings.

"What? When?"

"This weekend," he said. "I don't think I can…concentrate here. There's too much. This…makes it too much."

"Right," she said. "I just need my phone glued to me because I have to get that deal nailed down."

"I understand. We'll bring work with us." But the room felt like it was closing in on him, the whole city, just outside the windows, felt like it was folding on top of him. His mind was cluttered and he couldn't figure out how to sift through it. Especially not with the pounding that was starting in his head. With the way the light was starting to feel, like a knife going in through his eyes.

"We leave tomorrow."

Hannah nodded, for once without any kind of sassy comeback. "Okay."

CHAPTER TEN

"ARE you all right staying in here?"

Hannah looked around the frilly pink-and-white room. The room she and Eduardo had made love in. The room they'd conceived the baby in.

"As fine here as I would be anywhere," she said, her head spinning, a strange, heavy numbness invading her chest and spreading outward. She was so tired. Exhaustion seeped into her bones.

"I want to be close to you."

"I'm not going to do anything desperate, Eduardo."

"I know."

Except he didn't know. And that was fair enough, because she'd never really let him know her. He'd seen her naked and he still didn't know her. No one did. Not really. She wasn't sure she did anymore. Wasn't sure what she wanted. Wasn't sure if she could clear the next hurdle that had been placed in front of her.

Just the thought of what the next few months would bring, of what it would mean to watch her baby be carried from the room again, never holding him, never touching him, made her feel cold. Made her feel like the life was draining from her.

What if you kept him?

For a moment she imagined it. Holding her baby at her breast, looking into eyes that were dark like his father's. Having someone to love. Someone who would love her.

Her stomach seized, tears threatening to fall.

"I'm fine," she said, mostly for her own benefit. But she knew she was lying.

"Do you want to lie down for a while?"

"I'm not symptomatic yet."

"When does that usually start?"

"Six weeks or so," she said.

He frowned. "Do all women just…know this stuff? You don't seem like you would."

Shoot. Yes, she would have to tell him sometime. It wasn't like it would matter. Except it did. It was her pain. It had never been anyone else's.

"You'd be surprised," she said. "I am a little tired. I think I'll take a nap. We'll talk later?"

He nodded curtly. "If you feel up to it, I'd like to walk down to the beach with you."

"That would be great."

She ushered him out of the room and rested her back against the closed door. Her old life was crashing head-on into her new one, and she wasn't sure anymore where one ended and the other began.

It was her worst nightmare unfolding in front of her. And she wasn't sure there was anything she could do to stop it.

She woke up feeling sleepier than she had when she'd lain down. Her head was swimming, and it was dark outside. So she'd missed her walk. It was okay, though; she hadn't really felt up to talking to Eduardo. Not now. Not when she'd have to be honest with him.

A tear rolled down her face and back into her hair and she didn't bother to wipe it away. Eduardo was the only person she'd felt close to in so long, and even they were in opposition half the time.

Maybe she wasn't meant to be close to people. It was pretty obvious she didn't really know how to be. Even with Zach there had been calculated distance. They hadn't shared themselves. They'd met where they were at in life and moved forward, never digging deep, never really getting to know each other. And she'd been happy with that.

Eduardo pushed her; he made her angry. Made her feel passion and lose control. It didn't make her all that happy, and it had led to a pretty big mistake. But she did feel more genuine when she was with him. More herself.

She wasn't sure if that was a good thing or not.

She pulled her knees up to her chest and rolled to her side. She felt like she was breaking apart. For once she couldn't outthink a situation. Couldn't control it or change it. It was what it was. She was pregnant. With Eduardo's baby.

She sat up and wiped the tears from her cheeks. She needed to get her mind off it. She needed to be near Eduardo, and she couldn't fathom why. But it didn't matter why. She hurt everywhere. She felt like she was being scraped raw inside.

And she was so tired of being alone. She was always alone.

With shaking limbs she stood from the bed and padded across the room, to the door that separated her room from Eduardo's, walking into his room without knocking.

For a moment, she didn't see him. It was dark in his room, and he wasn't in the bed. Then she saw him, slumped in his chair, his hands gripping the armrests.

"Hi," she said, her voice sounding huskier than she intended it to.

He shifted. "Hannah? Are you feeling all right?"

"As well as can be expected. Yourself?"

"I had a migraine. I'm better now."

"Have you been drinking?"

"No. That makes it worse. Why?"

"Just…it's good to know. I…I really need you," she whispered.

"What?"

"I can't be alone. And I'm cold. I need you to make me

feel…make me feel again." She battled against the tears that were threatening to fall, threatening to choke her. "Make me warm."

He stood quickly and wrapped his arm around her waist, pulling her up against him. "Hannah…"

"I just want to stop thinking. For a minute. I just want to feel. You make me feel so good. When you touch me…" She swallowed hard. "I'm asking you for help now, Eduardo."

"Oh, Hannah."

He picked her up, holding her close to his chest, and she wrapped her arms around his neck. She'd never given a lot of thought to her feelings on over-the-top masculine displays of strength. Turned out, she liked them.

She placed her palms flat over his chest, over the hard muscles, maddeningly concealed by his thin T-shirt. She lowered her hands and found the hem of the shirt, sliding her fingertips up his hot, hair-roughened skin.

He groaned and set her down on the bed, tugging the shirt over his head. She could see the outline of his body, moonlight gleaming from the hard ridges of his chest and abs, his jeans low cut, delicious lines pointing right down to his erection.

And that was all she was going to think about. Just him.

"You're really sexy," she breathed.

He chuckled, his hands on his belt buckle. "So are you. Trade."

She tugged her shirt over her head and lay back, waiting for the rest of Eduardo to be revealed.

He shook his head. "Not enough."

"Grr." She got up on her knees and torqued her arms around, unhooking her bra and sending it sailing. "Better?"

The heat glittering in his dark eyes sent an answering fire down to her belly. And farther down.

A smile curved his lips. "Much better."

He worked his belt through the loops and tugged it free

Then shrugged off his pants and underwear in one deft motion.

"Come here," she said.

"Your wish is my command."

He joined her on the bed, his bare shaft hot against her stomach. "Oh, yes," she whispered, the edges of her mind getting fuzzy with arousal. This was what she needed.

He unbuttoned her jeans and tugged them down her legs, then quickly took her underwear down with them. He teased her with his fingers, his thumb sliding over her clitoris.

She arched into him, clawing at his back, letting her mind go blank of everything but the white-hot pleasure that was pouring through her.

Then he bracketed her face with his hands, kissing her. Deep. Long. Passionate. She clung to him, letting the kiss intensify, learning his rhythm, relearning her own.

This was less intimate than the way he'd touched her a moment ago, but also, somehow, infinitely more so. When he finally released her mouth to trail kisses down her neck, she was shaking, more turned on than she'd ever been in her life. On the verge of tears.

She forked her fingers through his hair, craving deeper contact, craving more.

He kissed her belly, heading lower.

"No," she breathed. "No time."

She needed him inside of her. As deep as he could be, as close as he could be. She hadn't needed anyone in longer than she could remember. She'd never been able to afford to.

"I need you," she said. Meaning it, with every fiber of her being. He continued down, a low chuckle escaping his lips. "No," she said. "This isn't…a game or anything. I need you."

He raised his head, moving back up her body, his dark eyes intense, locked with hers. He pushed her hair back from her face, then kissed her lightly on her lips. She parted her thighs and felt him at the entrance of her body.

"Yes," she whispered.

He slid slowly inside of her. With every inch she felt some of her emptiness fade, and when he was inside her completely, as close to her as two people could be, she felt like she understood sex in a new way entirely.

Sex had never been intimate for her. And she hadn't been after intimacy tonight. Back in high school she'd been after oblivion, a moment of happiness, of closeness even. But not true, deep intimacy.

But she felt it now. As if Eduardo had become a part of her. As if she would leave his bed changed.

He moved inside of her, every stroke perfection, driving her closer to the edge of bliss. Every thrust bringing him closer to her.

His pace increased and she locked her legs around his hips, moving with him; she arched back, her release crashing over her like a wave. He gripped the sheet by her head and shuddered out his own orgasm a moment later.

She lay against his chest, her heart pounding hard, her head swimming. She wanted to speak; she couldn't. A moment later she realized she was shaking. And crying, tears falling on his bare skin.

"I…" she started.

But there was nothing to say. She was overwhelmed. She was pregnant with this man's baby. This man who held her so tightly. Who made her feel close to someone for the first time ever.

No one had ever loved her. And she had never thought of it before. But now…now, in his arms, she wished so much that it could be different. That she could be different. That she could be loved.

He kept his arms wrapped tightly around her and held her close. She kept shaking and he reached down to grab the covers, drawing them up over both of them.

"Sleep now, *querida*. We'll talk more tomorrow."

She nodded wordlessly, unable to speak around the lump in her throat.

She curled up against him, inhaled the scent of him, so uniquely Eduardo. Then she closed her eyes and tried to fall asleep. Trying to fight off all of the demons that were threatening to tear her apart.

Eduardo woke up as the first rays of sun began to filter through the expansive windows of the room. He'd forgotten to close the blinds because his headache had hit after dark.

He rolled over to look at Hannah and his heart seized.

She was so beautiful. And achingly vulnerable. He didn't know how he'd missed it for so long. He'd imagined her invincible, a fair target to bring into his sphere. She could handle herself, after all, and he would never leave her empty-handed.

But he could see now that he'd been wrong. Very wrong.

He thought about what she'd said the day before. About him barely being able to run his business, much less run it with a baby around to distract him. She was right. And yet, when he thought back to his own childhood, the way his father had been, stern and distant, but steady and so very present, he couldn't imagine being anything less for his own child.

He had the resources to care for a son or daughter. And his mother would be thrilled.

And if you can't do it? If the crying gives you migraines and lack of sleep makes it impossible for you to concentrate? If it gets so bad you can't see? What will you do then?

He would figure it out. He had no other choice. They could get nannies, the best available. He would have to. But he could make it work.

He knew it now, with certainty. It had been too hard to process in his office, beneath the bright fluorescent lights. But now, in the gray light of dawn, with Hannah warm and naked by his side, it did seem clear.

He'd wanted to decide what to do about the baby before

anything else happened between them…but when she'd come to him, so vulnerable, so achingly sad, he hadn't been able to deny her. Especially as her misery seemed to be a reflection of his own.

She'd asked him to make her warm. She'd made him warm.

He moved his hand down to Hannah's stomach and his heart pounded faster. Harder.

"Are you awake?" he whispered.

Hannah's eyes opened slowly. "Oh…"

"You sound disappointed," he said.

She rolled over and buried her face in her pillow. "I slept with you again."

"I remember."

She rolled over again. "It wasn't a good idea. It…confuses things."

"Can things be any more confusing?"

"Oh, I don't know, but this can't possibly help clear it up."

"Okay, that's probably true." He moved into a sitting position, unconcerned with the fact that he was still naked. Hannah averted her eyes, clearly of a different opinion, clutching the sheets to her chest. "I'd like to talk to you. About the baby."

"I…" She bit her lip. "Now?"

"Why don't you go shower. I'll shower. We'll have breakfast. Then I'd like to walk with you for a while. On the beach."

She nodded slowly. "I can do that."

"Good." He leaned in and kissed her forehead, the move not planned. And he found he didn't regret it.

He got out of bed and walked toward his bathroom, taking a small amount of satisfaction in Hannah's muffled squeal, likely brought on by his continued nudity. He turned and saw her scrambling out of bed with the sheet still wrapped tight around her body.

"You might as well let it drop, Hannah. I've seen it all."

Something in her expression changed, a sad smile lifting the corner of her lips. "Not in daylight. I'll see you in a bit."

She turned, still covered, and walked out of the room.

Hannah was done showering before Eduardo, and had a few moments down in the breakfast area by herself. She nibbled on a bowl of fruit for a while, then asked one of Eduardo's staff if she could get some bacon. Bacon sounded good. It wasn't a pregnant craving, she was pretty sure it was too soon for that. She was just feeling horrible and trying to comfort herself with food.

She nibbled on the bacon while she thought about how today would play out. Yet again, it seemed impossible to plan.

She would have to tell Eduardo. There was really no way around it. Because she had to explain to him where she was coming from.

He appeared a few moments later, dressed in shorts and sandals, ready for a casual walk on the beach. She only had one pair of jeans, so she was going to have to settle for rolling them up past her ankles.

"I'm not really hungry," he said. "Are you ready?"

She picked up another bacon strip. "Yeah." She stood and took a deep breath, following him out the back door of the house. There was a little path that cut through the meadow and led down the hillside, tall grass rising up, making the walkway feel enclosed. Private.

The ground softened and turned from dirt to sand, the chilly, salty air stinging her cheeks. They were quiet until they reached the shore.

"How are you feeling now, Hannah?"

"Now that I've had a full twenty-four hours to process it?" she asked.

"Yes."

"Not great."

"Tell me," he said, still walking. Heading toward a grove

of trees that was at the far end of the beach. "Do you still want to give the baby up?"

Her throat tightened. "It's not a matter of want, Eduardo. It's about…about doing what's best for the baby. I wasn't very nice yesterday, to you, when I said that about caring for a baby and the company, but my point is still solid. I'm married to my work, and you're willing to do anything for your job. So when exactly are we going to find the time to raise a child? And with me in the U.S. and you here in Spain…"

"So, be here."

"Me? Move to Spain?"

"You've lived here before. You liked it."

She'd more than liked it. She loved Spain. In so many ways it felt like her home. "Yes," she said slowly, "but I have a job back in San Francisco, assuming they haven't cleaned out my desk."

"You've left plenty of jobs."

"That's not really the issue."

"Then what is?"

The truth hovered on the edge of her lips, but she couldn't quite bring herself to say it, not just yet.

"My father was very much committed to his business," Eduardo said. "He was still a good father."

"You were angry with him half the time."

"I know. Because I was young and stupid and entitled. And if there's one change I am thankful for in myself, it's that my fall seems to have knocked some of the jackass out of me."

She laughed. "Some, maybe. But you still have plenty."

They reached the little cluster of trees and they walked beneath them. Hannah looked up at the green leaves, a spiderweb of sunlight breaching the foliage.

"Do you know how all-consuming a baby will be?" she asked, her stomach churning.

"I'm not sure that I do. But no parent really does until they have one of their own."

It had been years since she'd thought of that long-ago baby as her son. She couldn't. Couldn't let herself have that connection to him. Because she knew better than most that it took more than blood to be a parent. For her son, his parents were the people who had raised him. Who had stayed up nights with him. She had simply carried him.

If only that were enough to abolish the connection she felt.

"I'm afraid," she whispered, tears clogging her throat.

"Of course you are, Hannah. Childbirth is…an unknown experience. Pregnancy is certainly…"

"No." She shook her head, trying to ignore the pain that was crawling through her veins. "I know all about being pregnant. About what it's like to feel your baby move inside you for the first time… It's…it's a miracle, Eduardo." She felt a tear slide down her cheek. "Labor is as awful as they say. But in the end there's this perfect little…life. And it's so worth it. All of it. The morning sickness, the stretch marks. The pain."

"Hannah," he said, his tone flat, cold.

"I was sixteen when I got pregnant," she said. She'd never voiced the words out loud before. Had never confided in anyone. "And I knew there was no way I could take care of a baby." Another tear fell and she didn't wipe it away.

"I gave him up. Because it was the right thing to do. But… but I'm not sure I can go through it again. I don't think I could give this one up, even if I should. And I'm afraid…I'm afraid that if I do keep this baby, I'll really understand what I gave up then."

CHAPTER ELEVEN

HANNAH felt emotion coming in thick, unendurable waves. She could drown in it, in the pain, the misery. The starkness of the truth. It was so very ugly, and yet, it was a part of her.

"Hannah that must have been…"

"There are days when I'm so glad that I did it. Because I was this poor, high school dropout with no future and what could I offer him? Nothing. Nothing but more of the same. More poverty. More…neglect maybe while I tried to work and earn enough money to keep us in whatever filthy apartment could afford. Was I going to take him back to the single-wide I shared with my dad? Expose him to secondhand smoke and mice and bugs and everything else we had to contend with?" She looked down. "But some people make it. I just…I knew I wasn't strong enough. I knew I didn't know how."

"What about the father?"

She shook her head, a faint feeling of embarrassment creeping over her, joining the misery. "I didn't really know him. He was this senior guy I hooked up with at a party. He wasn't my boyfriend. Obviously, I was very irresponsible. It wasn't the first time I'd done something like that, classic acting-out behaviors. I'm kind of a shameful stereotype. No attention from Dad so…anyway, you get the idea. He went away to college. I called about the baby but he…he didn't call back."

"He didn't call you back?"

"We were both young and stupid. He had college to look forward to. A way out of the hellhole we lived in and probably the last thing he wanted was to deal with having a kid back home. It doesn't excuse him but…I'm not mad at him for it. I…did it by myself."

"And after that, that was when you changed your name?"

She nodded, ready to tell now. "I needed to be someone different. I don't know how else to explain it. I just…I couldn't be…that girl anymore. The Johnsons, the adoptive parents, they paid for my prenatal care and my hospital bill, but they also had the agency send me a monetary gift. Something to help me start over. I felt like I had a choice in that moment. To go back to the place I'd always called home. Back to my old friends, who were still wasting any potential they might have had by partying it away. Back to a father who never seemed to notice what was happening with my life. Or I could try and take the fresh start. In that moment, everything seemed… new. For the first time, I felt like I could be anything. Do anything. I changed my name and figured out what I would have to do to get into college. Found the right people to help me forge the transcripts. And then I bought a plane ticket to Barcelona. And then I hit the ground running."

"And you've been running ever since."

She nodded. "I have been." She looked out at the sea, the white-capped waves rolling into the shore. "But I can't run from this."

"Neither can I. It's not in me. This is reality and we have to face it. But I'm certain we can make it work."

"I'm afraid that…it's going to bring it all back. I've spent so many years trying to let go. And it's a process. Like I said, some days I'm thankful. I'm glad for the stable life I'm sure he's had. Glad he's been able to grow up in comfort. Glad I was able to…to make something better of myself. But…"

"Come here." He sat down at the base of one of the trees and leaned against the smooth bark.

Hannah moved to where he was and sat. There was space between them; neither of them looked at each other. "Things are different now, Hannah. We can make this work. We'll do it together."

She put her hand on her stomach. "Can we?"

He put his hand over hers and a spark shot through her. "We will. We'll do it, because you're the strongest woman I've ever met. And I'm...not as much as I used to be but... But in some ways..."

"In some ways better," she said. Thinking of the Eduardo he had been. The laughing, mocking man who had taken nothing seriously.

"Yes, that, too."

She shivered. "I'm afraid of screwing a kid up. Like my parents did to me."

"I don't blame you."

"But your parents love you. You know how it's supposed to be."

He nodded slowly. "Yes. My parents do love me. They, especially my father, were never overly demonstrative, but I always knew that he had my best interests at heart. He made sure we were all cared for. Provided for. He was the pillar of my family. Still, I plagued him. I married an American girl he didn't approve of."

"Not at first," she said, remembering how things had been in the end. How Eduardo's father had told her she had one of the finest minds he'd ever encountered. That she could achieve great things if she kept going. "But in the end...well before I left you and made him hate me again...he treated me better than almost anyone else in my life. I'll always be grateful to him for his confidence in me."

"You know what you were missing growing up, Hannah, and I truly believe you'll know what needs to be given to your child."

She broke free of him, moving into a standing position

One thing was certain, she wasn't going to be able to think clearly while he was touching her.

"I hope you're right."

"Every parent starting out is afraid of whether or not they'll be good enough. So I hear."

"What if it affects your work?"

"It won't. I'll make sure that everything is taken care of. If things slip a bit, then they slip."

"But it's not what you want."

"Of course not. It's never been what I wanted. That's why I went to such great lengths to bring you back." A stark reminder that it had been her brains he wanted, not her body. Not that that was a bad thing. Really, it was flattering. Positive even. "I'm completely certain we can put the proper systems in place to ensure that nothing bad happens with the company."

She was glad he was feeling certain about something. She was feeling...dull. Achy. On edge. Far too close to having her past and future collide. To losing the detachment she'd made with that long-ago self.

"I remember his face," she said, not sure why she'd allowed the words to escape.

"Your child?"

She nodded. "He was a boy. They said that when he was born. And they lifted him up and I thought I could turn away quickly enough. That I wouldn't have to see him. That I could pretend it hadn't been real at all. But it was. He was." She blinked hard, trying to keep from dissolving completely. "I'll never forget his face."

"Perhaps you shouldn't."

She shook her head. "I don't want to anymore. But I did for a long time. I wished I could make it go away. Wished I didn't...ache for him. Like something was missing from inside of me."

"Is it like that? Still?"

She swallowed. "In some ways. But…I just…I have to let him go, don't I? I'm not his mother. Not really. I don't even know what they named him. I never held him or kissed him. I didn't watch him take his first steps. Or see him go to school for the first time. I never put a bandage on his scraped knees or…or…" She couldn't breathe. It took her a moment to realize it was because she was sobbing. Great gasps of air that came from deep inside of her and made her feel like she was breaking in two.

She sat down, on her knees in the sand, moisture seeping through the thick denim fabric of her pants. Her throat was burning, raw and painful, like she'd been screaming. But she hadn't been. She'd never allowed herself to let go so much. This was the first time she'd truly cried in years, not just tears, but with every piece of herself. This was the first time she'd cried for her son.

The first time she'd let herself fully realize what she'd lost.

Dimly she was aware of Eduardo hovering near her. He knelt down beside her, not touching her, and she was glad. Because if he did she would melt into him completely.

Finally, the storm passed, almost as quickly as it had hit. She shifted so that she was sitting on her backside, knees drawn up to her chest.

"I never told him I loved him," she said.

"He was a baby, Hannah," Eduardo said, his voice rusty.

"I know but…I don't even think I really let myself feel it." She looked up at him. "I did, though. I do."

"I know," he said.

Eduardo felt like his heart was going to hammer out of his chest. Fear. It was pure fear that had him shaking and on edge. He didn't know what to do with such raw emotion, didn't feel like he had the strength to handle it. What Hannah had been through…it was beyond him. What she had lost…it was so much greater than anything he had lost.

And yet, she knew, and he did, too, that she'd had very little choice.

He moved closer to her, unsure if he should touch her, take her in his arms, or not.

"Hannah, look at all you've accomplished in your life. You made the right choice. For both of you. So you could both live better."

"I know," she said, her voice firm. "I do know. But…just because a choice is right doesn't mean it won't hurt like hell."

"No, that is true."

"It hurts so much to love like this," she said softly. "To love a child. You're never the same again."

Another pang of fear hit him hard. "That's okay."

"You really think so?"

"I have to. No matter what, we've made a baby." She winced. "Sorry, cheesy choice of wording perhaps, but no matter what…there will…most likely be a baby. And we either face giving him up or keeping him. I think…I think we should keep him." The idea terrified him in many ways, but not more than feeling the sort of grief that came from Hannah in palpable waves.

Hannah wrapped her arms around herself like she was cold. "I…I think…"

"We'll do this, Hannah. Together. I'll be with you."

Her pale blue eyes, looking brighter thanks to the red rims they'd acquired during her crying jag, locked with his. "I trust you."

And he knew that that was probably the deepest compliment he had ever received. From Hannah or anyone.

He tried to block out the weight of it. The responsibility he might not be able to live up to. He winced against the pain in his head.

He would do it. He didn't have a choice.

Eduardo lifted his head from the floor. How was it possible for the medicine cabinet to be so far away? After the beach, his headache had steadily gotten worse until every fragment of light, every sound had become excruciating.

And he'd put off going for his medication. Put off acknowledging it because he didn't want Hannah to know.

His vision blurred and another stab of pain went through his head, through his body. Nausea rolled through him and he laid his head back down against the hard tile. He prayed that somehow the cold would work like an ice pack. That it would provide some relief. Enough that he could stand up and get his pills at least.

A fresh wave of pain hit him and he groaned, curling up, trying to shield himself from further attacks. It was impossible. He knew it, but it didn't stop him from trying.

If he could just stand up.

"Eduardo?"

Hannah's voice cut through the door. Cut through his skull. He wanted to tell her to go away, but just imagining the pain that would cause brought the acidic taste of bile to the back of his throat.

"Eduardo?" She was closer now, her voice sharper.

He growled against the floor, planting his hand in front of him, trying to push himself up. He was rewarded with another knife through his skull, so strong it put black spots in his vision.

"Go away, Hannah," he said. A rough sound escaped his lips as another shot of pain cracked through him. It hit him like a wall, the force of it enough to black out his sight entirely. He couldn't see anything. Couldn't move. Couldn't have found his way to the medicine cabinet now even if standing were a possibility.

"Are you okay? You're scaring me."

He pressed his forehead back down on the tile. He took a deep breath, steeling himself for the agony he was about to put himself in. But she couldn't see him. Not like this. On the floor, immobilized, sweating, shaking. Blind.

No. She couldn't see this.

"Go away, Hannah!" he roared, the shock of his own voice lancing him with intense physical torment that started at his head and worked through the rest of him. His face, his cheeks, were wet. From sweat or from unforgivable weakness, he didn't know.

"Eduardo, I am about to open the door. Sorry, but I am. You're freaking me out now."

She pushed the door open and he stretched his hand out, trying to stop it, but he was too weak to lift his arm. He was too weak in every way.

"Oh…are you…are you okay?" Hannah was down beside him, her voice too close, her hand on his face.

He shook his head, trying to find it in him to speak again. She was here. And he needed his pills. "Medicine cabinet," he said.

He heard her stand, the noises she made while rummaging through the medicine cabinet drumming in his head. He heard the water running and Hannah was kneeling beside him again.

Hannah looked down at Eduardo, panic racing through her. He'd mentioned migraines and she hoped that was all this was. Though…there was nothing minor about it, even if the symptoms weren't fatal.

She shifted so that she was sitting on her bottom behind Eduardo's head. Then she gripped him beneath his arms and tugged him up so that his head was resting on her thigh. His face was damp, with sweat and tears and her heart burned for him. His eyes were unfocused, open and staring.

She hated that she was seeing it. Not for her, but for him. Because she knew that this was flaying his pride, killing a part of him that was so essential to him.

She picked up the cup of water she'd set on the floor and tried to angle his head. She opened her hand and he opened his mouth as she put the pills on his tongue. She put the water glass to his lips and tilted it slowly. He swallowed the pills and his eyes fluttered closed, his head falling back to her lap.

She set the glass down and leaned back against the tub, her hands on his chest, feeling the steady beat of his heart beneath her hands. Every so often his muscles would tense, his face contorting, and her heart would burn.

The tile started to feel really hard, and the tub wasn't any better against her back, but she kept sitting there. Kept holding him.

There was nothing, not a sore butt or aching back, that was going to move her. Because Eduardo was hers. She tightened her hold on him and took a sharp, halting breath. She didn't know what that meant, she only knew that he was. That of all the people in the world, he was the only person who seemed to understand her. The only person who seemed to want to try.

Eduardo mattered. Her heart started beating faster as the realization worked its way through her. He mattered more than work. More than her personal success or her image. *He* mattered.

The beautiful, broken man in her arms was worth caring about. And she could. She did. No, he wasn't slick, urbane Eduardo from five years ago, but she didn't need him to be. That man hadn't called to her. That man hadn't reached her heart.

She moved her hand to his forehead and smoothed the lines there, trying to rub out his concerns. Trying to ease his pain.

Her heart tightened.

Maybe she could do it. Maybe they could do it.

One thing she knew for certain, as she sat there with her body aching, Eduardo in her arms, was that some people were worth caring for, worth working for. Eduardo was worth it. Their baby was worth it.

A sharp sense of longing, of tenderness, hit in her in the chest. She closed her eyes, letting a tear fall down her cheek. She lowered her head and rested her forehead on his.

She didn't know anything about marriage. Or about children. Or being a mother. But he made her want to try.

"Hannah?" When Eduardo woke up, it was dark. At least he hoped it was dark. His vision had gone before during migraines, but it never lasted long. He hoped it never did.

The fact that Hannah had seen him at his weakest...it galled him. And yet, he had needed her. That didn't make it feel any better.

"I'm right here," she said. She sounded tired, like she'd been sleeping.

It took him a moment to realize that he was in bed, and that she was sitting a few feet away.

"How did you manage to get me into bed?"

"Ah, gee, Eduardo, I've gotten you into bed a couple of times. I can't say it was all that hard."

"Hannah," he said, moving into a sitting position, every muscle in his body screaming at him, "I'm serious." His eyes started to adjust to the dim room, and he could see her, in his chair, her legs tucked up under her.

"Truthfully? You walked with me...you were just really out of it. And anyway, it's not that far."

"I don't want you to have to deal with things like this...."

"How often does this happen?" she asked.

"Migraines? Once every week or so. Migraines like that? It's been months since I've had to deal with anything on that level. They've gotten further apart but..."

"All this stress."

He shook his head. "Not necessarily."

"I've been thinking."

"You never stop thinking, *querida*."

"Granted. But I've been thinking specifically about our baby. And about our future."

He swallowed. "What about it?"

"We're already married."

"A fact we're both well aware of as it caused you grief a few weeks ago."

She nodded curtly. "Yes, but now I'm thinking it's advantageous."

"How do you mean?"

"We're having a baby."

"So many things manage to slip my mind, Hannah, and yet that one has not."

She laughed, a small, nervous sound. He wasn't used to Hannah sounding nervous. "I know...I— Do you want to talk later? I mean...that was a bad... It was bad. If you don't feel up to talking, I understand."

"Talk, Hannah."

"Okay. I think we should stay married. I think we should be a family."

"A...family? What do you think makes a family, Hannah? Marriage?"

She hopped out of the chair and started pacing. "I don't know, Eduardo. I...I don't really. I've never had a family. But on that note, I can tell you what doesn't make a family. A mother who never comes to see you. A father who can't be bothered to say four words to you on a daily basis. Do you know, he never did one thing for me? He bought frozen dinners and I heated them up for both of us. The school bus made sure I got to school. No one went to my parent-teacher conferences. I..." She took a breath. "I was seven when one of my friends said something about my hair not being brushed before I went to school. She started doing it for me on the bus. So, that's what family isn't. I'd really like to try and make a real family."

His heart hurt, for Hannah. The woman she was now, the little girl she'd been. He wanted to hold her close. Erase every bad thing that had ever happened to her. He wanted to care for her.

And then he remembered the events of the past few hours.

Remembered the fact that Hannah had just spent the afternoon caring for him.

He couldn't give her what she needed, what she deserved.

"Hannah, do you really understand what you just saw? When that happens...I can't move. I can't see. You want to try and make your perfect vision of family with me?"

"You're the one who wanted to try this. And I do, too," she said, conviction infusing her tone. "You said we'd do this together. I want to make this work. And the great thing is, we don't have to do anything. We're already married. We already talked about me coming to live in Barcelona. Really... really, it's perfect."

"And us, Hannah?" His whole body tightened when he thought of the other benefits of Hannah being his wife.

"I..."

Hannah felt like her insides had frozen. Of course sex would come into it. The sex between them was great. No question. And she wanted it, there was no question there, either. And if they were going to be married...well, it was only logical.

Then she thought back to that moment on the floor of the bathroom, when she'd held him in her arms. When she'd felt like he was part of her.

Just the thought of what it would be like to kiss him now, to be skin to skin with him now, when she felt so emotionally raw and stripped bare, when her defenses were gone, frightened her down to her soul.

"I can't think about it right now," she said. "That's just to say...I have to process one thing at a time. You and I will have...all the time ever to figure each other out."

Although, she was afraid she would need that much time just to sort herself out.

"That seems fair," he said, his voice rough.

"So...will you stay married to me?"

"Yes, Hannah," he said.

"Great. Good. That's…great. And good. Do you need anything?"

"No. Just sleep."

"Good, I'll leave you to that, then."

Hannah walked out of Eduardo's room and closed the door behind her. And only then did she realize she'd been holding her breath. She was going to have to get it together. She couldn't risk letting herself fall for him. She'd never believed in love, or at least she'd never believed that she could love anyone. That they could love her.

And she couldn't afford it. Couldn't afford to depend on him like that. To need him so much.

She thought back to that moment of fierce, pure possessiveness she'd felt, kneeling on the bathroom floor with him. That he was hers.

She tried to swallow past the lump in her throat. She would deal with the emotion stuff later. For now, she just had to focus on the positives. She was having a baby; she and Eduardo were doing the best thing possible for their baby. She had a plan.

She inhaled and exhaled slowly. Yes, she had a plan. And when she made plans, she kept them. A plan always fixed things.

Suddenly everything felt much more doable.

CHAPTER TWELVE

HANNAH hit the send button on her email and whimpered inwardly. She'd resigned from her job in San Francisco. Not the first job she'd resigned from. But she'd liked the job. She'd contacted a removal company about clearing out her apartment the day before, and had her now-ex-assistant working on listing the furniture and home for sale.

She was used to leaving, but it still felt strange. Sad.

The door to her new and now-more-permanent office at Vega opened and Eduardo entered on a loud and virulent curse.

"Why are you swearing? I'm the one that just resigned from my job." They'd been back in Barcelona for the whole week and they'd kept things very civilized and organized between them.

There was no mention of resuming a physical relationship. No mention of the future. And no mention of the migraine. She could handle that. Was using the time to try and heal, to try and rebuild her walls. To get a grip on the soft gooeyness that seemed to be overtaking her.

They had their system in place, her in her room, he in his, and they came to work together. And, it had even been decided she would be the new financial manager at Vega.

So, all in all, a good week. Even if she did feel confused and lonely. And a little nauseous.

"There's a…charity dinner tonight and I forgot about it. I

had it in my calendar but then I forgot to sync the calendar and so it didn't end up on my phone."

"Tonight?"

"Yes, after work."

"Well, that's not so bad. Go put on a tux and mingle for a couple of hours. It won't kill you."

"I'm not fun."

"You're not...boring."

"You have to come with me."

"No thanks."

"Hannah Vega, you have to come with me, because you are my wife. And my company and the success of it, is very important to you. Which means, the appearance of stability in my life should be very important to you. This is your son's or daughter's legacy, after all."

"Don't be a bear, Eduardo."

"I don't know another way to be. I told you, I'm not fun."

Her cheeks heated as she thought of some of the ways she'd had fun with Eduardo. Oh, no, she was not going there. No, no, no. "You'll be fine. We'll be fine. Not sure I'm up to going out, looking saucy and conspicuously avoiding drinking the champagne, but hey, why not?"

His expression lightened suddenly, concern filling his dark eyes. "I'm sorry, I didn't consider you might not be feeling up to it. I...forgot."

"Don't worry about it. I'm more worried about you. You're up to it?"

His expression darkened. "I'm fine."

"Good. Just tell me what color to wear, and I'll be ready by...when do you need?"

"Eight."

"Eight. I'm good at these kinds of things."

"I know you are," he said, his eyebrows drawing together a bit.

She wanted to go and touch him, comfort him. She wasn't

all that great at comforting people, not historically anyway, but she wanted to. Although, she wasn't sure what was allowed in the neutral zone that was their relationship. They weren't any closer than they'd been a week ago. They hadn't fought more, either. She actually missed fighting with him. Missed the spike of passion that had been between them in some form from the moment they'd met.

She missed the sex even more.

"So, just reap the benefits then and stop looking like the world is crumbling all around you." She stood up and took her purse off the hook behind her desk. "So, what color do you need me to wear?"

"Why?"

"I need to go shopping."

Something in his expression changed, darkened. Went back to how it had been before. And she liked it. "Wear red," he said.

She looked him up and down, heat firing in her blood. "Yeah. Maybe."

She swept past him and walked out of the office.

Eduardo was in hell. He was with the hottest woman in the room, in any room on the planet, he was certain, and yet, she was off-limits to him. Because she needed time to think about where things would go between them. Hell, he needed time. They weren't in a position to have a fun, heated affair. They were married. They were going to be parents.

It wasn't that he couldn't touch her. He had to touch her. She was his wife, and they were playing the reconciliation game. He realized that in many ways they were now playing it for life. No one was to suspect they weren't the loving couple they appeared to be. That he slept alone, with a hard-on that wouldn't quit.

Everyone had to see a committed, devoted couple. The press, most especially, had to see a committed, devoted couple.

But with Hannah dressed in a slinky red dress, with only one strap that gathered at her shoulder like a bow and made her look like a particularly tempting present, her curves hugged close and displayed perfectly by the close fit of the gown, the game was torture. And a simple touch wasn't enough.

"That dress makes quite the statement," he said, his eyes on the elegant curve of her neck. She was scanning the room, looking for the most influential people. At least, he imagined that's what she was doing. She had that way about her. Like she was always on alert. Always on show.

"That was the idea. And it matches your tie." She turned to face him, feathering her fingertips over the silk fabric of his necktie.

"I doubt anyone has noticed my tie."

"It's impossible not to notice a hot man in a great suit," she said, blue eyes raking over him, the appreciation in them open and undisguised. "So trust me, you've been noticed."

"To what do I owe the compliment?"

"Just honesty." Her smile widened and she took a step forward, bringing him with her as she intercepted an older man with a date some twenty years his junior.

They made casual conversation with him, Hannah enquiring after the man's grown children, asking him about his business. Eduardo followed her lead and managed to engage both the man and his date, whom he introduced as Laura, in a steady conversation for a few moments before they both moved on.

When they left, he frowned and leaned in to Hannah. "Why didn't he introduce himself?"

Hannah looked at him, her eyes wide. "That was Carlo Caretti."

He knew the name, and worse, he had the sinking feeling he'd met the man. On more than one occasion. In fact, several occasions. "He's placed some very large orders with

Vega for exclusive mobile phones for Caretti International,"
he said, everything slotting into place.

"Yes. He's a very big client for you. Has been for years."

"I haven't seen him since…"

"I know. It's fine. You covered fine."

He set his glass of champagne down. Hannah wasn't drinking; she couldn't drink. So he shouldn't, either. Which reminded him that he'd forgotten to ask how she felt.

"How are you?"

She waved her hand. "I'm fine."

"Not tired?"

"No. I like parties. Well, parties like this." She laughed. "Sort of over the whole high school undercover kegger."

"Been to a few, have you?"

She tossed him a look. "My former self? Yes. She enjoyed them. They made her forget how sad she was. Hannah Weston? No, she doesn't like them much."

Her admission hit him hard. More aching sadness for the strong, beautiful woman he called his wife. "What about Hannah Vega?"

"I haven't changed my name."

He frowned. "Will you?"

She blinked rapidly. "I…I hadn't really thought about it."

Another couple stopped and chatted with them for a while and thankfully, he'd never met them so he didn't feel stupid when they left. "I really didn't know them, right?" he asked, checking with Hannah.

She shook her head. "I don't think so. If you did, I don't know why, so they can't be that important. Ack, that sounds mean."

"Well, that's how you see things isn't it? In terms of business value."

She frowned. "Generally. I'm not sure I like it."

"I don't mind it."

"I don't see everything that way," she said, and he knew she meant the baby.

"I know you don't."

She bit her lip and nodded slowly. He wrapped his arm tightly around her waist and led her deeper into the opulent ballroom. People were milling around, looking at the artwork on the wall, placing written bids that were much higher than any of the work was worth. But proceeds went to a children's hospital charity and that meant generosity was high, and very few people actually cared what it was they were bidding on.

Hannah stopped in front of a painting of a woman. The woman was on a busy street, in a crowd. She was facing a different direction to everyone else, and there was space around her, while all the other people in the picture nearly blurred together into an indistinguishable mass.

"She's special," he said. She certainly stood out. She reminded him of Hannah. A woman who could never simply blend.

"She looks lonely to me," Hannah said.

He turned to look at her. She was staring at the painting, her attention rapt. "No one is touching her. No one's going with her."

"But she stands out," he said.

"By herself."

He extended his hand and brushed his thumb across her cheek. She turned to face him, eyes wide. "She's not alone."

She blinked. "I...I want to bid on this one." She took a slip of paper from the podium and wrote down a number she hid from him, then dropped the folded white square into the box.

"I think I'll place a bid, too." He got his own slip of paper and wrote his own bid on it. He was certain he would beat her. And then he would give it to her.

"You look confident there, Eduardo."

"I am," he said, dropping his bid into the box. "I think I'll win."

"Do you?"

"I do."

"A wager then."

"A wager?"

"Mmm-hmm. If I win, I get a favor. If you win, you get a favor."

"A favor?"

"A foot rub, a half day at work. Something. Be imaginative."

"I don't know if I'm imaginative."

"I'm sure you can be," she said.

"All right then, I take your bet."

She extended her hand and he shook it, then he leaned down and pressed his lips to her knuckles. Heat shot through him, down to his gut, gripping him tight with fiery fingers.

"Good," she said, her tone light, breathless. "When do they announce the winners?"

He checked his watch and the sign on the podium. "Bidding is closed in five minutes and it looks like they'll take about thirty minutes to announce the winners."

"Then we have some mingling time."

He could have groaned at that, but he kept his mind busy thinking of just what he would ask of her when he got his favor. A kiss maybe. More. The image of her lips on his body, on his shaft, as she'd done the first night they were together haunted him, intoxicated him.

They'd been strictly hands-off for the past week, and for good reason. And it was likely she hadn't intended the favor to be sexual, but damned if he could think of anything else.

He would ask for something else when he won. But for now he would let his mind wander.

The announcement was five minutes late, and in that space of five minutes he was more aware of the time than he'd been in his recent memory.

The man who was orchestrating the evening started reading off the auction winners and directing them to go to the back of the room to write their checks.

"Lot number fourteen goes to Hannah Vega," he said, barely taking a breath before moving on to fifteen.

Hannah shot him a triumphant smile. "I win." She breezed away from him, going to write her check and claim her spoils, he imagined. He followed after her.

"What did you bid?"

"A lot," she said, smiling sweetly.

"Why?"

"I can. I have a lot of money, Eduardo. But you know that."

"I know it, but I didn't know you were the type."

"I very much am. I give a lot to charity. And I really liked the painting."

"It looked like it made you sad."

She shrugged. "I connected with it. I'm going to hang it in our house."

"How much was your bid?" he repeated.

She gave him a figure that made his brows raise. They reached the back table and she dashed off a check and handed it to the woman manning the station.

"Would you like it delivered, Señora Vega?"

Hannah nodded. "I would, thank you." She bent and scribbled his address on a piece of paper. "To this address, please."

Eduardo took his own checkbook out and wrote a check for double what Hannah had bid on the painting. "I would like to add a contribution," he said, setting it on the table.

She lifted a brow but didn't say anything until they walked away. "Big man," she said.

"It's for a good cause, Hannah."

"Yes, but you mainly did it to show me up."

He shrugged. "I don't want people thinking you had to be the one to bid and pay."

"Does it matter?"

"Of course it does. I'm your husband, I'm supposed to take care of you."

She raised a brow and pursed her lips. "Oh, really. Well, all right then. I'm just glad you donated."

"Are you ready to go?"

She nodded. "If you are."

"I was ready to leave before we got here."

She laughed and took hold of his arm, giving little finger waves to everyone they passed by. "Don't look like such a storm cloud."

He forced a smile. "Better?" he asked.

"Much better," she said through her teeth.

They took a car back to his penthouse and she didn't make a mention of her favor the whole ride there. She was uncharacteristically quiet. Hannah was not known for her quiet.

When they got inside she leaned against the door, staring off into space, chewing her bottom lip.

"You must be tired," he said.

"A bit."

"Me, too. I'm going to head to bed. I'll see you in the morning, Hannah." After tonight, with her in that dress, with all of the touching and teasing that had happened at the charity event, it took every ounce of his strength to keep from going and kissing her.

"Wait," she said, just as he turned his back.

"What is it?" He turned to her, his heart pounding heavily.

"You still owe me a favor."

CHAPTER THIRTEEN

HANNAH felt like she was going to shake apart. At least, the shaking seemed to be happening from the inside out. There was small consolation in the fact that when she pushed off from the door and took a step toward him, her limbs didn't tremble.

"You're not getting out of it so easily," she said.

"Granting you your favor?"

She nodded, still not quite sure how she was going to execute the next part of her plan. Not quite sure when it had become her plan. She was hazy on the whole thing. But sometime between putting the huge figure down on her auction sheet and getting in the car with Eduardo, his heat so close to her she felt like she was burning up, she'd decided that her favor was going to involve getting him back into her arms. Back into her bed.

To what end? Oh, that she wasn't sure about.

About the only thing she was sure about was how much she wanted him. And she was ready to act on it.

"First things first, how much did you have to drink tonight?" she asked.

He lifted his chin, one dark brow lifted. "Why?"

"I'm stone-cold sober, a side effect of pregnancy, and I refuse to take advantage of a drunk man."

"I'm as sober as you are."

She nodded. "Excellent." She sounded so calm. Her voice

was odd to her own ears because it simply didn't match the jittery, fearful excitement that was rolling through her body. She looked around the penthouse, trying to plan her next move, trying to figure out what to ask him to do.

She closed her eyes and shook her head. She wasn't planning it. She was just going with what she wanted.

The idea of Eduardo as her personal playground was fairly enticing. The idea of getting just what she wanted from him. No-holds-barred access. She was on board with that.

She walked toward him, her heart pounding hard. "Take off your tie."

He raised his hand to the red knot at the base of his throat and paused. "Is that the favor? Because I was going to do this up in my room anyway."

"No. My favor comes in stages."

"Is that allowed?"

She smiled, a flush of warmth suffusing her. "Maybe not. But I'm up for a little rule breaking. How about you?"

He didn't move and for a moment, she was afraid he would say that he wasn't in the mood to break any rules. That they needed to keep things bland and passive and safe between them.

Then he started working the knot on the tie, the bit of red silk sliding down the front of his black jacket and pooling on the floor. He stood, waiting. For another command.

"Jacket," she said.

He obeyed.

"Now your shirt."

She watched, her heart in her throat as he undid the buttons at his cuffs, then worked the buttons at the front of the shirt, consigning it to the floor, as well. She was happy for the chance to look at him with the light on, to really take in the sight of his body. The sculpted, well-defined muscles, his broad masculine frame.

Just looking at him made her breasts ache, her nipples

tighten. She'd never wanted like this. Never before him, never in the years during their separation. She knew she never would again.

He put his hands on his belt and her eyes fell to the very clear outline of his erection. She sucked in a sharp breath. "Not yet."

He removed his hands. His eyes glittering in challenge. He was enjoying the game, she could tell. But she was also willing to bet he was waiting for the right moment to reverse it.

The thought sparked a flicker of heat low in her belly.

"Go sit on the couch."

He turned and walked toward the couch and she followed, her eyes on his backside.

"Checking me out?" he asked, sitting on the smooth leather couch, draping his arms across the back of it.

"Absolutely. And now I'm trying to decide what to do with you next."

She put her hands behind her back and gripped the tab of her zipper, lowering it slightly. The strap of her dress slipped, dropped so that the top fell dangerously low, draped over her breast, coming close to revealing the gossamer red bra she had beneath it.

Eduardo's face tensed, his hands curling into fists. He didn't move.

She arched and tugged the zipper down farther, letting the dress fall to her waist.

She heard his breath release in a sharp hiss.

"More?" she asked.

"You're the boss," he said, teeth gritted.

She smiled and brought the zipper down the rest of the way, letting the dress slide down her hips and pool at her feet. Showing him her thigh-high stockings and matching lace bra and panty set.

She walked over to the couch and sat next to him, his heat

warming her, the hunger in his gaze erasing any unease she might feel.

She put her hands on his chest and ran her fingertips over his finely sculpted muscles. And she didn't want to play games anymore.

"You're the sexiest man I've ever seen," she said, dipping her head and running her tongue over his nipple. He reached up and forked his fingers through her hair, holding her to him.

She pressed a kiss to his stomach, tight and flat, utter perfection. "I'm the luckiest woman alive, no question."

He laughed hoarsely. "I don't know about that, but I must be the luckiest man."

She put her hands on his belt buckle. "I've been told my mouth gets me into trouble."

"I would love to see that for myself," he said, voice tight.

She smiled and worked at his belt, then the closure of his pants. He helped her pull them off and then he was naked in front of her. She gripped his erection, squeezing, watching his head fall back, reveling in how labored his breathing became.

She leaned in and tasted him, gratified by the harsh sound of pleasure that escaped his lips. She pleasured him that way until he was shaking, until a fine sheen of sweat covered his olive skin.

"Hannah," he said roughly, "not yet, Hannah. Please."

She lifted her head and pressed a kiss to his stomach. "Not yet?"

"Not like that. I thought I owed you the favor?"

She laughed. "I didn't do anything I didn't want." She straightened and leaned in, kissing him on the lips, deep, passionate, pouring everything into it.

When they broke apart, they were both breathing hard. He held her chin between his thumb and forefinger, his dark eyes burning into hers. She felt a response in her chest, a strange tightness that made it hard to breathe. She wanted to cry, and laugh at the same time.

Instead, she kissed him again and he pulled her into his lap, his hands roaming over her curves, mouth and fingers teasing, tormenting, bringing her to the edge and then easing her back, building and retreating, the most perfect torture she could imagine.

She planted her hands on his shoulders, pressing herself tight up against him, his erection teasing her right where she was wet and ready for him.

He pressed a kiss to her collarbone, trailed a line with his tongue down to where the flimsy lace bra met the rounded curve of her breasts.

At the same time, he pushed his finger beneath the lacy edge of her panties and slid the tip of it over her clitoris, the strokes sending white heat through her, ramping up her arousal. She whimpered, tucked her head against his neck, kissing him there.

"I can't wait anymore," she said, her voice shaking. Gone was the control, the steadiness. She didn't have any of it now. She was too filled with her need for him to think, or seem cool. To wait to get the rest of her clothes off, her shoes off.

He tugged her panties to the side and pushed up inside of her. She gasped and arched against him as he filled her. The race to the peak was furious and fast. Eduardo gripped her hips pulling her down onto him as he thrust into her, his movements hard, lacking in finesse, utterly perfect.

She didn't want his control, because she didn't have any. She didn't want evidence of practiced sexual technique. She didn't want anything but him, out of control and just as dizzy with need for her as she was for him. She moved against him, tension drawing tight as a bowstring inside of her until it snapped, releasing her, letting her fall over the edge into bliss, her pleasure washing over her, leaving her spent, consumed in the aftermath.

He thrust up into her one last time, his fingers biting into her flesh, her name a harsh groan on his lips as he found his release.

He rested his head against hers, his breath harsh and hot, fanning over her cheek. Her arms wrapped around his neck, he lifted his hand, pushing her hair, which had come completely unpinned, from her face. His hands were shaking.

She leaned in and rested her head on his shoulder and he held her. While she held him. She never wanted to move. She just wanted to rest with him. She realized that the lights were on, bright and revealing. That she'd just lost her composure in his arms, utterly and completely, and that she wasn't embarrassed at all.

She'd been so afraid of a moment like this. Of being without her trappings. Without her makeup, and sleek hair. Without that suit of armor she kept on at all times. Keeping herself under tight control so that she would never, ever become that wild, stupid girl she'd been when she was growing up.

But she suddenly realized that she wasn't that girl anymore. She'd changed. She wasn't just stomping her down, or covering her up. But she had been holding down the real Hannah Weston. Choking the life out of her because she was so afraid.

So afraid of what? Of being hurt. Of caring.

Of loving.

And now, here she was, with the one man who knew her secrets, caring. Caring so much she felt as if it was pouring from her like blood. But she didn't feel as if it was running out, didn't feel as if it was leaving her weak.

She felt stronger than she had in a long time. Maybe stronger than she ever had. And she wasn't dressed for a business meeting; she wasn't giving someone the steely eye. She was mostly naked, curled up against Eduardo, on the edge of tears.

"Do you need me to move?" she asked, inhaling deeply, the scent of him filling her, making her chest feel like it was expanding.

"No," he said, tightening his hold on her.

"Mmm…good." She kissed his neck again. "I suppose things have the potential to get complicated now. But, on the plus side, the sex between us is very good."

He laughed, shaking beneath her, the low rumble sending a little thrill of pleasure through her. "You could say that."

"That will work, though. This will work."

"Hannah, you think too much. And at the moment, I can't think at all."

"Okay, I'll stop thinking." She shifted to the side and he put his hand on her stomach. She looked down at where his palm was, spread over her pale skin.

They looked up, eyes clashing, her heart squeezed.

"When I look at your face I keep expecting to see the girl I first met five years ago," he said. "In fact, I was counting on it."

"What do you mean?"

"I thought that by bringing you back…I thought if I had you back in my house, in my office, in my life, I might re-member what made me blackmail you into marrying me in the first place. The height of my entitlement. An act that so epitomized who I used to be. I thought if I could understand it, feel it again…"

"You were trying to go back," she said.

"Yes. But it didn't work, Hannah. Because I don't see you the same way now. Everything then…everything I was… it was about how it could benefit me. How people could be used to make my life more comfortable. More entertaining. I looked at you and saw a chance to play a game. Now I look and I see you. The real you."

Hannah blinked, trying to stop her eyes from stinging. "I think you're the only one who ever has."

He lifted his hand and looked down at her stomach, a faint frown visible on his face. He traced one faded, white line with the tip of his finger.

"Stretch marks," she said, for once not feeling cagey or weird about the past. "I got them pretty bad with…with him."

"Signs of your strength," he said, his voice rough.

"Or my weakness."

"Never that, Hannah. You are the strongest woman I've ever known. Everyone makes mistakes, but it takes someone truly great to go on and succeed in spite of them."

"I always think I succeeded because of them," she said, voicing a thought she'd never spoken out loud before. "Because getting pregnant the first time forced me to look at myself. To realize I was no better than my parents, who I despised so much. That I was just as irresponsible. That I would repeat the cycle unless I did something to break out of it."

"You did."

She nodded slowly. "Yes." More than that though, she felt like she'd only just really broken out. Yes, she'd gone and gotten an education. And yes, she'd gone and made money. But until this very moment, she doubted that she'd ever really cared for anyone. She doubted she'd ever loved.

She looked up at Eduardo again. She did now. She loved him.

"I…" She found she couldn't speak.

"I think it's time we took this to bed," he said. "And you can lose the shoes." He reached down and disposed of her spiky black heels. "The rest I'll be happy to take care of for you."

He lifted her up and she held on to him tight, unable to take her eyes off him, unable to stop turning over the immense, tender feeling that was spreading from her chest through the rest of her body.

She loved Eduardo. Love was different than she'd imagined.

It was better.

Two weeks passed and every night, Eduardo had Hannah in his bed. Every day, he tried to go to work and concentrate on what he was supposed to do. Sometimes he was more successful than others. He wasn't sure how much of it to blame on his new, unimproved brain and how much to blame on Hannah herself.

She was soft as silk, pale and perfect. The image of her, the thought of how her skin felt beneath his fingertips, seemed to invade his mind constantly. The taste of her, the overwhelming sensation of right when he slid inside of her wet heat.

Even now, as they waited at the exclusive doctor's office, his thoughts were on what was beneath the yellow silk dress she was wearing. Well, his thoughts were bouncing back and forth between that, and the health of their baby.

She was getting things confirmed today and it was enough to have him on edge. The pregnancy had been unintentional, but as they walked into the plush office he felt everything in him seize up and the realization of how important the baby had become to him hit him fully.

The nurse left them in the room and Hannah slipped out of her clothes, tugging a white linen hospital gown on over her body before lying back on the bed.

"Feeling good?" he asked, moving to stand by her head.

"Yeah," she said, her eyes wide. She looked nervous. The sight made his heart wrench up tight. He wasn't used to Hannah being nervous. Lately she'd been…softer. Not in an emotional wreck kind of way, but in a way that made her seem more real. More human. A way that made him want to protect her, shield her from the world. A way that made him want to hold her close and never let her go.

The doctor came in a few moments later and explained the Doppler machine to him before lifting Hannah's hospital gown and squirting a bit of clear gel onto her flat stomach.

"I see this isn't your first pregnancy, Hannah," Dr. Cordoba said.

Hannah shook her head. "No."

"Everything healthy with the last one?"

"Yes," Hannah said, her voice strong. Eduardo wanted to hug her. Kiss her. Tell her how brave she was.

"Good. Very good to know." The woman put the Doppler on Hannah's stomach, moved it lower. It made a kind of strange, white noise sound, changing slightly as she adjusted position.

His eyes were glued to Hannah's, even more specifically, to the little crease between her eyebrows. And then the sound changed to a fast, whooshing sound and the look on her face changed, a smile spreading her lips.

"That's it," she said, reaching for his hand.

He just stood and listened to the sound of his baby's heart filling the room. Listened to it all become real. To every intention of nannies and detachment vanishing, evaporating like smoke.

He felt like he was in a cloud, lost to reality, for the rest of the appointment. Everything was on track. She should come back next month. They'd do a sonogram to get measurements and confirm dates.

They walked out of the doctor's office and back out to the car, and he was thankful that today he'd used a driver. His head was too full to even consider driving at the moment.

He opened Hannah's door for her and settled in beside her. She leaned over and wrapped her arms around him, a sweet smile on her lips. "He's okay," she said. "I'm so glad I…I think part of me was afraid that…"

He wrapped his arm around her, even as fear flooded his chest. "You don't have to be afraid, Hannah."

"I know. Can we…can we stop by a courier's office?"

"Of course, what do you need?"

"I need…" She pulled her purse onto her lap and took a white envelope out, handing it to him. "I want to send this. … Would you read it?"

He opened up the envelope and took out a handwritten letter. He swallowed hard when he started reading, a lump settling in his throat that stayed with him through the entire letter.

It was to her son. A letter telling him about her circumstances. Telling him that she thought of him. That she hoped he was well. That she loved him.

"It's going to the adoption agency," she said. "That way if he ever wonders about me, he can go look at it but...but if he doesn't...then...I don't want to interrupt his life."

"I think it's perfect, Hannah," he said, his chest feeling tight.

"It's everything I felt like I needed to say. Everything I thought he might want to know. Mostly, I needed him to know that he wasn't unwanted. And that...that he has an extra person in the world who loves him and thinks about him."

He kissed her head. "Two."

"Two?"

"I'll think of him now. Always."

She smiled. "Thank you."

He nodded and brought her close to his body, ignoring the rush of fear that was burning through him. Reading Hannah's letter to a child she barely knew, seeing how much she loved him, even now, made him understand something that he hadn't wanted to understand.

A child would change things. It would change him.

And then there was Hannah. And somewhere, in all of that, was Vega. He was the man who was supposed to take care of all of that.

He closed his eyes and gritted his teeth, fighting hard against the migraine that was threatening to take him over again.

CHAPTER FOURTEEN

"EDUARDO, do you have the quarterly reports in from the retail stores?"

Hannah walked into his office looking every inch the cool businesswoman she was. Different, too. Her face glowed with…happiness.

She was a force of it. He couldn't ignore her, and he didn't want to.

He looked back at his computer screen and closed the window on the internet browser. He'd been looking at colleges. For their son or daughter who was a tiny embryo at that very moment.

He blinked and redirected his focus. "What?"

"The quarterly reports. I need them. Finances. Dollar signs. The thing you pay me for. I just need you to forward them to me. Last week. But unless you have a blue police box capable of time travel, I'll let it go."

"What?"

"Never mind. Do you have the reports or not?"

"I…somewhere. Hold on. They have to be in my in-box somewhere." She was watching him, her blue eyes trained on him. He waited to see impatience, and there was none. She was simply waiting. "Sorry, I'm not right on top of it, Hannah, I know you would be."

She waved a hand. "It's fine. I already did everything else

I had to do today. Anyway, I missed you, so it's nice to come and visit for a while."

She walked over to the desk, her delicate fingers resting on the wood, tracing idly over the designs in the grain. He gritted his teeth and tried to refocus his attention. He swore and slammed his hand down by his keyboard. Hannah jumped.

"I can't find them."

"Do a search."

Of course. He knew that. His mind was moving too slowly, and Hannah was too large in it. He couldn't focus. "Dammit, Hannah, do you mind not hovering?"

She frowned and he could have stabbed his own hand with a pen. "I'm sorry," he said, his voice rough.

"Are you having a hard time? Just let me find it for you."

"It's an email search. I can handle it." He typed in quarterly reports and it brought them up. Suddenly it was like the fog had cleared. He forwarded them to Hannah. "There, you have them now."

"Thank you."

"I'll see you when I'm through here."

She nodded, her lips turned down now. "Okay. See you."

She turned and walked out of his office and he leaned back in his chair, drawing his hand down his face. He was sweating. Why had that been so hard? Why had he forgotten the reports in the first place?

It was the distractions. All the time. All he could think about were Hannah and the baby. And when he wasn't thinking about them, he seemed to want to be thinking about them. So he found excuses to go to Hannah's office, he used Google to look up colleges and real estate listings in the city limits that weren't sky-high penthouses.

He'd thought he could do this. He had to do it. If he didn't, what legacy was there for his son or daughter? It mattered now, even more that he hang on to Vega. It wasn't about personal pride, it was about inheritance. About his child's right to not have their fool of a father destroy what could have been theirs.

Yes, he had a private fortune, but it was much less valuable than what he had here. The potential with Vega Communications was untapped. He knew it could be more. He'd always intended to make it more when his father was running it, and he knew it now. But if he continued to do stupid things like forgetting to forward financial reports, none of it would happen.

Hannah would have to remind him. Hold his hand. She was his wife, and he was meant to care for her. But he wasn't doing his job. He was failing her. He would fail her, continually. Until death did them part. He had tied her to him, tó a deficient man, when she was exceptional, brave and bright, brilliant beyond any he'd ever known.

He was sure that when he'd intercepted her on her wedding day she'd wished him to hell a thousand times. But for the first time, he wished himself there.

Eduardo was still tense when they got back to the penthouse. Tense didn't even begin to cover it. She was almost afraid to say anything for fear he would explode. Not that she couldn't handle him. But she was getting the increasingly worrying feeling that he wasn't happy. And that bothered her.

Because she was happy. Going to bed with him every night, waking up with him every morning. It was more than she'd ever imagined marriage to be. What he made her feel when he touched her was divine, but more than that was the connection between them.

She'd been skin to skin with men, boys really, before. She'd had lovers, if they could be called that. But she'd picked up and left them when they were through and felt...nothing. It had frightened her sometimes. When she was with them, she'd gotten the thrill, but it hadn't lingered, and they had never lingered in her mind, and certainly never her heart.

But Eduardo…he felt like he was a part of her. And she knew, knew for a fact, it had nothing to do with carrying his baby. She'd felt no mystical pull to the boy who'd gotten her pregnant the first time. No sense that she had a piece of him with her.

No, Eduardo was utterly unique and so was the connection she felt to him. It was deeper than sex. In fact, it had existed before the sex.

When the door closed behind them, he didn't speak, he just pulled her into his arms. His kiss was rough and demanding, his hands roaming over her curves, tugging at her shirt, her skirt. She pushed his jacket down his arms and onto the floor, devouring his mouth, conducting an exploration of her own.

They left a trail of clothes on their way to his bedroom. His movements were urgent, his mouth hard and hungry.

"There are ways I can care for you that no other man can," he said, his voice rough as he laid her down onto the bed. "There are things I can do." He put his hand down between her thighs and slid his fingers over the damp folds of her flesh. "Things I can make you feel, that no other man can make you feel."

She could only nod as he slid one finger inside of her.

"You want me?" he asked.

She nodded, her breath coming out on a sob. "Of course."

"Say it."

She opened her eyes, met with his intense, dark gaze. "I want you, Eduardo Vega. My husband."

A smile curved his mouth and he lowered his head, sucking hard on her nipple before continuing down, his mouth hot and demanding on her body, making her feel restless, so turned on she couldn't think or breathe.

When his mouth covered the heart of her she couldn't do anything but ride the wave of pleasure that threatened to carry her away.

Eduardo was drowning in her scent, her taste. His body

was on fire, his heart threatening to beat from his chest. He felt her tense beneath him, felt her body tighten as she found her release.

He pressed a kiss to her stomach and put his hand under her bottom, lifting her so that he could enter her in one smooth thrust. She arched against him, a hoarse cry escaping her lips that he captured with his own.

She was so tight and hot around him, her legs pinning him against her body, her small breasts, tight nipples, pressing into his chest. She tightened around his shaft and he just about lost it then and there. But he was going to make her come one more time.

He thrust hard into her and she tightened her hold on him, pressed wet kisses to his neck, whispering in his ear. How sexy he was. How good he felt.

And his blood roared in his ears, all thoughts of control and finesse lost in the rising tide of pleasure and urgency that was flooding him.

His orgasm overtook him like wildfire, impossible to stop, impossible to redirect, consuming everything in its path. He let out a short, sharp sound of pleasure as he spilled himself inside of her and he was aware, dimly, of Hannah shuddering out her own release.

He rested his head on her breasts, waited for his heart rate to return to normal. Waited for thoughts to start trickling through his brain.

All he had now was an intense emotion that seemed to be filling his chest. That seemed to be taking over.

He turned his face, inhaled her scent, let it fill him. She stroked his face, her hands soft, her touch soothing him down deep.

And he realized that no matter how many orgasms he'd given her, no matter how many he gave her over a lifetime, it wasn't proof that he was caring for her. Even now he was starving for her, for what she could give him. To have her arms around him, to have her hold him close.

And when the time came for another migraine, when he was curled up on the floor, unable to see, barely able to breathe, she would be the one who would have to hold him.

He would be a dead weight to her. To all she'd worked for. One more thing to hold Hannah back in life.

He would be damned if he did that to her. Of course, it was entirely possible he already was.

"You look extra broody this morning," Hannah said, walking into the kitchen and seeing Eduardo sitting at the table, his expression dark.

He lifted his cup of coffee to his lips and offered her a bored look.

"That's all you've got for me? At least say something rude," she said, rifling through the fridge for a bottle of milk. She liked that it was only the two of them living in the penthouse. He had staff that came in while they were gone, but otherwise it was just the two of them.

"Hannah, we need to talk."

She straightened then shut the fridge, the milk bottle clutched tightly in her hand. "What about?"

"About this arrangement."

"What about it?" She turned and opened one of the cabinets, reaching for a bowl, ignoring the unease that was making her stomach tighten.

"It's not working."

She dropped the cereal bowl she'd just grasped onto the counter and it clattered loudly against the hard surface, thankfully not shattering. "What?" She grabbed the bowl and stopped it from shivering against the tile. "I mean wh-wha about it isn't working? The amazing, soul-shaking sex? The relative harmony in which we live?"

"It's not that. It's… You were right. I'm not doing a goo

job of balancing domestic life with Vega and it has to change. It's going to get even harder when the baby's born."

"But…Eduardo…"

"I think it would be best if we kept things as simple as possible. Perhaps…perhaps it would be best if we didn't try to force a marriage between us. I've been looking for houses outside the city, but still close. A place more suitable to raising children. I would be happy to install you there with the child and a nanny. I could stay here during the work week."

"What? That doesn't make any sense, it doesn't… I mean… How can we…be a family if you don't even live with us?"

He stood up, slammed his palm down on the table, his expression thunderous. "I am not the man you should cast in your little sitcom, Hannah. I cannot give you whatever your vision is of what a perfect family should look like."

She gripped the edge of the counter, her heart pounding as she listened to him. Was that what she was doing? Was she trying to project her idea of perfection onto him? To force an idea that possibly wasn't real? Had that been what all of it was? Her trying to build a new fantasy?

The sharp pain in her heart told her no. That her feelings were real.

"You think you know the way the world works, Hannah," he continued, his voice a low growl. "You named yourself after a retail store because you thought it was fancy. You think black-and-white television shows are an example of how real life should work. That we can put a picket fence around the yard and get a dog and you can have all the things you've always fantasized about. You play so sophisticated, but in so many ways you're naive. A little girl playing dress-up."

"Is that what you think?" she said, her voice soft, anger rising up inside of her. Unreasonable, and unstoppable. And with it, pain, pain that she felt down so deep she wasn't sure she would ever find the bottom of it. "I'm going to let you have it now, Eduardo Vega, but this isn't just me spouting pithy one-liners to keep you from getting close. This is me being honest. I gave myself to you, and that wasn't pretend. That wasn't something I didn't understand, and you damn well gave yourself to me. So, now what? You're scared? You're freaked out because you forgot to hit Send on an email and now you're letting it get in your head."

"That's not all," he said, his voice fierce. "You know how bad it gets. You've seen."

"Yes, you had a migraine. A horrible one. You have them… I get it. But if I can handle it, then it's not up to you to say that I can't. You're making up excuses, and blaming things, blaming me, blaming you, for the fact that you're just scared because whatever this is between us…it's big. And you're scared of it."

"I'm going to get ready for work now, Hannah. You can call my driver and he'll take you later."

"Are you running?" she asked.

He whirled around to face her, his expression dark, dangerous. "I'm not running. I'm being reasonable. What did you think this would be?" he asked, his voice raw. "You're right. I can barely concentrate on the duties I already have. I don't have it in me, not the energy or the desire to be a husband to you. I can't…I can't take care of you."

Pain washed through Hannah, acute and sharp. "You don't…want to be my husband?"

"No, Hannah," he said, something in his tone jagged. Torn. "Okay."

"What?"

She shook her head. "Fine. Okay. Then I don't want you to be my husband. I'm not going to force it. It's funny…I was ready to marry Zack even though…even though he didn't know me. He didn't even especially want me. I mean…we weren't really lighting things on fire with our passion, you know? But that was okay with him. It's not okay with you and I only just realized that."

"What do you mean?"

"I won't be a duty to you. I want you to divorce me. And you be the best father you can be for our child. But I'm not going to be that wife you have to keep because you feel some sense of duty."

"All or nothing then."

"Yes." It broke her to say it, because there was a piece of her, that girl who was searching for permanent, for stable, who wanted desperately to cling to whatever he could give. Who wanted to marry the facade and forget the rest.

But the new Hannah, the one Eduardo had brought out, uncovered after so many years, she wanted more. She wanted it all. Not just duty, but love. Real love, not just a few hours of mindless pleasure every night. She wanted to share more than his bed. She wanted to share his heart. His life.

"Then it has to be nothing."

He turned and walked out of the room and she stood, watching the spot where he'd been, adjusting to him not being there.

When he got home from work, Hannah was gone. Not just gone for the moment, but gone. Her things were gone. The sweet sense of comfort he felt when he came home now was gone with her.

His head wasn't clearer. It pounded. Ached. Along with his entire body.

But then, he'd known that would be the case. Everything he'd said to her was utter bull. He went to his bar and poured himself a shot of tequila. Perfect for doling out the punishment he so richly deserved. If he imbibed enough tonight he wouldn't be able to move in the morning. Maybe it would even trigger another migraine. All the better. It would cover up the real reason he was curled up on the floor writhing in pain.

He carried the glass into his room with him and slammed it on his bedside table.

He'd blamed her. He'd told her she didn't know what she was getting into, and it was true. That he couldn't be everything for her, and that was true, too.

But he'd lied when he'd said he didn't want to be her husband.

He did. More than anything, he wanted to be by her side all of his life. But how could he do that when he wasn't everything a husband should be? His father had been so strong and capable; he'd cared for them all. He'd made sure his mother was beneath his protection, always. And he, Eduardo, was so...so weak.

He had feet of clay and he feared one day they would crumble beneath him.

He lay down in his bed and put his hand over his eyes, trying to dull the ache in his chest, trying to staunch the sudden flood of emotions that was washing through him like an endless river of pain.

Yes, he would have his child. He was thankful for that. He would be the best father he could be. But he wouldn't force Hannah to be with him. She would thank him later.

Dios, but he wanted her. If only this could somehow be enough. If only caring for her would make him worthy of her. After all she'd been through, the disgusting living conditions and neglect...

She deserved more. A champion. For someone to come in and make her life easier, not harder. She deserved a man who could be a strong father to their child. A man who could be a capable husband. A strong businessman who didn't make mistakes.

He wanted to howl at the irony. He'd had it. Back when he'd first married her, he'd had that capability. To be the man she deserved. And he hadn't cared. He hadn't tried. And now he was hampered, hampered by an altered mind, and now that he cared desperately about being everything for her, about loving her as she deserved, he couldn't.

He reached out and fumbled for his tequila but couldn't quite grasp the glass. He shoved it off the nightstand and lay back, embracing the pounding migraine that was starting behind his eyes and stabbing deeper with each passing moment.

He focused on it. Reveled in it.

Because it took the edge off the unendurable pain in his heart.

CHAPTER FIFTEEN

AFTER spending the day locked in his penthouse, he'd called his driver and made plans to go to the ranch the next day. He wasn't in the right frame of mind to drive up to the house. His head was pounding and he felt slow and thick.

Then he'd called around and found out Hannah was staying at a luxury hotel. He hoped they had sheets with a suitable thread count.

The thought made his eyes sting.

They would work it out to the point where they would see each other. He would buy her a house, get everything set for the baby. That would be worse in some ways. Seeing her, being so close, and not being able to have her.

Because of his own weakness. His own fault.

He wanted to peel his head open and pull his brain out. Fix it, get a new one. He hated it. Hated the feeling that he was trapped. Limited.

Hated being without her even more than that, because he felt like he was missing something of himself.

Because something had changed since Hannah had come back into his life. He didn't want to be the man he'd been anymore. That man had been a fool. Arrogant. Selfish. He no longer missed him, no longer wished he could be him.

An empty realization since the man he was now couldn't give her what she needed, either.

He exited the penthouse and got into the black town car

that was idling against the curb. He rested his head against the back of the seat and concentrated on the pounding in his head.

The car pulled away from the street and out into the flow of traffic. It didn't take long to get out of the city and he felt the pain in his head lessen, even as the one in his chest got worse.

He looked up for the first time, his eyes clashing with the blue eyes of the driver, reflected by the rearview mirror.

"Have I been kidnapped?" he asked, his voice sounding hollow, shocked, even to his own ears.

"*Kidnapped* is a harsh word," she said. "I prefer to think of it as being commandeered."

"Is it any different?"

"A bit."

His stomach tightened down. "What is it you want, *querida?*"

"Me? A fair hearing. You don't just get to decide how things are going to be. Or did you not get the memo that marriage is a partnership?"

"I believe I decided we wouldn't have a marriage."

"Yes, well, I don't agree. And if I recall, when I tried to marry someone else, you very much didn't agree, either. You told me we were married and that was my tough luck. So guess what, Eduardo? We're married. Tough luck. That means we talk this through and you don't just mandate."

"What did you do with my driver?" he asked.

"I paid him off. I'm very wealthy, you know. And persuasive."

"Hannah…"

"Back to the subject at hand, though." She maneuvered the car off the rural road, into a little alcove and put it in Park, killing the engine.

She unbuckled and got out, coming around to his side of the car and opening the door.

"As I was saying, you don't get to make all of the decisions in this relationship. I want some say, too." She lowered herself to her knees in front of him. "I'm really hard to live with sometimes. I'm stubborn, and I can be materialistic, and selfish. Until recently I was afraid to care for anyone, afraid to feel anything, because I couldn't control feelings. But not anymore. And it's because of you that I'm not afraid now."

His mouth dried. "How did I…how did I make you not afraid?"

"Because you have accepted me. No matter where I was at. No matter what I said. You didn't let me push you away. You didn't make me feel ashamed for what I'd done, for my fears. You were just…there. No one, not in my whole life, has ever simply accepted me. Has ever stood by and supported me. But you have. You've done that."

"But…Hannah…I can't…I can't take care of you. I can't be everything that a husband should be to you. I'm… I make mistakes."

"Yeah, so do I. Remember the fraud?"

"You did what you had to do."

"I'm not perfect. And neither are you, but that's okay. I love you, Eduardo. And when everything else in this world fails, that's what will remain. It's what will matter."

He lowered his head, pain seizing his chest. "You can't love me."

"Let me tell you something, Señor Vega. I try to control and reason everything so that it fits my idea of perfection. From my sheets to my name, I try to make it all my vision for what life should be. I can't do that with you. You aren't reasonable or controllable or perfect. You're better than that. You're you. And it's those little imperfect bits of you that make you the man I want. I don't need to be taken care of…I just need a partner. And I want you to be him."

He unbuckled his seat belt and pulled Hannah into the car, onto his lap, holding her close. "Hannah, I want so much to… I want to be your champion. To make everything easier for you. I don't want to be a burden."

"Do you want to know something? When I saw you having your migraine...when I held you against me...that was when I realized that I could be a mother. Not because I feel even remotely maternal about you, but because I realized that loving someone, being surrounded by the person you love, was so much more important than status. Than things. I've spent all of my life trying to fill this emptiness in me. I tried to do it by just giving in to whatever I wanted anytime I wanted it. Then I tried to do it by controlling myself. Controlling everything I did. I filled the void with things. With a penthouse with a view. But the satisfaction didn't last. It wasn't real. The one thing I've never had is love. And you've given it to me. You've shown me not just how it feels to be loved, but how beautiful it is to love. Eduardo, loving you could never be a burden." She pressed a kiss to his lips. "I wish you could feel it."

"What?" he asked, his voice rough.

"I wish you could feel what I feel. I feel like my heart was trapped in a cage. I wouldn't let myself have emotions. I wouldn't let myself care for anyone too deeply, wouldn't let myself have friends. I was strangling my heart, suffocating it. And you set it free." He looked at her eyes, pale and filled with tears, so sincere. "I'm free."

Something broke open inside of him. A stone wall that had been wrapped tightly around him. And he felt it, too. Felt like he'd walked out of a prison cell and into the sunlight for the first time in years. She'd spoken of that feeling once, and he felt it now. So real, so intense.

His heart thundered, his hands shaking as he stroked her hair. "Hannah...I... You love me?"

"Yes."

"Me. This me. Not the me that I was?"

"Eduardo, this man, the one you are right now, is the man I fell for. You're the one who changed me."

A wave of relief, so strong, so powerful, washed over him. "You want me like this?"

"Yes. Just like this. I don't think you're diminished, or wrong, in any way. You're just you."

He closed his eyes and rested his forehead against hers, his headache fading. "With you, Hannah, I imagine maybe I can just be me. The me I am now. I was...as afraid as you were of changing back into who you used to be, I was afraid I never would. But I think we were both being stupid."

"Do you?"

He nodded. "Like our past was a destination we could so easily get to. Like it was one I might want to get to. I thought that by bringing you back, by seeing your face, I would see the past. But now when I look at you I only see my future. I love you, Hannah."

She smiled, real, happy. "You mean, you really do want to be my husband?"

"Forever. I was just...too afraid. Of failing you. Of failing our child. I want to give you everything, and I'm afraid that I'm so much less than what you deserve. But I don't despise the man I am now... I don't want to go back. How can I when you love me? When you'll be in my future?" He took her chin between his thumb and forefinger.

"I will be," she whispered. "I promise."

"Sometimes I'll have headaches. I'll forget things. I'll make mistakes. But one thing I promise never to forget is how much I love you."

Hannah smiled, her blue eyes filled with joy. "I won't be perfect, either, but I will be myself. I will be committed fully to you."

"I promise the same."

Hannah looked around them, at the mountains, at the car, at him, and she laughed. "It's like making marriage vows all over again."

"Only these are very real," he said.

She nodded. "From my heart, I promise, Eduardo. I'll love you always. You know…no one has ever loved me before. But you were worth the wait."

His chest expanded, his heart overflowing with emotion, with love. "Never doubt that I love you. I do. More than anything. And our children will love you. Our lives will be filled with it."

"I want that, very much."

"And you will have it, my love." He leaned in and kissed her forehead. "I never imagined I could deserve such a strong, beautiful woman as my wife."

"Some might say we deserve each other, Eduardo," she said, a wicked little smile curving her lips.

"True."

"And it's a good thing we're both strong."

"Why is that?"

She pressed a kiss to his lips. "So we can take care of each other."

EPILOGUE

HANNAH looked up at the picture that had hung in their bedroom for the past ten years. When she'd first seen it, she'd thought the woman standing in the crowd looked alone. For some reason, she didn't think so now.

Maybe because she never felt alone. Just as Eduardo had promised, her life was filled with love now.

She looked down at the nightstand and opened up the drawer, and looked down at the letter that was there, a blue ribbon wrapped around the outside. The letter from Benjamin Johnson, who was now eighteen and headed off to college. The letter that thanked her. For giving him life. For giving him his family. She smiled down at the paper, her heart swelling with love, and slid the drawer closed.

"Mama!"

She heard screaming and shouting and a scuffle, then Eduardo's deep voice scolding in Spanish and four sets of little feet running, then a door slamming. She laughed and turned away from the painting just as her husband came into the room.

"Everything well with the troops?"

"Graciela had Juanita's doll. And the boys were simply choosing sides to create a scene," he said. "I sent them out. It's a nice day."

She turned to him, leaned against his solid strength. "I need your quarterly report," she said.

He dipped his head and kissed her on the nose. "I already sent it to you."

She smiled up at her husband, the father of her children, her business partner. "Well, now I have no reason to punish you."

His eyebrows arched. "You sound disappointed."

"I am."

"Thank you," he said.

"For what?"

He wrapped his arms around Hannah and she rested her head on his chest. "For being my partner."

She went up on her toes and pressed a kiss to his neck. "Always."

* * * * *

FOR THE SAKE
OF THEIR SON

CATHERINE MANN

For my children.

USA TODAY bestseller and *RITA*® Award winner **Catherine Mann** has penned over fifty novels, released in more than twenty countries. After years as a military spouse bringing up four children, Catherine is now a snowbird – sorta – splitting time between the Florida beach and somewhat chillier beach in her home state of South Carolina. The nest didn't stay empty long, though, as Catherine is an active board member for the *Sunshine State Animal Rescue*. www.CatherineMann.com

One

Elliot Starc had faced danger his whole life. First at the hands of his heavy-fisted father. Later as a Formula One race car driver who used his world travels to feed information to Interpol.

But he'd never expected to be kidnapped. Especially not in the middle of his best friend's bachelor party.

Mad as hell, Elliot struggled back to consciousness, only to realize his wrists were cuffed. Numb. He struggled against the restraints while trying to get his bearings, but his brain was still disoriented. Last he remembered, he'd been in Atlanta, Georgia, at a bachelor party and now he was cuffed and blindfolded, for God's sake. What the hell? He only knew that he was in the back of a vehicle that smelled of leather and luxury. Noise offered him little to go on. Just the purr of a finely tuned engine. The pop of an opening soda can. A low hum of music so faint it must be on a headset.

"He's awake," a deep voice whispered softly, too softly to be identified.

"Damn it," another voice hissed.

"Hey," Elliot shouted, except it wasn't a shout. More of a hoarse croak. He cleared his throat and tried again. "Whatever the hell is going on here, we can talk ransom—"

A long buzz sounded. Unmistakable. The closing of a privacy window. Then silence. Solitude, no chance of shouting jack to anyone in this...

A limo, perhaps? Who kidnapped someone using a limousine?

Once they stopped, he would be ready, though. The second he could see, he wouldn't even need his hands. He was trained in seven different forms of self-defense. He could use his feet, his shoulders and his body weight.

He would be damned before he let himself ever be helpless in a fight.

They'd pulled off an interstate at least twenty minutes ago, driving into the country as best he could tell. He had no way of judging north, south or west. He could be anywhere from Florida to Mississippi to South Carolina, and God knows he had enemies in every part of the world from his work with Interpol and his triumphs over competitors in the racing world.

And he had plenty of pissed-off ex-girlfriends.... He winced at the thought of females and Carolina so close together. Home. Too many memories. Bad ones—with just a single bright spot in the form of Lucy Ann Joyner, but he'd wrecked even that.

Crap.

Back to the present. Sunlight was just beginning to filter through the blindfold, sparking behind his eyes like shards of glinting glass.

One thing was certain. This car had good shock absorbers. Otherwise the rutted road they were traveling would have rattled his teeth.

Although his teeth were clenched mighty damn tight right now.

Even now, he still couldn't figure out how he'd been blindsided near the end of Rowan Boothe's bachelor party in an Atlanta casino. Elliot had ducked into the back to find a vintage Scotch. Before he could wrap his hand around the neck of the bottle, someone had knocked him out.

If only he knew the motive for his kidnapping. Was someone after his money? Or had someone uncovered his secret dealings with Interpol? If so, did they plan to exploit that connection?

He'd lived his life to the fullest, determined to do better than his wrong-side-of-the-tracks upbringing. He only had one regret: how his lifelong friendship with Lucy Ann had crashed and burned more fiercely than when he'd been sideswiped at the Australian Grand Prix last year—

The car jerked to a halt. He braced his feet to keep from rolling off onto the floor. He forced himself to stay relaxed so his abductors would think he was still asleep.

His muscles tensed for action, eager for the opportunity to confront his adversaries. Ready to pay back. He was trained from his work with Interpol, with lightning-fast instincts honed in his racing career. He wouldn't go down without a fight.

Since he'd left his dirt-poor roots behind, he'd been beating the odds. He'd dodged juvie by landing in a military reform school where he'd connected with a lifelong group of friends. Misfits like himself who disdained rules while living by a strict code of justice. They'd grown up to take different life paths, but stayed connected through their friendship and freelance work for Interpol. Not that they'd been much help to him while someone was nabbing him a few feet away from the bachelor party they were all attending.

The car door opened and someone leaned over him. Something tugged at the back of his brain, a sense that he should know this person. He scrambled to untangle the mystery before it was too late.

His blindfold was tugged up and off, and he took in the inside of a black limo, just as he'd suspected. His abductors, however, were a total surprise.

"Hello, Elliot, my man," said his old high school pal Malcolm Douglas, who'd asked him to fetch that bottle of Scotch back at the bachelor party. "Waking up okay?"

Conrad Hughes—another traitorous bastard friend— patted his face. "You look plenty awake to me."

Elliot bit back a curse. He'd been kidnapped by his own comrades from the bachelor party. "Somebody want to tell me what's going on here?"

He eyed Conrad and Malcolm, both of whom had been living it up with him at the casino well past midnight. Morning sunshine streamed over them, oak trees sprawling behind them. The scent of Carolina jasmine carried on the breeze. Why were they taking him on this strange road trip?

"Well?" he pressed again when neither of them answered. "What the hell are you two up to?" he asked, his anger barely contained. He wanted to kick their asses. "I hope you have a good reason for taking me out to the middle of nowhere."

Conrad clapped him on the back. "You'll see soon enough."

Elliot angled out of the car, hard as hell with his hands

cuffed in front of him. His loafers hit the dirt road, rocks and dust shifting under his feet as he stood in the middle of nowhere in a dense forest of pines and oaks. "You'll tell me now or I'll beat the crap out of both of you."

Malcolm lounged against the side of the black stretch limo. "Good luck trying with your hands cuffed. Keep talking like that and we'll hang on to the key for a good long while."

"Ha—funny—not." Elliot ground his teeth in frustration. "Isn't it supposed to be the groom who gets pranked?"

Conrad grinned. "Oh, don't worry. Rowan should be waking up and finding his new tattoo right about now."

Extending his cuffed wrists, Elliot asked, "And the reason for this? I'm not the one getting married."

Ever.

Malcolm pushed away, jerking his head to the side, gesturing toward the path leading into the dense cluster of more pine trees with an occasional magnolia reaching for the sun. "Instead of telling you why, we'll just let you look. Walk with us."

As if he had any choice. His friends clearly had some kind of game planned and they intended to see it through regardless. Sure, he'd been in a bear of a mood since his breakup with Gianna. Hell, even before that. Since Lucy Ann had quit her job as his assistant and walked out of his life for good.

God, he really needed to pour out some frustration behind the wheel, full out, racing to…anywhere.

A few steps deeper into the woods, his blood hummed with recognition. The land was more mature than the last time he'd been here, but he knew the area well enough. Home. Or rather it used to be home, back when he was a poor kid with a drunken father. This small South Carolina farm town outside of Columbia had been called God's land.

Elliot considered it a corner of hell.

Although hell was brimming with sunshine today.

He stepped toward a clearing and onto a familiar dirt driveway, with a ranch-style cabin and a fat oak at least a hundred years old in the middle. A tree he'd played under as a kid, wishing he could stay here forever because this little haven in hell was a lot safer than his home.

He'd hidden with Lucy Ann Joyner here at her aunt's farmhouse. Both of them enjoying the sanctuary of this place, even if only for a few hours. Why were his buds taking him down this memory lane detour?

Branches rustled, a creaking sound carrying on the breeze, drawing his gaze. A swing dangled from a thick branch, moving back and forth as a woman swayed, her back to them. He stopped cold. Suddenly the meaning of this journey was crystal clear. His friends were forcing a confrontation eleven months in the making since he and Lucy Ann were both too stubborn to take the first step.

Did she know he was coming? He swallowed hard at the notion that maybe she wanted him here after all. That her decision to slice him out of her life had changed. But if she had, then why not just drive up to the house?

He wasn't sure the past year could be that easily forgotten, but his gut twisted tight over just the thought of talking to her again.

His eyes soaked in the sight of her, taking her in like parched earth with water. He stared at the slim feminine back, the light brown hair swishing just past her shoulders. Damn, but it had been a long eleven months without her. His lifelong pal had bolted after one reckless—incredible—night that had ruined their friendship forever.

He'd given her space and still hadn't heard from her.

In the span of a day, the one person he'd trusted above everyone else had cut him off. He'd never let anyone get that close to him—not even his friends from the military reform school. He and Lucy Ann had a history, a shared link that went beyond a regular friendship.

Or so he'd thought.

As if drawn by a magnet, he walked closer to the swing, to the woman. His hands still linked in front of him, he moved silently, watching her. The bared lines of her throat evoked memories of her jasmine scent. The way her dress slipped ever so slightly off one shoulder reminded him of years past when she'd worn hand-me-downs from neighbors.

The rope tugged at the branch as she toe-tapped, back and forth. A gust of wind turned the swing spinning to face him.

His feet stumbled to a halt.

Yes, it was Lucy Ann, but not just her. Lucy Ann stared back at him with wide eyes, shocked eyes. She'd clearly been kept every bit as much in the dark as he had. Before he could finish processing his disappointment that she hadn't helped arrange this, his eyes took in the biggest shocker of all.

Lucy Ann's arms were curved around an infant swaddled in a blue plaid blanket as she breast-fed him.

Lucy Ann clutched her baby boy to her chest and stared in shock at Elliot Starc, her childhood friend, her former boss. Her onetime lover.

The father of her child.

She'd scripted the moment she would tell him about their son a million times in her mind, but never had it played out like this, with him showing up out of the blue. Handcuffed? Clearly, he hadn't planned on coming to see her. She'd tempted fate in waiting so long to tell him, then he'd pulled one of his disappearing acts and she couldn't find him.

Now there was no avoiding him.

Part of her ached to run to Elliot and trust in the friendship they'd once shared, a friendship built here, in the wooded farmland outside Columbia, South Carolina. But another part of her—the part that saw his two friends lurking and the handcuffs on her old pal—told her all she needed to know. Elliot hadn't suddenly seen the light and come running to apologize for being a first-class jerk. He'd been dragged kicking and screaming.

Well, screw him. She had her pride, too.

Only the baby in her arms kept her from bolting altogether into her aunt's cabin up the hill. Lucy Ann eased Eli from her breast and adjusted her clothes in place. Shifting her son to her shoulder, she patted his back, her eyes staying locked on Elliot, trying to gauge his mood.

The way his eyes narrowed told her loud and clear that she couldn't delay her explanation any longer. She should have told him about Eli sooner. In the early days of her pregnancy, she'd tried and chickened out. Then she'd gotten angry over his speedy rebound engagement to the goddess Gianna, and that made it easier to keep her distance a while longer. She wouldn't be the cause of breaking up his engagement—rat bastard. She would tell him once he was married and wouldn't feel obligated to offer her anything. Even though the thought of him marrying that too-perfect bombshell heiress made her vaguely nauseous.

Now, Elliot was here, so damn tall and muscular, his sandy brown hair closely shorn. His shoulders filled out the black button-down shirt, his jeans slung low on his hips. His five o'clock shadow and narrowed green eyes gave him a bad-boy air he'd worked his whole life to live up to.

She knew every inch of him, down to a scar on his elbow he'd told everyone he got from falling off his bike but he'd really gotten from the buckle on his father's belt during a beating. They shared so much history, and now they shared a child.

Standing, she pulled her gaze from him and focused on his old boarding school friends behind him, brooding Conrad Hughes and charmer Malcolm Douglas. Of course they'd dragged him here. These days both of them had sunk so deep into a pool of marital bliss, they seemed to think everyone else wanted to plunge in headfirst. No doubt they'd brought Elliot here with just that in mind.

Not a freakin' chance.

She wasn't even interested in dipping her toes into those waters and certainly not with Elliot, the biggest playboy in the free world.

"Gentlemen, do you think you could uncuff him, then leave so he and I can talk civilly?"

Conrad—a casino owner—fished out a key from his pocket and held it up. "Can do." He looked at Elliot. "I trust you're not going to do anything stupid like try to start a fight over our little prank here."

Prank? This was her life and they were playing with it. Anger sparked in her veins.

Elliot pulled a tight smile. "Of course not. I'm outnumbered. Now just undo the handcuffs. My arms are too numb to hit either of you anyway."

Malcolm plucked the keys from Conrad and opened the cuffs. Elliot massaged his wrists for a moment, still silent, then stretched his arms over his head.

Did he have to keep getting hotter every year? Especially not fair when she hadn't even had time to shower since yesterday thanks to her son's erratic sleeping schedule.

Moistening her dry mouth, Lucy Ann searched for a way to dispel the awkward air. "Malcolm, Conrad, I realize you meant well with this, but perhaps it's time for you both to leave. Elliot and I clearly have some things to discuss."

Eli burped. Lucy Ann rolled her eyes and cradled her son in the crook of her arm, too aware of the weight of Elliot's stare.

Malcolm thumped Elliot on the back. "You can thank us later."

Conrad leveled a somber steady look her way. "Call if you need anything. I mean that."

Without another word, both men disappeared back into the wooded perimeter as quickly as they'd arrived. For the first time in eleven months, she was alone with Elliot.

Well, not totally alone. She clutched Eli closer until he squirmed.

Elliot stuffed his hands in his pockets, still keeping his distance. "How long have you been staying with your aunt?"

"Since I left Monte Carlo." She'd been here the whole time, if he'd only bothered to look. Where else would she go? She had money saved up, but staying here made the most sense economically.

"How are you supporting yourself?"

"That's not your business." She lifted her chin. He had the ability to find out anything he wanted to know about her if he'd just looked, thanks to his Interpol connections.

Apparently, he hadn't even bothered to try. And that's what hurt the most. All these months, she'd thought he would check up on her. He would have seen she was pregnant. He would have wondered.

He would have come.

"Not my business?" He stalked a step closer, only a hint of anger showing in his carefully guarded eyes. "Really? I think we both know why it is so very much my business."

"I have plenty saved up from my years working for you." He'd insisted on paying her an outlandish salary to be his personal assistant. "And I'm doing virtual work to subsidize my income. I build and maintain websites. I make enough to get by." Her patience ran out with this small talk, the avoidance of discussing the baby sleeping in her arms. "You've had months to ask these questions and chose to remain silent. If anyone has a right to be angry, it's me."

"You didn't call either, and you have a much more compelling reason to communicate." He nodded toward Eli. "He is mine."

"You sound sure."

"I know you. I see the truth in your eyes," he said simply.

She couldn't argue with that. She swallowed once, twice, to clear her throat and gather her nerve. "His name is Eli. And yes, he's your son, two months old."

Elliot pulled his hands from his pockets. "I want to hold him."

Her stomach leaped into her throat. She'd envisioned this moment so many times, but living in it? She never could have imagined how deeply the emotions would rattle her. She passed over Eli to his father, watching Elliot's face. For once, she couldn't read him at all. So strange, considering how they'd once been so in sync they could finish each other's sentences, read a thought from a glance across a room.

Now, he was like a stranger.

Face a blank slate, Elliot held their son in broad, capable hands, palmed the baby's bottom and head as he studied the tiny cherub features. Eli still wore his blue footed sleeper from bedtime, his blond hair glistening as the sun sent dappled rays through the branches. The moment looked like a fairy tale, but felt so far from that her heart broke over how this should have, could have been.

Finally, Elliot looked up at her, his blasé mask sliding away to reveal eyes filled with ragged pain. His throat moved in a slow gulp of emotion. "Why did you keep this—Eli—from me?"

Guilt and frustration gnawed at her. She'd tried to contact him but knew she hadn't tried hard enough. Her pride... Damn it all. Her excuses all sounded weak now, even to her own ears.

"You were engaged to someone else. I didn't want to interfere in that."

"You never intended to tell me at all?" His voice went hoarse with disbelief, his eyes shooting back down to his son sleeping against his chest so contentedly as if he'd been there all along.

"Of course I planned to explain—after you were married." She dried her damp palms on her sundress. "I refused to be responsible for breaking up your great love match."

Okay, she couldn't keep the cynicism out of that last part, but he deserved it for his rebound relationship.

"My engagement to Gianna ended months ago. Why didn't you contact me?"

He had a point there. She ached to run, but he had her son. And as much as she hated to admit it to herself, she'd missed Elliot. They'd been so much a part of each other's lives for so long. The past months apart had been like a kind of withdrawal.

"Half the time I couldn't find you and the other half, your new personal secretary couldn't figure out where you were." And hadn't that pissed her off something fierce? Then worried her, because she knew about his sporadic missions for Interpol, and she also knew his reckless spirit.

"You can't have tried very hard, Lucy Ann. All you had to do was speak with any of my friends." His eyes narrowed. "Or did you? Is that why they brought me here today, because you reached out to them?"

She'd considered doing just that many times, only to balk at the last second. She wouldn't be manipulative. She'd planned to tell him face-to-face. And soon.

"I wish I could say yes, but I'm afraid not. One of them must have been checking up on me even if you never saw the need."

Oops. Where had that bitter jab come from?

He cocked an eyebrow. "This is about Eli. Not about the two of us."

"There is no 'two of us' anymore." She touched her son's head lightly, aching to take him back in her arms. "You ended that when you ran away scared after we had a reckless night of sex."

"I do *not* run away."

"Excuse me if your almighty ego is bruised." She crossed her arms over her chest, feeling as though they were in fifth grade again, arguing over whether the basketball was in or out of bounds.

Elliot sighed, looking around at the empty clearing. The limo's engine roared to life, then faded as it drove away without him. He turned back to Lucy Ann. "This isn't accomplishing anything. We need to talk reasonably about our child's future."

"I agree." Of course they had to talk, but right now her

heart was in her throat. She could barely think straight. She scooped her baby from his arms. "We'll talk tomorrow when we're both less rattled."

"How do I know you won't just disappear with my son?" He let go of Eli with obvious reluctance.

His son.

Already his voice echoed with possessiveness.

She clasped her son closer, breathing in the powder-fresh familiarity of him, the soft skin of his cheek pressed against her neck reassuringly. She could and she would manage her feelings for Elliot. Nothing and no one could be allowed to interfere with her child's future.

"I've been here all this time, Elliot. You just never chose to look." A bitter pill to swallow. She gestured up the empty dirt road. "Even now, you didn't choose. Your friends dumped you here on my doorstep."

Elliot walked a slow circle around her, his hand snagging the rope holding the swing until he stopped beside her. He had a way of moving with such fluidity, every step controlled, a strange contradiction in a man who always lived on the edge. Always flirting with chaos.

Her skin tingled to life with the memory of his touch, the wind teasing her with a hint of aftershave and musk.

She cleared her throat. "Elliot, I really think you should—"

"Lucy Ann," he interrupted, "in case it's escaped your notice, my friends left me here. Alone. No car." He leaned in closer, his hand still holding the rope for balance, so close she could almost feel the rasp of his five o'clock shadow. "So regardless of whether or not we talk, for now, you're stuck with me."

Two

Elliot held himself completely still, a feat of supreme control given the frustration racing through his veins. That Lucy Ann had hidden her pregnancy—his son—from him all this time threatened to send him to his knees. Somehow during this past year he'd never let go of the notion that everything would simply return to the way things had been before with them. Their friendship had carried him through the worst times of his life.

Now he knew there was no going back. Things between them had changed irrevocably.

They had a child together, a boy just inches away. Elliot clenched his hand around the rope. He needed to bide his time and proceed with caution. His lifelong friend had a million great qualities—but she was also stubborn as hell. A wrong step during this surprise meeting could have her digging in her heels.

He had to control his frustration, tamp down the anger

over all that she'd hidden from him. Staying levelheaded saved his life on more than one occasion on the racetrack. But never had the stakes been more important than now. No matter how robbed he felt, he couldn't let that show.

Life had taught him well how to hide his darker emotions.

So he waited, watching her face for some sign. The breeze lifted a strand of her hair, whipping it over his cheek. His pulse thumped harder.

"Well, Lucy Ann? What now?"

Her pupils widened in her golden-brown eyes, betraying her answering awareness a second before she bolted up from the swing. Elliot lurched forward as the swing freed. He released the rope and found his footing.

Lucy Ann glanced over her shoulder as she made her way to the graveled path. "Let's go inside."

"Where's your aunt?" He followed her, rocks crunching under his feet.

"At work." Lucy Ann walked up the steps leading to the prefab log cabin's long front porch. Time had worn the redwood look down to a rusty hue. "She still waits tables at the Pizza Shack."

"You used to send her money." He'd stumbled across the bank transaction by accident. Or maybe his accountant had made a point of letting him discover the transfers since Lucy Ann left so little for herself.

"Well, come to find out, Aunt Carla never used it," Lucy Ann said wryly, pushing the door open into the living room. The decor hadn't changed, the same brown plaid sofa with the same saggy middle, the same dusty Hummel figurines packed in a corner cabinet. He'd forgotten how Carla scoured yard sales religiously for the things, unable to afford them new.

They'd hidden here more than once as kids, then as

teenagers, plotting a way to escape their home lives. He eyed the son he'd barely met but who already filled his every plan going forward. "Your aunt's prideful, just like you."

"I accepted a job from you." She settled Eli into a portable crib by the couch.

"You worked your butt off and got your degree in computer technology." He admired the way she never took the easy way out. How she'd found a career for herself.

So why had she avoided talking to him? Surely not from any fear of confrontation. Her hair swung forward as she leaned into the baby crib, her dress clinging to her hips. His gaze hitched on the new curves.

Lucy Ann spun away from the crib and faced him again. "Are we going to keep making small talk or are you going to call a cab? I could drive you back into town."

"I'm not going anywhere."

Her eyebrows pinched together. "I thought we agreed to talk tomorrow."

"You decided. I never agreed." He dropped to sit on the sofa arm. If he sat in the middle, no telling how deep that sag would sink.

"You led me to believe…" She looked around as if searching for answers, but the Hummels stayed silent. "Damn it. You just wanted to get in the house."

Guilty as charged. "This really is the best place to discuss the future. Anywhere else and I'll have to be on the lookout for fans. We're in NASCAR country, you know. Not Formula One, but kissing cousins." He held up his hands. "Besides, my jackass buddies stranded me without my wallet."

She gasped. "You're joking."

"I wish." They must have taken it from his pocket while he was knocked out. He tamped down another surge of anger over being manipulated. If he'd just had some warning…

"Why did they do this to you—to both of us?" She sat on the other arm of the sofa, the worn width between them.

"Probably because they know how stubborn we are." He watched her face, trying to read the truth in the delicate lines, but he saw only exhaustion and dark circles. "Would you have ever told me about the baby?"

"You've asked me that already and I've answered. Of course I would have told you—" she shrugged "—eventually."

Finally he asked the question that had been plaguing him most. "How can I be sure?"

Shaking her head, she shrugged again. "You can't. You'll just have to trust me."

A wry smile tugged the corner of his mouth. "Trust has never been easy for either of us." But now that he was here and saw the truth, his decision was simple. "I want you and Eli to come with me, just for a few weeks while we make plans for the future."

"No." She crossed her arms over her chest.

"Ah, come on, Lucy Ann. Think about my request before you react."

"Okay. Thinking…" She tapped her temple, tapping, tapping. Her hand fell to her lap. "Still no."

God, her humor and spunk had lifted him out of hell so many times. He'd missed her since she'd stormed out of his life.…

But he'd also missed out on a lot more in not knowing about his son.

"I can never regain those first two months of Eli's life." A bitter pill he wasn't sure how to swallow down. "I need a chance to make up for that."

She shook her head slowly. "You can't be serious about taking a baby on the road."

"I'm dead serious." He wasn't leaving here without them. He couldn't just toss money down and go.

"Let me spell it out for you then. Elliot, this is the middle of your racing season." She spoke slowly, as she'd done when they were kids and she'd tutored him in multiplication tables. "You'll be traveling, working, running with a party crowd. I've seen it year after year, enough to know that's no environment for a baby."

And damn it, she was every bit as astute now as she'd been then. He lined up an argument, a way to bypass her concerns. "You saw my life when there wasn't a baby around—no kids around, actually. It *can* be different. *I* can be different, like other guys who bring their families on the circuit with them." He shifted to sit beside her. "I have a damn compelling reason to make changes in my life. This is the chance to show you that."

Twisting the skirt of her dress in nervous fingers, she studied him with her golden-brown gaze for so long he thought he'd won.

Then resolve hardened her eyes again. "Expecting someone to change only sets us both up for disappointment."

"Then you'll get to say 'I told you so.' You told me often enough in the past." He rested a hand on top of hers to still the nervous fidgeting, squeezing lightly. "The best that happens is I'm right and this works. We find a plan to be good parents to Eli even when we're jet-setting around the world. Remember how much fun we used to have together? I miss you, Lucy Ann."

He thumbed the inside of her wrist, measuring the speed of her pulse, the softness of her skin. He'd done everything he could to put her out of his mind, but with no luck. He'd been unfair to Gianna, leading her to think he was free. So many regrets. He was tired of them. "Lucy Ann…"

She yanked her hand free. "Stop it, Elliot. I've watched you seduce a lot of women over the years. Your games don't work with me. So don't even try the slick moves."

"You wound me." He clamped a hand over his heart in an attempt at melodrama to cover his disappointment.

She snorted. "Hardly. You don't fool me with the pained look. It's eleven months too late to be genuine."

"You would be wrong about that."

"No games." She shot to her feet. "We both need time to regroup and think. We need to continue this conversation later."

"Fair enough then." He sat on the sofa, stretching both arms out along the back.

She stomped her foot. "What are you doing?"

He picked up the remote from the coffee table and leaned back again into the deepest, saggiest part. "Making myself comfortable."

"For what?"

He thumbed on the television. "If I'm going to stick around until you're ready to talk, I might as well scout the good stations. Any beer in the fridge? Although wait, it's too early for that. How about coffee?"

"No." She snatched the remote control from his hand. "And stop it. I don't know what game you're playing but you can quit and *go*. In case that wasn't clear enough, leave and come back later. You can take my car."

He took the remote right back and channel surfed without looking away from the flat screen. "Thanks for the generous offer of transportation, but you said we can't take Eli on the road and I only just met my son. I'm not leaving him now. How about the coffee?"

"Like hell."

"I don't need cream. Black will do just fine."

"Argh!" She slumped against the archway between the living room and kitchen. "Quit being ridiculous about the coffee. You know you're not staying here."

He set aside the remote, smiling as some morning talk show droned in the background. "So you'll come with me after all. Good."

"You're crazy. You know that, right?"

"No newsflash there, sweetheart. A few too many concussions." He stood. "Forget the suitcase."

"Run that by me again?"

"Don't bother with packing. I'll buy everything you need, everything new. Let's just grab a couple of diapers for the rug rat and go."

Her acceptance was becoming more and more important by the second. He needed her with him. He had to figure out a way to tie their lives together again so his son would know a father, a mother and a normal life.

"Stop! Stop trying to control my life." She stared at him sadly. "Elliot, I appreciate all you did for me in the past, but I don't need rescuing anymore."

"Last time I checked, I wasn't offering a rescue. Just a partnership."

If humor and pigheadedness didn't work, time to go back to other tactics. No great hardship really, since the attraction crackled between them every bit as tangibly now as it had the night they'd impulsively landed in bed together after a successful win. He sauntered closer. "As I recall, last time we were together, we shared control quite…nicely. And now that I think of it, we really don't need those clothes after all."

* * *

The rough upholstery of the sofa rasped against the backs of Lucy Ann's legs, her skin oversensitive, tingling to life after just a few words from Elliot. Damn it, she refused to be seduced by him again. The way her body betrayed her infuriated her down to her toes, which curled in her sandals.

Sure, he was beach-boy handsome, mesmerizingly sexy and blindingly charming. Women around the world could attest to his allure. However, in spite of her one unforgettable moment of weakness, she refused to be one of those fawning females throwing themselves at his feet.

No matter how deeply her body betrayed her every time he walked in the room.

She shot from the sofa, pacing restlessly since she couldn't bring herself to leave her son alone, even though he slept. Damn Elliot and the draw of attraction that had plagued her since the day they'd gone skinny-dipping at fourteen and she realized they weren't kids anymore.

Shutting off those thoughts, she pivoted on the coarse shag carpet to face him. "This is not the time or the place for sexual innuendo."

"Honey—" his arms stretched along the back of the sofa "—it's never a bad time for sensuality. For nuances. For seduction."

The humor in his eyes took the edge of arrogance off his words. "If you're aiming to persuade me to leave with you, you're going about it completely the wrong way."

"There's no denying we slept together."

"Clearly." She nodded toward the Pack 'n Play where their son slept contentedly, unaware that his little world had just been turned upside down.

"There's no denying that it was good between us. Very good."

Elliot's husky words snapped her attention back to his face. There wasn't a hint of humor in sight. Awareness tingled to the roots of her hair.

Swallowing hard, she sank into an old cane rocker. "It was impulsive. We were both tipsy and sentimental and reckless." The rush of that evening sang through her memory, the celebration of his win, reminiscing about his first dirt track race, a little wine, too much whimsy, then far too few clothes.... "I refuse to regret that night or call our...encounter...a mistake since I have Eli. But I do not intend to repeat the experience."

"Now that's just a damn shame. What a waste of good sexual chemistry."

"Will you please stop?" Her hands fisted on the arms of the wooden rocker. "We got along just fine as friends for thirty years."

"Are you saying we can be friends again?" He leaned forward, elbows on his knees. "No more hiding out and keeping big fat secrets from each other?"

His words carried too much truth for comfort. "You're twisting my words around."

"God's honest truth, Lucy Ann." He sighed. "I'm trying to call a truce so we can figure out how to plan our son's future."

"By telling me to ditch my clothes? You obviously missed class the day they taught the definition of truce."

"Okay, you're right. That wasn't fair of me." He thrust his hands through his hair. "I'm not thinking as clearly as I would like. Learning about Eli has been a shock to say the least."

"I can understand that." Her hands unfurled to grip the rocker. "And I am so very sorry for any pain this has caused you."

"Given that I've lost the first two months of my son's

life, the least you can do is give me four weeks together. Since you're working from home here, you'll be able to work on the road, as well. But if going on the race circuit is a deal breaker, I'll bow out this season."

She jolted in surprise that he would risk all he'd worked so hard to achieve, a career he so deeply loved. "What about your sponsors? Your reputation?"

"This is your call."

"That's not fair to make an ultimatum like that, to put it on me."

"I'm asking, and I'm offering you choices."

Choices? Hardly. She knew how important his racing career was to him. And she couldn't help but admit to feeling a bit of pride in having helped him along the way. There was no way she could let him back out now.

She tossed up her hands. "Fine. Eli and I will travel with you on the race circuit for the next four weeks so you can figure out whatever it is you want to know and make your plans. You win. You always do."

Winning didn't feel much like a victory tonight.

Elliot poured himself a drink from the wet bar at his hotel. He and Lucy Ann had struck a bargain that he would stay at a nearby historic home that had been converted into a hotel while she made arrangements to leave in the morning. He'd called for a car service to pick him up, making use of his credit card numbers, memorized, a fact he hadn't bothered mentioning to Lucy Ann earlier. Although she should have known. Had she selectively forgotten or had she been that rattled?

The half hour waiting for the car had been spent silently staring at his son while Eli slept and Lucy Ann hid in the other room under the guise of packing.

Elliot's head was still reeling. He had been knocked

unconscious and kidnapped, and found out he had an
unknown son all in one day. He tipped back the glass of
bourbon, emptying it and pouring another to savor, more
slowly, while he sat out on the garden balcony where he
would get better cell phone reception.

He dropped into a wrought-iron chair and let the Carolina moon pour over him. His home state brought such
a mix of happy and sad memories. He was always better served just staying the hell away. He tugged his cell
from his waistband, tucked his Bluetooth in his ear and
thumbed autodial three for Malcolm Douglas.

The ringing stopped two buzzes in. "Brother, how's
it going?"

"How do you think it's going, Douglas? My head hurts
and I'm pissed off." Anger was stoked back to life just
thinking about his friends' arrogant stunt, the way they'd
played with his life. "You could have just told me about
the baby."

Malcolm chuckled softly. "Wouldn't have been half
as fun that way."

"Fun? You think this is some kind of game? You're a
sick bastard." The thought of them plotting this out while
he partied blissfully unaware had him working hard to
keep his breath steady. He and his friends had played
some harsh jokes on one another in the past, but nothing
like this. "How long have you known?"

"For about a week," the chart-topping musician answered unrepentantly.

"A week." Seven days he could have had with his
son. Seven days his best friends kept the largest of secrets from him. Anger flamed through him. Was there
nobody left in this world he could trust? He clenched his
hand around the glass tumbler until it threatened to shatter. "And you said nothing at all."

"I know it seems twisted, but we talked it through," he said, all humor gone, his smooth tones completely serious for once. "We thought this was the best way. You're too good at playing it cool with advance notice. You would have just made her mad."

"Like I didn't already do that?" He set aside the half-drunk glass of bourbon, the top-shelf brand wasted on him in his current mood.

"You confronted her with honesty," Malcolm answered reasonably. "If we'd given you time to think, you'd have gotten your pride up. You would have been angry and bullish. You can be rather pigheaded, you know."

"If I'm such a jackass, then why are we still friends?"

"Because I'm a jackass, too." Malcolm paused before continuing somberly. "You would have done the same for me. I know what it's like not to see your child, to have missed out on time you can never get back…"

Malcolm's voice choked off with emotion. He and his wife had been high school sweethearts who'd had to give up a baby girl for adoption since they were too young to provide a life for their daughter. Now they had twins—a boy and a girl—they loved dearly, but they still grieved for that first child, even knowing they'd made the right decision for her.

Although Malcolm and Celia had both known about *their* child from the start.

Elliot forked his hands through his buzzed hair, kept closely shorn since he'd let his thoughts of Lucy Ann distract him and he'd caught his car on fire just before Christmas—nearly caught himself on fire, as well.

He'd scorched his hair; the call had been that damn close.

"I just can't wrap my brain around the fact she's kept his existence from me for so long."

Malcolm snorted. "I can't believe the two of you slept together."

A growl rumbled low in his throat. "You're close to overstepping the bounds of our friendship with talk like that."

"Ahhh." He chuckled. "So you do care about her more than you've let on."

"We were…friends. Lifelong friends. That's no secret." He and Lucy Ann shared so much history it was impossible to unravel events from the past without thinking about each other. "The fact that there was briefly more…I can't deny that, either."

"You must not have been up to snuff for her to run so fast."

Anger hissed between Elliot's teeth, and he resisted the urge to pitch his Bluetooth over the balcony. "Now you have crossed the line. If we were sitting in the same place right now, my fist would be in your face."

"Fair enough." Douglas laughed softly again. "Like I said. You do care more than a little, more than any 'buddy.' And you can't refute it. Admit it, Elliot. I've just played you, my friend."

No use denying he'd been outmaneuvered by someone who knew him too well.

And as for what Malcolm had said? That he cared for Lucy Ann? Cared? Yes. He had. And like every other time in his life he'd cared, things had gone south.

If he wanted to sort through this mess and create any kind of future with Eli and Lucy Ann, he had to think more and care less.

Three

Lucy Ann shaded her eyes against the rising sun. For the third time in twenty-four hours a limousine pulled up her dusty road, oak trees creating a canopy for the long driveway. The first time had occurred yesterday when Elliot had arrived, then when he'd left, and now, he was returning.

Her simple semihermit life working from home with her son was drawing to a close in another few minutes.

Aunt Carla cradled Eli in her arms. Carla never seemed to age, her hair a perpetual shade halfway between gray and brown. She refused to waste money to have it colored. Her arms were ropy and strong from years of carting around trays of pizzas and sodas. Her skin was prematurely wrinkled from too much hard work, time in the Carolina sun—and a perpetual smile.

She was a tough, good woman who'd been there for Lucy Ann all her life. Too bad Carla couldn't have been her mother. Heaven knows she'd prayed for that often enough.

Carla smiled down at little Eli, his fist curled around her finger. "I'm sure I'm going to miss you both. It's been a treat having a baby around again."

She'd never had a child of her own, but was renowned for opening her home to family members in need. She wasn't a problem-solver so much as a temporary oasis. Very temporary, as the limo drew closer down the half-mile driveway.

"You're sweet to make it sound like we haven't taken over your house." Lucy Ann tugged her roller bag through the door, *kerthunking* it over a bump, casting one last glance back at the tiny haven of Hummels and the saggy sofa.

"Sugar, you know I only wish I could've done more for you this time and when you were young." Carla swayed from side to side, wearing her standard high-waisted jeans and a seasonal shirt—a pink Easter bunny on today's tee.

"You've always been there for me." Lucy Ann sat on top of her luggage, her eyes on the nearing limo. "I don't take that for granted."

"I haven't always been there for you and we both know it," Carla answered, her eyes shadowed with memories they both didn't like to revisit.

"You did the best you could. I know that." Since Lucy Ann's mother had legal guardianship and child services wouldn't believe any of the claims of neglect, much less allegations of abuse by stepfathers, there wasn't anything Lucy Ann could do other than escape to Carla—or to Elliot.

Her mother and her last stepfather had died in a boating accident, so there was nothing to be gained from dwelling on the past. Her mom had no more power over her than Lucy Ann allowed her. "Truly, Carla, the past is best left there."

"Glad to know you feel that way. I hope you learned that from me." Carla tugged on Lucy Ann's low ponytail. "If you can forgive me, why can't you forgive Elliot?"

Good question. She slouched back with a sigh. "If I could answer that, then I guess my heart wouldn't be breaking in two right now."

Her aunt hauled her in for a one-armed hug while she cradled the baby in the other. "I would fix this for you if I could."

"Come with us," Lucy Ann blurted. "I've asked you before and I know all your reasons for saying no. You love your home and your life and weekly bingo. But will you change your mind this time?" She angled back, hoping. "Will you come with us? We're family."

"Ah, sweet niece." Carla shook her head. "This is your life, your second chance, your adventure. Be careful. Be smart. And remember you're a damn amazing woman. He would be a lucky man to win you back."

Just the thought... No. "That's not why I'm going with him." She took Eli from her aunt. "My trip is only about planning a future for my son, for figuring out a way to blend Elliot's life with my new life."

"You used to be a major part of his world."

"I was his glorified secretary." A way for him to give her money while salving her conscience. At least she'd lived frugally and used the time to earn a degree so she could be self-sufficient. The stretch limo slowed along the last patch of gravel in front of the house.

"You were his best friend and confidant... And apparently something more at least once."

"I'm not sure what point you are trying to make, but

if you're going to make it, do so fast." She nodded to the opening limo door. "We're out of time."

"You two got along fabulously for decades and there's an obvious attraction. Why can't you have more?" Her aunt tipped her head, eyeing Elliot stepping from the vehicle. The car door slammed.

Sunshine sent dappled rays along his sandy-brown hair, over his honed body in casual jeans and a white polo that fit his muscled arms. She'd leaned on those broad shoulders for years without hesitation, but now all she could think about was the delicious feel of those arms around her. The flex of those muscles as he stretched over her.

Lucy Ann tore her eyes away and back to her aunt. "Have more?" That hadn't ended well for either of them. "Are you serious?"

"Why wouldn't I be?"

"He hasn't come looking for me for nearly a year. He let me go." Something that had hurt every day of the eleven months that passed. She waved toward him talking to his chauffeur. "He's only here now because his friends threw him on my doorstep."

"You're holding back because of your pride?" Her aunt tut-tutted. "You're throwing him and a possible future away because of pride?"

"Listen to me. *He* threw *me* away." She'd been an afterthought or nuisance to people her whole life. She wouldn't let her son live the same second-class existence. Panic began to set in. "Now that I think of it, I'm not sure why I even agreed to go with him—"

"Stop. Hold on." Carla grabbed her niece by the shoulders and steadied her. "Forget I said anything at all. Of course you have every reason to be upset. Go with him and figure out how to manage your son's future. And I'll always be here if you decide to return."

"If?" Lucy Ann rolled her eyes. "You mean when."

Carla pointed to the limo and the broad-shouldered man walking toward them. "Do you really think Elliot's going to want his son to grow up here?"

"Um, I mean, I hadn't thought…"

True panic set in as Lucy Ann realized she no longer had exclusive say over her baby's life. Of course Elliot would have different plans for his child. He'd spent his entire life planning how to get out of here, devising ways to build a fortune, and he'd succeeded.

Eli was a part of that now. And no matter how much she wanted to deny it, her life could never be simple again.

Elliot sprawled in the backseat of the limo while Lucy Ann adjusted the straps on Eli's infant seat, checking each buckle to ensure it fit with obvious seasoned practice. Her loose ponytail swung forward, the dome light bringing out the hints of honey in her light brown hair.

He dug his fingers into the butter-soft leather to keep from stroking the length of her hair, to see if it was as silky as he remembered. He needed to bide his time. He had her and the baby with him. That was a huge victory, especially after their stubborn year apart.

And now?

He had to figure out a way to make her stay. To go back to the way things were…except he knew things couldn't be exactly the same. Not after they'd slept together. Although he would have to tread warily there. He couldn't see her cheering over a "friends with benefits" arrangement. He'd have to take it a step at a time to gauge her mood. She needed to be reminded of all the history they shared, all the ways they got along so well.

She tucked a homemade quilt over Eli's tiny legs before shifting to sit beside him. Elliot knocked on the driver's window and the vehicle started forward on their journey to the airport.

"Lucy Ann, you didn't have to stay up late packing that suitcase." He looked at the discarded cashmere baby blanket she left folded to the side. "I told you I would take care of buying everything he needs."

His son would never ride a secondhand bike he'd unearthed at the junkyard. A sense of possessiveness stirred inside him. He'd ordered the best of the best for his child—from the car seat to a travel bed. Clothes. Toys. A stroller. He'd consulted his friends' wives for advice—easy enough since his buddies and their wives were all propagating like rabbits these days.

Apparently, so was he.

Lucy Ann rested a hand on the faded quilt with tiny blue sailboats. "Eli doesn't know if something is expensive or a bargain. He only knows if something feels or smells familiar. He's got enough change in his life right now."

"Is that a dig at me?" He studied her, trying to get a read on her mood. She seemed more reserved than yesterday, worried even.

"Not a dig at all. It's a fact." She eyed him with confusion.

"He has you as a constant."

"Damn straight he does," she said with a mama-bear ferocity that lit a fire inside him. Her strength, the light in her eyes, stirred him.

Then it hit him. She was in protective mode because she saw him as a threat. She actually thought he might try to take her child away from her. Nothing could be further from the truth. He wanted to parent the child *with* her.

He angled his head to capture her gaze fully. "I'm not trying to take him away from you. I just want to be a part of his life."

"Of course. That was always my intention," she said, her eyes still guarded, wary. "I know trust is difficult right now, but I hope you will believe me that I want you to have regular visitation."

Ah, already she was trying to set boundaries rather than thinking about possibilities. But he knew better than to fight with her. Finesse always worked better than head-on confrontation. He pointed to the elementary school they'd attended together, the same redbrick building but with a new playground. "We share a lot of history and now we share a son. Even a year apart isn't going to erase everything else."

"I understand that."

"Do you?" He moved closer to her.

Her body went rigid as she held herself still, keeping a couple of inches of space between them. "Remember when we were children, in kindergarten?"

Following her train of thought was tougher than maneuvering through race traffic, but at least she was talking to him. "Which particular day in kindergarten?"

She looked down at her hands twisted in her lap, her nails short and painted with a pretty orange. "You were lying belly flat on a skateboard racing down a hill."

That day eased to the front of his mind. "I fell off, flat on my ass." He winced. "Broke my arm."

"All the girls wanted to sign your cast." She looked sideways at him, smiling. "Even then you were a chick magnet."

"They just wanted to use their markers," he said dismissively.

She looked up to meet his eyes fully for the first time since they'd climbed into the limousine. "I knew that your arm was already broken."

"You never said a word to me." He rubbed his forearm absently.

"You would have been embarrassed if I confronted you, and you would have lied to me. We didn't talk as openly then about our home lives." She tucked the blanket more securely around the baby's feet as Eli sucked a pacifier in his sleep. "We were new friends who shared a jelly sandwich at lunch."

"We were new friends and yet you were right about the arm." He looked at his son's tiny hands and wondered how any father could ever strike out at such innocence. Sweat beaded his forehead at even the thought.

"I told my mom though, after school," Lucy Ann's eyes fell to his wrist. "She wasn't as...distant in those days."

The weight of her gaze was like a stroke along his skin, her words salve to a past wound. "I didn't know you said anything to anyone."

"Her word didn't carry much sway, or maybe she didn't fight that hard." She shrugged, the strap of her sundress sliding. "Either way, nothing happened. So I went to the principal."

"My spunky advocate." God, he'd missed her. And yet he'd always thought he knew everything about her and here she had something new to share. "Guess that explains why they pulled me out of class to interview me about my arm."

"You didn't tell the principal the truth though, did you?

I kept waiting for something big to happen. My five-year-old imagination was running wild."

For one instant in that meeting he had considered talking, but the thoughts of afterward had frozen any words in his throat like a lodged wad of that shared jelly sandwich. "I was still too scared of what would happen to my mother if I talked. Of what he would do to her."

Sympathy flickered in her brown eyes. "We discussed so many things as kids, always avoiding anything to do with our home lives. Our friendship was a haven for me then."

He'd felt the same. But that meeting with the principal had made him bolder later, except he'd chosen the wrong person to tell. Someone loyal to his father, which only brought on another beating.

"You had your secrets, too. I could always sense when you were holding back."

"Then apparently we didn't have any secrets from each other after all." She winced, her hand going to her son's car seat. "Not until this year."

The limo jostled along a pothole on the country road. Their legs brushed and his arm shot out to rest along the back of her seat. She jolted for an instant, her breath hitching. He stared back, keeping his arm in place until her shoulders relaxed.

"Oh, Elliot." She sagged back. "We're a mess, you and I, with screwed-up pasts and not much to go on as an example for building a future."

The worry coating her words stabbed at him. He cupped her arm lightly, the feel of her so damn right tucked to him. "We need to figure out how to straighten ourselves out to be good parents. For Eli."

"It won't be all that difficult to outdo our parents."

"Eli deserves a lot better than just a step above our

folks." The feel of her hair along his wrist soothed old wounds, the way she'd always done for him. But more than that, the feel of her now, with the new memories, with that night between them...

His pulse pounded in his ears, his body stirring.... He wanted her. And right now, he didn't see a reason why they couldn't have everything. They shared a similar past and they shared a child.

He just had to convince Lucy Ann. "I agree with you there. That's why it's important for us to use this time together wisely. Figure out how to be the parents he deserves. Figure out how to be a team, the partners he needs."

"I'm here, in the car with you, committed to spending the next four weeks with you." She tipped her face up to his, the jasmine scent of her swirling all around him. "What more do you want from me?"

"I want us to be friends again, Lucy Ann," he answered honestly, his voice raw. "Friends. Not just parents passing a kid back and forth to each other. I want things the way they were before between us."

Her pupils widened with emotion. "Exactly the way we were before? Is that even possible?"

"Not exactly as before," he conceded, easy enough to do when he knew his plans for something better between them.

He angled closer, stroking her ponytail over her shoulder in a sweep he wanted to take farther down her back to her waist. He burned all the way to his gut, needing to pull her closer.

"We'll be friends and more. We can go back to that night together, pick up from there. Because heaven help me, if we're being totally honest, then yes. I want you back in my bed again."

Four

The caress of Elliot's hand along her hair sent tingles all the way to her toes. She wanted to believe the deep desire was simply a result of nearly a year without sex, but she knew her body longed for this particular man. For the pleasure of his caress over her bare skin.

Except then she wouldn't be able to think straight. Now more than ever, she needed to keep a level head for her child. She loved her son more than life, and she had some serious fences to mend with Elliot to secure a peaceful future for Eli.

Lucy Ann clasped Elliot's wrist and moved it aside. "You can't be serious."

"I'm completely serious." His fingers twisted in her ponytail.

"Let. Go. Now," she said succinctly, barely able to keep herself from grabbing his shirt and hauling him in for a kiss. "Sex will only complicate matters."

"Or it could simplify things." He released her hair slowly, his stroke tantalizing all the way down her arm.

Biting her lip, she squeezed her eyes shut, too enticed by the green glow of desire in his eyes.

"Lucy Ann?" His bourbon-smooth tones intoxicated the parched senses that had missed him every day of the past eleven months. "What are you thinking?"

Her head angled ever so slightly toward his touch. "My aunt said the same thing about the bonus of friends becoming…more."

He laughed softly, the heat of his breath warming her throat and broadcasting just how close he'd moved to her, so close he could kiss the exposed flesh. "Your aunt has always been a smart woman. Although I sure as hell didn't talk to her about you and I becoming lovers."

She opened her eyes slowly, steeling herself. "You need to quit saying things like that or I'm going to have the car stopped right now. I will walk home with my baby if I have to. You and I need boundaries for this to work."

His gaze fell to her mouth for an instant that felt stretched to eternity before he angled back, leather seat creaking. "We'll have to agree to disagree."

Her exhale was shakier than she would have liked, betraying her. "You can cut the innocent act. I've seen your playboy moves over the years. Your practiced charm isn't going to work with me." Not again, anyway. "And it wouldn't have worked before if I hadn't been so taken away by sentimentality and a particularly strong vintage liqueur."

Furrows dug deep trenches in his forehead. "Lucy Ann, I am deeply sorry if I took advantage of our friendship—"

"I told you that night. No apologies." His apologies had been mortifying then, especially when she'd been hoping for a repeat only to learn he was full of regrets. He'd stung her pride and her heart. Not that she ever intended to let him know as much. "There were two of us in bed that night, and I refuse to call it a mistake. But it won't happen again, remember? We decided that then."

Or rather *he* had decided and *she* had pretended to go along to save face over her weakness when it came to this man.

His eyes went smoky. "I remember a lot of other things about that night."

Already she could feel herself weakening, wanting to read more into his every word and slightest action. She had to stop this intimacy, this romanticism, now.

"Enough talking about the past. This is about our future. Eli's future." She put on her best logical, personal-assistant voice she'd used a million times to place distance between them. "Where are we going first? I have to confess I haven't kept track of the race dates this year."

"Races later," he said simply as the car reached the airport. "First, we have a wedding to attend."

Her gut tightened at his surprise announcement. "A wedding?"

Lucy Ann hated weddings. Even when the wedding was for a longtime friend. Elliot's high school alumni pal—Dr. Rowan Boothe—was marrying none other than an African princess, who also happened to be a Ph.D. research scientist.

She hated to feel ungrateful, though, since this was the international event of the year, with a lavish ceremony in East Africa, steeped in colorful garb and local delicacies. Invitations were coveted, and media cameras hovered at a respectable distance, monitored by an elite security team that made the packed day run smoothly well into the evening. Tuxedos, formal gowns and traditional tribal wraps provided a magnificent blend of beauty that reflected the couple's modern tastes while acknowledging time-honored customs.

Sitting at the moonlit reception on the palace lawns by the beach, her baby asleep in a stroller, Lucy Ann sipped her glass of spiced fruit juice. She kept a smile plastered on her face as if her showing up here with Elliot and their son was nothing out of the ordinary. Regional music with drums and flutes carried on the air along with laughter and celebration. She refused to let her bad mood ruin the day for the happy bride and groom. Apparently, Elliot had been "kidnapped" from Rowan's bachelor party.

Now he'd returned for the wedding—with her and the baby. No one had asked, but their eyes all made it clear they knew. The fact that he'd thrust their messed-up relationship right into the spotlight frustrated her. But he'd insisted it was better to do it sooner rather than later. Why delay the inevitable?

He'd even arranged for formal dresses for her to pick from. She'd had no choice but to oblige him since her only formals were basic black, far too somber for a wedding. She'd gravitated toward simple wear in the past, never wanting to stand out. Although in this colorful event, her pale lavender gown wasn't too glaring. Still, she felt a little conspicuous because it was strapless and floor-length with a beaded bodice. Breast-feeding had given her new cleavage.

A fact that hadn't gone unnoticed, given the heated looks Elliot kept sliding her way.

But her mood was too sour to dwell on those steamy glances. Especially when he looked so mouth-wateringly handsome in a tuxedo, freshly shaven and smiling. It was as if the past eleven months apart didn't exist, as if they'd just shared the same bed, the same glass of wine. They'd been close friends for so long, peeling him from her thoughts was easier said than done.

She just wanted the marriage festivities to be over, then hopefully she would feel less vulnerable, more in control.

Weddings were happy occasions for some, evoking dreams or bringing back happy memories. Not for her. When she saw the white lace, flowers and a towering cake, she could only remember each time her mama said "I do." All four times. Each man was worse than the one before, until child services stepped in and said drug addict stepdaddy number four had to go if Lucy Ann's mother wanted to keep her child.

Mama chose hubby.

Lucy Ann finally went to live with her aunt for good—no more dodging groping hands or awkward requests to sit on "daddy's" lap. Her aunt loved her, cared for her, but Carla had others to care for, as well—Grandma and an older bachelor uncle.

No one put Lucy Ann first or loved her most. Not until this baby. She would do anything for Eli. Anything. Even swallow her pride and let Elliot back in her life.

Still, keeping on a happy face throughout the wedding was hard. All wedding phobia aside, she worked to appreciate the wedding as an event. She had to learn the art of detaching her emotions from her brain if she expected to make it through the next four weeks with her heart intact.

"Lucy Ann?" A familiar female voice startled her, and she set her juice aside to find Hillary Donavan standing beside her.

Hillary was married to another of Elliot's school friends, Troy Donavan, more commonly known as the

Robin Hood Hacker. As a computer-savvy teen he'd wreaked all sorts of havoc. Now he was a billionaire software developer. He'd recently married Hillary, an events planner, who looked as elegant as ever in a green Grecian-style silk dress.

The red-haired beauty dropped into a chair beside the stroller. "Do you mind if I hide out here with you and the baby for a while? My part in orchestrating this nationally televised wedding is done, thank heavens."

"You did a lovely job blending local traditions with a modern flair. No doubt magazine covers will be packed with photos."

"They didn't give me much time to plan since they made their engagement announcement just after Christmas, but I'm pleased with the results. I hope they are, too."

"I'm sure they are, although they can only see each other." Lucy Ann's stomach tightened, remembering her mother's adoring looks for each new man.

"To think they were professional adversaries for so long…now the sparks between them are so tangible I'm thinking I didn't need to order the firework display for a finale."

Lucy Ann pulled a tight smile, doing her best to be polite. "Romance is in the air."

"I hope this isn't going too late for you and the little guy." She flicked her red hair over her shoulder. "You must be exhausted from your flight."

"He's asleep. We'll be fine." If she left, Elliot would feel obligated to leave, as well. And right now she was too emotionally raw to be alone with him. Surely Hillary had to have some idea of how difficult this was for her, since the alum buddies had been party to the kidnapping.

Her eyes slid to the clutch of pals, the five men who'd been sent to a military reform school together.

Their bond was tight. Unbreakable.

They stood together at the beachside under a cabana wearing matching tuxedos, all five of them too damn rich and handsome for their own good. Luckily for the susceptible female population, the other four were now firmly taken, married and completely in love with their brides. The personification of bad boys redeemed, but still edgy.

Exciting.

The Alpha Brotherhood rarely gathered in one place, but when they did, they were a sight to behold. They'd all landed in trouble with the law as teens, but they'd been sent to a military reform school rather than juvie. Computer whiz Troy Donavan had broken into the Department of Defense's computer system to expose corruption. Casino magnate Conrad Hughes had used insider trading tips to manipulate the stock market. He'd only barely redeemed himself by tanking corporations that used child-labor sweatshops in other countries. World famous soft rock/jazz musician Malcolm Douglas had been sent away on drug charges as a teenager, although she'd learned later that he'd been playing the piano in a bar underage and got nabbed in the bust.

The groom—Dr. Rowan Boothe—had a history a bit more troubled. He'd been convicted of driving while drunk. He'd been part of an accident he'd taken the blame for so his overage brother wouldn't go to jail—then his brother had died a year later driving drunk into a tree. Now Rowan used all his money to start clinics in third-world countries.

They all had their burdens to bear, and that guilt motivated them to make amends now. Through their freelance work with Interpol. Through charitable donations beyond anything anyone would believe unless they saw the accounting books.

Now, they'd all settled down and gotten married, starting families of their own. Was that a part of what compelled Elliot to push for more with her? A need to fit in with his Alpha Brothers as they moved on to the next phase of their lives?

Lucy Ann looked back at Hillary. "Did you know what Malcolm and Conrad were up to yesterday?"

"I didn't know exactly, not until Troy told me, and they were already on their way. I can't say I approve of their tactics, but it was too late for me to do anything. You appear to be okay." Hillary leaned on her elbows, angling closer, her eyes concerned. "Is that an act?"

"What do you think?"

She clasped Lucy Ann's hand. "I'm sorry. I should have realized this calm of yours is just a cover. We're kindred spirits, you and I, ever organized, even in how we show ourselves to the world." She squeezed once before letting go. "Do you want to talk? Need a shoulder? I'm here."

"There's nothing anyone can do now. It's up to Elliot and me to figure out how to move forward. If I'd let him know earlier…"

"Friend, you and I both know how difficult it can be to contact them when the colonel calls for one of their missions. They disappear. They're unreachable." She smiled sadly. "It takes something as earth-shattering as, well, a surprise baby to get them to break the code of silence."

"How do you live with that, as a part of a committed relationship?"

She couldn't bring herself to ask what it felt like to be married to a man who kept such a chunk of his life separate. She'd known as a friend and as a personal assistant that Elliot's old headmaster later recruited previous students as freelancers for Interpol. She'd kept thoughts about that segmented away, since it did not pertain to her job or their life on the race circuit.

But now, there was no denying that her life was tied to Elliot's in a much deeper way.

"I love Troy, the man he is. The man he's always been," Hillary said. "We grow, we mature, but our basic natures stay the same. And I love who that man is."

Lucy Ann could almost—almost—grasp the promise in that, except she knew Hillary helped her husband on some of those missions, doing a bit of freelance work of her own.

Lucy Ann stared down into the amber swirl of her juice glass. "Is it so wrong to want an ordinary life? I don't mean to sound ungrateful, but *normal,* boring, well, I've never had that. I crave it for myself and my child, but it feels so unattainable."

"That's a tough one, isn't it? These men are many things, but normal—delightfully boring—doesn't show up anywhere on that list."

Where did that leave her? In search of what she couldn't have? Or a hypocrite for not accepting Elliot the way he had accepted her all her life? She ran from him. As much as she swore that he pushed her away, she knew. She'd run just as fast and hard as he'd pushed.

"Thank you for the advice, Hillary."

Her friend sighed. "I'm not sure how much help I've been. But if you need to talk more, I'm here for you. I won't betray your confidences."

"I appreciate that," Lucy Ann said, and meant it, only just realizing how few female friends she'd ever had. Elliot had been her best friend and she'd allowed that to close her off to other avenues of support.

"Good, very good. We women need to stick together, make a sisterhood pact of our own." She winked before ducking toward the stroller. "Little Eli is adorable, and I'm glad you're here."

Lucy Ann appreciated the gesture, and she wanted to trust. She wanted to believe there could be a sisterhood of support in dealing with these men—even though she wouldn't be married to Elliot. Still, their lives were entwined because of their child.

A part of her still wondered, doubted. The wives of Elliot's friends had reached out initially after she left, but eventually they'd stopped. Could she really be a part of their sisterhood?

"Thank you, Hillary," she said simply, her eyes sliding back to Elliot standing with his friends.

Her hand moved protectively over to the handle of her son's stroller, her throat constricting as she took in the gleaming good looks of her baby's father. Even his laugh seemed to make the stars shimmer brighter.

And how frivolous a thought was that?

She definitely needed to keep her head on straight and her heart locked away. She refused to be anyone's obligation or burden ever again.

Elliot hoped Rowan and Mariama's marriage ceremony would soften Lucy Ann's mood. After all, weren't weddings supposed to make women sentimental? He'd watched her chatting with his friends' wives and tried to gauge her reaction. She knew them all from her time working as his assistant, and seeing this big extended family connected by friendship rather than blood should appeal to her. They'd talked about leaving their pasts behind countless times as kids.

They could fit right in here with their son. A practical decision. A fun life.

So why wasn't she smiling as the bride and groom drove away in a BMW convertible, the bride's veil trailing in the wind?

Shouldering free of the crowd, Elliot made his way toward Lucy Ann, who stood on the periphery, their son in a stroller beside her. Even though he'd arranged for a nanny who'd once worked for a British duke, Lucy Ann said she couldn't let her son stay with a total stranger. She would need to conduct her own interview tomorrow. If the woman met her standards, she could help during Eli's naps so Lucy Ann could keep up with the work obligations she hadn't been able to put on hold. The encounter still made Elliot grin when he thought of her refusing to be intimidated by the very determined Mary Poppins.

He stopped beside Lucy Ann, enjoying the way the moonlight caressed her bare shoulders. Her hair was loose and lifting in the night wind. Every breath he took drew in hints of her, of Carolina jasmine. His body throbbed to life with a reminder of what they could have together, something so damn amazing he'd spent eleven months running from the power of it.

Now, fate had landed him here with her. Running wasn't an option, and he found that for once he didn't mind fate kicking him in the ass.

Elliot rested his hand on the stroller beside hers, watching every nuance of her reaction. "Are you ready to call it a day and return to our suite, or would you like to take a walk?"

She licked her lips nervously. "Um, I think a walk, perhaps."

So she wasn't ready to be alone with him just yet? A promising sign, actually; she wanted him still, even if she wasn't ready to act on that desire. Fine, then. He could use the moon and stars to romance her, the music from a steel drum band serenading them.

"A walk it is, then, Lucy dear," he asserted.

"Where can we go with a baby?"

He glanced around at the party with guests still dancing along the cabana-filled beach. Tables of food were still laden with half shares of delicacies, fruits and meats. A fountain spewing wine echoed the rush of waves along the shore. Mansions dotted the rocky seashore, with a planked path leading to docks.

"This way." He gestured toward the shoreline boardwalk, all but deserted this late at night. "I'll push the stroller."

He stepped behind the baby carriage. Lucy Ann had no choice but to step aside or they would be stuck hip to hip, step for step.

Five minutes later, they'd left the remnants of the reception behind, the stroller wheels rumbling softly along the wooden walkway. To anyone looking from the looming mansions above, lights shining from the windows like eyes, he and Lucy Ann would appear a happy family walking with their son.

Tonight more than ever he was aware of his single status. Yet again, he'd stood to the side as another friend got married. Leaving only him as a bachelor. But he was a father now. There was no more running from fears of becoming his father. He had to be a man worthy of this child. His child with Lucy Ann.

She walked beside him, the sea breeze brushing her gauzy dress along his leg in phantom caresses. "You're quite good at managing that stroller. I'm surprised. It took me longer than I expected to get the knack of not knocking over everything in my path."

He smiled at her, stuffing down a spark of anger along with the urge to remind her that he would have helped in those early days if she'd only let him know. "It's just like maneuvering a race car."

"Of course. That makes sense."

"More sense than me being at ease with a child? I'm determined to get this right, Lucy Ann, don't doubt that for a second." Steely determination fueled his words.

"You used to say you never wanted kids of your own."

Could those words have made her wary of telling him? There had been a time when they shared everything with each other.

He reminded her, "You always insisted that you didn't want children, either."

"I didn't want to risk putting any child in my mother's path." She rubbed her hand along her collarbone, the one she'd cracked as a child. "I'm an adult now and my mother's passed away. But we're talking about *you* and your insistence that you didn't want kids."

"I didn't. Then." If things hadn't changed, he still might have said the same, but one look in Eli's wide brown eyes and his world had altered in an instant. "I don't run away from responsibilities."

"You ran away before—" She stopped short, cursing softly. "Forget I said that."

Halting, he pulled his hands from the stroller, the baby sleeping and the carriage tucked protectively between them and the railing.

Elliot took her by the shoulders. Her soft bare shoulders. So vulnerable. So...*her*. "Say it outright, Lucy Ann. I left *you* behind when I left Columbia behind, when I let myself get sloppy and caught, when I risked jail because anything seemed better than staying with my father. For a selfish instant, I forgot about what that would mean for you. And I've regretted that every day of my life."

The admission was ripped from his throat; deeper still, torn all the way from his gut. Except there was no one but Lucy Ann to hear him on the deserted walkway. Stone houses dotted the bluff, quarters for guests and staff, all structures up on the bluff with a few lights winking in the night. Most people still partied on at the reception.

"I understand that you feel guilty. Like you have to make up for things. But you need to stop thinking that way. I'm responsible for my own life." She cupped his face, her eyes softening. "Besides, if you'd stayed, you wouldn't have this amazing career that also gave me a chance to break free. So I guess it all worked out in the end."

"Yet you ended up returning home when you left me." Hell, he should be honest now while he had the chance. He didn't want to waste an instant or risk the baby waking up and interrupting them. "When I stupidly pushed you away."

Her arm dropped away again. "I returned with a degree and the ability to support myself and my child. That's significant and I appreciate it." Her hands fisted at her sides. "I don't want to be your obligation."

"You want a life of your own, other than being my assistant. I understand that." He kept his voice low, which brought her closer to listen over the crash of waves below the boardwalk. He liked having her close again. "Let's talk it through, like we would have in the old days."

"You're being so—" she scowled "—so reasonable."

"You say that like it's a dirty word. Why is that a bad thing?" Because God help him, he was feeling anything but reasonable. If she wanted passion and emotion, he was more than willing to pour all of that into seducing her. He just had to be sure before he made a move.

A wrong step could set back his cause.

"Don't try to manipulate me with all the logical reasons why I should stay. I want you to be honest about what you're thinking. What you *want* for your future."

"When it comes to the future, I don't know what I want, Lucy Ann, beyond making sure you and Eli are safe, provided for, never afraid. I'm flying by the seat of my pants here, trying my best to figure out how to get through this being-a-father thing." Honesty was ripping a hole in him. He wanted to go back to logic.

Or passion.

Her chest rose and fell faster with emotion, a flush spreading across her skin in the moon's glow. "How would things have been different if I had come to you, back when I found out I was pregnant?"

"I would have proposed right away," he said without hesitation.

"I would have said no," she answered just as quickly.

He stepped closer. "I would have been persistent in trying to wear you down."

"How would you have managed that?"

The wind tore at her dress, whipping the skirt forward to tangle in his legs, all but binding them together with silken bands.

He angled his face closer to hers, his mouth so close he could claim her if he moved even a whisker closer. "I would have tried to romance you with flowers, candy and jewels." He watched the way her pupils widened with awareness as his words heated her cheek. "Then I would have realized you're unconventional and I would have changed tactics."

"Such as?" she whispered, the scent of fruit juice on her breath, dampening her lips. "Be honest."

"Hell, Lucy Ann, if you want honesty, here it is." His hand slid up her bare arm, along her shoulder, under her hair, to cup the back of her neck, and God, it felt good to touch her after so long apart. It felt right. "I just want to kiss you again."

Five

Lucy Ann gripped Elliot's shoulders, her fingers digging in deep by instinct even as her brain shouted "bad idea."

Her body melted into his, the hard planes of his muscular chest absorbing the curves of her, her breasts hypersensitive to the feel of him. And his hands… A sigh floated from her into him. His hands were gentle and warm and sure along her neck and into her hair, massaging her scalp. Her knees went weak, and he slid an arm down to band around her waist, securing her to him.

How could he crumble her defenses with just one touch of his mouth to hers? But she couldn't deny it. A moonlight stroll, a starlight kiss along the shore had her dreaming romantic notions. Made her want more.

Want him.

His tongue stroked along the seam of her mouth, and she opened without hesitation, taking him every bit as much as he took her. Stroking and tasting. There was a certain safety in the moment, out here in the open, since there was no way things could go further. Distant guest houses, the echoes of the reception carrying on the wind and of course the baby with them kept her from being totally swept away.

Her hands glided down his sides to tuck into his back pockets, to cup the taut muscles that she'd admired on more than one occasion. Hell, the whole female population had admired that butt thanks to a modeling gig he'd taken early in his career to help fund his racing. She'd ribbed him about those underwear ads, even knowing he was blindingly hot. She'd deluded herself into believing she was objective, immune to his sensuality, which went beyond mere good looks.

The man had a rugged charisma that oozed machismo.

Heaven help her, she wanted to dive right in and swim around, luxuriating in the sensations. The tingling in her breasts sparked through her, gathering lower with a familiar intensity she recognized too well after their night together.

This had to stop. Now. Because mistakes she'd made this time wouldn't just hurt her—or Elliot. They had a child to consider. A precious innocent life only a hand's reach away.

With more than a little regret, she ended the kiss, nipping his sensuous bottom lip one last time. His growl of frustration rumbled his chest against hers, but he didn't stop her. Her head fell to rest on his shoulder as she inhaled the scent of sea air tinged with the musk of his sweat. As Elliot cupped the back of her head in a broad palm, his ragged breaths reassured her he was every bit as affected by the kiss. An exciting and yet dangerous reality that confused her after the way they'd parted a year ago.

She needed space to think through this. Maybe watching the wedding and seeing all those happy couples had affected her more than she realized. Even just standing here in his arms with the feel of his arousal pressing against her stomach, she was in serious danger of making a bad choice if she stayed with him a moment longer.

Flattening her palms to his chest, Lucy Ann pushed, praying her legs would hold when he backed away.

She swayed for an instant before steeling her spine. "Elliot, this—" she gestured between them, then touched her kissed tender lips softly "—this wasn't part of our bargain when we left South Carolina. Or was it?"

The night breeze felt cooler now, the sea air chilly.

His eyes stayed inscrutable as he stuffed his hands in his tuxedo pockets, the harsh planes of his face shadowed by moonlight. "Are you accusing me of plotting a seduction?"

"*Plotting* is a harsh word," she conceded, her eyes flitting to the baby in his stroller as she scrambled to regain control of her thoughts, "but I think you're not above planning to do whatever it takes to get your way. That's who you are. Can you deny it?"

His eyes glinted with determination—and anger? "I won't deny wanting to sleep with you. The way you kissed me back gives me the impression you're on board with that notion."

Her heartbeat quickened with visions of how easy it would be to fall into bed with him. To pick up where they'd left off a year ago. If only she had any sense he wanted her for more than a connection to his son.

"That's the point, Elliot. It doesn't matter what *we* want. This month together is supposed to be about building a future for *Eli*. More of—" she gestured between them, her heart tripping over itself at just the mention of their kiss, their attraction "—playing with fire only risks an unstable future for our son. We need to recapture our friendship. Nothing more."

Her limbs felt weak at even the mention of *more*.

He arched an arrogant eyebrow. "I disagree that they're mutually exclusive."

"If you push me on this, I'll have to leave the tour and return to South Carolina." She'd seen too often how easily he seduced women. He was a charmer, without question, and she refused to be like her mother, swept away into reckless relationships again and again. She had a level head and she needed to keep it. "Elliot, do you hear me? I need to know we're on the same page about these next four weeks."

He studied her through narrowed eyes for the crash of four rolling waves before he shrugged. "I will respect your wishes, and I will keep my hands to myself." He smiled, pulling his hands from his pockets and holding them up. "Unless you change your mind, of course."

"I won't," she said quickly, almost too forcefully for her own peace of mind. That old Shakespeare quote came back to her, taunting her, *Methinks the lady doth protest too much.*

"Whoa, whoa, hold on now." Elliot patted the air. "I'm not trying to make you dig in your stubborn heels, so let's end this conversation and call it a day. We can talk more tomorrow, in the light of day."

"Less ambiance would be wise." Except she knew he looked hunky in any light, any situation.

Regardless of how much she wanted to go back, she realized that wasn't possible. They'd crossed a line the night they went too far celebrating his win and her completing her final exams.

It had never happened before she had a plan for her

own future. The catalyst had been completing her degree, feeling that for the first time since they were kids, she met him on an even footing. She'd allowed her walls to come down. She'd allowed herself to acknowledge what she'd been hiding all her adult life. She was every bit as attracted to Elliot Starc as his fawning groupies.

What if she was no different from her mother?

The thought alone had her staggering for steady ground. She grabbed the stroller just to be on the safe side. "I'm going back to the room now. It's time to settle Eli for the night. I need to catch up on some work before I go to sleep. And I do mean sleep."

"Understood," he said simply from beside her. "I'll walk back with you."

The heat of him reached her even though their bodies didn't touch. Just occupying the same space as him offered a hefty temptation right now.

She shook her head, the glide of her hair along her bared shoulders teasing her oversensitized skin. "I'd rather go alone. The palace is in sight and the area's safe."

"As you wish." He stepped back with a nod and a half bow. "We'll talk tomorrow on the way to Spain." He said it as a promise, not a request.

"Okay then," she conceded softly over her shoulder as she pushed the stroller, wheeling it toward the palace where they were staying in one of the many guest suites. Her body still hummed from the kiss, but her mind filled with questions and reservations.

She and Elliot had been platonic friends for years, comfortable with each other. As kids, they'd gone skinny-dipping, built forts in the woods, comforted each other during countless crises and disappointments. He'd been her best friend…right up to the moment he wasn't. Where had this crazy attraction between them come from?

The wheels of the stroller whirred along the walkway as fast as the memories spinning through her. That night eleven months ago when they'd been together had been spontaneous but amazing. She'd wondered if maybe there could be more between them. The whole friends-with-benefits had sounded appealing, taking it a day at a time until they sorted out the bombshell that had been dropped into their relationship: a sexual chemistry that still boggled her mind.

And yet Elliot's reaction the next day had made her realize there could be no future for them. Her euphoria had evaporated with the morning light.

She'd woken before him and gone to the kitchen to make coffee and pile some pastries on a plate. The front door to his suite had opened and she'd assumed it must be the maid. Anyone who entered the room had to have a key and a security code.

However, the woman who'd walked in hadn't been wearing a uniform. She—Gianna—had worn a trench coat and nothing else. If only it had been a crazed fan. But Lucy Ann had quickly deduced Gianna was the new female in Elliot's life. He hadn't even denied it. There was no misunderstanding.

God, it had been so damn cliché her stomach had roiled. Elliot came out of the bedroom and Gianna had turned paler than the towel around Elliot's waist.

He'd kept his calm. Apologized to Gianna for the awkward situation, but she'd burst into tears and run. He'd told Lucy Ann there was nothing between him and his girlfriend anymore, not after what happened the night before with Lucy Ann.

But she'd told him he should have let Gianna know that first, and she was a hundred percent right. He'd agreed and apologized.

That hadn't been enough for her. The fact that he could be seeing one woman, even superficially, and go to bed with another? No, no and hell, no. That was something she couldn't forgive. Not after how all those men had cheated on her mom with little regard for vows or promises. And her mother kept forgiving the first unfaithful jerk, and then the next.

If Elliot could behave this way now, how could she trust him later? What if he got "swept away" by someone else and figured he would clue her in later? She'd called him dishonorable.

And in an instant, with that one word, a lifetime friendship crumbled.

She'd thrown on her clothes and left. Elliot's engagement to Gianna a month later had only sealed Lucy Ann's resolve to stay away. They hadn't spoken again until the day he'd shown up in Carla's yard.

Now, after more impulsive kisses, she found herself wanting to crawl right back into bed with him. Lucy Ann powered the stroller closer to the party and their quarters, drawing in one deep breath of salty air after another, willing her pulse to steady. Wishing the urge to be with Elliot was as easily controlled.

With each step, she continued the chant in her brain, the vow not to repeat her mother's mistakes.

Wind tearing at his tuxedo jacket, Elliot watched Lucy Ann push the stroller down the planked walkway, then past the party. He didn't take his eyes off her or his son until he saw they'd safely reached the palace, even though he now had bodyguards watching his family 24/7. His family?

Hell, yes, his family.

Eli was his son. And Lucy Ann had been his only real

family for most of his life. No matter how angry he got at her for holding back on telling him about Eli, Elliot also couldn't forgive himself for staying away from her. He'd let her down in a major way more than once, from his teenage years up to now. She had reason not to trust him.

He needed to earn back her trust. He owed her that and so much more.

His shoulders heaving with a sigh, he started toward the wedding reception. The bride and groom had left, but the partying would go long into the night. It wasn't every day a princess got married. People would expect a celebration to end all celebrations.

A sole person peeled away from the festivities and ambled toward him. From the signature streamlined fedora, he recognized his old school pal Troy Donavan. Troy was one of the originals from their high school band, the Alpha Brotherhood, a group of misfits who found kindred spirits in one another and their need to push boundaries, to expose hypocrisy—the greatest of crimes in their eyes.

Troy pulled up alongside him, passing him a drink. "Reconciliation not going too well?"

"What makes you say that?" He took the thick cut glass filled with a locally brewed beer.

"She's returning to her room alone after a wedding." Troy tipped his glass as if in a toast toward the guests. "More people get lucky after weddings than any other event known to mankind. That's why you brought Lucy Ann here, isn't it? To get her in the romantic mood."

Had he? He'd told himself he wanted her to see his friends settling down. For her to understand he could do the same. But he wasn't sure how much he felt like sharing, especially when his thoughts were still jumbled.

"I brought Lucy Ann to the wedding because I couldn't

miss the event. The timing has more to do with how you all colluded to pull off that kidnapping stunt."

"You're still pissed off? Sorry, dude, truly," he said, wincing. "I thought you and Malcolm talked that all out."

"Blah, blah, blah, my good pals wanted to get an unguarded reaction. I heard." And it still didn't sit well. He'd trusted these guys since high school, over fifteen years, and hell, yeah, he felt like they'd let him down. "But I also heard that Lucy Ann contacted the Brotherhood over a week ago. That's a week I lost with my son. A week she was alone caring for him. Would you be okay with that?"

"Fair enough. You have reason to be angry with us." Troy nudged his fedora back on his head. "But don't forget to take some of the blame yourself. She was your friend all your life, and you just let her go. You're going to have a tough as hell time convincing her you've magically changed your mind now and you would have wanted her back even without the kid."

The truth pinched. "Tell me something I don't know."

"Okay then. Here's a bit of advice."

"Everyone seems full of it," Elliot responded, tongue in cheek.

Troy laughed softly, leaning back against a wrought-iron railing. "Fine. I'm full of it. Always have been. Now, on to my two cents."

"By all means." Elliot knocked back another swallow of the local beer.

"You're a father now." Troy rolled his glass between his palms. "Be that boy's father and let everything else fall into place."

A sigh rattled through Elliot. "You make it sound so simple."

Troy's smile faded, no joking in sight. "Think how different our lives would have been with different parents.

Things came together when Salvatore gave us direction. Be there for your son."

"Relationships aren't saved by having a child together." His parents had gotten married because he was on the way. His mother had eventually walked out and left him behind.

"True enough. But they sure as hell are broken up by fighting over the child. Be smart in how you work together when it comes to Eli and it might go a long way toward smoothing things out with Lucy Ann." Troy ran a finger along the collar of his tuxedo shirt, edging a little more air for himself around his tie. "If not, you've got a solid relationship with your kid, and that's the most important thing."

Was his focus all wrong by trying to make things right with Lucy Ann? Elliot had to admit Troy's plan made some sense. The stakes were too important to risk screwing up with his son. "When did you get to be such a relationship sage?"

"Hillary's a smart woman, and I'm smart enough to listen to her." His sober expression held only for a second longer before he returned to the more lighthearted Troy they were all accustomed to. "Now more than ever I need to listen to Hillary's needs since she's pregnant."

"Congratulations to you both." Elliot clapped Troy on the back, glad for his friend even as he wondered what it might have been like to be by Lucy Ann's side while she was expecting Eli. "Who'd have predicted all this home and hearth for us a few years ago?"

"Colonel Salvatore's going to have to find some new recruits."

"You're not pulling Interpol missions?" That surprised him. Elliot understood Hillary's stepping out of fieldwork while pregnant. But he wouldn't have thought Troy would ever back off the edge.

"There are other ways I can help with my tech work. Who knows, maybe I'll even take on the mentorship role like Salvatore someday. But I'm off the clock now and missing my wife." Troy walked backward, waving once before he sprinted toward the party.

Elliot knew his friend was right. The advice made sense. Focus on the baby. But that didn't stop him from wanting Lucy Ann in his bed again. The notion of just letting everything fall into place was completely alien to his nature. He'd never been the laid-back sort like Troy. Elliot needed to move, act, win.

He needed Lucy Ann back in his life.

For months he'd told himself the power of Lucy Ann's kiss, of the sex they'd shared nearly a year ago, had been a hazy memory distorted by alcohol. But now, with his body still throbbing from the kiss they'd just shared, his hair still mussed, the memory of their hands running frenetically—hungrily—over each other, he knew. Booze had nothing to do with the explosive chemistry between them. Although Gianna's arrival had sure as hell provided a splash of ice water on the morning-after moment.

He'd screwed up by not breaking things off with Gianna before he let anything happen between him and Lucy Ann. He still wasn't sure why he and Gianna had reconciled afterward. He hadn't been fair to either woman. The dishonor in that weighed on him every damn day.

At least he'd finally done right by Gianna when they'd broken up. Now, he had to make things right with Lucy Ann.

Their kiss ten minutes ago couldn't lead to anything more, not tonight. He accepted that. It was still too early in his campaign to win her over. But a kiss? He could have that much for now at least. A taste of her, a hint of what more they could have together.

A hint of Lucy Ann was so much more than everything with any other woman.

She was so much a part of his life. Why the hell had he let her go?

This didn't have to be complicated. Friendship. Sex. Travel the world and live an exciting life together. He had a fortune at his disposal. They could stay anywhere, hire teachers to travel with them. Eli would have the best of everything and an education gleaned from seeing the world rather than just reading about it. Surely Lucy Ann would see that positively.

How could she say no to a future so much more secure than what they'd grown up with? He'd been an idiot not to press his case with her last time. But when she'd left before, he'd thought to give her space. This time, he would be more persistent.

Besides, last time he'd been a jerk and tried to goad her into returning by making the news with moving on—a total jackass decision he never would have made if he'd thought for a second that Lucy Ann might be pregnant.

Now, he would be wiser. Smoother.

He would win her over. They'd been partners before. They could be partners again.

Lucy Ann peered out the window of the private jet as they left Africa behind.

Time for their real journey to begin. It had been challenging enough being together with his friends, celebrating the kind of happily ever after that wasn't in the cards for her. But now came the bigger challenge—finding a way to parent while Elliot competed in the Formula One circuit. A different country every week—Spain, Monaco, Canada, England. Parties and revelry and yes, decadence, too. She felt guilty for enjoying it all, but she couldn't deny that she'd missed the travel, experiencing different cultures without a concern for cost. Plus, his close-knit group of friends gave them a band of companionship no matter what corner of the earth he traveled to during racing season.

She sank deeper into the luxury of the leather sofa, the sleek chrome-and-white interior familiar from their countless trips in the past, with one tremendous exception. Their son was secured into his car seat beside her, sleeping in his new race car pj's with a lamb's wool blanket draped over his legs. She touched his impossibly soft cheek, stroking his chubby features with a soothing hand, cupping his head, the dusting of blond hair so like his father's.

Her eyes skated to Elliot standing in the open bulkhead, talking to the pilot. Her former best friend and boss grew hotter with each year that passed—not fair. That didn't stop her from taking in the sight of him in low-slung jeans and a black button-down shirt with the sleeves rolled up. Italian leather loafers. He looked every bit the world-famous race car driver and heartthrob.

How long would Elliot's resolution to build a family life for Eli last? Maybe that's what this trip was about. Proving to *him* it couldn't be done. She wouldn't keep his son from him, but she refused to expose her child to a chaotic life. Eli needed and deserved stability.

And what did she want?

She pressed a hand to her stomach, her belly full of butterflies that had nothing to do with a jolt of turbulence. Just the thought of kissing Elliot last night... She dug her fingers into the supple leather sofa to keep from reaching for him as he walked toward her.

"Would you like something to eat or drink?" he asked, pausing by the kitchenette. "Or something to read?"

She knew from prior trips that he kept a well-stocked library of the classics as well as the latest bestsellers loaded on ereaders for himself and fellow travelers. In school, he'd always won the class contest for most books read in a year. He told her once those stories offered him an escape from his day-to-day life.

"No, thank you. The brunch before we left was amazing."

True enough, although she hadn't actually eaten much. She'd been so caught up in replaying the night before. In watching his friends' happy marriages with their children and babies on the way until her heart ached from all she wanted for her son.

For herself, as well.

Elliot slid onto the sofa beside her, leaning over her to adjust the blanket covering Eli's legs. "Tell me about his routine."

She sat upright, not expecting that question at all. "You want to know about Eli's schedule? Why?"

"He's my son." His throat moved with a long swallow of emotion at the simple sentence. "I should know what he needs."

"He has a mom, and he even has a nanny now." The British nanny was currently in the sleeping quarters reading or napping or whatever nannies did when they realized mothers needed a breather from having them around all the time.

Elliot tapped Lucy Ann's chin until she looked at him again. "And he has a dad."

"Of course," she agreed, knowing it was best for Eli,

but unused to sharing him. "If you're asking for diaper duty, you're more than welcome to it."

Would he realize her halfhearted attempt at a joke was meant to ease this tenacious tension between them? They used to be so in tune with each other.

"Diaper duty? Um, I was thinking about feeding and naps, that kind of thing."

"He breastfeeds," she said bluntly.

His eyes fell to her chest. The stroke of his gaze made her body hum as tangibly as the airplane engines.

Elliot finally cleared his throat and said, "Well, that could be problematic for me. But I can bring him to you. I can burp him afterward. He still needs to be burped, right?"

"Unless you want to be covered in baby spit-up." She crossed her arms over her chest.

He pulled his eyes up to her face. "Does he bottle-feed, too? If so, I can help out that way."

Fine, he wanted to play this game, then she would meet him point for point. "You genuinely think you can wake up during the night and then race the next day?"

"If you can function on minimal sleep, then so can I. You need to accept that we're in this together now."

He sounded serious. But then other than his playboy ways, he was a good man. A good friend. A philanthropist who chose to stay anonymous with his donations. She knew about them only through her work as his assistant.

"That's why I agreed to come with you, for Eli and in honor of our friendship in the past."

"Good, good. I'm glad you haven't forgotten those years. That friendship is something we can build on. But I'm not going to deny the attraction, Lucy Ann." He slid his arm along the back of the sofa seat, stretching his legs out in front of him. "I can't. You've always been pretty, but you looked incredible last night. Motherhood suits you."

"Flattery?" She picked up his arm and moved it to his lap. "Like flowers and candy? An obvious arm along the back? Surely you've got better moves than that."

"Are you saying compliments are wasted on you?" He picked up a lock of her hair, teasing it between two fingers. "What if I'm telling the truth about how beautiful you are and how much I want to touch you?"

She rolled her eyes, even though she could swear electricity crackled up the strand of hair he held. "I've watched your moves on women for years, remember?"

"It's not a move." He released the lock and smoothed it into the rest before crossing his arms. "If I were planning a calculated seduction for you, I would have catered a dinner, with a violin."

She crinkled her nose. "A violin? Really?"

"No privacy. Right." His emerald eyes studied her, the wheels in his brain clearly churning. "Maybe I would kiss you on the cheek, distract you by nuzzling your ear while tucking concert tickets into your pocket."

"Concert tickets?" She lifted an eyebrow with interest. They'd gone to free concerts in the park when they were teenagers.

"We would fly out to a show in another country, France or Japan perhaps."

She shook her head. "You're going way overboard. Too obvious. Rein it in, be personal."

"Flowers…" He snapped his fingers. "No wait. A single flower, something different, like a sprig of jasmine because the scent reminds me of you."

That silenced her for a moment. "You know my perfume?"

He dipped his head toward her ever so slightly as if

catching a whiff of her fragrance even now. "I know you smell like home in all the good ways. And I have some very good memories of home. They all include you."

Damn him, he was getting to her. His words affected her but she refused to let him see that. She schooled her features, smiling slightly. "Your moves have improved."

"I'm only speaking the truth." His words rang with honesty, his eyes heated with attraction.

"I do appreciate that about you, how we used to be able to tell each other anything." Their friendship had given her more than support. He'd given her hope that they could leave their pasts behind in a cloud of dust. "If we can agree to be honest now, that will work best."

"And no more secrets."

She could swear a whisper of hurt smoked through his eyes.

Guilt stabbed through her all over again. She owed him and there was no escaping that. "I truly am sorry I held back about Eli. That was wrong of me. Can you forgive me?"

"I have to, don't I?"

"No." She swallowed hard. "You don't."

"If I want us to be at peace—" he reached out and took her hand, the calluses on his fingertips a sweet abrasion along her skin "—then yes, I do."

She wasn't sure how that honest answer settled within her because it implied he wasn't really okay with what she'd done. He was only moving past it out of necessity. The way he'd shrugged off all the wrongs his father had done because he had no choice.

Guilt hammered her harder with every heartbeat, and she didn't have a clue how to make this right with him. She had as little practice with forgiveness and restitution as he did.

So she simply said, "Peace is a very good thing."

"Peace doesn't have to be bland." His thumb stroked the inside of her wrist.

Her pulse kicked up under his gentle stroking. "I didn't say that."

"Your tone totally implied it. You all but said 'boring.'" His shoulder brushed hers as he settled in closer, seducing her with his words, his husky tones every bit as much as his touch. "A truce can give freedom for all sorts of things we never considered before."

"News flash, Elliot. The kissing part. We've considered that before."

"Nice." He clasped her wrist. "You're injecting some of your spunky nature into the peace. That's good. Exciting. As brilliantly shiny as your hair with those new streaks of honey added by the Carolina sun."

Ah, now she knew why he'd been playing with her hair. "Added by my hairdresser."

"Liar."

"How do you know?"

"Because I'm willing to bet you've been squirrelling away every penny you make. I can read you—most of the time." He skimmed his hand up her arm to stroke her hair back over her shoulder. "While I know that you want me, I can't gauge what you intend to do about that, because make no mistake, I want us to pursue that. I said before that motherhood agrees with you and I meant it. You drove me crazy last night in that evening gown."

He continued to stroke her arm, but she couldn't help but think if she moved even a little, his hand would brush her breast. Even the phantom notion of that touch had her tingling with need.

She worked to keep her voice dry—and to keep from grabbing him by the shirtfront and hauling him toward her. "You're taking charming to a new level. I'm impressed."

"Good. But are you seduced?"

"You're good, and I'm enticed," she said, figuring she might as well be honest. No use denying the obvious. "But Elliot, this isn't a fairy tale. Our future is not going to be some fairy tale."

He smiled slowly, his green eyes lighting with a promise as his hand slid away. "It can be."

Without another word, he leaned back and closed his eyes. Going to sleep? Her whole body was on fire from his touch, his words—his seduction. And he'd simply gone to sleep. She wanted to shout in frustration.

Worse yet, she wanted him to recline her back on the sofa and make love to her as thoroughly as he'd done eleven months ago.

Six

By nightfall in Spain, Elliot wondered how Lucy Ann would react to their lodgings for the night. The limousine wound deeper into the historic district, farther from the racetrack than they normally stayed. But he had new ideas for these next few weeks, based on what Lucy Ann had said on the plane.

After the fairy-tale discussion, inspiration had struck. He'd forced himself to make a tactical retreat so he could regroup. Best not to risk pushing her further and having her shut him down altogether before he could put his plan into action to persuade her to stay longer than the month.

Once she was tucked into the back room on the airplane to nurse Eli, Elliot had made a few calls and set the wheels in motion to change their accommodations along the way. A large bank account and a hefty dose of fame worked wonders for making things happen fast. He just hoped his new agenda would impress Lucy Ann. Winning her over was becoming more pressing by the second. Not just for Eli but because Elliot's life had been damn empty without her. He hadn't realized just how much until he had her back. The way her presence made everything around him more vibrant. Hell, even her organized nature, which he used to tease her about. She brought a focus, a grounding and a beauty to his world that he didn't want to lose again.

Failure was not an option.

He'd made himself a checklist, just like he kept for his work. People thought he was impulsive, reckless even, but there was a science to his job. Mathematics. Calculations. He studied all the details and contingencies until they became so deeply ingrained they were instinct.

Still, he refused to become complacent. He reviewed that checklist before every race as if he were a rookie driver. Now he needed to apply the same principles to winning back Lucy Ann's friendship…and more.

Their new "hotel" took shape on the top of the hill, the Spanish sunset adding the perfect dusky aura to their new accommodations.

In the seat across from him, Lucy Ann sat up straighter, looking from the window to him with confusion stamped on her lovely face.

"This isn't where you usually stay. This is…a castle."

"Exactly."

The restored medieval castle provided safety and space, privacy and romance. He could give her the fairy tale while making sure Lucy Ann and their son were protected. He could—and would—provide all the things a real partner and father provided. He would be everything his father wasn't.

"Change of plans for our stay."

"Because…?"

"We need more space and less chance of interruptions." He couldn't wait to have her all to himself. Damn, he'd missed her.

"But pandering to the paparazzi plays an important role in your PR." She hugged the diaper bag closer to her chest; the baby's bag, her camera and her computer had been the only things she'd insisted on bringing with her from home.

"Pandering?" He forced himself to focus on her words rather than the sound of her voice. Her lyrical Southern drawl was like honey along his starved senses. "That's not a word I'm particularly comfortable with. Playing along with them, perhaps. Regardless, they don't own me, and I absolutely will not allow them to have access to you and our son on anything other than our own terms."

"Wow, okay." Her eyes went wide before she grinned wryly. "But did you have to rent a castle?"

He wondered if he'd screwed up by going overboard, but her smile reassured him he'd struck gold by surprising her.

"It's a castle converted to a hotel, although yes, it's more secure and roomier." Safer, but also with romantic overtones he hoped would score points. "I thought in each place we stay, we could explore a different option for traveling with a child."

"This is…an interesting option," she conceded as the limousine cruised along the sweeping driveway leading up to the towering stone castle. Ivy scrolled up toward the turrets, the walls beneath baked brown with time. Only a few more minutes and the chauffeur would open the door.

Elliot chose his words wisely to set the stage before they went inside. "Remember how when we were kids, we hid in the woods and tossed blankets over branches? I called them forts, but you called them castles. I was cool with that as long as I got to be a knight rather than some pansy prince."

They'd climbed into those castle forts where he'd read for hours while she colored or drew pictures.

"Pansy prince?" She chuckled, tapping his chest. "You *are* anti-fairy-tale. What happened to the kid who used to lose himself in storybooks?"

He captured her finger and held on for a second before linking hands. "There are knights in fairy tales. And there are definitely castles."

"Is that what this is about?" She left her hand in his. "Showing me a fairy tale?"

"Think about coming here in the future with Eli." He stared at his son's sleeping face and images filled his head of their child walking, playing, a toddler with his hair and Lucy Ann's freckles. "Our son can pretend to be a knight or a prince, whatever he chooses, in a real castle. How freaking cool is that?"

"Very cool." A smile teased her kissable pink lips. "But this place is a long way from our tattered quilt forts in the woods."

His own smile faded. "Different from our childhood is a very good thing."

Her whole body swayed toward him, and she cupped his face. "Elliot, it's good that our child won't suffer the way we did, but what your father did to you…that had nothing to do with money."

Lucy Ann's sympathy, the pain for him that shone in her eyes, rocked the ground under him. He needed to regain control. He'd left that part of his life behind and he had no desire to revisit it even in his thoughts. So he deflected as he always did, keeping things light.

"I like it when you get prissy." He winked. "That's really sexy."

"Elliot, this isn't the time to joke around. We have some very serious decisions to make this month."

"I'm completely serious. Cross my heart." He pressed their clasped hands against his chest. "It makes me want to ruffle your feathers."

"Stop. It." She tugged free. "We're talking about Eli. Not us."

"That's why we're at a castle, for Eli," he insisted as the limousine stopped in front of the sprawling fortress. "Einstein said, 'The true sign of intelligence is not knowledge but imagination.' That's what we can offer our son with this unique lifestyle. The opportunity to explore his imagination around the world, to see those things that we only read about. You don't have to answer. Just think on it while we're here."

With the baby nursing, Lucy Ann curled up in her massive bed. She took comfort in the routine of feeding her child, the sweet softness of his precious cheek against her breast. With her life turning upside down so fast, she needed something familiar to hold on to.

The medieval decor wrapped her in a timeless fantasy she wasn't quite sure how to deal with. The castle had tapestries on the wall and sconces with bulbs that flickered like flames. Her four-poster bed had heavy drapes around it, the wooden pillars as thick as any warrior's chest. An arm's reach away waited a bassinet, a shiny reproduction of an antique wooden cradle for Eli.

Her eyes gravitated toward the tapestry across the room telling a love story about a knight romancing a maiden by a river. Elliot had chosen well. She couldn't help but be charmed by this place. Even her supper was served authentically in a trencher, with water in a goblet.

A plush, woven rug on the stone floor, along with

the low snap of the fire in the hearth, kept out the chilly spring night. The sound system piped madrigal music as if the group played in a courtyard below.

Through the slightly opened door, she saw the sitting room where Elliot was parked at a desk, his computer in front of him. Reviewing stats on his competitors? Or a million other details related to the racing season? She missed being a part of all that, but he had a new assistant, a guy who did his job so seamlessly he blended into the background.

And speaking of work, she had some of her own to complete. Once Eli finished nursing and went to bed there would be nothing for her to do but complete the two projects she hadn't been able to put on hold.

She'd expected Elliot to try to make a move on her once they got inside, but the suite had three bedrooms off the living area. One for her and one for him. The British nanny he'd hired had settled into the third, turning in after Lucy Ann made it clear Eli would stay with his mother tonight. While Mrs. Clayworth kept a professional face in place, the furrows along her forehead made it clear that she wondered at the lack of work on this job.

This whole setup delivered everything Elliot had promised, a unique luxury she could see her son enjoying someday. Any family would relish these fairy-tale accommodations. It was beyond tempting.

Elliot was beyond tempting.

Lucy Ann tore her eyes from her lifetime friend and onetime lover. This month was going to be a lot more difficult than she'd anticipated.

Desperate for some grounding in reality before she weakened, she reached for her phone, for the present, and called her aunt Carla.

* * *

She'd made it through the night, even if the covers on the bed behind her were a rumpled mess from her restless tossing and turning.

Lucy Ann sat at the desk at the tower window with her laptop, grateful to Carla for the bolstering. Too bad she couldn't come join them on this trip, but Carla was emphatic. She loved her home and her life. She was staying where she belonged.

Who could blame her? A sense of belonging was a rare gift Lucy Ann hadn't quite figured out how to capture yet. In South Carolina, she'd dreamed of getting out, and here she craved the familiarity of home.

Which made her feel like a total ingrate.

She was living the easy life, one any new mother would embrace. How ironic that at home she'd spent every day exhausted, feeling like Eli's naps were always a few minutes too short to accomplish what she needed to do. And now, she spent most of her time waiting for him to wake up.

She closed her laptop, caught up on work, dressed for the day, waiting to leave for Elliot's race. She still couldn't wrap her brain around how different this trip was from ones she'd shared with Elliot in the past. Staring out the window in their tower suite, she watched the sun cresting higher over the manicured grounds.

Last night, she'd actually slept in a castle. The restored structure was the epitome of luxury and history all rolled into one. She'd even pulled out her camera and snapped some photos to use for a client's web design. Her fingers already itched to get to the computer and play with the images, but Elliot was due back soon.

He'd gone to the track for prelim work, his race scheduled for tomorrow. Normally he arrived even earlier before an event, but the wedding had muddled his schedule. God, she hoped his concentration was rock solid. The thought of him in a wreck because she'd damaged his focus sent her stomach roiling. Why hadn't she considered this before? She should have told him about Eli earlier for so many reasons.

She was familiar with everything about his work world. She'd been his personal assistant for over a decade, in charge of every detail of his career, his life. And even in their time apart she'd kept up with him and the racing world online. Formula One racing in Spain alternated locations every year, Barcelona to Valencia and back again. She knew his preferences for routes like Valencia, with the street track bordering the harbor. She was used to being busy, in charge—not sitting around a castle twiddling her thumbs, eating fruit and cheese from medieval pottery.

Being waited on by staff, nannies and chauffeurs, being at loose ends, felt alien, to say the least. But she'd agreed to give him a chance this month. She would stick to her word.

As if conjured from her thoughts, Elliot appeared in the arched doorway between the living area and her bedroom. Jeans hugged his lean hips, his turtleneck shirt hugging a well-defined chest. Her mouth watered as she considered what he would do if she walked across the room, leaned against his chest to kiss him, tucked her hands in his back pockets and savored the chemistry simmering between them.

She swallowed hard. "Are you here for lunch?"

"I'm here for you and Eli." He held out a cashmere sweater of his. "In case you get chilly on our outing."

"Outing?" she asked to avoid taking the sweater until she could figure out what to do next.

She'd worn pieces of Elliot's clothes countless times over the years without a second thought, but the notion of wrapping his sweater around her now felt so intimate that desire pooled between her legs. However, to reject the sweater would make an issue of it, revealing feelings that made her too vulnerable, a passion she still didn't know how to control yet.

Gingerly, she took the sweater from him, the cashmere still warm from his touch. "Where are we going?"

He smiled mysteriously. "It's another surprise for you and Eli."

"Can't I even have a hint?" She hugged the sweater close, finding she was enjoying his game more than she should.

"We're going to play." He scooped his son up from the cradle in sure hands. "Right, Eli, buddy? We're going to take good care of your mama today. If she agrees to come with me, of course."

The sight of their son cradled in Elliot's broad hands brought her heart into her throat. She'd imagined moments like this, dreamed of how she would introduce him to their child. Day after day, her plan had altered as she delayed yet again.

And why? Truly, why? She still wasn't sure she understood why she'd made all the decisions she'd made these past months. She needed to use her time wisely to figure out the best way to navigate their future.

She tugged on the sweater. "Who am I to argue with such a tempting offer? Let's go play."

They left the suite and traveled down the sweeping stone stairway without a word, passing other guests as well as the staff dressed in period garb. The massive front doors even creaked as they swept open to reveal the waiting limousine.

Stepping out into the sunshine, she took in the incredible lawns. The modern-day buzz of cars and airplanes mixed with the historical landscaping that followed details down to the drawbridge over a moat.

The chauffeur opened the limo door for her. Lucy Ann slid inside, then extended her arms for her child. Elliot passed over Eli as easily as if they were a regular family.

Lucy Ann hugged her son close for a second, breathing in the baby-powder-fresh scent of him before securing Eli into his car seat. "Shouldn't you be preparing for race day?"

Getting his head together. Resting. Focusing.

"I know what I need to do," he answered as if reading her mind. He sat across from her, his long legs extended, his eyes holding hers. "That doesn't mean we can't have time together today."

"I don't want to be the cause of your exhaustion or lack of focus because you felt the need to entertain me." She'd been so hurt and angry for a year, she'd lost sight of other feelings. Race day was exciting and terrifying at the same time. "I've been a part of your world for too long to let you be reckless."

"Trust me. I have more reason than ever to be careful. You and Eli are my complete and total focus now."

There was no mistaking the certainty and resolve in his voice. Her fears eased somewhat, which made room for her questions about the day to come back to the fore. "At least tell me something about your plans for today. Starting with, where are we going?"

He leaned to open the minifridge and pulled out two water bottles. "Unless you object, we are going to the San Miguel de los Reyes Monastery."

She sat up straighter, surprised, intrigued. She took

the water bottle from him. "I'm not sure I understand your plan...."

"The monastery has been converted into a library. We've never had a chance to visit before on other trips." He twisted open his spring water. "In fact, as I look back, we both worked nonstop, all the time. As I reevaluate, I'm realizing now a little sightseeing won't set us behind."

"That's certainly a one-eighty from the past. You've always been a very driven man—no pun intended." She smiled at her halfhearted joke, feeling more than a little off balance by this change in Elliot. "I'll just say thank-you. This is a very thoughtful idea. Although I'm curious. What made you decide on this particular outing when there are so many more obvious tourist sites we haven't visited?"

"You sparked the idea when we were on the airplane, actually." He rolled the bottle between his palms. "You mentioned not believing in fairy tales anymore. That is why I chose the castle. Fairy tales are important for any kid...and I think we've both lost sight of that."

"We're adults." With adult wants and needs. Like the need to peel off his forest-green turtleneck and faded jeans.

"Even as kids, we were winging it with those fairy tales. Then we both grew jaded so young." He shrugged muscular shoulders. "So it's time for us to learn more about fairy tales so we can be good parents. Speaking of which, is Eli buckled in?"

"Of course."

"Good." He tapped on the window for the chauffeur to go. "Just in case you were wondering, I'm calling this the *Beauty and the Beast* plan."

They were honest-to-goodness going to a library. She sagged back, stunned and charmed all at once.

God, she thought she'd seen all his moves over the years—moves he'd used on other women. He'd always been more...boisterous. More obvious.

This was different. Subtle. Damn good.

"So I'm to be Belle to your beast."

"A Southern belle, yes, and you've called me a beast in the past. Besides, you know how much I enjoy books and history. I thought you might find some interesting photo opportunities along the way."

"You really are okay with a pedestrian stroll through a library." The Elliot she'd known all her life had always been on the go, scaling the tallest tree, racing down the steepest hill, looking for the edgiest challenge. But he did enjoy unwinding with a good book, too. She forgot about that side of him sometimes.

"I'm not a Cro-Magnon...even though I'm playing the beast. I do read. I even use a napkin at dinnertime." He waggled his eyebrows at her, his old playful nature more evident.

She wished she could have just slugged him on the shoulder as if they were thirteen again. Things had been simpler then on some levels—and yet not easy at all on others.

"You're right. I shouldn't have been surprised."

"Let's stop making assumptions about each other from now on about a lot of things. We've been friends for years, but even friends change, grow, even a man like me can mature when he's ready. Thanks to you and Eli, I'm ready now."

She wanted to believe him, to believe in him. She wanted to shake off a past where the people she cared about always let her down. Hundreds of times over the past eleven months she'd guessed at what his reaction would be if she told him about the baby.

She'd known he would come through for her. The part that kept haunting her, that kept her from trying... She could never figure out how she would know if he'd come through out of duty or something more.

The thought that she could yearn for more between the two of them scared her even now. She was much better off taking this one day at a time.

"Okay, Elliot—" she spread her arms wide "—I'm all-in...for our day at the monastery."

As she settled in for her date, she couldn't help wondering which was tougher: resisting the fairy-tale man who seemed content to ignore the past year or facing the reality of her lifelong friend who had every reason to be truly angry with her.

Regardless, at some point the past would catch up with both of them. They could only play games for so long before they had to deal with their shared parenthood.

Wearing a baseball cap with the brim tugged low, Elliot soaked in the sight of Lucy Ann's appreciation of the frescoes and ancient tomes as she filled a memory card with photos of the monastery turned library. He should have thought to do this for her sooner. The place was relatively deserted, a large facility with plenty of places for tourists to spread out. A school tour had passed earlier, but the echoes of giggles had faded thirty minutes ago. No one recognized him, and the bodyguards hung back unobtrusively. For all intents and purposes, he and Lucy Ann were just a regular family on vacation.

Why had he never thought to bring her to places like this before? He'd convinced himself he was taking care of her by offering her a job and a life following him around the world. But somehow he'd missed out on giving her so much more. He'd let her down when they were teenagers and he'd gotten arrested, leaving her alone to deal with her family. Now to find out he'd been selfish as an adult too. That didn't sit well with him.

So he had more to fix. He and Lucy Ann were bound by their child for life, but he didn't intend to take that part for granted. He would work his tail off to be more for her this time.

He set the brake on the stroller by a looming marble angel. "You're quiet. Anything I can get for you?"

She glanced away from her camera, looking back over her shoulder at him. "Everything's perfect. Thank you. I'm enjoying the peace. And the frescoes as well as the ornately bound books. This was a wonderful idea for how to spend the afternoon."

Yet all day long she'd kept that camera between them, snapping photos. For work? For pleasure?

Or to keep from looking at him?

Tired of the awkward silence, he pushed on, "If you're having fun, then why aren't you smiling?"

She lowered the camera slowly, pivoting to face him. Her eyes were wary. "I'm not sure what you mean."

"Lucy Ann, it's me here. Elliot. Can we pretend it's fifteen years ago and just be honest with each other?"

She nibbled her bottom lip for a moment before blurting out, "I appreciate what you're doing, that you're trying, but I keep waiting for the explosion."

He scratched over his closely shorn hair, which brought memories of sprinting away from a burning car. "I thought we cleared that up in the limo. I'm not going to wreck tomorrow."

"And I'm not talking about that now." She tucked the camera away slowly, pausing as an older couple meandered past looking at a brochure map of the museum. Once they cleared the small chapel area, she turned back to him and said softly, "I'm talking about an explosion of anger. You have to be mad at me for not telling you about Eli sooner. I accept that it was wrong of me not to try harder. I just keep wondering when the argument will happen."

God, was she really expecting him to go ballistic on her? He would never, never be like his father. He used his racing as an outlet for those aggressive feelings. He did what he needed to do to stay in control. Always.

Maybe he wasn't as focused as he claimed to be, because if he'd been thinking straight he would have realized that Lucy Ann would misunderstand. She'd spent her life on shaky ground growing up, her mother hooking up with a different boyfriend or husband every week. Beyond that, she'd always stepped in for others, a quiet warrior in her own right.

"You always did take the blame for things."

"What does that have to do with today?"

He gestured for her to sit on a pew, then joined her. "When we were kids, you took the blame for things I did—like breaking the aquarium and letting the snake loose in the school."

She smiled nostalgically. "And cutting off Sharilynn's braid. Not a nice thing to do at all, by the way."

"She was mean to you. She deserved it." He and Lucy Ann had been each other's champions in those days. "But you shouldn't have told the teacher you did it. You ended up cleaning the erasers for a week."

"I enjoyed staying after school. And my mom didn't do anything except laugh, then make me write an apology and do some extra chores." She looked down at her hands twisted in her lap. "Your father wouldn't have laughed if the school called him."

"You're right there." He scooped up her hand and held

on. It was getting easier and easier for them to be together again. As much as he hated revisiting the past, if
it worked to bring her back into his life, he would walk
over hot coals in hell for her. "You protected me every
bit as much as I tried to protect you."

"But your risk was so much higher…with your dad."
She squeezed his hand. "You did the knightly thing. That
meant a lot to a scrawny girl no one noticed except to
make fun of her clothes or her mom."

He looked up at Lucy Ann quickly. Somehow he'd forgotten that part of her past. He always saw her as quietly
feisty. "What elementary school boy cares about someone's clothes?"

"True enough, I guess." She studied him through the
sweep of long eyelashes. "I never quite understood why
you decided we would be friends—before we started taking the blame for each other's transgressions."

Why? He thought back to that time, to the day he saw
her sitting at the computer station, her legs swinging, too
short to reach the ground. The rest of the class was running around their desks while the teacher stepped out to
speak with a parent. "You were peaceful. I wasn't. We
balanced each other out. We can have that again."

"You're pushing." She tugged her hand.

He held firm. "Less than a minute ago, you told me I
have the right to be mad at you."

"And I have the right to apologize and walk away."

Her quick retort surprised him. The Lucy Ann of the
past would have been passive rather than confrontational.
Like leaving for a year and having his baby. "Yeah, you're
good at that, avoiding."

"There." She looked up quickly. "Tell me off. Be
angry. Do anything other than smile and pretend every-

thing's okay between us while we tour around the world like some dream couple."

Her fire bemused him and mesmerized him. "You are the most confusing woman I have ever met."

"Good." She stood up quickly, tugging her camera bag back onto her shoulder. "Women have always fallen into your arms far too easily. Time to finish the tour."

Seven

Lucy Ann swaddled her son in a fluffy towel after his bath while the nanny, Mrs. Clayworth, placed a fresh diaper and sleeper on the changing table. After the full day touring, then dinner with the nanny so Lucy Ann could get to know her better, she felt more comfortable with the woman.

Elliot's thoughtfulness and care for their son's future touched her. He'd charmed Mrs. Clayworth, yet asked perceptive questions. The woman appeared soft and like someone out of a Disney movie, but over the hours it became clear she was more than a stereotype. More than a résumé as a pediatric nurse. She was an avid musician and a hiker who enjoyed the world travel that came with her job. She spent her days off trekking through different local sites or attending concerts.

Lucy Ann liked the woman more and more with every

minute that passed. "Mrs. Clayworth, so you really were a nanny for royalty? That had to have been exciting."

Her eyes twinkled as she held out her arms for Eli. "You have seen my list of references. But that's just about the parents." She tucked Eli against her shoulder with expert hands, patting his back. "A baby doesn't care anything about lineage or credentials. Only that he or she is dry, fed, cuddled and loved."

"I can see clearly enough that you have a gift with babies."

The nanny's patience had been admirable when, just after supper, Eli cried himself purple over a bout of gas.

"I had two of my own. The child care career started once they left for the university. I used to be a pediatric nurse and while the money was good, it wasn't enough. I had bills to pay because of my loser ex-husband, and thanks to my daughter's connections with a blue-blooded roommate, I lucked into a career I thoroughly enjoy."

Having lived the past months as a single mom, Lucy Ann sympathized. Except she had always had the safety net of calling Elliot. She'd had her aunt's help, as well. What if she'd had nowhere to go and no one's help? The thought made her stomach knot with apprehension. That didn't mean she would stay with Elliot just because of her bills—but she certainly needed to make more concrete plans.

"I want the best for my son, too."

"Well, as much as I like my job, you have to know the best can't always be bought with money."

So very true. Lucy Ann took Eli back to dress him in his teddy bear sleeper. "You remind me of my aunt."

"I hope that's a compliment." She tucked the towel into the laundry chute.

"It is. Aunt Carla is my favorite relative." Not that

there was a lot of stiff competition. She traced the appliquéd teddy bear on the pj's and thought of her aunt's closet full of themed clothes. "She always wears these chipper seasonal T-shirts and sweatshirts. She has a thick Southern accent and deep-fries everything, including pickles. I know on the outside it sounds like the two of you are nothing alike, but on the inside, there's a calming spirit about you both."

"Then I will most certainly take that as a compliment, love." She walked to the pitcher on the desk by the window and poured a glass of water. "I respect that you're taking your time to get to know me and to see how I handle your son. Not all parents are as careful with their wee ones."

Mrs. Clayworth placed the glass beside the ornately carved rocker thoughtfully, even though Lucy Ann hadn't mentioned how thirsty she got when she nursed Eli. Money couldn't buy happiness, but having extra hands sure made life easier. She snapped Eli's sleeper up to his neck.

"I do trust Elliot's judgment. I've known him all my life. We've relied on each other for so much." There had been a time when she thought there was nothing he could do that would drive a wedge between them. "Except now there's this new dynamic to adjust to with Eli. But then you probably see that all the time."

Lucy Ann scooped up her son and settled into the wooden rocker, hoping she wasn't the only new mother to have conflicted feelings about her role. As much as she loved nursing her baby, she couldn't deny the occasional twinge of sadness that the same body Elliot once touched with passion had been relegated to a far more utilitarian purpose.

"You're a new mum." Mrs. Clayworth passed a burp cloth. "That's a huge and blessed change."

"My own mother wasn't much of a role model." She adjusted her shirt, and Eli hungrily latched on.

"And this favorite aunt of yours?" The nanny adjusted the bedding in the cradle, draping a fresh blanket over the end, before taking on the many other countless details in wrapping up the day.

"She helped as much as she could, but my mother resented the connection sometimes." Especially when her mom was between boyfriends and lonely. Then suddenly it wasn't so convenient to have Lucy Ann hang out with Aunt Carla. "I've been reading everything I can find on parenting. I even took some classes at the hospital, but there are too many things to cover in books or courses."

"Amen, dear."

Having this woman to lean on was...incredible, to say the least. Elliot was clearly working the fairy tale–like life from all angles.

She would be pridefully foolish to ignore the resources this woman brought to the table. Isolating herself for the past eleven months had been a mistake. Lucy Ann needed to correct that tendency and find balance. She needed to learn to accept help and let others into her life. Starting now seemed like a good idea.

She couldn't deny that all this "playing house" with Elliot was beginning to chip away at her reservations and her resolve to keep her distance. Elliot had said they needed to use this time to figure out how to parent Eli. She knew now they also needed to use this time to learn how to be in the same room with each other without melting into a pool of hormones. Time to quit running from the attraction and face it. Deal with it.

"And that's where your experience comes in. I would

be foolish not to learn from you." Lucy Ann paused, patting Eli's pedaling feet. "Why do you look so surprised?"

"Mothers seek help from me, not advice. You are a unique one."

"Would you mind staying for a while so we can talk?"

"Of course. I don't mind at all."

Lucy Ann gestured to the wingback chair on the other side of the fireplace. "I'd like to ask you a few questions."

"About babies?" she asked, sitting.

"Nope, I'd like to ask your advice on men."

The winner's trophy always felt so good in his hands, but today...the victory felt hollow in comparison with what he really wanted. More time with Lucy Ann.

Elliot held the trophy high with one hand, his helmet tucked under his other arm.

His *Beauty and the Beast* plan had gone well. They'd spent a low-key day together. Her pensive expression gave him hope he was on the right path. If she was ready to check out and return to Columbia, there would have been decisiveness on her face. But he was making headway with her. He could see that. He just needed to keep pushing forward with his plans, steady on. And try like hell to ignore the urge to kiss her every second they were together.

A wiry reporter pushed a microphone forward through the throng of fans and press all shouting congratulations. "Mr. Starc, tell us about the new lady in your life."

"Is it true she was your former assistant?"

"Where has she been this year?"

"Did she quit or was she fired?"

"Lovers' spat?"

"Which designer deserves credit for her makeover?"

Makeover? What the hell were they talking about?

To him, she was Lucy Ann—always pretty and special. And even though she had come out of her shell some in the past year, that didn't change the core essence of her, the woman he'd always known and admired.

Sure, her new curves added a bombshell quality. And the clothes his new assistant had ordered were flashier. None of that mattered to him. He'd wanted her before. He wanted her still.

The wiry reporter shoved the mic closer. "Are you sure the baby is yours?"

That question pulled him up short in anger. "I understand that the press thinks the personal life of anyone with a little fame is fair game. But when it comes to my family, I will not tolerate slanderous statements. If you want access to me, you will respect my son and his mother. And now it's time for me to celebrate with my family. Interviews are over."

He heard his assistant hiss in protest over the way he'd handled the question. The paparazzi expected to be fed, not spanked.

Shouldering through the crowd, Elliot kept his eyes locked on Lucy Ann in his private box, watching. Had she heard the questions through the speaker box? He hoped not. He didn't want anything to mar the evening he had planned. She'd actually consented to let the nanny watch Eli. Elliot would have her all to himself.

He kept walking, pushing through the throng.

"Congratulations, Starc," another reporter persisted. "How are you planning to celebrate?"

"How long do you expect your winning streak to run?"

"Is the woman and your kid the reason your engagement broke off?"

He continued to "no comment" his way all the way up the steps, into a secure hallway and to the private view-

ing box in the grandstand where Lucy Ann waited with
a couple of honored guests, local royalty and politicians
he only just managed to acknowledge with a quick greeting and thanks for attending. His entire focus locked on
Lucy Ann.

"You won," she squealed, her smile enveloping him
every bit as much as if she'd hugged him. Her red wraparound dress clung to her body, outlining every curve.

He would give up his trophy in a heartbeat to tug that
tie with his teeth until her dress fell open.

"I think we should go." Before he embarrassed them
both in front of reporters and esteemed guests.

He couldn't wait to get her alone. All he'd been able
to think about during the race was getting back to Lucy
Ann so he could continue his campaign. Move things
closer to the point where he could kiss her as he wanted.

"Right." She leaned to pluck her purse from her seat.
"The after-parties."

"Not tonight," he said softly for her ears only. "I have
other plans."

"You have responsibilities to your career. I understand that."

He pulled her closer, whispering, "The press is particularly ravenous today. We need to go through the private elevator."

Her eyebrows pinched together. "I'm not so sure that's
the best idea."

Damn it, was she going to bail on him before he even
had a chance to get started? He would just have to figure out a way around it. "What do you propose we do
instead?"

She tugged his arm, the warmth of her touch reaching
through his race jacket as she pulled him closer to the ob-

servation window. "You taught me long ago that the best way to get rid of the hungry press is to feed them tidbits."

The tip of her tongue touched her top lip briefly before she arched up on her toes to kiss him. He stood stock-still in shock for a second before—hell, yeah—he was all-in. His arms banded around her waist. She leaned into him, looping her arms his neck. He could almost imagine the cameras clicking as fast as his heartbeat, picking up speed with every moment he had Lucy Ann in his arms.

He didn't know what had changed her mind, but he was damn glad.

Her fingers played along his hair and he remembered the feel of her combing her hands through it the night they'd made love. He'd kept his hair longer then, before the accident.

Lucy Ann sighed into his mouth as she began to pull back with a smile. "That should keep the media vultures happy for a good long while." She nipped his bottom lip playfully before asking, "Are you ready to celebrate your win?"

Lucy Ann stepped out onto the castle balcony, the night air cool, the stone flooring under her feet even cooler but not cold enough to send her back inside. She walked to the half wall along the balcony and let the breeze lift her hair and ruffle through her dress before turning back to the table.

Elliot was showering off the scent of gasoline. He'd already ordered supper. The meal waited for them, savory Spanish spices drifting along the air.

There was no question that Elliot had ordered the dinner spread personally. The table was laden with her favorites, right down to a flan for dessert. Elliot remembered. She'd spent so much time as his assistant making sure to remember every detail of his life, she hadn't considered he'd been paying just as close attention to her.

She trailed her fingers along the edge of her water goblet. The sounds below—other guests coming and going, laughing and talking—mingled with the sound system wafting more madrigal tunes into the night. She didn't even have the nursery monitor with her for the first time since… She couldn't remember when. Mrs. Clayworth had already planned to watch Eli tonight since Lucy Ann had expected to go to an after-race party with Elliot.

Then she'd kissed him.

Halfway through that impulsive gesture, Lucy Ann realized that holding back was no longer an option. Sleeping with Elliot again was all but inevitable. The longer she waited, the more intense the fallout would be. They needed to figure out this crazy attraction now, while their son was still young enough not to know if things didn't work out.

Her stomach knotted with nerves. But the attraction was only getting stronger the longer she denied herself. It was only a matter of time—

As if conjured from that wish, Elliot stood in the balcony doorway, so fresh from the shower his short hair still held a hint of water. He'd changed into simple black pants and a white shirt with the sleeves rolled up. With the night shadows and flickering sconce lights he had a timeless air—the Elliot from the past mixing with the man he'd become.

She wanted them both.

Lucy Ann swallowed nervously and searched for something to say to break the crackling silence between them. "I can't believe the press actually left us alone after the race."

"We did slip away out a back entrance."

"That never stopped them before."

"I ordered extra security." He stalked toward her slowly. "I don't want anyone hassling you or Eli. Our lives are private now. I'm done playing the paparazzi game. At least we know this place is secure."

"As private as the woods we hid in as kids."

How many times had he made her feel safe? As if those quilted walls could hold out the world while they huddled inside reading books and coloring pictures like regular kids.

He stopped in front of her, his hand brushing back a stray lock of her hair. "Why did you kiss me after the race?"

"To keep the press content." To let other women know he was taken? "Because I wanted to."

He tugged the lock of hair lightly. "I meant why did you bite me?"

A laugh rolled free and rode the breeze. "Oh, that. Can't have everything going your way."

"You're more confident these days." His emerald eyes glinted with curiosity—and promise.

"Motherhood has given me purpose." Even now, the need to settle her life for her child pushed her to move faster with Elliot, to figure out one way or another.

To take what she could from this time together in case everything imploded later.

"I like seeing you more comfortable in your skin." He sat on the balcony half wall with unerring balance and confidence. "Letting the rest of the world see the woman you are."

As much as she feared trusting a man—trusting Elliot—she couldn't help but wonder if he would continue trying to spin a fairy-tale future for them long beyond tonight and ignore the fact that she had been the unnoticed Cinderella all her life. She wanted a man who noticed the real her—not the fairy tale. Not the fantasy. If she was honest, she was still afraid his sexual interest had come too late to feel authentic.

"You make me sound like I was a mouse before—someone in need of a makeover, like that reporter said."

He cursed softly. "You heard their questions?"

"The TV system in the private box was piping in feed from the winner's circle." She rolled her eyes. "It was a backhanded compliment of sorts."

"Don't ever forget I saw the glow long before."

She couldn't help but ask, "If you saw my glow, then why did it take you all those years to make a move on me?"

"If I remember correctly, you made the first move."

She winced, some of her confidence fading at the thought that they could have still been just friends if she hadn't impulsively kissed him that night they'd been drunk, celebrating and nostalgic. "Thanks for reminding me how I made a fool of myself."

"You're misunderstanding." He linked fingers with her, tugging her closer. "I've always found you attractive, but you were off-limits. Something much more valuable than a lover—those are a dime a dozen. You were, you are, my friend."

She wanted to believe him. "A dime a dozen. Nice."

"Lucy Ann, stop." He squeezed her hand. "I don't want to fight with you. It doesn't have to be that way for us this time. Trust me. I have a plan."

She'd planned to seduce him, keep things light, and he was going serious on her. She tried to lighten the mood again. "What fairy tale does this night come from?"

"It could be reality."

"You disappoint me." She leaned closer until their

chests just brushed. Her breasts beaded in response. "Tonight, I want the fairy tale."

He blinked in surprise. "Okay, fair enough." He stood, tugging her to the middle of the balcony. "We're in the middle of Cinderella's ball."

Appropriate, given her thoughts earlier. "Well, the clock is definitely ticking since Eli still wakes up in the middle of the night."

"Then we should make the most of this evening." The moonlight cast a glow around them, adding to the magical air of the night. "Are you ready for supper?"

"Honestly?" She swayed in time with the classical music.

"I wouldn't have asked if I hadn't wanted to know. I don't think you know how much I want to make you happy."

She stepped closer, lifting their hands. "Then let's dance."

"I can accommodate." He brought her hand to rest on his shoulder, his palm sliding warmly along her waist. "I owe you for homecoming our sophomore year in high school. You had that pretty dress your aunt made. She showed me so I could make sure the flowers on your wrist corsage matched just the right shade of blue."

"I can't believe you still remember about a high school dance." Or that he remembered the color of her dress.

"I got arrested for car theft and stood you up." He rested his chin on top of her head. "That tends to make a night particularly memorable."

"I knew it was really your friends that night, not you."

He angled back to look in her warm chocolate-brown eyes. "Why didn't you tell me you thought that?"

"You would have argued with me about some technical detail." She teased, all the while too aware of the freshly showered scent of him. "You were even more stubborn in those days."

"I *did* steal that car." He tugged her closer and stole her breath so she couldn't speak. "And it wasn't a technicality. I wanted to take you to the dance in decent wheels. I figured the used car dealership would never know as long as I returned it in the morning."

"I wouldn't have cared what kind of car we had that night."

"I know. But I cared. And ended up spending the night in jail before the car dealer dismissed the charges—God only knows why." He laughed darkly. "That night in jail was the best night's sleep I'd gotten in a long time, being out of my father's house."

God, he was breaking her heart. Their childhoods were so damaged, had they even stood a chance at a healthy adult relationship with each other? She rested her head on his shoulder and let him talk, taking in the steady beat of his pulse to help steady her own.

"I felt like such a bastard for sleeping, for being grateful for a night's break from my dad when I'd let you down."

Let her down? He'd been her port in the storm, her safe harbor. "Elliot," she said softly, "it was a silly dance. I was more worried about how your father would react to your arrest."

"I wanted to give you everything," he said, ignoring her comment about his dad. "But I let you down time after time."

This conversation was straying so far from her plans for seduction, her plans to work out the sensual ache inside her. "This isn't the sort of thing Prince Charming says to Cinderella at the ball."

"My point is that I'm trying to give you everything

now, if you'll just let me." He nuzzled her hair. "Just tell me what you want."

Every cell in her body shouted for her to say she wanted him to peel off her dress and make love to her against the castle wall. Instead, she found herself whispering, "All I want is for Eli to be happy and to lead a normal life."

"You think this isn't normal." His feet matched steps with hers as the music flowed into their every move.

A castle? A monastery library? "Well, this isn't your average trip to a bookstore or corner library, that's for sure."

"There are playgrounds here as well as libraries. We just have to find them for Eli."

Lucy Ann felt a stab of guilt. Elliot was thinking of their son and she'd been thinking about sex. "You make it sound so simple."

"It can be."

If only she could buy into his notion of keeping things simple long-term. "Except I never contacted you about being pregnant."

"And I didn't come after you like I should have. I let my pride get stung, and hurt another woman in the process."

She hadn't considered the fact that Gianna had been wronged in this situation. "What happens in the future if you find someone else…or if I do?"

"You want monogamy?" he asked. "I can do that."

"You say that so quickly, but you're also the one spinning fairy tales and games." She looked up at him. "I'm asking honest questions now."

She wondered why she was pushing so hard for answers to questions that could send him running. Was she on a self-destructive path in spite of her plans to be with him? Then again, this level of honesty between them had been a long time coming.

His feet stopped. He cupped her face until their eyes met. "Believe this. You're the only woman I want. You're sure as hell more woman than I can handle, so if you will stay with me, then monogamy is a piece of cake."

"Are you proposing?"

"I'm proposing we stay together, sleep together, be friends, lovers, parents."

He wasn't proposing. This wasn't Cinderella's ball after all. They were making an arrangement of convenience—to enjoy sex and friendship.

She didn't believe in fairy tales, damn it. So she should take exactly what he offered. But she intended to make sure he understood that convenience did not mean she would simply follow his lead.

Eight

Lucy Ann stepped out of his arms, and a protest roared inside Elliot. Damn it, was she leaving? Rejecting him in spite of everything they'd just said to each other? He set his jaw and stuffed his hands into his pockets to keep from turning into an idiot, a fool begging her to stay.

Except she didn't move any farther away. She locked eyes with him, her pupils wide—from the dark or from desire? He sure as hell hoped for the latter. Her hand went to the tie of her silky wraparound dress and she tugged.

His jaw dropped. "Um, Lucy Ann? Are you about to, uh—?"

"Yes, Elliot, I am." She pulled open the dress, revealing red satin underwear and an enticing expanse of creamy freckled skin.

His brain went on stun. All he could do was stare—and appreciate. Her bra cupped full breasts so perfectly his hands ached to hold and test their weight, to caress her until she sighed in arousal.

She shrugged and the dress started to slide down, down—

Out here.

In the open.

He bolted forward, a last scrap of sense telling him to shield her gorgeous body. He clasped her shoulders and pulled her to him, stopping the dress from falling away. "Lucy Ann, we're on a balcony. Outside."

A purr rippled up her throat as she wriggled against his throbbing erection. "I know."

Her fragrance beckoned, along with access to silky skin. His mouth watered. That last bit of his sense was going to give up the fight any second.

"We need to go back into our suite."

"I know that, too. So take me inside. Your room or mine. You choose as long as we're together and naked very soon." She leaned into him, her breasts pressing against his chest. "Unless you've changed your mind."

The need to possess tensed all his muscles, the adrenaline rush stronger than coming into a final turn neck and neck.

"Hell, no, I haven't changed my mind. We'll go to my room because there are condoms in my nightstand. And before you ask, yes, I've been wanting and planning to take you to bed again every minute of our journey." He scooped her up into his arms and shouldered the doors open into their suite. The sitting area loomed quiet and empty. "Thank God Mrs. Claymore isn't up looking for a midnight snack."

Her hair trailing loose over his shoulder, Lucy Ann kissed his neck in a series of nibbles up to his ear. "You're supposed to be the race car driver who lives on the edge.

and yet you're the one being careful. That's actually quite romantic."

"For you. Always careful for you." Except he hadn't been. He'd left her alone as a teen, gotten her pregnant and stayed away for nearly a year. He refused to let her down again in any way. She deserved better from him.

Lucy Ann deserved the best. Period.

She slid her hand behind his head and brought him closer for a kiss. He took her mouth as fully as he ached to take her body. With every step closer to his bedroom, his body throbbed harder and faster for her. The last few steps to the king-size bed felt like a mile. The massive headboard took up nearly the whole wall, the four posters carved like trees reaching up to the canopy. He was glad now he'd brought her here, a place they'd never been, a fantasy locale for a woman who deserved to be pampered, adored.

Treasured.

He set her on her feet carefully, handling her like spun glass. She tossed the dress aside in a silky flutter of red.

Nibbling her bottom lip and releasing it slowly, seductively, Lucy Ann kicked her high heels off with a flick of each foot. "One of us is *very* overdressed."

"You don't say."

"I do." She hooked her finger in the collar of his shirt and tugged down. Hard. Popping the buttons free in a burst that scattered them along the floor.

Ooooo-kay. So much for spun glass. His libido ramped into high gear. "You seem to be taking charge so nicely I thought you might help me take care of that."

He looked forward to losing more buttons in her deft hands.

"Hmm," she hummed, backing toward the bed until her knees bumped the wooden steps. "If I'm taking charge, then I want you to take off the rest of your clothes while I watch."

"I believe I can comply with that request." Shrugging off his destroyed shirt, he couldn't take his eyes from her as she settled onto the middle of the gold comforter, surrounded by tapestry pillows and a faux-fur throw. He toed off his loafers, his bare feet sinking into the thick Persian rug.

She reclined on the bed, pushing her heels into the mattress to scoot farther up until she could lean against the headboard. "You could have continued your underwear model days and made a mint, you know."

His hands stopped on his belt buckle. "You're killing the mood for me, Lucy Ann. I prefer to forget that brief chapter of my life."

"Briefs?" She giggled at her own pun. "You're right. You're definitely more of a boxers kind of guy now."

Fine, then. She seemed to want to keep this lighthearted, avoiding the heavier subjects they'd touched on while dancing. Now that he thought of it, they'd never gotten around to dinner, either. Which gave him an idea, one he'd be better off starting while he still had his clothes on.

"Stay there, just like that," he said. "I'll be right back."

Belt buckle clanking and loose, he sprinted out to the balcony. He picked up the platter of fruit and cheese and tucked the two plates of flan on top. Balancing the makeshift feast, he padded toward their room, careful not to wake the nanny or Eli.

Backing inside, he elbowed the door closed carefully. Turning, he breathed a sigh of relief to find Lucy Ann waiting. He hadn't really expected her to leave…except for a hint of an instant he'd thought about how quickly she'd run from what they shared last time.

She tipped her head to the side, her honey-streaked brown hair gliding along her shoulder like melted caramel. "You want to eat dinner now?"

He gave her his best bad boy grin. "If you're my plate, then yes, ma'am, I think this is a fine time for us to have supper."

"Okay then. Wouldn't want to mess up our clothes." She tugged off her bra and shimmied out of her panties, her lush curves bared and... Wow.

He almost dropped the damn tray.

Regaining his footing, he set the food on the edge of the bed without once taking his eyes off the long lines of her legs leading up to her caramel curls. He was definitely overdressed for what he had in mind.

He tugged off his slacks along with his boxers. His erection sprang free.

She smiled, her eyes roving over him in an appreciative sweep that made him throb harder. "Elliot?"

"Yes?" He clasped her foot in his hand, lifting it and kissing the inside of her ankle where a delicate chain with a fairy charm surprised him on such a practical woman. What else had he missed about Lucy Ann in the year they'd been apart?

"Do you know what would make this perfect?"

He kissed the inside of her calf. "Name it. I'll make it happen."

"More lights."

He looked up from her leg to her confident eyes reflecting the bedside lamp. "Lights?"

"It's been quite a while since I saw you naked, and last time was rather hurried and with bad lighting."

She was a total and complete turn-on. Everything about her.

"Can do," he said.

He placed her leg back on the bed and turned on the massive cast-iron chandelier full of replica candles that supplemented the glow of the bedside lamp. The rich colors of the bed and the heavy curtains swept back on either side somehow made Lucy Ann seem all the more pale and naked, her creamy flesh as tempting as anything he'd ever seen. The feel of her gaze on him heated his blood to molten lava, his whole body on fire for her.

But no way in hell would he let himself lose control. He took the time to reach for the bedside table, past his vintage copy of *Don Quixote*. Dipping into the drawer, he pulled out a condom. He dropped it on the bed before hitching a knee on the edge and joining her on the mattress. Taking his time, even as urgency thrummed through him, he explored every curve, enjoying the way goose bumps rose along her bared flesh.

She met him stroke for stroke, caress for caress, until he couldn't tell for certain who was mirroring whom. Their hands moved in tandem, their sighs syncing up, until they both breathed faster. He lost track of how long they just enjoyed each other, touching and seeking their fill. At some point, she rolled the condom over him, but he only half registered it since pleasure pulsed through him at her touch—and at the feel of her slick desire on his fingertips as he traced and teased between her legs.

Holding himself in check grew tougher by the second so he angled away, reaching for the platter of food on the corner of the bed.

He pushed the tray along the bed to put it in better reach. Then he plucked a strawberry and placed the plump fruit between his teeth. He slid over her, blanketing her. He throbbed between her legs, nudging, wanting. He leaned closer and pressed the strawberry to her mouth. Her lips parted to close over the plump fruit until they met in a kiss.

She bit into the strawberry and he thrust inside her. The fruity flavor burst over his taste buds at the same time sensation sparked through him. Pleasure. The feel of her clamping around him, holding him deep inside her as a "yes" hissed between her teeth. Her head pressed back into the bolster, her eyes sliding closed.

He moved as her jaw worked, chewing the strawberry. Her head arched back, her throat gliding with a slow swallow. Her breasts pushed upward, beading tight and hard.

Inviting.

Leaning on one elbow, he reached for another berry. He squeezed the fruit in his fist, dribbling the juice over her nipple. She gasped in response. He flicked his tongue over her, tasting her, rolling the beaded tip in his mouth until she moaned for more. The taste of ripe fruit and a hint of something more had him ready to come apart inside her already.

Thrusting over and over, he pushed aside the need to finish, hard and fast. Aching to make this last, for her and for him.

How could he possibly have stayed away from her for so long? For any time at all? How could he have thought for even a second he could be with anyone other than her? They were linked together. They always had been, for as far back as he could remember.

She was his, damn it.

The thought rocketed through him, followed closely by her sighs and moans of completion. Her hands flung out, twisting in the comforter, her teeth sinking deep into her bottom lip as she bit back the cry that might wake others.

Seeing the flush of pleasure wash over her skin

snapped the reins on his restraint and he came, the hot pulse jetting from him into her. Deeper, and yet somehow not deep enough as he already wanted her again.

As his arms gave way and he sank to rest fully on top of her, he could only think, damn straight, she was his.

But he hadn't been able to keep Lucy Ann before. How in the hell was he going to manage to keep the new, more confident woman in his arms?

A woman who didn't need anything from him.

Tingling with anticipation, Lucy Ann angled toward Elliot. "I need another bite now or I am absolutely going to pass out."

She gripped his wrist and guided his spoonful of flan toward her mouth as he chuckled softly. She closed her lips over it and savored the creamy caramel pudding. All of her senses were on hyperalert since she and Elliot had made love—twice. The scent of strawberries still clung to the sheets even though they'd showered together, making love in the large stone spa before coming back to bed.

Eventually, she would have to sleep or she would be a completely ineffective mother. But for now, she wasn't ready to let go of this fantasy night, making love with Elliot in a castle.

The luxurious sheets teased her already-sensitive skin, and she gave herself a moment to soak in the gorgeous surroundings. Beyond Elliot. The man was temptation enough, but he'd brought her to this decadent haven where she could stare up at carvings of a Dionysian revel on the bedposts or lose herself in the images of a colorful, wall-sized tapestry depicting a medieval feast. The figures were almost life-size, gathered around a table, an elegant lord and lady in the middle and an array of characters all around from lecherous knight to teasing serving maid. Even the scent of dried herbs and flowers that emanated from the linens immersed her in a fantasy world.

One she never wanted to end.

She scooped her spoon through the flan and offered a bite to her own sexy knight. "I have to say our dance tonight ended much better than our sophomore homecoming ever could have."

"You're right about that." He dipped his spoon into the dessert for her, picking up the rhythm of feeding each other. "Lady, you are rocking the hell out of that sheet."

He filled her whole fairy-tale fantasy well with his broad shoulders and muscular chest, the sheet wrapped around his waist. There was a timeless quality about this place that she embraced. It kept her from looking into the future. She intended to make the absolute most of this chance to be together.

They'd had sex before. They knew each other's bodies intimately. Yet there was a newness about this moment. She looked different now that she'd had a baby. Her body had changed. *She* had changed in other ways, as well. She had a growing confidence now, personally and professionally.

Lucy Ann searched Elliot's eyes…and found nothing but desire. His gaze stroked over her with appreciation and yes, even possession—stoking the heat still simmering inside her.

"I have to confess something." She angled forward to accept the next bite he fed her.

His face went somber in a flash even as he took the spoonful of flan she brought to his mouth. He swallowed, then said, "Tell me whatever you need to. I'm not going anywhere."

She carefully set her utensil onto the platter by the last strawberry, her body humming with the memory of the moment they'd shared the fruit, the moment he'd thrust inside her. The intensity of it all threatened to overwhelm her. She desperately needed to lighten the moment before they waded into deeper waters.

"I may like simplicity in many parts of my life—" she paused for effect, then stretched out like a lazy cat until the sheet slithered away from her breasts "—but I am totally addicted to expensive linens."

"God, Lucy Ann." He hauled her against his side, her nipples beading tighter at the feel of his bare skin. "You scared the hell out of me with talk of confessions."

"I'm serious as a heart attack here." She rested her cheek on his chest, the warmth of him seeping into her. "Every night when I crawled into bed—and trust me, cheap mattresses also suck a lot more than I remembered—those itchy sheets made me long for Egyptian cotton."

"Ahhh, now I understand." He tugged the comforter over them. "The fairy tale here is *The Princess and the Pea*. I will be very sure you always have the best mattresses and sheets that money can buy." He patted her butt.

"My prince," she said, joking to keep talk of the future light for now, all the while knowing that inevitably they would have to steer the conversation in another direction. "I don't think I ever said congratulations on your win today. I'm sorry you missed out on the parties tonight."

"I'm not sorry at all." He stroked back her hair, extending the length with his fingers and letting damp strands glide free. "This is exactly where I wanted to be. Celebrating with you, without clothes—best party ever."

"You do deserve to celebrate your success though. You've come a long way through sheer determination." She hooked a leg over his, enjoying the way they fit.

"Although I have to say, I've always been surprised you chose Formula One over the NASCAR route, given your early days racing the dirt-track circuit."

Why had she never thought to question him about this before? She'd simply followed, accepting. He'd always taken the lead in life and on the track.

He'd begun racing with adults at fourteen years old, then picked it up again when he graduated from the military high school in North Carolina. He was a poster boy for the reformative success of the school even without people knowing he periodically helped out Interpol.

Elliot rested his chin on her head, his breath warm on her scalp. "I guess I have a confession of my own to make. I wanted to go to college and major in English. But I had to make a living. I went back to racing after school because my credit was shot."

English? It made sense given the way he'd always kept a book close at hand, and yet she couldn't believe he'd never mentioned that dream. A whole new side of Elliot emerged, making her wonder what else he'd kept secret.

"Because of your arrest history?"

His chest rose and fell with a heavy sigh. "Because my father took out credit cards in my name."

Her eyes closing, she hugged an arm tighter around him. "I'm so sorry. Nothing should surprise me when it comes to that man, but it still sucks to hear. I'm just so glad you got away from him."

"You should be mad at me for leaving you," he repeated, his voice hoarse. "I let you down."

"I don't agree." She kissed his chest before continuing. "You did what you needed to. I missed you when they sent you to North Carolina, but I understood."

"All the same, you were still hurt by what I did. I could see that then. I can even feel it now. Tell me the truth."

So much for keeping things light. They would always have to cycle around to the weightier stuff eventually. "I understand why you needed a way out, believe me, I do. I just wish you'd spoken to me, given me an opportunity to weigh in and figure out how we could both leave. That place was bearable with you around. Without you…"

She squeezed her eyes closed, burying her face in his chest, absorbing the vibrant strength of him to ward off the chill seeping into her bones.

"I like to think if I could go back and change the past that I would. Except I did the same thing all over again. I let you go. You deserve to be put first in someone's life, someone who won't let you down."

Where was he going with this? Where did she *want* him to go?

After that, he stayed silent so long she thought for a moment he had drifted off midthought, then his hand started to rove along her spine slowly. Not in a seductive way; more of a touch of connection.

He kissed the top of her head, whispering into her hair still damp from their shared shower, "I didn't want to leave you back in high school. You have to know that." His voice went ragged with emotion. "But I didn't have anything to offer you if we left together. And I couldn't stay any longer. I just couldn't see another way out except to get arrested."

She struggled to sift through his words, to understand what he was trying to tell her. "You stole cars on purpose, hoping the cops would catch you?"

"That pretty much sums it up." His hand slid to rest on her hip, his voice strangely calm in contrast to his racing heart. "After that first night in jail, I started stealing cars on a regular basis. I didn't expect to be so good at it. I thought I would get caught much earlier."

"Why did you want to get caught?" she repeated, needing to understand, wondering how she didn't know this about him. She'd thought they told each other everything.

"I figured jail was safer than home," he said simply. "I didn't worry so much about myself with my dad, but I worried what he would do to the people around me."

"You mean me and your mother?"

He nodded against her head. "Remember when we went on that trip to the beach and my old rebuilt truck broke down?"

"You mean when the tires fell off." Only his incredible reflexes had kept them from crashing into a ditch. It had been a near miss.

"Right. When the first one fell off, I thought what crappy luck. Then the second one came off, too…."

Her stomach lurched at the memory. "We were lucky we didn't get T-boned in traffic. You had fast instincts, even then."

His arms twitched around her, holding her too tightly. "I found out that my father had taken out a life insurance policy on me."

She gasped, rising up on her elbows to look him in the eyes. His expression was completely devoid of emotion, but she could see the horror that must be on her face reflected in his eyes.

"Elliot, do you really believe your father tried to kill you?"

"I'm sure of it," he said with certainty, pushing up to sit, the covers rustling and twisting around their legs.

"You had to have been so scared."

Why hadn't he told her? Although the second she finished that thought, she already knew the answer. He didn't want to put her at risk. Debating the fact now, insisting he should have told the police, seemed moot after so long. Better to just listen and figure out why he was telling her this now.

"I didn't have the money to strike out on my own. I knew the odds of teens on the street." His head fell back against the carved headboard. "I figured the kids in juvie couldn't be as bad as my old man."

"Except you were sent to military reform school instead."

Thank heavens, too, since his life had been turned around because of his time in that school, thanks to his friends and the headmaster. The system did work for the best sometimes. Someone somewhere had seen the good deep inside of Elliot.

"I finally caught a lucky break." He cupped the back of her head, his fingers massaging her scalp. "I'm just so damn sorry I had to leave you behind. I see now I should have figured out another way."

"It all worked out—"

"Did it?" he asked, his eyes haunted. "Your mom's boyfriends... We've talked about so much over the years but we've never discussed that time when I was away."

Slowly, she realized what he was asking, and the thought that he'd worried about her, about that, for all these years... Her heart broke for him and the worries he'd had. She wondered if that's why he'd been so protective, giving her a job, keeping her with him—out of guilt?

"Elliot, the guys my mom saw were jerks, yes, and a few of them even tried to cop a feel, but none of them were violent. Some may have been perverts but they weren't rapists. So I was able to take care of myself by avoiding them. I escaped to Aunt Carla's until things settled down or until Mom and her latest guy broke up."

"You shouldn't have had to handle it yourself, to hide from your own home." Anger and guilt weighted his words and tightened his jaw until the tendons flexed along his neck. "Your mother should have been there for you. *I* should have been there."

She didn't want him to feel guilty or to feel sorry for her. Angling up, she cupped his face in her hands. "I don't want you to feel obligated to be my protector."

"I don't know what else I can be for you." His voice was ragged with emotion, his eyes haunted.

They could have been teenagers again, the two of them clinging to each other because there was so little else for them. So much pain. So much betrayal by parents who should have valued them and kept them safe. Her shared past with Elliot wrapped around her so tightly she felt bound to him in a way she couldn't find words to explain but felt compelled to express, even if only physically.

Soaking in the feel of bare flesh meeting flesh, Lucy Ann kissed Elliot, fully, deeply. She savored the taste of flan and strawberries and *him*. A far more intoxicating combination than any alcohol.

And he was all hers, for tonight.

Nine

Their tongues met and tangled as Lucy Ann angled her mouth over Elliot's. They fit so seamlessly together as she tried to give him some sort of comfort, even if only in the form of distraction. Sex didn't solve problems, but it sure made the delaying a hell of a lot more pleasurable. Her mind filled with the sensation of him, the scents of them together.

His hands banded around her waist, and he urged her over him. She swung her leg over his lap, straddling him. His arousal pressed between her legs, nudging against the tight bundle of nerves at her core.

She writhed against him, her body on fire for him. "I need… I want…"

"Tell me, Lucy Ann," he said between kisses and nips, tasting along her neck, "tell me what you want."

She didn't even know what would settle out their lives or how to untangle the mess they'd made of their world.

Not to mention their emotions. "Right now, I just need you inside me."

"That's not what I meant." He held her with those mesmerizing green eyes, familiar eyes that had been a part of her life for as long as she could remember.

"Shh, don't ruin this." She pressed two fingers to his lips. She didn't want to risk their conversation leading down a dangerous path as it had eleven months ago.

Even thinking about their fight chilled her. That argument had led to the most painful time in her life, the time without the best friend she'd ever had. They couldn't go that route again. They had Eli to consider.

And as for their own feelings?

She shied away from those thoughts, determined to live in the moment. She shifted to reach in the bedside table drawer for another condom. He plucked it from between her fingers and sheathed himself quickly, efficiently, before positioning her over him again. Slowly, carefully—blissfully—she lowered herself onto him, taking the length of him inside her until he touched just... the right...spot.

Yessss.

Her eyelids grew heavy but the way he searched her face compelled her to keep her eyes open, to stare back at him as she rolled her hips to meet his thrusts. Every stroke sent ripples of pleasure tingling through her as they synced up into a perfect rhythm. Her palms flattened against his chest, her fingers digging into the bunched muscles twitching under her touch. A purr of feminine satisfaction whispered free as she reveled in the fact that she made him feel every bit as out of control as he made her feel.

His hands dug into her hips then eased, caressing up her sides then forward to cup her breasts. She sighed at the gentle rasp of his callused fingers touching her so instinctively, his thumbs gliding over nipples until she feared she would come apart now. Too soon. She ached for this to last, to hang on to the blissful forgetfulness they could find in each other's arms. She flowed forward to cover him, moving slower, holding back.

Elliot's arms slid around her, and he drew her earlobe between his teeth. Just an earlobe. Yet her whole body tensed up with that final bit of sensation that sent her hurtling into fulfillment. Her nails dug into his shoulders, and she cried out as her release crested.

He rolled her over, and she pushed back, tumbling them again until the silver tray went crashing to the floor, the twang of pewter plates clanking. He kissed her hard, taking her cries of completion into his mouth. As orgasm gripped her again and again, his arms twitched around her, his body pulsing, his groans mingling with hers until she melted in the aftermath.

Panting, she lay beside him, her leg hitched over his hip, an arm draped over him. Her whole body was limp from exhaustion. She barely registered him pulling the comforter over her again.

Maybe they could make this friendship work, friendship combined with amazing sex. Being apart hadn't made either of them happy.

Could this be enough? Friendship and sex? Could they learn to trust each other again as they once had?

They had the rest of the month together to figure out the details. If only they could have sex until they couldn't think about the future.

His breath settled into an even pattern with a soft snore. What a time to realize she'd never slept with him before. She'd seen him nap plenty of times, falling asleep with a book on his chest, but never once had she stayed through the night with him.

For now, it was best she keep it that way. No matter how tempted she was to indulge herself, she wouldn't make the mistakes of her past again. Not with Eli to think about.

Careful not to wake her generous, sexy lover, she eased from the bed, tiptoeing around the scattered cutlery and dishes that looked a lot like the disjointed parts of her life. Beautiful pieces, but such a jumbled mess there was no way to put everything back together.

"Lucy Ann?" Elliot called in a groggy voice. He reached out for her. "Come back to bed."

She pulled on her red wraparound dress and tied it quickly before gathering her underwear. "I need to go to Eli. I'll see you in the morning."

Her bra and panties in her hand, she raced from his room and tried to convince herself she wasn't making an even bigger mess of her life by running like a coward.

"Welcome to Monte Carlo, Eli," Elliot said to his son, carrying the baby in the crook of his arm, walking the floor with his cranky child while everyone else slept. He'd heard Eli squawk and managed to scoop him up before Lucy Ann woke.

But then she was sprawled out on her bed, looking dead to the world after their trip to Monte Carlo—with a colicky kid.

The day had been so busy with travel, he hadn't had a chance to speak to Lucy Ann alone. But then she hadn't gone out of her way to make that possible, either. If he hadn't known better, he would have thought she was hiding from him.

Only there was no reason for her to do so. The sex

last night had been awesome. They hadn't argued. Hell, he didn't know what was wrong, but her silence today couldn't be missed.

Compounding matters, Eli had become progressively irritable as the day passed. By the time his private plane had landed in Monte Carlo, Elliot was ready to call a doctor. Lucy Ann and the nanny had both reassured him that Eli was simply suffering from gas and exhaustion over having his routine disrupted.

Of course that only proved Lucy Ann's point that a child shouldn't be living on the road, but damn it all, Elliot wasn't ready to admit defeat. Especially not after last night. He and Lucy Ann were so close to connecting again.

He'd hoped Monte Carlo would go a long way toward scoring points in his campaign. He owned a place here. A home with friends who lived in the area. Sure it was a condominium and his friend owned a casino. But his friend was a dad already. And the flat was spacious, with a large garden terrace. He would have to add some kind of safety feature to the railing before Eli became mobile. He scanned the bachelor pad with new eyes and he saw a million details in a different light. Rather than fat leather sofas and heavy wooden antiques, he saw sharp edges and climbing hazards.

"What do you think, Eli?" he asked his son, staring down into the tiny features all scrunched up and angry. "Are you feeling any better? I'm thinking it may be time for you to eat, but I hate to wake your mama. What do you say I get you one of those bottles with expressed milk?"

Eli blinked back up at him with wide eyes, his fists and feet pumping.

He'd always thought babies all looked the same, like

tiny old men. Except now he knew he could pick out Eli from dozens of other babies in a heartbeat.

How strange to see parts of himself and Lucy Ann mixed together in that tiny face. Yet the longer he looked, the more that mixture became just Eli. The kid had only been in his life for a week. Yet now there didn't seem to be a pre-Eli time. Any thoughts prior to seeing him were now colored by the presence of him. As if he had somehow already existed on some plane just waiting to make an appearance.

Eli's face scrunched up tighter in that sign he was about to scream bloody murder. Elliot tucked his son against his shoulder and patted his back while walking to the fridge to get one of the bottles he'd seen Lucy Ann store there.

He pulled it out, started to give it to his son...then remembered something about cold bottles not being good. He hadn't paid a lot of attention when his friends took care of baby stuff, but something must have permeated his brain. Enough so that he tugged his cell phone from his pocket and thumbed speed dial for his buddy Conrad Hughes. He always stayed up late. Conrad had said once that life as a casino magnate had permanently adjusted his internal clock.

The phone rang only once. "This is Hughes. Speak to me, Elliot."

"I need advice."

"Sure, financial? Work? Name it."

"Um, babies." He stared at the baby and the bottle on the marble slab counter. Life had definitely changed. "Maybe you should put Jayne on the line."

"I'm insulted," Conrad joked, casino bells and music drifting over the airwaves. "Ask your question. Besides, Jayne's asleep. Worn out from the kiddo."

"The nanny's sick and Lucy Ann really needs to sleep in." He swayed from side to side. "She's been trying to keep up with her work, the baby, the traveling."

"And your question?"

"Oh, right. I forgot. Sleep deprivation's kicking in, I think," he admitted, not that he would say a word to Lucy Ann after the way she was freaking out over him having a wreck.

"Happens to the best of us, brother. You were just the last man to fall."

"Back to my question. When I give the baby a bottle of this breast milk from the refrigerator, do I heat it in the microwave? And I swear if you laugh, I'm going to kick your ass later."

"I'm only laughing on the inside. Never out loud." Conrad didn't have to laugh. Amusement drenched his words.

"I can live with that." As long as he got the advice.

"Run warm water over the bottle. No microwave. Do not heat it in water on the stove," Conrad rattled off like a pro. "If he doesn't eat it all, pour it out. You can't save and reuse it. Oh, and shake it up."

"You're too good at this," Elliot couldn't resist saying as he turned on the faucet.

"Practice."

"This has to be the strangest conversation of my life." He played his fingers through the water to test the temperature and found it was warming quickly. He tucked the bottled milk underneath the spewing faucet with one hand, still holding his son to his shoulder with the other.

"It'll be commonplace before you know it."

Would it? "I hope so."

The sound of casino bells softened, as if Conrad had

gone into another room. "What about you and Lucy Ann?"

Elliot weighed his answer carefully before saying simply, "We're together."

"Together-together?" Conrad asked.

Elliot glanced through the living area at the closed bedroom door and the baby in his arms. "I'm working on it."

"You've fallen for her." His friend made it more of a statement than a question.

So why couldn't he bring himself to simply agree? "Lucy Ann and I have been best friends all our lives. We have chemistry."

Best friends. His brothers all called themselves best friends, but now he realized he'd never quite paired up with a best bud the way they all had. He was a part of the group. But Lucy Ann was his best friend, always had been.

"You'd better come up with a smoother answer than that if you ever get around to proposing to her. Women expect more than 'you're a great friend and we're super together in the sack.'"

Proposing? The word *marriage* hadn't crossed his mind, and he realized now that it should have. He should have led with that from the start. He should have been an honorable, stand-up kind of guy and offered her a ring rather than a month-long sex fest.

"I'm not that much of an idiot."

He hoped.

"So you are thinking about proposing."

He was now. The notion fit neatly in his brain, like the missing piece to a puzzle he'd been trying to complete since Lucy Ann left a year ago.

"I want my son to have a family, and I want Lucy Ann to be happy." He turned off the water and felt the bottle. Seemed warm. He shook it as instructed. "I'm just not sure I know how to make that happen. Not many long-term role models for happily ever after on my family tree."

"Marriage is work, no question." Conrad whistled softly on a long exhale. "I screwed up my own pretty bad once, so maybe I'm not the right guy to ask for advice."

Conrad and Jayne had been separated for three years before reuniting.

"But you fixed your marriage. So you're probably the best person to ask." Elliot was getting into this whole mentor notion. Why hadn't he thought to seek out some help before? He took his son and the bottle back into the living room of his bachelor pad, now strewn with baby gear. "How do you make it right when you've messed up this bad? When you've let so much time pass?"

"Grovel," Conrad said simply.

"That's it?" Elliot asked incredulously, dropping into his favorite recliner. He settled his son in the crook of his arm and tucked the bottle in his mouth. "That's your advice? Grovel?"

"It's not just a word. You owe her for being a jackass this past year. Like I said before. Relationships are work, man. Hard work. Tougher than any Interpol assignment old headmaster Colonel Salvatore could ever give us. But the payoff is huge if you can get it right."

"I hope so."

"Hey, I gotta go. Text just came in. Kid's awake and Jayne doesn't believe in nighttime nannies. So we're in the walking dead stage of parenthood right now." He didn't sound at all unhappy about it. "Don't forget. Shake the milk and burp the kid if you want to keep your suit clean."

Shake. Burp. Grovel. "I won't forget."

Lucy Ann blinked at the morning sun piercing the slight part in her curtains. She'd slept in this room in Elliot's posh Monte Carlo digs more times than she could remember. He'd even had her choose her own decor since they spent a lot of off-season time here, too.

She'd chosen an über-feminine French toile in pinks and raspberries, complete with an ornate white bed— Renaissance antiques. And the best of the best mattresses. She stretched, luxuriating in the well-rested feeling, undoubtedly a by-product of the awesome bed and even more incredible sex. She couldn't remember how long it had been since she'd woken up refreshed rather than dragging, exhausted. Certainly not since Eli had been born—

Blinking, she took in the morning sun, then gasped. "Eli!"

She jumped from the bed and raced over to the portable crib Elliot had ordered set up in advance. Had her baby slept through the night? She looked in the crib and found it empty. Her heart lurched up to her throat.

Her bare feet slipping on the hardwood floor, she raced out to the living room and stopped short. Elliot sat in his favorite recliner, holding their son. He looked so at ease with the baby cradled in the crook of his arm. An empty bottle sat on the table beside them.

Elliot toyed with his son's foot. "I have plans for you, little man. There are so many books to read. *Gulliver's Travels* and *Lord of the Rings* were favorites of mine as a kid. And we'll play with Matchbox cars when you're older. Or maybe you'll like trains or airplanes? Your choice."

Relaxing, Lucy Ann sagged against the door frame in relief. "You're gender stereotyping our child."

Glancing up, Elliot smiled at her, so handsome with a five o'clock shadow peppering his jaw and baby spit-up dotting his shoulder it was all she could do not to kiss him.

"Good morning, beautiful," he said, his eyes sliding over her silky nightshirt with an appreciation that all but mentally pulled the gown right off her. "Eli can be a chef or whatever he wants, as long as he's happy."

"Glad to hear you say that." She padded barefoot across the room and sat on the massive tapestry otto-man between the sofa and chairs. "I can't believe I slept in so late this morning."

"Eli and I managed just fine. And if I ran into prob-lems, I had plenty of backup."

"I concede you chose well with the nanny." She wasn't used to taking help with Eli, but she could get addicted to this kind of assistance quickly. "Mrs. Clayworth's amaz-ing and a great help without being intrusive."

"You're not upset that I didn't wake you?"

She swept her tangled hair back over her shoulders. "I can't think any mother of an infant would be upset over an extra two hours of sleep."

"Glad you're happy, Sleeping Beauty." His heated gaze slid over the satin clinging to her breasts.

"Ah, your fairy-tale romancing theme."

He arched an eyebrow. "You catch on fast. If you were to stay with me for the whole racing season, we could play Aladdin and his lamp."

His talk of the future made her…uncomfortable. She was just getting used to the shift in their relationship adding a sexual level on a day-to-day basis. So she ig-nored the part about staying longer and focused on the fairy tale. "You've been fantasizing about me as a belly dancer?"

"Now that you mention it…"

"Lucky for us both, I'm rested and ready." She curled her toes into the hand-knotted silk Persian rug that would one day be littered with toys. "You're going to be a wonderful father."

As the words fell from her mouth she knew them to be true, not a doubt in her mind. And somehow she'd slid into talking about the future anyway.

"Well, I sure as hell learned a lot from my father about how not to be a dad." His gaze fell away from her and back to their child. "And the things I didn't learn, I intend to find out, even if that means taking a class or reading every parenting book on the shelves since I never had much of a role model."

Clearly, he was worried about this. She leaned forward to touch his knee. "Does that mean I'm doomed to be a crummy mother?"

"Of course not." He covered her hand with his. "Okay, I see your point. And thanks for the vote of confidence."

"For what it's worth, I do think you've had a very good role model." She linked fingers with him. "The colonel. Your old headmaster has been there for you, the way my aunt has for me. Doing the best they could within a flawed system that sent them broken children to fix."

"I don't like to think of myself as broken." His jaw clenched.

"It's okay, you know—" she rubbed his knee "—to be sad or angry about the past."

"It's a lot easier to just speed around the track, even smash into walls, rather than rage at the world." His throat moved with a long swallow.

"I'm not so sure I like that coping mechanism. I would

be so sad if anything happened to you." And wasn't that the understatement of the year? She had to admit, though, she'd been worrying more about him lately, fearing the distractions she brought to his life, also fearing he might have beat the odds one time too many.

He squeezed her hand, his eyes as serious as she'd ever seen them. "I would quit racing. For you."

"And I would never ask you to do that. Not for me."

"So you would ask for Eli?"

She churned his question around in her mind, unable to come up with an answer that didn't involve a lengthy discussion of the future.

"I think this is entirely too serious a conversation before I've had breakfast."

Scooping up her son from Elliot's arms, she made tracks for the kitchen, unable to deny the truth. Even though she stayed in the condo, she was running from him now every bit as much as she'd run eleven months ago.

Ten

Steering through the narrow streets of Monte Carlo, Elliot drove his new Mercedes S65 AMG along the cliff road leading to the Hughes mansion. His Maserati wouldn't hold a baby seat, so he'd needed a sedan that combined space and safety with his love of finely tuned automobiles. He felt downright domesticated driving Lucy Ann and their son to a lunch with friends. She was meeting with Jayne Hughes and Jayne's baby girl while he went over to the track.

Last time he'd traveled this winding road, he'd been driving Jayne and Conrad to the hospital—Conrad had been too much of a mess to climb behind the wheel of his SUV. Jayne had been in labor. She'd delivered their baby girl seventeen minutes after they'd arrived at the hospital.

How strange to think he knew more about his friend's first kid coming into the world than he knew about the birth of his own son.

His fingers clenched around the steering wheel as they wound up a cliff-side road overlooking the sea. "Tell me about the day Eli was born."

"Are you asking me because you're angry or because you want to know?"

A good question. It wouldn't help to say both probably came into play, so he opted for, "I will always regret that I wasn't there when he came into this world, that I missed out on those first days of his life. But I understand that if we're going to move forward here, I can't let that eat at me. We both are going to have to give a little here. So the answer to your question is, I want to know because I'm curious about all things relating to Eli."

She touched his knee lightly. "Thank you for being honest."

"That's the only way we're going to get through this, don't you think?"

He glanced over at her quickly, taking in the beautiful lines of her face with the sunlight streaming through the window.

Why had it taken him so long to notice?

"Okay..." She inhaled a shaky breath. "I had an appointment the week of my due date. I really expected to go longer since so many first-time moms go overdue. But the doctor was concerned about Eli's heart rate. He did an ultrasound and saw the placenta was separating from the uterine wall— Am I getting too gross for you here?"

"Keep talking," he commanded, hating that he hadn't been there to make things easier, less frightening for her. If he hadn't been so pigheaded, he would have been there to protect her. Assure her.

"The doctor scheduled me for an immediate cesarean section. I didn't even get to go home for my toothbrush," she joked in an attempt to lighten the mood.

He wasn't laughing. "That had to be scary for you. I wish I could have been with you. We helped each other through a lot of tough times over the years."

"I did try to call you," she confessed softly, "right before I went in. But your phone went straight to voice mail. I tried after, too…I assumed you were off on an Interpol secret 'walkabout' for Colonel Salvatore."

"I was." He'd done the math in his head. Knew the case he'd been working at the time.

"I know I could have pushed harder and found you." She shook her head regretfully. "I didn't even leave a message. I'm so sorry for that. You may be able to move past it, but I'm not sure I'll ever forgive myself."

He stayed silent, not sure what to say to make this right for both of them.

"What would we have done if Malcolm and Conrad hadn't kidnapped you from the bachelor party?"

Damn good question. "I like to think I would have come to my senses and checked on you. I don't know how the hell I let eleven months pass."

"Or how you found a fiancée so fast," she blurted out. "You proposed to another woman barely three months after we slept together. Yes, that's a problem for me."

He weighed his words carefully. "This may sound strange, but Gianna was the one who got shortchanged. I obviously didn't care about her the way I should have. I wasn't fair to her."

Her smile was tight. "Excuse me if I'm not overly concerned about being fair to Gianna. And from what I read in the news, she broke things off with you. Not the other way around. If she hadn't left, would you have married her?"

Stunned, he downshifted around a corner. She'd read about his breakup? She'd left, but kept tabs on him. If only he'd done the same with her, he would have known about Eli. As much as Elliot wanted to blame a remote Interpol stint for keeping him out of touch, he knew he should have followed up with Lucy Ann.

Then why hadn't he? She'd been so good to him, always there for him, always forgiving him. Damn it, he didn't deserve her— Could that have been part of why he'd stayed away? Out of guilt for taking so much from her all their lives?

That she could think he still wanted Gianna, especially after what he and Lucy Ann had just shared... Incomprehensible.

"No. I didn't want to marry her. We broke off the engagement. I knew it was inevitable. She just spoke first."

She nodded tightly. "Fine, I appreciate your honesty. I'm still not totally okay with the fact that you raced right back to her after we... Well, I'm just not okay with it. But I'm working on it."

Conrad had told him to grovel. Elliot scrounged inside himself for a way to give her what she needed.

"Fair enough. At least I know where I stand with you." He stared at the road ahead, struggling. Groveling was tougher than he'd expected after the way his father had beaten him to his knees so many times. "That was the hardest part about growing up with my old man. The uncertainty. I'm not saying it would have been okay if he'd punched me on a regular basis. But the sick feeling in my gut as I tried to gauge his moods? That was a crappy way to live."

"I'm so sorry." Her hand fell to rest on his knee again. This time she didn't pull away.

"I know. You saved my sanity back then." He placed his hand over hers. "I always knew it was you who let the air out of my dad's tires that time in sixth grade."

She sat upright. "How did you know?"

"Because you did it while I was away on that science fair trip. So I couldn't be blamed or catch the brunt of his anger." He rubbed her hand along the spot on her finger where he should have put a ring already. "Do I have the details correct?"

"That was the idea. Couldn't have your father get away with everything."

"He didn't. Not in the end." There'd never been a chance to make peace with his bastard of an old man—never a chance to confront him, either.

"I guess there's a sad sort of poetic justice that he died in a bar fight while you were off at reform school."

Her words surprised him. "You're a bloodthirsty one."

"When it comes to protecting the people in my life? Absolutely."

She was freaking amazing. He couldn't deny the rush of admiration for the woman she'd become—that she'd always been, just hidden under the weight of her own problems.

And on the heels of that thought, more guilt piled on top of him for all the ways he'd let her down. Damn it all, he had to figure out how to make this right with her. He had to pull out all the stops as Conrad advised.

Full throttle.

He had to win her over to be his wife.

Lucy Ann sat on the terrace with Jayne Hughes, wondering how a woman who'd been separated for three years could now be such a happily contented wife and new mother. What was her secret? How had they overcome the odds?

There was no denying the peaceful air that radiated off the bombshell blonde with her baby girl cradled in a sling. The Hughes family split their time between their home in Monte Carlo and a home in Africa, where Jayne worked as a nurse at a free clinic her husband funded along with another Alpha Brother. She made it all look effortless whether she was serving up luncheon on fine china or cracking open a boxed lunch under a sprawling shea butter tree.

Lucy Ann patted her colicky son on his precious little back. He seemed to have settled to sleep draped over her knees, which wasn't particularly comfortable, but she wasn't budging an inch as long as he was happy.

Jayne paused in her lengthy ramble about the latest addition to the pediatrics wing at the clinic to tug something from under the plate of petits fours. "Oh, I almost forgot to give you this pamphlet for Elliot."

"For Elliot?" She took it from Jayne, the woman's short nails hinting at her more practical side. "On breast-feeding?"

"He called Conrad with questions the other night." She adjusted her daughter to the other breast in such a smooth transition the cloth baby sling covered all. "I don't know why he didn't just look it up on Google. Anyhow, this should tell him everything he needs to know."

"Thank you." She tucked the pamphlet in her purse, careful not to disturb her son. "He didn't tell me he called your husband for help."

"He was probably too embarrassed. Men can be proud that way." She sipped her ice water, sun glinting off the Waterford crystal that Lucy Ann recalled choosing for a wedding gift to the couple.

There'd been a time when tasks like that—picking out expensive trinkets for Elliot's wealthy friends—had made her nervous. As if the wrong crystal pattern could call her out as an interloper in Elliot Starc's elegant world.

But it had taken walking away from the glitz and glamour to help her see it for what it really was…superficial trappings that didn't mean a lot in the long run. Lucy Ann was far more impressed with Jayne's nursing capabilities and her motherhood savvy than with what kind of place setting graced her table.

"There's a lot to learn about parenting," Lucy Ann acknowledged. "Especially for someone who didn't grow up around other kids." She would have been overwhelmed without Aunt Carla's help.

And wasn't it funny to think that, even though she'd traveled the globe with Elliot for a decade, she'd still learned the most important things back home in South Carolina?

"I think it's wonderful that he's trying. A lot of men would just dump all the tough stuff onto a nanny." Jayne shot a glance over her shoulder through the open balcony doors, somehow knowing Conrad had arrived without even looking.

"I just suggested that it wouldn't hurt to let someone else change the diapers," said Mr. Tall, Dark and Brooding. "Who the hell wants to change a diaper? That doesn't make me a bad human being."

Lucy Ann had to admit, "He has a point."

Jayne set her glass down. "Don't encourage him."

Conrad chuckled as he reached for his daughter. "Lucy Ann, let me know when you're done. I promised Elliot I would drive you and the kidlet back to the condo. He said he's running late at the track. Have fun, ladies. The princess and I are going to read the *Wall Street Journal*."

Conrad disappeared back into the house with his daughter, words about stocks and short sales carrying on the wind spoken in a singsong tone as if telling her a nursery rhyme.

Lucy Ann leaned back in the chair and turned her water glass on the table, watching the sunlight refracting prisms off the cut crystal. "I envy your tight-knit support group. Elliot and I didn't have a lot of friends when we were growing up. He was the kid always in trouble so parents didn't invite him over. And I was too shy to make friends."

"You're not shy anymore," Jayne pointed out.

"Not that I let people see."

"We've known you for years. I would hope you could consider us your friends, too."

They'd known each other, but she'd been Elliot's employee. It wasn't that his friends had deliberately excluded her, but Conrad had been separated for years, and only recently had the rest of them started marrying. She knew it would be easier for all of them if she made the effort here.

"We'll certainly cross paths because of Eli," Lucy Ann said simply.

"And Elliot?"

The conversation was starting to get too personal for her comfort. "We're still working on that."

"But you're making progress."

"Have you been reading the tabloids?"

"I don't bother with those." Jayne waved dismissively. "I saw the way you two looked at each other when Elliot dropped you off."

In spite of herself, Lucy Ann found herself aching to talk to someone after all, and Jayne seemed the best candidate. "He's into the thrill of the chase right now. Things will go back to normal eventually."

"I'm not so sure I agree. He seems different to me." Jayne's pensive look faded into a grin. "They all have to grow up and settle down sometime."

"What about—" She didn't feel comfortable discussing the guys' Interpol work out in the open, so she simply said, "Working with the colonel after graduation and following a call to right bigger wrongs? How do they give that up to be regular family guys?"

"Good question." Jayne pinched the silver tongs to shuffle a petit four and fruit onto a dessert plate. "Some still take an active part once they're married, but once the children start coming, things do change. They shift to pulling the strings. They become more like Salvatore."

"Mine is a bit wilder than yours." When had she started thinking of Elliot as *hers*? Although on some level he'd been hers since they were children. "I mean, seriously, he crashes cars into walls for a living."

"You've known that about him from the start. So why are things different now?"

"I don't know how to reconcile our friendship with everything else that's happened." The whole "friends with benefits" thing was easier said than done.

"By 'everything else' you mean the smoking hot sex, of course." Jayne grinned impishly before popping a grape in her mouth.

"I had forgotten how outspoken you can be."

"Comes with the territory of loving men like these. They don't always perceive subtleties."

True enough. Lucy Ann speared a chocolate strawberry and willed herself not to blush at the heated memories the fruit evoked. "Outspoken or not, I'm still no closer to an answer."

Jayne nudged the gold-rimmed china plate aside and leaned her arms on the table. "You don't have to reconcile the two ways of being. It's already done—or it will be once you stop fighting."

Could Jayne be right? Maybe the time had come to

truly give him a chance. To see if he was right. To see if they could really have a fairy-tale life together.

Fear knotted her gut, but Lucy Ann wasn't the shy little girl anymore. She was a confident woman and she was all-in.

Elliot shrugged out of his black leather jacket with a wince as he stepped into the dark apartment. He'd done his prelim runs as always, checklists complete, car scrutinized to the last detail, and yet somehow he'd damn near wiped out on a practice run.

Every muscle in his body ached from reactionary tensing. Thank goodness Lucy Ann hadn't been there as she would have been in the past as his assistant. He didn't want her worrying. He didn't want to risk a confrontation.

He tossed the jacket over his arm, walking carefully so he wouldn't wake anyone up. His foot hooked on something in the dark. He bit back a curse and looked down to find…a book? He reached to pick up an ornately bound copy of *Hansel and Gretel*. He started to stand up again and looked ahead to find a trail of books, all leading toward his bedroom. He picked up one book after the other, each a different fairy tale, until he pushed open his door.

His room was empty.

Frowning, he scanned the space and… "Aha…"

More books led to the bathroom, and now that he listened, he could hear the shower running. He set the stack on the chest of drawers and gathered up the last few "crumbs" on his trail, a copy of *Rapunzel* and a Victorian version of *Rumpelstiltskin*. Pushing his way slowly into the bathroom, he smiled at the shadowy outline behind the foggy glass wall. The multiple showerheads shot spray over Lucy Ann as she hummed. She didn't seem to notice he'd arrived.

He peeled off his clothes without making a sound and padded barefoot into the slate-tiled space. He opened the door and stepped into the steam. Lucy Ann stopped singing, but she didn't turn around. The only acknowledgment she gave to his arrival was a hand reaching for him. He linked fingers with her and stepped under the warm jets. The heat melted away the stress from his muscles, allowing a new tension to take hold. He saw the condom packet in the soap dish and realized just how thoroughly she'd thought this through.

He pressed against her back, wrapping his arms around her. Already, his erection throbbed hard and ready, pressed between them.

He sipped water from just behind her ear. "I'm trying to think of what fairy tale you're fantasizing about, and for water, I can only come up with the *Frog Prince*."

Angling her head to give him better access to her neck, she combed her fingers over his damp hair. "We're writing our own fantasy tonight."

Growling his approval, he slicked his hands over her, taking in the feel of her breasts peaking against his palms. His blood fired hotter through his veins than the water sluicing over them. He slipped a hand between her thighs, stroking satin, finding that sweet bundle of nerves. Banding his arm tighter around her waist, he continued to circle and tease, feeling her arousal lubricate his touch. She sagged back against him, her legs parting to give him easier access.

With her bottom nestled against him, he held on to control by a thread. Each roll of her hips as she milked the most from her pleasure threatened to send him over the edge. But he held back his own release, giving her hers. He tucked two fingers inside her, his thumb still working along that pebbled tightness.

Her sighs and purrs filled the cubicle, the jasmine scent of her riding the steam. Every sound of her impending arousal shot a bolt of pleasure through him, his blood pounding thicker through his veins. Until, yes, she cried out, coming apart in his arms. Her fingernails dug deep into his thighs, cutting half-moons into his flesh as she arched into her orgasm.

He savored every shiver of bliss rippling her body until he couldn't wait any longer. He took the condom from the soap tray and sheathed himself. He pressed her against the shower stall wall, her palms flattened to the stone. Standing behind her, he nudged her legs apart and angled until... He slid home, deep inside her, clamped by damp silken walls as hot and moist as the shower.

Sensation engulfed him, threatened to shake the ground under him as he pushed inside her again and again. Things moved so damn fast... He was so close... Then he heard the sound of her unraveling in his arms. The echoes of her release sent him over the edge. Ecstasy rocked his balance. He flattened a hand against the warm wall to keep from falling over as his completion pulsed until his heartbeat pounded in his ears. Shifting, he pulled out of her, keeping one arm around her.

Slowly, his world expanded beyond just the two of them, and he became aware of the water sheeting over them. The patter of droplets hitting the door and floor.

Tucking her close again, he thought about his near miss at the track today and all the relationship advice from his friends. He'd waited too long these past eleven months to make sure she stayed with him. Permanently. He wouldn't let another minute pass without moving forward with their lives.

He nuzzled her ear. "What kind of house do you want?"

"House?" she asked, her knees buckling.

He steadied her. "I want to build a real house for us, Lucy Ann. Not just condos or rented places here and there."

"Umm..." She licked her lips. The beads on her temple mingled perspiration with water. "What city would you choose?"

He had penthouse suites around the world, but nowhere he stayed long enough to call home. And none of them had the room for a boy to run and play.

"I need a home. We need a home for our son."

"You keep assuming we'll stay together."

Already his proposal was going astray. Could be because most of the blood in his brain was surging south. "Where do you want to live? I'll build two houses next door if that's the way you want it." Living near each other would give him more time to win her over, because he was fast realizing he couldn't give her up. "I have connections with a friend who restores historic homes."

She turned in his arms, pressing her fingers to his lips. "Can we just keep making love instead?"

Banding her wrist in his hand, he kissed it, determined not to let this chance slip away, not to let *her* slip away again. "Let's get married."

She leaned into him, whispering against his mouth as she stroked down between them, molding her palm to the shape of him. "You may have missed the memo..." She caressed up and down, again and again. "But you don't have to propose to get me to sleep with you."

He angled away, staring straight in her eyes, her eyelashes spiky wet. "I'm not joking, so I would appreciate it if you took my proposal seriously."

"Really? Now?" She stepped back, the water showering between them. "You mean this. For Eli, of course."

"Of course Eli factors into the equation." He studied her carefully blank expression. "But it's also because you and I fit as a couple on so many levels. We've been friends forever, and our chemistry... Well, that speaks for itself. We just have to figure out how not to fight afterward and we'll have forever locked and loaded."

The more he talked, the more it felt right.

"Forever?" Her knees folded, and she sat on the stone seat in the corner, her hair dripping water. "Do you think that's even possible for people like you and me?"

"Why shouldn't it be?" He knelt in front of her.

"Because of our pasts." She stroked over his wet hair, cupping his neck, her eyes so bittersweet they tore him to bits. "Our parents. Our own histories. I refuse to spend the rest of my life wondering when the next Gianna is going to walk through the door."

Gianna? He hadn't even thought of her other than when Lucy Ann mentioned her. But looking back, he realized how bad his engagement would have looked to her, how that must have played a role in her keeping quiet about the pregnancy.

This was likely where the groveling came in. "I'm sorry."

"For which part? The engagement? Or the fact you didn't contact me— Hell, forget I said that." She leaned forward to kiss him.

If they kissed, the discussion would be over, opportunity missed. He scooped her up in his arms and pivoted, settling her into his lap as he sat on the stone seat in the corner.

She squawked in protest but he pressed on. "You expected me to follow you? Even after you said—and I quote—'I don't ever want to lay eyes on your irresponsible ass ever again'?"

"And you've never said anything in the heat of the moment that you regretted later?"

Groveling was all well and good, but he wasn't taking the full blame for what shook down these past months. "If you regretted those words, it sure would have been helpful if you'd let me know."

"This is my whole point. We're both so proud, neither one of us could take the steps needed to repair the damage we did. Yes, I am admitting that we both were hurt. Even though you seemed to recover fast with Gianna—" she gave him that tight smile again "—I acknowledge that losing our friendship hurt you, as well. But friendship isn't enough to build a marriage on. So can we please go back to the friends-with-benefits arrangement?"

"Damn it, Lucy Ann—"

She traced his face with her fingers. "Do you know what I think?" She didn't wait for him to answer. "I think you don't believe in fairy tales after all. The dates, the romance... It has actually been a game for you after all. A challenge, a competition. Something to win. Not Cinderella or Sleeping Beauty."

"I suspect I've been led into a trap." He'd thought he'd been following all the right signs and taking the steps to fix this, but he'd only seemed to dig a bigger hole for himself.

"Well, you followed my bread crumbs." Her joke fell flat between them, her eyes so much sadder than he'd ever dreamed he could make them.

"So you're sure you don't want to marry me?"

She hesitated, her pulse leaping in her neck. "I'm sure I don't want you to propose to me."

Her rejection stunned him. Somehow he'd expected her to say yes. He'd thought... Hell, he'd taken her for granted all over again and he didn't know how to fix this. Not now. He needed time to regroup. "If I agree to stop pressing for marriage, can we keep having incredible sex with each other?"

"'Til the end of the month."

"Sex for a few weeks? You're okay with sleeping together with an exit strategy already in place?"

"That's my offer." She slid from his lap, stepping back. Away. Putting distance between them on more than just one level. "Take it or leave it."

"Lucy Ann, I'm happy as hell to take you again and again until we're both too exhausted to argue." Although right now, he couldn't deny it. He wanted more from her. "But eventually we're going to have to talk."

Eleven

Lucy sprawled on top of Elliot in bed, satiated, groggy and almost dry from their shower, but not ready for their evening together to end. Elliot seemed content to let the proposal discussion go—for tonight. So this could well be the last uncomplicated chance she had to be with him.

The ceiling fan *click, click, clicked* away their precious remaining seconds together, the lights of Monaco glittering through the open French doors, the Cote d'Azur providing a breathtaking vista. Who wouldn't want to share this life with him? Why couldn't she just accept his proposal? She hated how his offer of marriage made her clench her gut in fear. She should be happy. Celebrating. This would be the easy answer to bringing up Eli together. They were best friends. Incredible lovers. Why not go with the flow? They could take a day to see Cannes with the baby, and she could snap pictures...savor the things she'd been too busy to notice in the early years of traveling with Elliot.

Yet something held her back. She couldn't push the word *yes* free. Every time she tried, her throat closed up. She trusted him…yet the thought of reliving the past eleven months again, of living without him…

Her fingers glided along his closely shorn hair. "You could have been killed that day your hair got singed."

"You're not going to get rid of me that easily," he said with a low chuckle and a stroke down her spine.

Ice chilled the blood in her veins at his words. "That wasn't funny."

"I'm just trying to lighten the mood." He angled back to kiss the tip of her nose, then look into her eyes. "I'm okay, Lucy Ann. Not a scratch on me that day."

She'd been in South Carolina when it had happened, her belly swelling with his child and her heart heavy with the decision of when to tell him about the baby. "That doesn't make it any less terrifying."

He grinned smugly. "You do care."

"Of course I care what happens to you. I always have. There's no denying our history, our friendship, how well we know each other." How could he doubt that, no matter what else they'd been through? "But I know something else. You're only interested in me now because I'm telling you no. You don't like being the one left behind."

Breathlessly, she finished her rant, stunned at herself. Her mouth had been ahead of her brain. She hadn't even realized she felt that way until the words came rolling out.

"That's not a very nice thing to say," he said tightly.

"But is it true?" She cupped his face.

He pulled her hands down gently and kissed both palms. "I already offered to stop racing. I meant it. I'm

a father now and I understand that comes with responsibilities."

Responsibilities? Is that what they were to him? But
then, in a way, that's what she'd always been since he
got out of reform school, since he'd offered her a job
as his assistant even though at the time she hadn't been
qualified for the job. He'd given it to her out of friendship—and, yes, the sense of obligation they felt to look
out for each other.

That had been enough for a long time, more than either
of them had gotten from anyone else in their lives. But
right now with her heart in her throat, obligation didn't
feel like nearly enough to build a life on.

She slid off him, the cooling breeze from the fan chill-
ing her bared flesh. "Do whatever you want."

"What did I say wrong? You want me to quit and I
offer and now you're angry?"

"I didn't say I want you to quit." She opted for the simpler answer. "I understand how important your career is
to you. You have a competitive nature and that's not a
bad thing. It's made you an incredibly successful man."

"You mentioned my competitiveness earlier. Lucy
Ann, that's not why I—"

She rolled to her side and pressed her fingers to his
mouth before he could get back to the proposal subject
again. "You've channeled your edginess and your drive
to win. That's not a bad thing." She tapped his bottom
lip. "Enough talk. You should rest up now so you're focused for the race."

And so she could escape to her room, away from the
building temptation to take what he offered and worry
about the consequences later. Except with Elliot's muscled arm draped over her waist, she couldn't quite bring
herself to move out of his embrace. His hand moved along

her back soothingly. Slowly, her body began to relax, melting into the fantastic mattress.

"Lucy Ann? You're right, you know." Elliot's words were so low she almost didn't hear him.

"Right about what?" she asked, groggy, almost asleep.

"I like to win— Wait. Scratch that. I *need* to win."

Opening her eyes, she didn't move, just stared at his chest and listened. There was no escaping this conversation. Wherever it led them.

"There are two kinds of people in the world. Ones who have known physical pain and those who never will. Being beaten…" He swallowed hard, his heart hammering so loudly she could feel her pulse sync up with his, racing, knowing just what that word *beating* meant to him growing up. "That does something to your soul. Changes you. You can heal. You can move on. But you're forever changed by that moment you finally break, crying for it to stop."

His voice stayed emotionless, but what he said sliced through her all the more because of the steely control he forced on himself.

Her hand fluttered to rest on his heart as she pressed a kiss to his shoulder. "Oh, God, Elliot—"

"Don't speak. Not yet." He linked his fingers with hers. "The thing is, we all like to think we're strong enough to hold out when that person brings on the belt, the shoe, the branch, or hell, even a hand used as a weapon. And there's a rush in holding out at first, deluding yourself into believing you can actually win."

She willed herself to stay completely still, barely breathing, while he poured out the truth she'd always known. She'd even seen the marks he'd refused to acknowledge. Hearing him talk about it, though, shredded her heart, every revelation making her ache for what he'd suffered growing up. She also knew he wouldn't accept her sympathy now any more than he had then. So she gave him the only thing she could—total silence while he spoke.

"The person with the weapon is after one thing," he shared, referring to his father in such a vague sense as if that gave him distance, protection. "It isn't actually about the pain. It's about submission."

She couldn't hold back the flinch or a whimper of sympathy.

Elliot tipped her chin until she looked at him. "But you see, it's okay now. When I'm out there racing, it's my chance to win. No one, not one damn soul, will ever beat me again."

She held her breath, wrestling with what to do next, how they could go forward. This wasn't the time to pledge futures, but it also wasn't the time to walk away. Growing up, she'd always known how to be there for him. At this moment, she didn't have a clue.

The squawk of their son over the nursery monitor jolted them both. And she wasn't sure who was more relieved.

Her or Elliot.

Elliot barely tasted the gourmet brunch catered privately at a crowded café near the race day venue. With two hundred thousand people pouring into the small principality for the circuit's most famous event, there were fans and media everywhere. At least his friends and mentor seemed to be enjoying themselves. He wanted to chalk up his lack of enthusiasm to sleep deprivation.

Race day in Monaco had always been one of Elliot's favorites, from the way the sun glinted just right off the streets to the energy of the crowds. The circuit was considered one of the most challenging Formula One routes—narrow roads, tight turns and changing elevations made it all the more exciting, edgy, demanding.

And just that fast, Lucy Ann's words haunted him, how she'd accused him of searching out challenges. How she'd accused him of seeing her as a challenge. Damn it all, he just wanted them to build a future together.

What would she be thinking, sitting in the stands today with his school friends and their wives?

He glanced at her across the table, strain showing in the creases along her forehead and the dark smudges under her eyes. He wanted to take Eli from her arms so she could rest, but wasn't sure if she would object. He didn't want to cause a scene or upset her more.

With a mumbled excuse, he scraped back his chair and left the table. He needed air. Space.

He angled his way out of the room—damn, he had too many curious friends these days—and into the deserted patio garden in the back. All the patrons had flocked out front to the street side to watch the crowds already claiming their places to watch the race. But back here, olive trees and rosebushes packed the small space so densely he almost didn't see his old high school headmaster— now an Interpol handler—sitting on a bench sending text messages.

Colonel Salvatore sat beside his preteen son, who was every bit as fixated on his Game Boy as his father was on his phone. A couple of empty plates rested between them.

How had he missed them leaving the table? Damn, his mind wasn't where it was supposed to be.

Colonel Salvatore stood, mumbled something to his son, then walked toward Elliot without once looking up from his phone. The guy always had been the master of multitasking. Very little slipped by him. Ever.

The older man finally tucked away his cell phone and nodded. "We couldn't sit still," he said diplomatically, "so we're out here playing 'Angry Monkeys' or something like that."

"I'm sure you both enjoyed the food more here where it's quieter," he said diplomatically. "I could sure use parenting advice if you've got some to offer up."

Salvatore straightened his standard red tie. He wore the same color gray suit as always, like a retirement uniform. "Why don't you ask the guys inside?"

"They only have babies. They're new parents." Like him. Treading water as fast as he could and still choking. "You have an older boy."

"A son I rarely see due to my work schedule." He winced. "So again I say, I'm not the one to help."

"Then your first piece of advice would be for me to spend time with him."

"I guess it would." He glanced over at his son, whose thumbs were flying over the buttons. "Gifts don't make up for absence. Although don't underestimate the power of a well-chosen video game."

"Thank God we have the inside scoop with Troy's latest inventions." Maybe that's who he needed to be talking to. Maybe Troy could invent a baby app. Elliot shoved a hand over his hair, realizing how ridiculous the thought sounded. He must be sleep-deprived. "I'm a little short on role models in the father department—other than you."

Salvatore's eyebrows went up at the unexpected compliment. "Um, uh, thank you," he stuttered uncharacteristically.

"Advice then?"

"Don't screw up."

"That's it?" Elliot barked. "Don't screw up?"

"Fine, I'll spell it out for you." Salvatore smiled as if

he'd been toying with him all along. Then the grin faded. "You've had to steal everything you've ever wanted in life. From food to cars to friends—to your freedom."

"I'm past that."

"Are you?" The savvy Interpol handler leaned against the centuries-old brick wall, an ivy trellis beside him. "It's difficult for me to see beyond the boy you were when you arrived at my school as a teenager hell-bent on self-destructing."

"Self-destructing?" he said defensively. "I'm not sure I follow." He was all about winning.

"You stole that car on purpose to escape your father, and you feel guilty as hell for leaving Lucy Ann behind," Salvatore said so damn perceptively he might as well have been listening in on Elliot's recent conversations. "You expected to go to jail as punishment and since that didn't happen, you've been trying to prove to the world just how bad you are. You pushed Lucy Ann away by getting engaged to Gianna."

"When did you find time to get your psychology degree between being a headmaster and an Interpol handler?"

"There you go again, trying to prove what a smart-ass you are."

Damn it. Didn't it suck to realize how well he played to type? He took a steadying breath and focused.

"I'm trying to do the right thing by Lucy Ann now. I want to live up to my obligations."

"The right thing." The colonel scratched a hand over gray hair buzzed as short of Elliot's. "What is that?"

"Provide for our son... Marry her... Damn it, colonel, clearly you think I'm tanking here. Is it fun watching me flounder?"

"If I tell you what to do, you won't learn a thing. A

mentor guides, steers. Think of it as a race," he said with a nod—which Elliot knew from years in the man's office meant this conversation was over. Colonel Salvatore fished out his phone and headed back to sit silently beside his son.

Elliot pinched the bridge of his nose and pivoted toward the iron gate that led to the back street. He needed to get his head on straight before the race. Hell, he needed to get his head back on straight, period. Because right now, he could have sworn he must be hallucinating.

Beyond the iron gate, he saw a curly-haired brunette who looked startlingly like his former fiancée. He narrowed his eyes, looking closer, shock knocking him back a step as Gianna crossed the street on the arm of a Brazilian Formula One champion.

Lucy Ann usually found race day exciting, but she couldn't shake the feeling of impending doom. The sense that she and Elliot weren't going to figure out how to make things work between them before the end of their time together. Thank goodness Mrs. Clayworth had taken the baby back to the condo to nap, because Lucy Ann was beyond distracted.

Sitting in the private viewing box with Elliot's friends and the relatives of other drivers, she tried to stifle her fears, to reassure herself that she and Elliot could find a way to parent together—possibly even learn to form a relationship as a couple. That she could figure out how to heal the wounds from his past, which still haunted everything he did.

The buzz of conversation increased behind her, a frenzy of whispers and mumbles in multiple languages. She turned away from the viewing window and monitors broadcasting prerace hubbub, newscasters speaking in French, English, Spanish and a couple of languages she didn't recognize. She looked past the catering staff carrying glasses of champagne to the entrance. A gasp caught in her throat.

Gianna? Here?

The other woman worked her way down the steps, her dark curls bouncing. Shock, followed by a burst of anger, rippled through Lucy Ann as she watched Gianna stride confidently closer. Her white dress clung to her teeny-tiny body. Clearly those hips had never given birth. And Lucy Ann was long past her days of wearing anything white thanks to baby spit-up. Not that she would trade her son for a size-zero figure and a closet full of white clothes.

Above all, she did not want a scene in front of the media. Gianna's eyes were locked on her, her path determined. If the woman thought she could intimidate, she was sorely mistaken.

Lucy Ann shot to her feet and marched up the stairs, her low heels clicking. She threw her arms wide and said loud enough for all to hear, "Gianna, so glad you could make it."

Stunned, the woman almost tripped over her own stilettos. "Um, I—"

Lucy Ann hugged her hard and whispered in her ear, "We're going to have a quick little private chat and, above all, we will not cause a scene before the race."

She knew how fast gossip spread and she didn't intend to let any negative energy ripple through the crowd. And she definitely didn't intend for anyone to see her lose her calm. She hauled the other woman down the hall and into a ladies' room, locking the door behind them.

Once she was sure no one else was in the small sitting area or in the stalls, she confronted Elliot's former fiancée. "Why are you here?"

Gianna shook her curls. "I'm here with a retired Brazilian racer. I was simply coming by to say hello."

"I'm not buying that." Lucy Ann stared back at the other woman and found she wasn't jealous so much as angry that someone was trying mess with her happiness—hers, Elliot's and Eli's.

The fake smile finally faded from Gianna's face. "I came back because now it's a fair fight."

At least the woman wasn't denying it. "I'm not sure I follow your logic."

"Before, when I found out about you and the baby—"

Lucy gasped. "You knew?"

"I found out by accident. I got nosy about you, looked into your life…" She shrugged. "I was devastated, but I broke off the engagement."

"Whoa, hold on." Lucy Ann held up a hand. "I don't understand. Elliot said you broke up because of his Interpol work. That you couldn't handle the danger."

She rolled her dramatic Italian eyes. "Men are so very easy to deceive. I broke the engagement because I couldn't be the one to tell him about your pregnancy. I couldn't be 'that' woman. The one who broke up true love. The evil one in the triangle. But I also couldn't marry him knowing he might still want you or his child."

"So you left." Lucy Ann's legs gave way and she sagged back against the steel door.

"I loved him enough to leave and let him figure this out on his own."

If she'd really loved him, Gianna would have told him about his child, but then Lucy Ann figured who was she to throw stones on that issue? "Do you still love Elliot?"

"Yes, I do."

She searched the woman's eyes and saw…genuine heartache. "You're not at all what I expected."

Gianna's pouty smile faltered. "And you're everything I feared."

So where did they go from here? That question hammered through Lucy Ann's mind so loudly it took her a moment to realize the noise was real. Feet drummed overhead with the sound of people running. People screaming?

She looked quickly at Gianna, whose eyes were already widening in confusion, as well. Lucy Ann turned on her heels, unlocked the door and found mass confusion. Spectators and security running. Reporters rushing with their cameras at the ready, shouting questions and directions in different languages.

Lucy Ann grabbed the arm of a passing guard. "What's going on?"

"Ma'am, there's been an accident in the lineup. Please return to your seat and let us do our jobs," the guard said hurriedly and pulled away, melting into the crowd.

"An accident?" Her stomach lurched with fear.

There were other drivers. Many other drivers. And an accident while lining up would be slow? Right? Unless someone was doing a preliminary warm-up lap.... So many horrifying scenarios played through her mind, all of them involving Elliot. She shoved into the crush, searching for a path through to her viewing area or to the nearest telecast screen. Finally, she spotted a wide-screen TV mounted in a corner, broadcasting images of flames.

The words scrolling across the bottom blared what she already knew deep in her terrified heart.

Elliot had crashed.

Twelve

Her heart in her throat, Lucy Ann pushed past Gianna
and shouldered through the bustling crush of panicked
observers. She reached into her tailored jacket and pulled
out her pass giving her unlimited access. She couldn't
just sit in the private viewing area and wait for someone
to call her. What if Elliot needed her? She refused to accept the possibility that he could be dead. Even the word
made her throat close up tight.

Her low pumps clicked on the stairs as she raced
through various checkpoints, flashing the access pass
every step of the way.

Finally, thank God, finally, she ran out onto the street
level where security guards created an impenetrable wall.
The wind whipped her yellow sundress around her legs as
she sprinted. Her pulse pounding in her ears, she searched
the lanes of race cars, looking for flames. But she found
no signs of a major explosion.

A siren's wail sliced through her. An ambulance navigated past a throng of race personnel spraying down the street with fire extinguishers. The vehicle moved toward two race cars, one on its side, the other sideways as if it had spun out into a skid. As much as she wanted to deny what her eyes saw, the car on its side belonged to Elliot.

Emergency workers crawled all over the vehicle, prying open the door. Blinking back burning tears, Lucy Ann strained against an arm holding her back, desperate to see. Her shouts were swallowed up in the roar of activity until she couldn't even hear her own incoherent pleas.

The door flew open, and her breath lodged somewhere in her throat. She couldn't breathe, gasp or shout. Just wait.

Rescue workers reached inside, then hauled Elliot out.

Alive.

She sagged against the person behind her. She glanced back to find Elliot's Interpol handler, Colonel Salvatore, at her side. He braced her reassuringly, his eyes locked on the battered race car. Elliot was moving, slowly but steadily. The rescue workers tried to keep his arms over their shoulders so they could walk him to a waiting ambulance. But he shook his head, easing them aside and standing on his own two feet. He pulled off his helmet and waved to the crowd, signaling that all was okay.

The crowd roared, a round of applause thundering, the reverberations shuddering through her along with her relief. His gaze homed in on her. Lucy Ann felt the impact all the way to her toes. Elliot was alive. Again and again, the thought echoed through her mind in a continual loop of reassurance, because heaven help her, she loved him. Truly loved him. That knowledge rolled through her, settled into her, in a fit that told her what she'd known all along.

They'd always loved each other.

At this moment, she didn't doubt that he loved her back. No matter what problems, disagreements or betrayals they might have weathered, the bond was there. She wished she could rejoice in that, but the fear was still rooted deep inside her, the inescapable sense of foreboding.

Elliot pushed past the emergency personnel and... heaven only knew who else because she couldn't bring herself to look at anyone except Elliot walking toward her, the scent of smoke tingling in her nose as the sea breeze blew in. The sun shone down on the man she loved, bright Mediterranean rays glinting off the silver trim on his racing gear with each bold step closer.

She vaguely registered the colonel flashing some kind of badge that had the security cop stepping aside and letting her stumble past. She regained her footing and sprinted toward Elliot.

"Thank God you're okay." Slamming into his chest, she wrapped her arms around him.

He kissed her once, firmly, reassuringly, then walked her away from the sidelines, the crowd parting, or maybe someone made the path for them. She couldn't think of anything but the man beside her, the warmth of him, the sound of his heartbeat, the scent of his aftershave and perspiration.

Tears of relief streaming down her face, she didn't bother asking where they were going. She trusted him, the father of her child, and honestly didn't care where they went as long as she could keep her hands on him, her cheek pressed to his chest, the fire-retardant material of his uniform bristly against her skin. He pushed through a door into a private office. She didn't care whose or how he'd chosen the stark space filled with only a wooden desk, a black leather sofa and framed racing photos.

Briskly, he closed and locked the door. "Lucy Ann, deep breaths or you're going to pass out. I'm okay." His voice soothed over her in waves. "It was just a minor accident. The other guy's axle broke and he slammed into me. Everyone's fine."

She swiped her wrists over her damp eyes, undoubtedly smearing mascara all over her face. "When there's smoke—possibly fire—involved, I wouldn't call that minor."

Elliot cradled her face in his gloved hands. "My hair didn't even get singed."

"I'm not in a joking mood." She sketched jerky hands over him, needing to touch him.

"Then help me out." He stalled one of her hands and kissed her palm. "What can I say to reassure you?"

"Nothing," she decided. "There's nothing to say right now."

It was a time for action.

She tugged her hand free and looped her arms around his neck again and drew his face down to hers. She kissed him. More than a kiss. A declaration and affirmation that he was alive. She needed to connect with him, even if only on a physical level.

"Lucy Ann," he muttered against her mouth, "are you sure you know what you're doing?"

"Are you planning to go back to the race?" she asked, gripping his shoulders.

"My car's in no shape to race. You know that. But are you cert—"

She kissed him quiet. She was so tired of doubts and questions and reservations. Most of all, she couldn't bear for this to be about the past anymore. To feel more pain for him. For herself. For how damn awful their childhoods had been—his even worse than hers.

Hell, she'd lived through those years with him, doing her best to protect him by taking the brunt of the blame when she could. But when the adults wouldn't step up and make things right, there was only so much a kid could do.

They weren't children any longer, but she still couldn't stand to think of him getting hurt in any way. She would do anything to keep danger away, to make them both forget everything.

At this moment, that "anything" involved mind-blowing sex against the door. Fast and intense. No fun games or pretty fairy tales. This was reality.

She tugged at his zipper, and he didn't protest this time. He simply drew back long enough to tug his racing gloves off with his teeth. With her spine pressed to the door, he bunched up her silky dress until a cool breeze blew across her legs. A second later, he twisted and snapped her panties free, the scrap of lace giving way to him as fully as she did.

But she took as much as she gave. She nudged the zipper wider, nudging his uniform aside until she released his erection, steely and hot in her hand. Then, he was inside her.

Her head thunked against the metal panel, her eyes sliding closed as she lost herself in sensation. She glided a foot along his calf, up farther until her leg hitched around him, drawing him deeper, deeper in a frenzied meeting of their bodies.

All too soon, the pleasure built to a crescendo, a wave swelling on the tide of emotions, fear and adrenaline. And yes, love. She buried her face in his shoulder, trying to hold back the shout rolling up her throat. His hoarse encouragement in her ear sent pleasure crashing over her. Feeling him tense in her arms, shudder with his own completion, sent a fresh tingle of aftershocks through her. Her body clamped around him in an instinctive need to keep him with her.

With each panting breath, she drew in the scent of them. His forehead fell to rest against the door, her fingers playing with the close-shorn hair at the base of his neck. Slowly, her senses allowed in the rest of the world, the dim echo outside reminding her they couldn't hide in here forever.

They couldn't hide from the truth any longer.

Even as she took him now, felt the familiar draw of this man she'd known for as long as she could remember, she also realized she didn't belong here in this world now. She couldn't keep him because she couldn't stay.

No matter how intrinsic the connection and attraction between them, this wasn't the life she'd dreamed of when they'd built those fairy-tale forts and castles. In her fantasies, they'd all just looked like a real home. A safe haven.

She loved him. She always had. But she'd spent most of her adult life following him. It was time to take charge of her life, for herself and for her son.

It was time to go home.

As Elliot angled back and started to smile at her, she captured his face in her hands and shook her head.

"Elliot, I can't do this anymore, trying to build a life on fairy tales. I need something more, a real life, and maybe that sounds boring to you, but I know who I am now. I know the life I want to live and it isn't here."

His eyes searched hers, confused and a little angry. "Lucy Ann—"

She pressed her fingers to his mouth. "I don't want

to argue with you. Not like last time. We can't do that to each other again—or to Eli."

He clasped her hand, a pulse throbbing double time in his neck. "Are you sure there's nothing I can do to change your mind?"

God, she wanted to believe he could, but right now with the scent of smoke clinging to his clothes and the adrenaline still crackling in the air, she couldn't see any other way. "No, Elliot. I'm afraid not."

Slowly, he released her hand. His face went somber, resigned. He understood her in that same perfect and tragic way she understood him. He already knew.

They'd just said goodbye.

The next day, Elliot didn't know how he was going to say goodbye. But the time had come. He sat on Aunt Carla's front porch swing while Lucy Ann fed Eli and put him down for a nap.

God, why couldn't he and Lucy Ann have had some massive argument that made it easier to walk away, like before?

Instead, there had been this quiet, painful realization that she was leaving him. No matter how many fairy-tale endings he tried to create for her, she'd seen through them all. After their crazy, out-of-control encounter against the door, they'd returned to the hotel. She'd packed. He'd arranged for his private jet to fly them home to South Carolina.

Lucy Ann had made a token offer to travel on her own, not to disrupt his schedule—not to distract him. The implication had been there. The accident had happened because his life was fracturing. He couldn't deny it.

But he'd damn well insisted on bringing them back here himself.

The front door creaked open, and he looked up sharply. Lucy Ann's aunt walked through. He sagged back in his swing, relieved to have the inevitable farewell delayed for a few more minutes. He knew Lucy Ann would let him be a part of his son's world, but this was not how he wanted their lives to play out.

Carla settled next to him on the swing, her T-shirt appliquéd with little spring chickens. "Glad to know you survived in one piece."

"It was a minor accident," he insisted again, the wind rustling the oak trees in time with the groan of the chains holding the swing. The scent of Carolina jasmine reminded him of Lucy Ann.

"I meant that kidnapping stunt your friends staged. Turning your whole life upside down."

Right now, it didn't feel like he'd walked away unscathed. The weight on his chest pressed heavier with every second, hadn't let up since he'd been pulled from his damaged car. "I'll provide for Lucy Ann and Eli."

"That was never in question." She patted his knee. "I'm glad you got out of here all those years ago."

"I thought you wanted Lucy Ann to stay? That's always been my impression over the years."

"I do believe she belongs here. But we're not talking about her." She folded her arms over the row of cheerful chickens. "I'm talking about what you needed as a teenager. You had to leave first before you could find any peace here. Although, perhaps it was important for Lucy Ann to leave for a while, as well."

There was something in her voice—a kindred spirit? An understanding? Her life hadn't been easy either, and he found himself saying, "You didn't go."

"I couldn't. Not when Lucy Ann needed me. She was my one shot at motherhood since I couldn't have kids of my own." She shrugged. "Once she left with you, I'd already settled in. I'm on my own now."

"I just assumed you didn't want kids." He was realizing how little time he'd spent talking to this woman who'd given him safe harbor, the woman who'd been there for Lucy Ann and Eli. He didn't have much in the way of positive experience with blood relatives, but it was undoubtedly time to figure that out.

"I would have adopted," Carla confided, "but my husband had a record. Some youthful indiscretions with breaking and entering. Years later it didn't seem like it should have mattered to the adoption agencies that he'd broken into the country club to dump a bunch of Tootsie Rolls in the pool."

Elliot grinned nostalgically. "Sounds like he would have made a great addition to the Alpha Brotherhood."

And might Elliot have found a mentor with Lucy Ann's uncle as well if he'd taken the time to try?

"I wish Lucy Ann could have had those kinds of friendships for herself. She was lost after you left," Carla said pointedly. "She didn't find her confidence until later."

What was she talking about? "Lucy Ann is the strongest, most confident person I've ever met. I wouldn't have made it without her."

He looked into those woods and thought about the dream world she'd given him as a kid, more effective an escape than even his favorite book.

"You protected her, but always saw her strengths. That's a wonderful thing." Carla pinned him with unrelenting brown eyes much like her stubborn niece's. "But you also never saw her vulnerabilities or insecurities. She's not perfect, Elliot. You need to stop expecting her to be your fairy-tale princess and just let her be human."

What the hell was she talking about? He didn't have time to ask because she pushed up from the swing and left him sitting there, alone. Nothing but the creak of the swing and the rustle of branches overhead kept him company. There was so much noise in this ends-of-the-earth place.

Carla's words floated around in his brain like dust searching for a place to land. Damn it all, he knew Lucy Ann better than anyone. He saw her strengths and yes, her flaws, too. Everyone had flaws. He didn't expect her to be perfect. He loved her just the way she—

He loved her.

The dust in his brain settled. The world clarified, taking shape around those three words. He loved her. It felt so simple to acknowledge, he wondered why he hadn't put the form to their relationship before. Why hadn't he just told her?

The trees swayed harder in the wind that predicted a storm. He couldn't remember when he'd ever told anyone he loved them. But he must have, a long time ago. Kids told their parents they loved them. Although now that he thought about it, right there likely laid the answer for why the word *love* had dried up inside him.

He'd told himself he wanted to be a better parent than his father—a better man than his father. Now he realized being a better man didn't have a thing to do with leaving this porch or this town. Running away didn't change him. This place had never been the problem.

He had been the problem. And the time had come to make some real changes in himself, changes that would make him the father Eli deserved. Changes that would make him the man Lucy Ann deserved.

Finally, he understood how to build their life together.

* * *

The time was rapidly approaching to say goodbye to Elliot.

Her mind full of regrets and second thoughts, Lucy Ann rocked in the old bentwood antique in her room at Carla's, Eli on her shoulder. She held him to comfort herself since he'd long since settled into a deep sleep. She planned to find a place of her own within the next two weeks, no leaning on her aunt this time.

The past day since they'd left Monte Carlo after the horrifying accident had zipped by in such a haze of pain and worry. Her heart still hadn't completely settled into a steady beat after Elliot's accident. Right up to the last second, she'd hoped he would come up with a Hail Mary plan for them to build a real life together for Eli. She loved Elliot with all her heart, but she couldn't deny her responsibilities to her son. He needed a stable life.

To be honest, so did she.

There was a time she'd dreamed of escaping simple roots like the cabin in the woods, and now she saw the value of the old brass bed that had given her a safe place to slip away. The Dutch doll quilt draped over the footboard had been made for her by her aunt for her eighth birthday. She soaked in the good memories and the love in this place now, appreciating them with new eyes—but still that didn't ease the unbearable pain in her breaking heart as she hoped against all hope for a last-minute solution.

Footsteps sounded in the hall—even, manly and familiar. She would recognize the sound of Elliot anywhere. She had only a second to blink back the sting of tears before the door opened.

Elliot filled the frame, his broad-shouldered body that of a mature man, although in faded jeans and a simple gray T-shirt, he looked more like *her* Elliot. As if this weren't already difficult enough.

She smoothed a hand along Eli's back, soaking in more comfort from his baby-powder-fresh scent. "Did you want to hold him before you go?"

"Actually, I thought you and I could go for a walk first and talk about our future," he said, his handsome face inscrutable.

What else could there be left to say? She wasn't sure her heart could take any more, although another part of her urged her to continue even through the ache, just to be with him for a few minutes longer.

"Sure," she answered, deciding he must want to discuss visitation with Eli. She wouldn't keep him from his son. She'd made a horrible mistake in delaying telling Elliot for even a day. She owed him her cooperation now. "Yes, we should talk about the future, but before we do that, I need to know where you stand with Gianna. She approached me at the stadium just before your wreck." The next part was tougher to share but had to be addressed. "She said she's still in love with you."

His forehead furrowed. "I'm sorry you had to go through that, but let's be very clear. I do *not* love Gianna and I never did, not really. I did her a grave injustice by rebounding into a relationship with her because I was hurting over our breakup." The carefully controlled expression faded and honest emotion stamped itself clearly in his eyes. "That's a mistake I will not repeat. She is completely in the past. My future is with you and Eli. Which is what I want to speak with you about. Now, can we walk?"

"Of course," she said, relief that one hurdle was past and that she wouldn't have to worry about Gianna popping up in their lives again.

Standing, Lucy Ann placed her snoozing son in his portable crib set up beside her bed. She felt Elliot behind her a second before he smoothed a hand over their son's head affectionately, then turned to leave.

Wordlessly, she followed Elliot past the Hummel collection and outside, striding beside him down the porch steps, toward a path leading into the woods. Funny how she knew without hesitation this was where they would walk, their same footpath and forest hideout from their childhood years. Oak trees created a tunnel arch over the dappled trail, jasmine vines climbing and blooming. Gray and orange shadows played hide-and-seek as the sunset pushed through the branches. Pine trees reached for the sky. She'd forgotten how peaceful this place was.

Of course she also knew she'd walked the same course over the past year searching for this peace. Elliot's presence brought the moment to shimmering life as he walked beside her, his hands in his pockets. She assumed he had a destination in mind since they still weren't talking. A dozen steps later they came around a bend and—

Four of her aunt's quilts were draped over the branches, creating a fort just like the ones they'd built in the past. Another blanket covered the floor of their forest castle.

Lucy Ann gasped, surprised. Enchanted. And so moved that fresh tears stung her eyes.

Elliot held out a hand and she took it. The warmth and familiarity of his touch wrapped around her, seeping into her veins. She wasn't sure where he was going with this planned conversation, but she knew she couldn't turn back. She needed to see it through and prayed that somehow he'd found a way for them all to be together.

He guided her to their fort, and she sat cross-legged, her body moving on instinct from hundreds of similar hideaways here. He took his place beside her, no fancy trappings but no less beautiful than the places they'd traveled.

"Elliot, I hope you know that I am so very sorry for not telling you about Eli sooner," she said softly, earnestly. "If I had it to do over again, I swear to you I would handle things differently. I know I can't prove that, but I mean it—"

He covered her hand with his, their fingers linking. "I believe you."

The honesty in his voice as he spoke those three words healed something inside her she hadn't realized was hurting until now. "Thank you, Elliot. Your forgiveness means more to me than I can say."

His chest rose and fell with a deep sigh. "I'm done with racing. There's no reason to continue putting my life at risk in the car—or with Interpol, for that matter."

The declaration made her selfishly want to grasp at what he offered. But she knew forcing him into the decision would backfire for both of them. "Thank you for offering again, but as I said before, I don't want you to make that sacrifice for me. I don't want you to do something that's going to make you unhappy, because in the end that's not going to work for either of us—"

"This isn't about you. It isn't even about Eli, although I would do anything for either of you." He squeezed her fingers until she looked into his eyes. "This decision is about me. Interpol has other freelancers to call upon. I mean it when I say I'm through with the racing circuit. I don't need the money, the notoriety. The risk or the chaos. I have everything I want with you and Eli."

"But please know I'm not asking that sacrifice from you." Although, oh, God, it meant so much to her that he'd offered.

He lifted her hand and kissed the inside of her wrist.

"Being with you isn't a sacrifice. Having you, I gain everything."

Seeing the forgiveness that flooded his eyes, so quickly, without hesitation, she realized for the first time how much more difficult her deception must have been for him, given his past. All his life he'd been let down by people who were supposed to love him and protect him. His father had beaten him and for years he'd taken it to shield his mother. His mother hadn't protected him. Beyond that, his mother had walked out, leaving him behind. On the most fundamental levels, he'd been betrayed. He'd spent most of his adult years choosing relationships with women that were destined to fail.

And when their friendship moved to a deeper level, he'd self-destructed again by staying away. He'd been just as scared as she was about believing in the connection they'd shared the night they'd made love.

She knew him so well, yet she'd turned off all her intuition about him and run.

"Life doesn't have to be about absolutes. Your world or my world, a castle or a fort. There are ways to compromise."

Hope flared in his green eyes. "What are you suggesting?"

"You can have me." She slid her arms around his neck. "Even if we're apart for some of the year, we can make that work. We don't have to follow you every day, but Eli and I can still travel."

"I know you didn't ask me to give it up," he interrupted. "But it's what I want—a solid base for our son and any other children we have. I'm done running away. It's time for us to build a home. We've been dreaming of this since we tossed blankets over branches in the forest as kids. Lucy Ann," he repeated, "it's time for me to come home and make that dream come true. I love you, Lucy Ann, and I want you to be my wife."

How could she do anything but embrace this beautiful future he'd just offered them both? Her heart's desire had come true. And now, she was ready, she'd found her strength and footing, to be partners with this man for life.

"I've loved you all my life, Elliot Starc. There is no other answer than yes. Yes, let's build our life together, a fairy tale on our own terms."

The sigh of relief that racked his body made her realize he'd been every bit as afraid of losing this chance. She pressed her lips to his and sealed their future together as best friends, lovers, soul mates.

He swept back her hair and said against her mouth, "Right here, on this spot, let's build that house."

"Here?" She appreciated the sacrifice he was making, returning here to a town with so many ghosts and working to find peace. "What if we take our blankets and explore the South Carolina coast together until we find the perfect spot—a place with a little bit of home, but a place that's also new to us where we can start fresh."

"I like the way you dream, Lucy Ann. Sounds perfect." He smiled with happiness and a newfound peace. "We'll build that home, a place for our son to play, and if we have other children, where they can all grow secure." He looked back at her, love as tangible in his eyes as those dreams for their future. "What do you think?"

"I believe you write the most amazing happily ever after ever."

Epilogue

Elliot Starc had faced danger his whole life. First at the hands of his heavy-fisted father. Later as a Formula One race car driver who used his world travels to feed information to Interpol.

But he'd never expected to be kidnapped. Especially not in the middle of his son's second birthday party.

Apparently, about thirty seconds ago, one of his friends had snuck up behind him and tied a bandanna over his eyes. He wasn't sure who since he could only hear a bunch of toddlers giggling.

Elliot lost his bearings as two of his buddies turned him around, his deck shoes digging into the sand, waves rolling along the shore of his beach house. "Are we playing blind man's bluff or pin the tail on the donkey?"

"Neither." The breeze carried Lucy Ann's voice along with her jasmine scent. "We're playing guess this object."

Something fuzzy and stuffed landed in his hands.

Some kind of toy maybe? He frowned, no clue what he held, which brought more laughter from his Alpha Brotherhood buddies who'd all gathered here with their families. Thank goodness he and Lucy Ann had plenty of room in their home and the guest house.

He'd bought beach property on a Low Country Carolina island, private enough to attract other celebrities who wanted normalcy in their lives. He and Lucy had built a house. Not as grand as he'd wanted to offer her, but he understood the place was a reflection of how they lived now. She'd scaled him back each step of the way on upgrades, reminding him of their new priorities. Their marriage and family topped the list—which meant no scrimping on space, even if he'd had to forgo a few extravagant extras.

As for upgrades, that money could be spent on other things. They'd started a scholarship foundation. Lucy Ann's organizational and promotional skills had the foundation running like clockwork, doubling in size. They'd kept to their plans to travel, working their schedule around his life, which had taken a surprising turn. Since he didn't have to worry about money, thanks to his investments, he'd started college, working toward a degree in English. He was studying the classics along with creative writing, and enjoying every minute of it. Lucy Ann had predicted he would one day be a college professor and novelist.

His wonderful wife was a smart woman and a big dreamer.

There was a lot to be said for focus. Although with each of the brothers focused on a different part of the world, they had a lot of ground covered. Colonel Salvatore had taught them well, giving them a firm foundation to build happy, productive lives even after their Interpol days were past.

Famous musician Malcolm Douglas and his wife were

currently sponsoring a charity tour with their children in tow, and if it went as well as they expected, it would be an annual affair. The Doctors Boothe had opened another clinic in Africa last month along with the Monte Carlo mega-rich Hughes family—their daughters along for the ribbon-cutting. Computer whiz Troy Donavan and his wife, Hillary, had a genius son who kept them both on their toes.

"Elliot." Lucy Ann's whisper caressed his ear. "You're not playing the game."

He peeled off his blindfold to find his beautiful wife standing in front of him. His eyes took in the sight of her in a yellow bikini with a crocheted cover-up. "I surrender."

She tucked her hand in his pocket and stole the toy from his hand, tucking it behind her back. "You're not getting off that easily."

Colonel Salvatore chuckled from a beach chair where he wore something other than his gray suit for once—gray swim trunks and T-shirt, but still. Not a suit. But they were all taking things easier these days. "You never did like to play by the rules."

Aunt Carla lifted a soda in toast from her towel under a beach umbrella. "I can attest to that."

Elliot reached toward Lucy Ann for the mysterious fuzzy toy. "Come on. Game over."

She backed up, laughing. "Catch me if you want it now."

She was light on her feet, and he still enjoyed the thrill of the chase when it came to his wife. Jogging a few yards before he caught her, Elliot swept her up into his arms and carried her behind a sand dune where he could kiss her properly as he'd been aching to do all day. Except his house was so full of friends and family.

With the waves crashing and sea grass rustling, Elliot kissed her as he'd done thousands of times and looked forward to doing thousands more until they drew their last breath. God, he loved this woman.

Slowly, he lowered her feet to the ground, and she molded her body to his. If there wasn't a party going on a few yards away, he would have taken this a lot further. Later, he promised himself, later he would bring her out to a cabana and make love to her with the sound of the ocean to serenade them—his studies in English and creative writing were making him downright poetic these days.

For now though, he had a mission. He caressed up her arm until he found her hand. With quick reflexes honed on the racetrack, he filched the mystery toy from her fingers. Although he had to admit, she didn't put up much of a fight.

He slid his hand back around, opened his fist and found...a baby toy. Specifically, a fuzzy yellow rabbit. "You're—"

"Pregnant," she finished the sentence with a shining smile. "Four weeks. I only just found out for sure."

They'd been trying for six months, and now their dream to give Eli a brother or a sister was coming true. He hugged her, lifting her feet off the ground and spinning her around.

Once her feet settled on the sand again, she said, "When we were kids, we dreamed of fairy tales. How funny that we didn't start believing them until we became adults."

His palm slid over her stomach. "Real life with you and our family beats any fairy tale, hands down."

* * * * *

Join Britain's BIGGEST Romance Book Club

- **EXCLUSIVE offers** every month

- **FREE delivery direct** to your door

- **NEVER MISS a title**

- **EARN Bonus Book** points

Call Customer Services
0844 844 1358*

or visit
lsandboon.co.uk/subscriptions

* This call will cost you 7 pence per minute plus your phone company's price per minute access charge.